FELA

JOHN COLLINS

FOREWORD BY BANNING EYRE

DISCOGRAPHY BY RONNIE GRAHAM

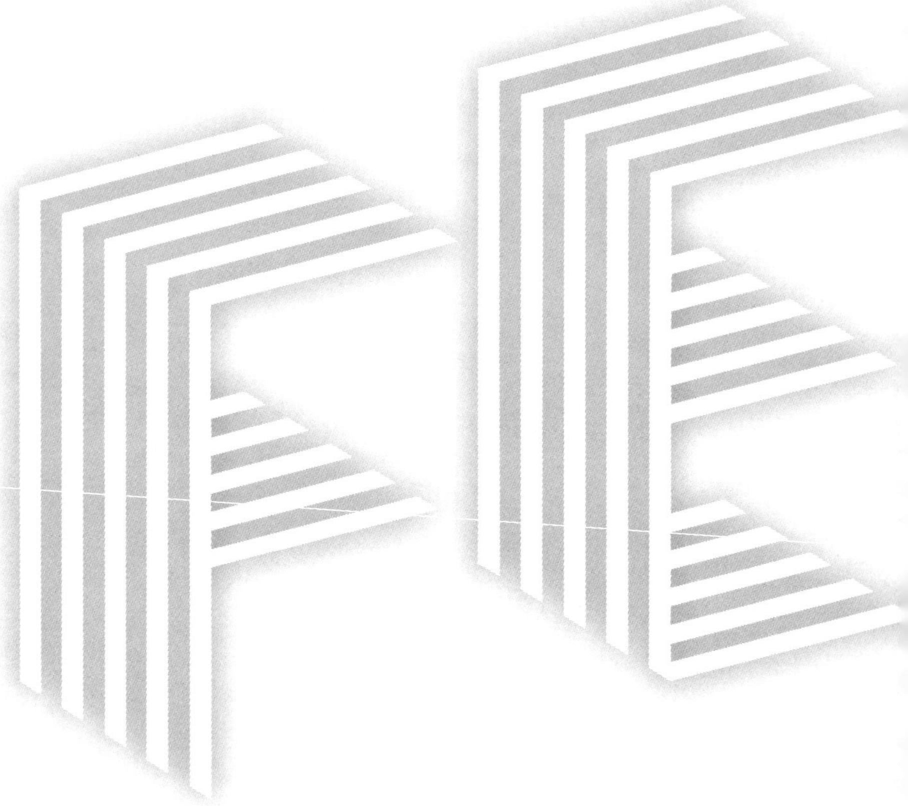

KALAKUTA NOTES SECOND EDITION

Wesleyan University Press Middletown, Connecticut

Wesleyan University Press
Middletown CT 06459
www.wesleyan.edu/wespress

Manufactured in the United States of America
Designed by Mindy Basinger Hill
Typeset in Albertina MT Pro

New, revised, and expanded edition of *Fela: Kalakuta Notes*, © KIT Publishers, 2009.

Wesleyan University Press is a member of the Green Press Initiative. The paper used in this book meets their minimum requirement for recycled paper.

Library of Congress
Cataloging-in-Publication Data

Collins, John, 1944–
Fela: Kalakuta notes / John Collins; foreword by Banning Eyre; discography by Ronnie Graham.—Second edition.
pages cm.—(Music/Interview)
Includes bibliographical references and index.
ISBN 978-0-8195-7539-5 (pbk.: alk. paper)—
ISBN 978-0-8195-7540-1 (ebook)
1. Fela, 1938–1997. 2. Musicians—Nigeria—Biography. I. Title.

ML410.F2955C67 2015
781.63092—dc23
[B] 2014042402

5 4 3 2 1

TO MY WIFE AND SON,

DOVI HELEN AND

THOMAS KOJO COLLINS

CONTENTS

Foreword by Banning Eyre ix

Introduction 1

PART ONE *Early Days*

1. The Birth of Afrobeat 27
2. Joe Mensah Remembers 41
3. Fela in Ghana 49
4. Stan Plange Remembers 55

PART TWO *Confrontation*

5. The Kalakuta Is Born 67
6. "J. B." Talks about Fela 73
7. The Kalakuta Republic 81
8. The Black President 114
9. Amsterdam and After 125

PART THREE *Retrospect*

10. Mac Tontoh on Fela 139

11. Frank Talk about Fela 152

12. Obiba Plays It Again 165

13. Smart Binete Sorts It Out 174

14. Anku Checks Out the Beat 178

15. Nana Danso Orchestrates 183

16. Some Early Afro-Fusion Pioneers 197

17. Interview with Fela 204

18. Afterthoughts and Updates 209

19. Felabrations at Home and Abroad 238

Chronology 259

Notes 269

Selected Bibliography 281

Discography 285

Appendix A: "Shuffering and Shmiling" Score 303

Index 309

FOREWORD

Fela Kuti (1938–1997) and Afrobeat are here to stay. It is fair to say that no African musician has ever exerted such a powerful cultural force during his lifetime and left such an extensive and resonant international legacy after his death. Rather than fading, Fela's stature and influence worldwide keeps growing year by year as young musicians come together to form Afrobeat bands, DJs and remixers chop and dice Fela classics, and all known art forms—dance, poetry, theater, film, photography, painting—come together in myriad annual expressions of "Felabration." Much has been written about Fela, his life and work, and much more will be in the future. But this book assumes a unique place in the Fela literary canon because of its author, a man with the perspective, knowledge, and access to Fela's story to render it with the style of a novelist, the precision and detail of a historian, and the musical insight of an insider to the creative process.

John Collins went to Ghana as a child when his father, Edmund Collins, brought the family there from England to help set up the University of Ghana's philosophy department in 1952. Collins's mother took him back to England for schooling, but he rejoined his father in Accra in 1969 and has mostly lived there ever since, becoming a naturalized Ghanaian. Collins is today a renowned archivist, producer, author, and a professor at the University of Ghana. But before he was any of these things, he was a musician, a classically trained guitarist who became swept up in jazz, blues, and rock 'n' roll before chancing into an opportunity to tour Ghana with the Jaguar Jokers Concert Party, which combined highlife music with local theater. For Collins, becoming part of a highlife band in the early years of Ghana's independence made him feel like an Englishman joining a sixteenth-century commedia dell'arte group with its itinerant lifestyle and improvised musical plays.

Collins absorbed everything, the intricacies of the music, the themes and messages in the concert party plays, the personalities, humor, triumphs, and scandals of the artists he came to know. Bemused and curious, he formed strong and lasting friendships with musicians he would later immortalize in recordings and writings. He came to understand that he was a privileged witness to a vanishing era of music, one created out of the tumultuous collapse of European colonialism in West Africa and the chaotic exuberance of the young nations that emerged there. All this was the prelude to his meeting Fela.

Fela was no superstar when he first came to Ghana in the 1960s. He was a young bandleader with new ideas, scrambling for work like many others. Collins and the people he interviews in these pages help us to know this Fela, a fascinating figure largely obscured from our view by the dramas that dominate his narrative. And as these dramas unfolded, once again, Collins would witness history, this time at Fela's side, and he writes about it clearly and incisively, leveraging insight no mere researcher or ethnomusicologist can match.

The core of this book is Collins's interviews, which provide firsthand descriptions of Fela's early and mid career, and—especially—Collins's own account of events leading up to two raids on Fela's Kalakuta Republic compound, in 1974 and 1977. The fact that these accounts were written close to the actual events is crucial. The young writer understands the sounds, the trends, the key players in highlife, Afro-soul, Afro-funk, and all the various genres that feed into Fela's Afrobeat sound. And he understands the political context, having lived through the transformation from colonial rule to independence. Writing in the 1970s, Collins cannot know where Fela's story is going, but he senses its import, and observes precisely without emotionalizing. He is honest, neither a sycophant nor a critic. These qualities make his accounts riveting to read—the real stuff of history.

In a fundamental way, Fela's art and story are a reaction to Nigeria's transformation from colonial rule to independence. But Collins leaves heady analysis to others. Instead, he writes what he sees, wonderfully combining the distance of a Western observer and the familiarity of a participant in the art and history he is observing. The 1977 raid on Fela's compound is a landmark moment in African cultural history. By pure chance, Collins was there just before it happened, dispassionately noting visual details, exchanges, and conversations, mundane events that make the larger story newly palpable and terrifying.

Collins leaves many contradictions for others to resolve. Was Fela a good trumpet player or not? Both opinions are expressed passionately. Who coined the term "Afrobeat"? Collins expresses his opinion, but almost in passing. His principle mission here is to report, not to analyze. He incorporates humor, brings characters to life, and observes very difficult events in spare, steely prose that inspires a reader's trust and discourages any easy judgment. Collins appears to have no agenda beyond observation, an impressive achievement in such a combative milieu.

Beyond his own writings, Collins draws on his long friendships with other players in the Fela story, presenting interviews conducted at various times and places. We revisit key events from different perspectives, acquiring new detail and nuance each time. Collins's knowledge of, and affection for, Fela's family members adds depth and power to his account. Once again, he tells us what he sees and feels, very specifically, avoiding conclusions and generalizations. In this way, we move through Fela's career, from his earliest days as a wannabe bandleader in Accra, to his enshrinement in a triangular granite tomb at the newly opened Kalakuta Museum in Lagos.

Once you come to know Fela, it is easy to form strong opinions about him. His brash and brilliant music bears the stamp of his headstrong personality. He was arrogant. He was politically incorrect on issues such as gender, sex, and AIDS, which ultimately felled him. He could be abusive to those around him, even those in his band. None of this fazes Collins, but neither does he hold back compromising details nor make excuses for them. This book stands as a useful antidote to Fela hagiography, whether penned by music writers entranced amid the spell cast by Fela's best band, Africa 70, or whether played out with mystical adulation in a Broadway play. Here we find a remarkable, self-possessed, visionary, wise but also shockingly flawed man. And if, in the end, we don't know exactly how to feel about Fela, that seems entirely appropriate.

The later portions of this book document the record of the Fela legacy, nothing short of staggering in its dimensions. Just in the five years since this book was originally published, there have been enough developments in the "Fela legacy" to pack another fact-filled chapter. From all this detail emerges the real story of Fela, a story about art, not a man. As Collins enumerates all the musical subgenres in which Fela's music now resonates—from Afrobeat in Brooklyn or Tokyo to the latest variant of "hiplife" in Accra—we marvel at the fragmentary complexity of today's popular music landscape. It is almost impossible to imagine any musician today making as much, or as lasting, cultural noise as Fela did. The man may be gone, but the story continues.

Banning Eyre

SENIOR EDITOR OF AFROPOP.ORG

FELA

INTRODUCTION

Fela Anikulapo-Kuti was Africa's archetypal Pan-African protest singer whose lyrics condemned neocolonialism in general and the Nigerian authorities in particular. During his turbulent lifetime, and particularly since his death in 1997, this controversial Nigerian creator of Afrobeat and spokesman for the poor and downtrodden masses, or "sufferheads," of Africa, has generated an enormous level of international interest. He has been the subject of many books and PhD dissertations and thousands of column inches of newsprint, both in Nigeria and elsewhere. In the mid-1980s he became an official "prisoner of conscience" of Amnesty International. Throughout his stormy career he has been the source of more wild and uninformed gossip than almost any musician of the twentieth century.

Fela, the "chief priest" of Afrobeat; the aspiring "Black President"; "Anikulapo," who carries death in his pocket; "Abami Edo," "the weird one and strange being," died in Lagos aged fifty-eight on August 2, 1997. Fela did two remarkable and unique things in his life. First of all, he almost singlehandedly created Afrobeat, a major new genre of African popular music that is adored by fans throughout Africa and that has influenced numerous African and international musicians. Second, with his unsurpassed militancy, he took African music into the arena of direct political action; a fighting spirit reflected in his own contrary lifestyle and his catalogue of antiestablishment songs dedicated to Pan-Africanism and the Nigerian masses.

Fela was a musical warrior who drew heavily on age-old connections between music, militancy, and violence. Lyrically, his music dwelt on the confrontational aspects of life, from which he obtained enormous inspiration. Indeed, if there was not sufficient confrontation to inspire a song, he would create that confrontation first—a unique creative device that often resulted in direct battles with the Nigerian authorities. In his songs Fela went much farther than the oft-quoted pantheon of international protest singers such as Bob Dylan, James Brown, and Bob Marley. Whereas their confrontations with established authority were couched in terms of "The Times They Are A-Changin,'" "Say It Loud—I'm Black and I'm Proud," and the evils of "Babylon," Fela's songs not only protested against various forms of injustice but often fiercely attacked specific agencies such as "Alagbon Close," which mocked the police criminal investigation department (CID) headquarters in Lagos where Fela was imprisoned in 1974. His 1976 *Zombie* album was an insulting caricature of the Nigerian army mentality that became a battle cry across a continent that was plagued by military regimes at the time. Sometimes he named names. His song "Coffin for Head of State" was directed against Nigeria's then military ruler (and later civilian president) General Olusegun Obasanjo. "International Thief Thief (ITT)" criticized the US multinational company, International Telephone & Telegraph Corporation, which set up a telecommunications system in Nigeria under Chief Moshood Abiola, who later stood for president of Nigeria.

As the dust settles over Fela's fiery, promiscuous, rascally, and egoistic lifestyle, his Afrobeat groove lives on. He will always be remembered as the most radical musical spokesman of the African poor. His peppery character in the African soup continues to be sorely missed.

Fela's Family Background in Abeokuta

Fela was born on October 15, 1938, in Abeokuta, a Yoruba town about fifty miles north of Lagos that is famous for its natural fortress, Abeokuta Rock.

Fela's birth name was Olufela Olusegun Oludotun Ransome-Kuti. His older sister was Oludulopa, or Dolu, who became a nurse, and his older and younger brothers were Olikoye and Bekolari, who both became medical doctors. The famous poet-novelist and Nobel Prize laureate Wole Soyinka was Fela's cousin and was also raised in Abeokuta.

Fela's maternal grandfather was Pastor Thomas, a Yoruba slave freed in Sierra Leone. Fela's paternal grandfather was the Anglican priest, the Reverend J. J. Ransome-Kuti, a principal figure in the Christianization of the Yoruba who was also a pianist and composed many Yoruba hymns and patriotic anthems. Forty-four of these were recorded by the Zonophone/EMI company of Britain in the mid-1920s, and these included sacred songs with piano, two funeral laments, and two patriotic songs with piano—one being the Abeokuta National Anthem "K'Olurun Da Oba Si."[1] Fela's father was the Anglican Reverend Oludotun Ransome-Kuti, a schoolteacher, music tutor, and a strict disciplinarian who became headmaster of the Abeokuta Grammar School that the young Fela attended and from where he obtained his music skills.

Besides the local hymns and Western-type music training coming from Fela's father and grandfather, Fela was, as a youth, also exposed to other musical forms prominent in Abeokuta at the time, such as Yoruba juju guitar-band music, Yoruba-Muslim *sakara* and *apala* popular-music styles, and the deeper Yoruba drum and dance music of the Egungun and Gelede masquerade cults that were dedicated to the ancestors and fertility.

Fela's mother, Funmilayo Ransome-Kuti (née Thomas), was a nationalist and women's rights activist. In 1947–48 Funmilayo led a number of mass demonstrations of local Egba market women who opposed the

British-instigated plan of taxing them via the *alake* (king) of Abeokuta, Olapado Ademola. Their demonstrations were successful, and these events are captured in Wole Soyinka's autobiographical novel *Ake: Years of Childhood.*[2] Shortly after, Fela's mother went on to found the Nigerian Women's Union and then became an executive of the Women's International Democratic Federation, and in this capacity visited Moscow, Eastern Europe, and Beijing between 1953 and 1961.[3] She met Mao Zedong, was the first Nigerian woman to visit Russia, where she received the Lenin Peace Prize, and was the first woman to drive a car in Nigeria. When the country became independent in 1960 she became one of Nigeria's few women chiefs. Funmilayo was also a supporter of one of the leading figures of modern Nigerian nationalism, Dr. Nnamdi Azikiwe, or "Zik," and her nationalist inclinations also resulted in her (and also Fela) meeting Nkrumah, for instance, when the Ghanaian leader made trip to Lagos by boat in 1957.[4]

Fela's younger brother, Dr. Beko Ransome-Kuti, also inherited his mother's radical streak. During the 1970s Beko was running his free Junction Clinic for the poor of Mushin at Fela's Kalakuta Republic, which, in fact, was their mother's Lagos house. Beko was also the general secretary of the radical Nigerian Medical Association, and after the burning of the Kalakuta and his clinic by the Nigerian army in 1977 he was radicalized and became chairman of the Nigerian Campaign for Democracy and so was imprisoned from 1995 to 1998. This was during the brutal Abacha military regime when Fela was also imprisoned on several occasions.

Fela's Musical Background: Highlife, Jazz, and Soul

By 1954 Fela had completed his primary education at his father's school and for four years attended the Abeokuta Secondary School. In 1955 Fela's father died, and so Fela began making occasional trips to Lagos where he became friends with Jimo Kombi, or "J. K.," Braimah, who finished school

Victor Olaiya's highlife band around 1960. Fela sang with them occasionally in the 1950s. Olaiya is in the center of the picture on trumpet.

in 1956, became a clerk in a Lagos court, and in his spare time sang for various highlife dance bands in Lagos. One of these was Victor Olaiya's Cool Cats, and the precocious Fela sometimes accompanied him to these shows. After the death of Fela's father, his mother relocated to the family house at 14A Agege Motor Road, Surulere (which later became the Kalakuta Republic). By 1957 Fela had finished his schooling and so went to stay with his mother in Lagos and work there in a government commercial industry office. It was at this time Fela joined Olaiya's band as a singer who, in turn had been influenced in the 1950s by Ghana's pioneering highlife dance-band musician E. T. Mensah, who took his Tempos dance band on numerous tours of Nigeria beginning in 1951.

Nigerian highlife itself originally came from Ghana in three waves. First was the 1938 Nigerian tour of the Cape Coast Sugar Babies dance orchestra; this was followed by the low-class *konkoma* (*konkomba*) form of highlife brought by Ghanaian migrant workers that did away with expensive Western instruments by using local percussion and voices;

and finally the 1950 tours by the Tempos dance band that will be referred to again below.

Although the term "highlife" was not coined in Ghana until the early to mid-1920s, the origins of it go back much earlier. In the late nineteenth century British-trained Ghanaian regimental brass-band musicians at Cape Coast and El Mina Castle began creating their own syncopated and polyphonic style of brass-band music, with the catalyst being the 5,000 to 7,000 West Indian soldiers who were stationed at these castle forts during the Ashanti Wars of 1873–1901. The Afro-Caribbean tunes and syncopated rhythms that these colonial black troops from the English-speaking Caribbean played in their spare time provided an alternative model of brass-band music, as compared to the British marching songs done in strict time. As a result, coastal African brass musicians first copied Afro-Caribbean rhythms and melodies and then, within ten years or so, went on to invent a proto-form of highlife called *adaha* music in the 1880s.

Around the same time, African sailors (and in particular the coastal Kru or Croo of Liberia) employed on British and American ships during the nineteenth century adopted sailors' instruments and on the high seas created a distinct African way of playing the guitar that they spread down the western and central African coast. These guitar techniques fed into the emerging popular "palm-wine" guitar music of Sierra Leone (Krio *maringa* music), Ghana (Fanti *osibisaaba*), and Nigeria (Yoruba juju music).

Juju music itself was a fusion of sailors' palm-wine guitar music, Sierra Leone derived *ashiko* music and local "native blues," and Yoruba praise singing. It first appeared in Lagos and Ibadan in the 1930s and was pioneered by the likes of Tunde King and Ayinde Bakere. Later Bakere and Akanbi Ege Wright introduced amplified guitars, and during the 1950s to 1970s this guitar-band music was developed by Tunde Nightingale, I. K. Dairo, Ebenezer Obey, Sunny Adé, and others.[5]

The word *highlife* emerged in Ghana after 1914, when many ballroom-dance orchestras were set up by and for the local elites; these included the

Cape Coast Sugar Babies Orchestra and fans in Enugu in 1938.

British officer training a Gold Coast marching band in the early 1900s.

The Ghanaian Kumasi Trio guitar band in 1928, composed of three Fanti musicians based in Kumasi. The leader, Kwame Asare (a.k.a. Jacob Sam), is on the right.

Juju band at Lido nightclub opposite the old Africa Shrine, 1974.

Tempos band with its leader E. T. Mensah seated in the middle.

Excelsior Orchestra, the Jazz Kings, the Accra Orchestra, and the Cape Coast Sugar Babies. At first these musicians did not play local music, but by the early 1920s they began to orchestrate some of the *adaha, osibisaaba,* and other local street songs. In fact, the name "highlife" was coined not by the well-to-do performers and audiences of these prestigious orchestras but rather by the poor who gathered outside for free shows on the nearby streets and pavements: the sailors, fishermen, ex-soldiers, migrants, and area boys who were the original purveyors, and audiences for, the existing forms of local popular music.[6]

During the Second World War Allied troops were stationed in many African countries and they brought swing-jazz records with them. In Ghana this resulted in a new type of highlife band modeled on a small swing combo that replaced the earlier large and mostly symphony-like ballroom-dance orchestras. It was the wartime Tempos dance band that pioneered this development.

The Tempos initially consisted of Ghanaians and white army musicians who played swing for the thousands of Allied troops stationed in Ghana between 1939 and 1945. But when the white soldiers left, the Tempos survived as an all-Ghanaian band, and under the leadership of Kofi Ghanaba (Guy Warren), and then E. T. Mensah, this outfit made the breakthrough into a new sound, which fused highlife music with jazz, calypso, and Latin music. By the early fifties other dance bands modeled on the Tempos were appearing in Ghana, such as the Red Spots, Joe Kelly's Band, the Rhythm Aces, and Black Beats. In 1951 the Tempos, now under the leadership of E. T. Mensah, made their first trip to Nigeria.

It was largely through the 1950s tours of the Tempos that highlife dance-band music spread from Ghana to Nigeria. There musicians like Bobby Benson, Rex Lawson, Victor Olaiya, Bill Friday, Roy Chicago, Eddie Okonta, and Zeal Onyia quickly Nigerianized highlife, which became entrenched in western, midwestern, and southeastern Nigeria.

All this development of dance-band highlife in Ghana and Nigeria was going on in the early fifties and was being put together by young musicians who supported the independence struggle. As a result, their new sound that employed Western jazz instrumentation but played African music became the "sound symbol" or "sound track" for the early independence era of both of these two countries.

For instance, Ghana's Kwame Nkrumah used highlife music for state and international functions, set up government highlife bands, and encouraged these bands to Africanize their music.[7] On the eve of Nigeria's independence in 1960 irate Nigerian musicians marched with their union through Lagos to demand that highlife be played at the National Independence Dance, rather than the planned performance by the British Edmundo Ross band. According to the Ghanaian guitarist Stan Plange,[8] who was in Lagos then as guitarist with Bill Friday's Downbeats band, almost a thousand members of the Nigerian musicians' union marched from the Empire Hotel, Idioro, to Government House to petition the

Bobby Benson and E. T. Mensah in the early 1950s.

prime minister, Tafawa Balewa. He agreed that local highlife rather than imported Latin and swing music should be played. So local highlife artists such as Victor Olaiya, Zeal Onyia, and Chris Ajilo played at this important national event.

During the 1960s Western pop music began to be picked up by the youth of Ghana, Nigeria, and other countries in Africa. First came rock 'n' roll and the associated "twist" dance, followed by soul music of James Brown and Wilson Pickett. At first local artists simply copied this imported music. Rock bands in Ghana included the Avengers and Psychedelic Aliens; then from Gambia came the Super Eagles (led by Badou Jobe and Paps Touray); from Sierra Leone, Geraldo Pino's Heartbeats (that included Francis Fuster); and from Nigeria, the Clusters, Segun Bucknor's Hot Four, and Sonny Okosun's Postmen. Local soul artists and bands included Elvis J. Brown, Pepe Dynamite, and Stanley Todd's El Pollos of Ghana and the Hykkers and Tony Benson's Strangers of Nigeria, with Joni Haastrup being acclaimed as Nigeria's James Brown. Even earlier,

Geraldo Pino, leader of the
Sierra Leonian band The Heartbeats.

in Sierra Leone, Pino's Heartbeats switched from pop to soul music and became West Africa's first homegrown soul band. They then promptly left Freetown for Ghana and then Nigeria, taking live performances of this black American dance music with them.

By the late 1960s there was a creative explosion among African musicians who had been influenced by rock and soul music introduced through records and films. First, early rock 'n' roll and its associated twist dance became a craze with urban African youth. This was followed by the progressive and psychedelic rock music of the later Beatles, Eric Clapton's Cream (that included the drummer Ginger Baker), Jimi Hendrix, Sly and the Family Stone, as well as the Latin-rock fusion of Santana—all of which fostered a more experimental spirit among young African pop musicians. Enhancing this impact on African musicians was that both Ginger Baker and Paul McCartney worked in Nigeria in 1971 and 1973, respectively, while Santana played in Ghana in 1971. At the same time soul music and its "funk" offshoot with their extended dance grooves and associated "Afro" fashions became the craze of urban African youth. Soul also spread an Afrocentric "roots" message as found, for instance, in the "Say It Loud—I'm Black and I'm Proud" lyrics of James Brown. In fact his records became so popular that he and his J.B.'s band toured Nigeria in 1970.

As a result of the back-to-roots and innovative energy contained in these new forms of imported popular music, many young African artists who had been copying rock and soul music began to dig into their own indigenous musical resources and develop various new forms of Afropop music, such as Afro-rock, Afro-soul, Afro-funk, and Afrobeat. Afro-rock was created around 1969–70 by the London-based group Osibisa that included Ghanaian, West Indian, and Nigerian musicians and was led by three Ghanaian ex-highlife dance-band musicians: Mac Tonto, Sol Amarfio, and Teddy Osei.

Their international success encouraged numerous other Afro-rock

Ghanaian dancer Tawia Brown (*second from right*) and friends at the Africa Shrine. For the Bunzus and Basa-Basa shows at the Africa Shrine and Papingo nightclub, Tawia Brown would do a floor show in between sets.

bands that formed in the early and mid-1970s, such as South Africa's Harare and Juluka (Johnny Clegg and Sipho Mchunu), Thomas Mapfumo's Hallelujah Chicken Run Band and Acid Band in Zimbabwe, Ebenezer Kojo Samuels' Kapingbdi group in Liberia, and the Super Combo of Sierra Leone. In Ghana there was as Boombaya, the Zonglo Biiz, Hedzoleh, Basa-Basa, and the Bunzus. Nigeria saw the formation of Tee Macs Afro-Collection, BLO, Ofege, Sonny Okosun (his *ozzidi* style), Ofo and the Black Company, Mono Mono, and the Funkees.

At roughly the same time that Afro-rock was emerging, different Africanized versions of soul, or "Afro-soul," were appearing in many African countries. In the Democratic Republic of the Congo the guitarist Dr. Nico Kassandra released his popular soul number "Suki Shy Man" in 1969, the

Cameroonian saxophonist Manu Dibango released his "Soul Makossa" in 1972, and by 1974 Moses Ngenya's and his Soul Brothers of South Africa were blending soul with local township mbaqanga music.

In Ghana there was the Afro-soul of the Magic Aliens, El Pollos, and Tommy Darling's Wantu Wazuri, followed by the Afro-funk and funky highlifes of Ebo Taylor, Bob Pinodo, and Gyedu-Blay Amboley. Nigerian experimentations with Afro-soul music likewise began in the late 1960s and included those of the highlife guitarist Victor Uwaifo (his *mutaba* style), the highlife saxophonist Orlando Julius, the pop and soul musician Segun Bucknor—and of course the highlife musician Fela Kuti, who coined the term "Afrobeat" in 1968.

As will be discussed in this book, Fela actually combined a number of musical styles into his Afrobeat that, besides highlife and soul music, also include three other important ingredients. First there was jazz music, with Fela employing the modal jazz approach of artists such as Miles Davis and John Coltrane, who created melodies based on improvising around and moving between two modes or tone centers rather than following a single scale and strict chord changes. Incidentally, this use of modal melodies that move between two tones rather than following a Western-type chord progression (e.g., I–IV–V) away from and back to a single tone center, makes modal jazz rather similar to African traditional music. As such, Afrobeat created a convergence between modal jazz and African music. Another jazz feature found in Afrobeat is that its rhythmic basis was created by the half Ghanaian–half Nigerian trap drummer Tony Allen, who played in a modern-jazz style—moving away from simply providing regular dance rhythms to also including improvisations, polyrhythmic high-hat pulses, and offbeat accents that supplied rhythmic space and ventilation for the dance groove. Allen also developed the double bass-drum technique so distinctive of his Afrobeat style in which he does a double kick on the bass pedal a sixteenth note apart, which usually falls right at the beginning of the four-bar measure and propels the rhythm emphatically forward.

Besides highlife, soul, and jazz, another source that Fela drew on for his Afrobeat was traditional Yoruba music making, which included the modal melodic movements already mentioned as well as other traditional features such as call-and-response between chorus and singer/soloist and the use of a pentatonic singing style that Fela blended in with the minor blues scale. These traditional elements were enhanced by Fela's adding two hand drums to his ensemble around 1970–71.

The last ingredient of Afrobeat was that Fela often gave his compositions a Latin touch. This was partly a result of the long-term impact from the 1930s of Afro-Cuban (later called salsa) music on West African dance-band musicians. But also important was the presence from the late nineteenth century of many thousands of freed Brazilian slaves (Aguda people) who brought their samba music and masquerades with them—and which became part of the Lagos musical landscape. Indeed, current Felabrations in Lagos that commemorate Fela's birthday include a carnival parade that draws on this Brazilian heritage.

Fela began experimenting with his new Afrobeat style in the late 1960s with his Koola Lobitos band, but really put the sound together when he was in the United States in 1969–70. It was also there he changed the name of his group to Nigeria 70, and on returning to Nigeria changed it yet again to Africa 70. His Afrobeat spread far and wide and influenced many African artists and bands. There was the Poly-Rhythmic Orchestra of Cotonu in the Benin Republic, the music of the South African jazz trumpeter Hugh Masekela, and the Big Beats, Sawaaba Sounds, and Nana Ampadu's African Brothers (with his "Afrohili" style of guitar-band music) in Ghana. In Nigeria there were the Lijadu Sisters and the Hausa Afrobeat of Bala Miller's Northern Pyramids.

In Nigeria a number of Yoruba juju-music guitar-band artists were also influenced in the early to mid-1970s by Fela's Afrobeat—and these included Pick Peters, Prince Adekunle, and Sunny Adé with his "synchro system" style.

Emmanuel Odunesu of the EMI Studio in Lagos.

Fela's Political Background: Nkrumah and the Early Independence Era of Ghana and Nigeria

Fela was born one year before the outbreak of the Second World War during which Africa supplied raw materials and about 300,000 soldiers to the Allied war effort. The war weakened the British and French, and as a result their colonies were granted independence, beginning with British India in 1948, followed by Caribbean and African countries during the late fifties and sixties.

The first African country to gain independence was Ghana in 1957, and the preceding nationalist upsurge was triggered by a peaceful demonstration in 1948 of Ghanaian ex-servicemen who had fought in the British army in Burma and the Far East against the Japanese[9] and were demanding back pay. Several were shot, and this resulted in widespread rioting and the looting of European shops. The British lost their colonial nerve and allowed elections to be held in 1952. Despite the fact that the British had jailed the radical Ghanaian nationalist Kwame Nkrumah who wanted independence "now," he won the election—and the country was given internal self-rule in 1952 and full independence in 1957. Ghanaian independence was followed by the independence of Guinea from France in 1958, and Nkrumah helped its new president Sékou Touré after the French had wrecked the country in a fit of pique when it had dared to say *non* to General de Gaulle's referendum on retaining close ties with France.[10]

Like Ghana, Nigeria supplied raw materials and soldiers for the British war effort; in fact over, half of the 100,000 Anglophone West African soldiers who fought in Burma were Nigerian—where they became known as "boma boys."[11] Also like Ghana, Nigeria had a tradition of anticolonial activists, for instance, the previously mentioned Nnamdi "Zik" Azikiwe who, like Nkrumah, attended university in the United States. Following his studies (in 1934), Azikiwe became the editor for the *African Morning Post* of Accra, Ghana. But when he was imprisoned for publishing what the British thought to be a seditious article, he returned to Nigeria in 1937 where he founded the *West African Pilot* newspaper that fostered Nigerian nationalism.

Also like Ghana, Nigeria had been radicalized by the war, and this growing militancy was evidenced in 1945 by two developments. That year Zik and Herbert Macaulay founded the independence party called the National Council of Nigeria and the Cameroons (NCNC) that Funmilayo Ransome-Kuti supported. Second, there were a number of big strikes that year by Nigerian workers. There was a general strike led by the Nigerian Trade Union Congress (led by Michael Imoudu) that involved tens of thousands of railway, transport, dock, and civil service workers. Nigerian popular artists of the times even became involved in this dispute, such as the leader of the Nigerian popular theater movement, Hubert Ogunde, who produced the sensational play, *Strike and Hunger.* Ogunde would eventually be arrested on charges of sedition for his play *Bread and Bullets* about the 1950 Enugu coal strike.[12]

By the 1950s there were three main political parties operating in Nigeria that were demanding independence: Azikiwe's (NCNC) had control of the Eastern Region government; the Northern Peoples Congress (NPC) centered on the Northern Region; and the Action Group (AG) was based in the Yoruba Western Region. Internal self-rule was granted in the late 1950s, and in October 1960 the country obtained full independence as the Federation of Nigeria. The first government was an alliance of the eastern-based NCNC and the northern NPC, with Abubakar Tafawa Balewa as Nigeria's first prime minister and Azikiwe as the governor-general. When Nigeria declared itself a Republic in 1963, Azikiwe would become the country's first president, serving until 1966 when the first of many military coups took place in Nigeria.

During these years, when Fela and the Koola Lobitos were playing in Lagos, the city was the highlife hub for both eastern and western Nigerian highlife musicians. After the 1967–70 Nigerian Civil War, many Igbo and other eastern Nigerian highlife musicians and bands relocated to the east.

Fela was also influenced by the recorded music (and occasional trips to Nigeria) by Ghanaian highlife dance bands such as the Tempos, who in the early sixties became closely associated with the great Pan-African thinker Kwame Nkrumah. Furthermore, from the late 1960s onward, Fela made numerous trips to Ghana where he was particularly impressed by the music of the Uhuru big band, sometimes stayed at their premises in Accra—and at one point in his early career even thought of relocating to Ghana.

Ghana was the first West African country to become independent, it was home to Kwame Nkrumah, and it was the birthplace of highlife—it's easy to see how Fela became such a Ghanaphile. When Fela later became politically conscious he became an Nkrumahist. Indeed, he constructed a Pan-African shrine in the early 1970s at his Africa Shrine Club that was centered on images of Nkrumah.

My Encounters with Fela

It was around 1970 or '71 that I first heard Fela's songs "Mister Who Are You?" and "Jeun K'oku" (also called "Chop and Quench") from singles friends brought back from Nigeria to Ghana. However, it was only in 1972 that I first saw him play when I was a student at the University of Ghana at Legon and he and his Africa 70 band played at the university cafeteria, with Fela on keyboards and tenor saxophone.

Then in November 1974 I played for a week in Lagos with the Ghanaian Bunzus Band at Fela's Africa Shrine Club and Victor Olaiya's Papingo Nightclub. During this time, the police raided the old Kalakuta Republic. After his acquittal Fela assisted us in the recordings that we and our sister band Basa-Basa and our manager Faisal Helwani were making at the at the EMI studio in Lagos.

In December 1975 I again met Fela in Lagos when I was on my way to Benin City to work with and write about the highlife musician Victor Uwaifo. I interviewed Fela on this occasion. This was probably around the time that Fela began discussing with the Ghanaian poet and screenwriter Alex Oduro the possibility of making a film of Fela's life.

Early in 1976 I met Fela several times in Ghana when he came to Accra to play at Helwani's Napoleon Club jazz jam-session nights. On these trips Fela did his "yabbis" for the university students, telling them how the Western world had deliberately hidden the long history of Africa. He called these sessions "Who No Know Go Know" after his 1975 album of that name.

In June 1976 Fela returned to Ghana to plan "The Black President" film, in which I played a British colonial education inspector. It was in December 1976 that Fela arrived in Ghana to begin the actual shooting of

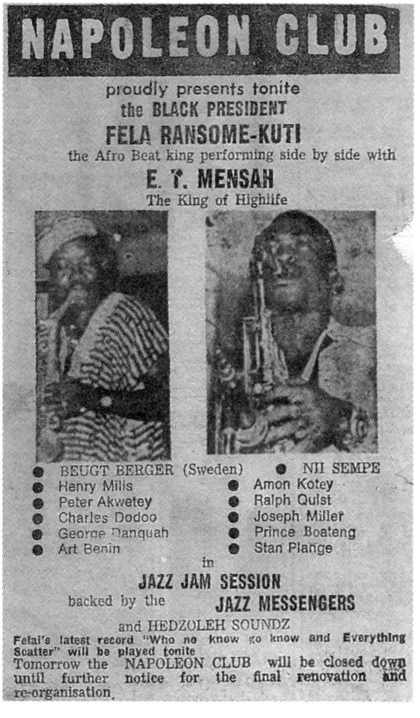

Basa-Basa guys and bus (*above*) in between Accra and Lagos. The Basa-Basa band went with the Bunzus band to Nigeria to play and record.

Poster (*left*) for a Fela show at the Napoleon Club jazz night, 1976.

the film, and it was on this occasion that I introduced him to the famous Ghanaian guitar-band highlife musician E. K. Nyame, whose songs had been popular in Nigeria when Fela was young.

I spent the month of January 1977 in Nigeria acting in "The Black President," and during this trip I met Fela's wife, Remi, his mother, Funmilayo, his sister, Dolu, his brother Beko, and his three children: Yeni, Femi, and Sola. Later that year and also in 1978, I met Fela several times when he was going back and forth between Accra and Lagos doing the overdubs of the destroyed sound track of "The Black President" film at the Ghana Film Studio in Accra.

In 1981 I met Fela and his Egypt 80 band in Holland at the Amsterdam Woods summer festival and later took a group of Dutch journalists to meet him at his hotel. He had just released his album *International Thief Thief* (ITT).

A Note on Sources

In addition to my own reminiscences, diaries, journalistic works, and interviews, this book also draws on Ghanaian and Nigerian newspapers. I conducted an interview with Fela in 1975. The two interviews with Faisal Helwani were shortly after Fela's death. I also enjoyed long conversations with two eminent Ghanaian musicians, Stan Plange and Joe Mensah, both of whom knew Fela intimately in his early days. I spoke to George Gardner, Fela's Ghanaian lawyer during the late 1970s. Fela employed several Ghanaian musicians in his band, and I have included an important interview with his 1970s conga player, "J. B." Koranteng, as well as Fela's 1980s' percussionists Frank Siisi-Yoyo and Obiba Sly Collins. Nigerians I talked to include Fela's lifelong friend J. K. Braimah; the musicologist Meki Nzewi; the Afro-fusion artist Tee Mac Omatshola; Smart Binete, who organized Fela's last Ghanaian tour; and the percussionist Bayo Martins, who at one point in the early 1960s played with Fela. I interviewed the Ghanaian musicians Mac Tontoh of the Uhuru highlife dance band (later the Osibisa Afro-rock band), and Nana Danso, whose Pan-African Orchestra includes instrumental versions of some of Fela's songs—as well communicating with Johnny Opoku Akyeampong (Jon C. G. N. Goldy) and Alfred "Kari" Bannerman, who worked alongside Fela in the late 1960s. I also interviewed the late Professor Willie Anku of the University of Ghana, who has transcribed several of Fela's songs.

For additional context I have included some comments by the Ghanaian drummer Kofi Ghanaba (Guy Warren), who as early as the 1950s and '60s was producing his own distinct style of Afro-jazz, and the Nigerian keyboard player Segun Bucknor, who created a form of Afro-soul in the late 1960s.

PART ONE EARLY DAYS

1

THE BIRTH OF AFROBEAT

Fela in London

In 1958 Fela's mother encouraged him to go to England to study medicine or law. He went to study at Trinity College in London, but against her and the rest of his family's wishes he switched to music. At Trinity, he got his training in formal music and trumpet and also fell in love with jazz and with the highlife of the London-based Nigerian musician Ambrose Campbell and his West African Swing Stars (or Rhythm Brothers). In 1961, Fela formed a jazz quintet and then in 1962 the Highlife Rakers. Later he formed the Koola Lobitos, with his close friend "Alhaji" J. K. Braimah on guitar and Bayo Martins on drums. According to Martins, Fela was "a cool and clean non-smoking, non-alcohol-drinking teetotaler." In a 1982 interview with Carlos Moore, Braimah makes a similar observation, stating that although Fela was a ruffian he "looked like a nice, clean boy . . . a perfect square."[1]

Fela and his cousin, Wole Soyinka, shared a flat in the White City area of West London. It was in London that Fela met his wife Remi, who had Nigerian, British, and Native American ancestry. Even though she says Fela was a rascal and teddy boy (a sort of early English juvenile-delinquent

Twenty-one-year-old Fela as a student at Trinity College in London in 1958.

rocker), she fell in love with him. They got married in 1961 and had three children. Yeni and her brother Femi were born in London in 1960 and 1962, respectively. Their younger sister, Sola, was born in 1963 in Lagos.

Returning Home

When he went home to Lagos in 1963 he continued to experiment with jazz. I will let the music journalist Benson Idonije explain this story.[2]

> When Fela came from London in 1963 he came to Nigeria as a jazz musician, even though he had played highlife in London. He abandoned highlife and played strict jazz after he met in London the West Indian saxophonist Joe Harriott who used to play Charlie Parker–style bebop, and the West Indian trumpeter Shake Keane who played like Miles Davis. Though Fela was good

enough to play with them, he disgraced himself as he couldn't cope with the improvisation. But that encouraged him to practice to play jazz and he went on to redeem himself. Before he left London he joined some West Indians to make a strict jazz album, which he brought to Nigeria.

So when he came back to Nigeria he didn't like highlife at all, and he met me as I was presenting a jazz program on radio called NBC *Jazz Club.* He came to meet me in the studio and introduced himself and so I interviewed him on the program and we became friends. Then he started coming to my house and in 1963 we formed the Fela Ransome-Kuti Quintet [with Benson as its manager]. This Quintet had a base at the Victor Olaiya's Cool Cats Inn where we were playing every Monday night. In the group Fela was playing trumpet and piano. On bass was Emmanuel Ngomalio, on drums was a guy called John Bull, on guitar Don Amechi, a fantastic guitarist, and we also had this organist Sid Moss. In later years we had the saxist Igo Chiko and other musicians were coming as guests; like Zeal Onyia on trumpet and Art Alade and Wole Bucknor on piano, Bayo Martins on drums—then later Steve Rhodes [piano].

The Koola Lobitos

With J. K. Braimah and some others in his jazz quintet, Fela re-formed the Koola Lobitos dance band, and he called his music "highlife-jazz." Fela played trumpet and keyboards, and the group was based at the Kadu Club. They played alongside King of Twist Chubby Checker and the young Jamaican ska artist Millie Small, who both toured Nigeria in the mid-1960s.

At the same time, Fela was working as a music producer at the Nigerian Broadcasting Corporation (NBC), a job he considered dull and deadening—and was sacked after a few years. Dr. Meki Nswewi (a musicologist at University of Nigeria, Nsukka, and now South Africa) was Fela's colleague then. As he recalled:

> Nothing was very radical about Fela in those days [1965]. He was running his Koola Lobitos group at the Kakadu Club at a hotel he had taken over on Macaulay Street. Fela had a very good Yoruba sax player called Igo Chiko whom I later recruited for some university drama productions. In Studio A of NBC there was a grand piano and Fela would go in there and experiment with his compositions during office time. He was concerned with trying to find a sound, as he wasn't happy with his jazz-highlife.
>
> The NBC also had a good record library, which the British had set up [and which Fela used]. Fela was also having problems with the NBC. The organist, Mr. Ola-Deyi, was in charge of the Music Department, and, as he was a fairly old man, he didn't like Fela whom he thought didn't take things seriously—coming late for work, etc. . . . Also, in those days no one was getting paid music royalties, and Fela was agitating for royalties to be paid for his music. So his records were not played. Another reason for this banning was that he was beginning to use a language they called "not to be broadcast."[3]

It was after leaving his job at the NBC in 1965 that Fela again reorganized the Koola Lobitos and this time brought in the drummer Tony Allen. One of the first Koola Lobitos hits of the time (1967) was the jazzy highlife "Yeshe Yeshe." But although Fela was to become popular in Nigeria in the 1970s he was then relatively unknown. And it was in Ghana—the birthplace of dance band highlife—that his music first really caught on. Koola Lobitos made many trips to Ghana from 1967, the first being with Nigerian trumpeter Zeal Onyia.

Ghanaphilia

Fela came to like Ghana so much that when he was in Lagos he had to have a constant supply of Ghanaian tea bread and Okususeku's gin sent to him. He also fell in love with Ghanaian women and the country's legacy of Nkrumaism. It was Fela's friend Faisal Helwani and his F Promotions Company that organized these early tours. As Helwani recalls:

The Nigerian promoter Chris Okoli came to Ghana in 1964–65 with Fela's manager or agent, Steve Rhodes. I went to Nigeria with them, as I wanted to bring some Nigerian musicians to Ghana. Ghana was like Hollywood for Nigeria at that time. So Chris Okoli introduced me to Fela at the Kakadu Club and we became friends straightaway and he became like a brother to me.

I visited him a few times in Lagos before promoting him here in Ghana. At the beginning Fela had a lot of sense of humor. As for the womanizing—it was there, but he was married and was living with his wife. He was jovial and liked to have a good time. At that time Fela was not into politics.

Then I started promoting him here in 1967 and the Ghanaian tours made him popular in his own country. He liked to work for me, as I never cheated him. If I'm on tour I pay him in advance, rain or shine. On one of these tours that I brought him to Ghana for, out of fourteen days it rained heavily for thirteen. There was only one day left for the tour to end and my hope was on that day, which was in Kumasi. I went down to Kumasi with Fela and another band called the Shambros (the resident highlife band of the Lido nightclub in Accra) in two busloads. The weather seemed OK and we said thank God. But as we reached the outskirts of Kumasi it started to piss down.

We set up our equipment to play but the rain wouldn't stop. By 9:30 p.m. only two people had bought tickets. Now, how to pay accommodation? No money. So I decided to drive back to Accra as we had a hotel booked there. I paid the two people their ticket money and dashed them taxi money to go home. Now, driving back to Accra from Kumasi and when we were almost at the doorstep of Nkawkaw more than halfway back, we saw this huge tree that had fallen across the road, completely blocking it. Now we had to drive back to Kumasi and take the Obuasi road to Accra through Cape Coast. While I'm going through all this agony Fela was sitting next to me in the Benz bus with half a bottle of Okukuseku gin. He said: "Ha-ha-ha promoter, rain beat you, me I've got my money." The next day I still had a balance to collect for Fela, so I sold one of my taxis to pay him. Fela always respects me for that.[4]

El Sombreros, the Koola Lobitos, and the Latin Touch

El Sombreros, a youthful pop band that played mainly rock music and soul, were put together and promoted by Faisal Helwani to support a Ghanaian tour of Fela's Koola Lobitos in late summer of 1968. This is what one of its members, Johnny Opoku-Akyeampong (Jon Goldy),[5] told me about the group:

> The line-up of El Sombreros was Bray on drums, Kojo Simpson on bass, Turkson on rhythm guitar, Alfred Bannerman on lead guitar,[6] me on vocals, and a female singer called Annshirley Amihere who was a shit-hot soul singer. Our signature tune was "Take Five" an old jazz tune. We also played other jazz-influenced tunes like Jimmy Smith's version of "Got My Mojo Working." Faisal and his F Promotions organized the tour, which consisted of three gigs only. The first one was at the Lido nightclub, then Kumasi City Hotel and The Star Hotel, respectively. There was an MC in tow who traveled with us known as Big J and even a journalist known as Jackie. The Koola Lobitos stayed at the Grand Hotel during the tour.

This is what Johnny told me of Fela's character at the time:

> I think Fela had a sense of his own destiny even back then, and no one could mess with him. I found him and his musicians to be quite high-spirited, at times irreverent and a lot of slapstick humor. But on stage they were a tightly disciplined band. Fela was already sporting his tight-fitting James Brown–like costumes back then. The music was basically the Nigerian style highlife with a jazzy feel to it. Even back then you could tell he was a superb arranger. His approach then was a typical Western-style format similar to the Sammy Obot–Uhuru [big band] style, but less swing big-band style and certainly not like the guitar-band style typical of other Nigerian artists. Also at that juncture the African shamanic feel was not yet in evidence in the mix. Fela was a shit-hot trumpeter who always strained to push the limits

of the music within the conventional highlife structure. As for the political stance I saw nothing like that during '68 during the tour.[7]

This is what Alfred "Kari" Bannerman told me:

> I remember Fela would sometimes start the band off on a tune, go to the bar and down a full glass of transparent liquid, and then to my surprise go back on stage to play blistering solos on his trumpet! Many years on Dele Sosimi pointed out to me what I thought was gin was actually a glass of water, as Fela didn't drink[8]—but smoked all right. At the time having left the GBC [Ghana Broadcasting Corporation Band] where long chord progressions were the order of the day, I was taken in by the two-chord modal nature of Fela's compositions. But things were tough as this was before the onslaught of Afrobeat and they [i.e., the shows] were sparsely attended. The guitar the Koola Lobitos used had a nail sticking out, holding neck to body![9]

The reason Helwani chose the name El Sombreros for the pop group was that at the time Latin- and Spanish-sounding names were a vogue with some pop bands in Ghana and in fact the country's leading soul band was called El Pollos. Likewise the Sierra Leonian leader of the soul-ish Heartbeats band, Gerald Pine, called himself Geraldo Pino. Furthermore, Fela's band was called the Koola Lobitos. So Faisal Helwani insisted that the name of the Fela's youthful support band (originally called the Beavers) should likewise have a Spanish-sounding name and that the El Sombreros should wear Latin-style costumes. Here are Bannerman's views on this:

> I really didn't like the shiny, frilly multicolored costume, plus [sombrero-type] hat. We were playing "Jumping Jack Flash," the Rolling Stones, etc. But it wasn't something that jelled with my soul, and who would like to be part of a band named like they were Mexicans? On the other hand, Fela I found intriguing and very smart as he had his signature designed shirts, which were almost collarless.

Despite the fact that the Koola Lobitos did not sport Latin costumes they were in fact influenced by Latin music to some degree—as in the late 1960s Fela was not only drawing on jazz, soul, and R & B, but also on Latin salsa music: as in the songs "Oritshe/Orise" and "We Dele."[10] "We Dele" is in a minor-key bluesy-jazz style, and "Orise" is more highlifish, but both use Latin-style horns to accompany and/or respond to the vocals.

This Latin touch in Fela's music may have come from several sources. Fela was an avid listener of modern jazz, and the Cuban mambo had made a big impact on jazz from the late forties, such as with the "Cubop" associated with Dizzy Gillespie, the Cuban percussionist Chano Pozo, and Stan Kenton's Afro-Cubists band. Then came the "pachanga" dance craze of the 1960s that swept across the globe, including Africa,[11] followed in the late sixties by the salsa (hot sauce) music that was created in New York with its large Latino population. Salsa went on to influence American soul and R & B when Cuban congas were added to rock and funk bands, and there was a new Latin "bugalu" dance craze among the youth that went international.

The Latin tinge is reflected in a number of the Afrobeat songs Fela composed after 1970. One is "Jeun Ko'ku," which opens with a Latin horn fanfare and utilizes a Caribbean clave rhythm. Other Latin and Latin-jazz-influenced songs are the mid-1970s "Water No Get Enemy," "I No Get Eye For Back," "Who No Know Go Know," and "Na Poi."

Despite the Spanish tinge in Fela's music, his main musical direction in 1968 was highlife-jazz and soul.

This is what Johnny Opoku-Ayeampong has to say on the matter:

> In 1968 he seemed to be looking for a new sound and had split the repertoire into the jazz highlife which we already knew, and something more soulish. So it was of two types, something called Afro-highlife and the other genre was dubbed Afro-soul. For me the Afro-highlife was only slightly different from the Afro-soul, which I preferred because it was less jazzy, less

highlifish, and perhaps a bit more danceable—though not quite as funky as the American soul which by then had literally taking over most of our mixed repertoire at the time. It could have been deliberate as throughout all his music, one could detect that he wanted to be different, but it was quite subtle in those days. Also I think the Afro-soul was mostly sung in English or pidgin and the Afro-highlife mostly in Yoruba. Musically I did not immediately warm up to him because for most of us teenage musicians horns and highlife were not exciting and challenging enough. Also we had no horn players in our midst and other horn players around were older, too formal in their approach and would only play in B♭, C#, etc.—which was a pain for the average guitarist. We were then doing all the horn parts on the guitars until we progressed to the organ, mainly due to the advent of the Heartbeats influence [resident in Ghana 1964–68]. However at the gig at the Lido Fela played alone on the piano—a jazzy bluesy piece which suddenly gained my utmost respect and admiration.

Opoku-Akyeampong did not see Fela play again until early 1971 when Fela came to Ghana again and did one of his shows at the Labadi Pleasure Beach in Accra. By this time the Fela's band was called the Africa 70, the soul and funk influence was more pronounced, and Afrobeat had crystallized. According to Opoku-Akyeampong Fela had by then become so popular that there were huge crowds at the event, and here he describes the music.

One thing which struck me after absorbing the early music was the undeniable influence of James Brown, like his danceable 1967 "Cold Sweat" single and albums which I loved that he released in 1968–69. That's where Fela got his rhythm section, [where] the bass, drums, and guitars came from. Perhaps Fela "Africanized" it the more with the percussion, but the rest was all his own creation. Of course none of this detracts from this great man's musical genius. If anything it is a true testament to his creativity, and I wish he had acknowledged it as such. . . . Again Fela accidentally coinvented jazz-funk. No one but James Brown had attempted anything quite like that before '71. And I don't recall J. B. doing anymore of those instrumentals. But I must be careful here to say that Booker T. and the M.G.'s also did some inspiring dance instrumentals even before 1971, but they were not jazz oriented as such. But the rest of jazz-funk proliferated with Grover Washington and the others throughout the 1970s.

Soul, Funk, and Crossover Sounds

In the late 1960s new outside musical influences began to affect Fela's music. Soul music, and the associated Afro fashion, was introduced to Nigeria in 1966 by the Heartbeats band of Sierra Leone[12] led by Geraldo Pino (Gerald Pine). A period of experimentation took place between 1967 and 1969, with Lagos artists such as Fela, Segun Bucknor, and Orlando Julius creating various blends of Afro-soul. Orlando changed the name of his highlife band to the Afro Sounders in 1967, while Segun changed his band's name from Soul Assembly to Revolution in 1969. Fela was experimenting with soulish songs like "My Baby Don't Love Me," "Everyday I Got My Blues," and also "Home Cooking" in which he actually uses the word "Afrobeat."

It is likely that is was in 1968 that Fela started to call this new style that combined highlife, jazz, salsa, and soul "Afrobeat" and launched it at the Kakadu Club, which that year he began to call his Afro-Spot.[13] According to the 1982 interview with Fela by Carlos Moore,[14] Fela coined the name Afrobeat to distinguish his sound from the soulish sound of Geraldo Pino, whose Heartbeats were very big in Nigeria at the time.[15] Again, according to Carlos Moore, Fela was in a club in Accra listening to James Brown's soul music on a record player in 1968 with the Ghanaian/Nigerian music producer Raymond Aziz when he invented the name.[16] Incidentally, it was only in 1970 that James Brown actually played in Africa—when he toured Nigeria in December of that year.

Although Fela's Afrobeat was beginning to emerge by the late sixties, its lyrics were not at first so politically and socially confrontational as they

Sandra Iszadore began Fela's political radicalization and collaborated with him musically.

were to become later. Fela's politicization and radicalization was accelerated when he went to the United States in August 1969 for ten months.

While there he and his eight-strong Koola Lobotis group made a record called "Keep Nigeria One," a patriotic song that supported the federal government during the 1967–70 Nigerian Civil War. He also met the African American singer Sandra Iszadore (Smith) at a show of the National Association for the Advancement of Colored People (NAACP) in Los Angeles. Sandra was associated with the militant Black Panther movement of Stokely Carmichael and others, and she gave Fela *The Autobiography of Malcolm X* to read. It was then that Fela began to be "exposed to African history," as he puts it. It was in the United States that his first real Afrobeat style—influenced by both soul-funk and modal jazz—came together. It was also while in Los Angeles that he began to call his band Nigeria 70.

The Africa Shrine, Africa 70, and Anikulapo-Kuti Are Born

Fela returned to Nigeria in 1970 with his new Afrobeat sound, and at first he and his Nigeria 70 band continued operating his Afro-Spot club at the Kakudu Club. This is a description of how the musician Tee Mac Omatshola first encountered Fela and his club at that time.[17]

> My mother, Suzanna Iseli Fregene Omateye, had the exclusive hairdressing Salon Bolaji, and I just returned from Switzerland having obtained a degree in economics and a master's degree in the flute. I took up a job with UTC (a Swiss department store group in Lagos) and was just forming the Afro Collection.[18] I went from the UTC head office every lunchtime to my mother's salon to eat some food. So in August 1970 I went there on a Friday and saw a slim gentleman sitting there. My mother introduced me to him as the son of her good friend Mrs. Funmilayo Ransome-Kuti who was the first Nigerian lady to drive a car (and my mother was the second). She told me that her girls were doing the hair for Fela's wife, and so I sat beside of Fela and we talked. I told him that I studied classical music in Switzerland and France and he told me that he is playing Afrobeat and jazz. He invited me to come to his Afro-Spot club next evening where his manager Felix received me. I was taken to Fela's dressing room filled with girls. Fela sat there with a big joint in his mouth; it smelled bad and I asked him what the hell he was smoking! He said, "Natural Nigerian grass!" I joined him on stage [later] with my flute and I had the feeling that my fingers were playing on their own. Fela and the band loved my performance and I played many more times with him in the next twenty years.

I should add that Sandra Iszadore briefly joined Fela in Lagos in 1970. In fact he even made one song with Iszadore on a later trip by her called "Upside Down" that was released by Decca West Africa in 1976. This is about a man who travels the world where the telephones, light supply, transport system, etc. all work in an orderly way. However, when he comes back to Africa he sees plenty of land but no food, plenty of villages but no roads, plenty of open space but no houses. In short, education, agriculture, communications, and the power supply are in confusion. Fela's reference to electrical failures is a quip on the state of NEPA, the Nigerian Electrical Supply Authority, which in the 1970s broke down ten to twenty times a day.

It was in 1971 that Fela moved from the Kakadu Club to the larger Surulere Club, changed the name of his band from the Nigeria 70 to the Africa 70, and renamed his Afro-Spot venue the Africa Shrine, which included a small shrine. By this time he had developed the idea of his "comprehensive show" in which his band would take a break in the middle of the dance set, change into animal skins, and return to play a floor show that included dancing and funny novelty acts. According to the band's hand-drummer Daniel "J. B." Koranteng, Fela wore a costume made out of snakeskin, another musician a leopard skin, while J. B. himself wore one made from a lion skin.

In 1971 Fela teamed up with Ginger Baker (formerly with Eric Clapton's band Cream). The British rock drummer had crossed the Sahara Desert that year and made a film of the journey,[19] as well as making a visit to Ghana's veteran master drummer Kofi Ghanaba (Guy Warren). Baker subsequently went into partnership with a Nigerian and helped set up Nigeria's first multitrack studio, ARC Studio

During the summer of 1971 the Africa 70 played in London with Ginger Baker at the Abbey Road Studios in London to record the album *Fela Live with Ginger Baker.* It was there that Fela first met Paul McCartney, who later, in 1973, was to visit Lagos on a recording trip with his band Wings and who got into a confrontation with and Fela at the Afro-Spot club in Lagos when Fela accused McCartney of trying to steal or woo away some members of the Africa 70.[20]

In London the Africa 70 played at the Cue Club, the Four Aces, and 100 Club and also toured the country. "J. B." Koranteng told me that when they played in Wales and the band marched up to the stage for their "comprehensive show" section of the performance dressed in animal skins, the crowd panicked. Some started rushing for the door and others tried to jump out of windows, until Ginger Baker cooled them down and explained it was all part of the show.

It was in 1972 that Fela released his much-loved Yoruba Afrobeat "Sa-

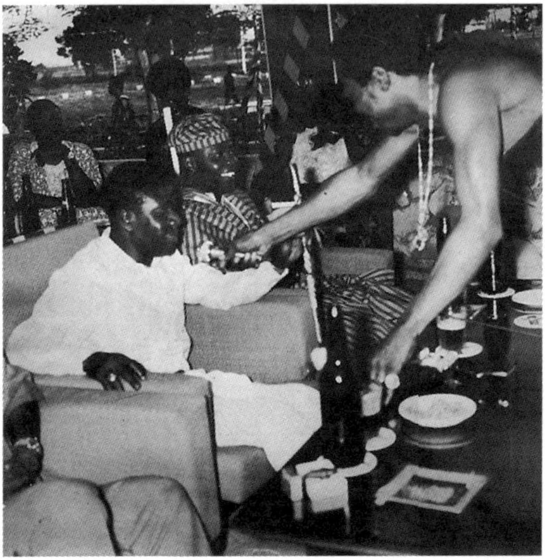

Fela talking to the Ghanaian military head of state Colonel Acheampong during a show in Accra in 1972.

kara Oleje" about loudmouthed braggarts. That was also the year that the Africa 70 toured Ghana in a program organized by Stan Plange and Faisal Helwani. This included a performance for the leader Colonel Acheampong, as the new military government of Ghana was pro-Nkrumahist and still radical at that time. So Fela was quite comfortable performing for this military leader. Fela also played for and "yabbied" the university students at the Legon campus and the African Youth Command in Tema.

In 1972 J. K. joined Fela after returning from abroad, and in late 1973 Fela relocated the Africa Shrine to the Empire Hotel in Mushin, diagonally opposite his house. There too he set up an actual shrine dedicated to Kwame Nkrumah and surrounded by the flags of some of Africa's independent nations. By then the Africa 70 band was becoming more radical in its Yoruba and pidgin English lyrics, and between 1972 and 1974 the group began making extensive tours of West Africa. It was in 1975 that Fela Africanized his name by removing the colonial "Ransome" from his surname Ransome-Kuti and substituting it with "Anikulapo," which means "he who holds death in his pocket or pouch."

2

JOE MENSAH REMEMBERS

The late Joe Mensah was a pioneering Ghanaian highlife singer who released eleven albums and several singles. He began his musical career with the Broadway Dance Band in the 1950s. This was against his parents' wishes, so as a teenager he left Ghana for Lagos in 1958, where he joined Chief Billy Friday's Downbeat Highlife Band. It was then that Joe became a close friend of the young Fela, just before Joe went to further his studies in London. Joe returned home three years later and rejoined Broadway, renamed Uhuru, in 1963. In the same year he recorded his famous "Uhuru Special" (with "Bosoe" on the flip side) in Lagos with the Uhuru members under the name Big Beats. In 1964 he left for the United States to study civil engineering and pursue his musical career. However, he made many trips to West Africa, and in the early 1970s, with the help of Fela's horn section, he recorded in Lagos with the Ghanaian band Sweet Talks. He returned to Ghana in 1992, becoming president of the musicians' union of Ghana. Sadly, Joe died in 2002 after a short illness. This interview was recorded at the MUSIGA offices on September 2, 1998.

Tell me how you first got to know Fela.

We [a group of Ghanaian musicians] got to Lagos in early 1958 to join the Downbeats that resided at a nightclub called Nat's Club de Paris at 80 Ojuelegbe Road in Surulere. It was not far from Fela's home as he was staying with his mother at the family house [working as a clerk with the Ministry of Commerce]. We played at the club about four times a week, and one evening, I think it was a Sunday, we played our usual gig. At the end of one of the songs I sang I saw somebody come on stage, put his head between my legs and carry me on his shoulders. He took me through the audience and was saying to the crowd: "You people, have you heard any voice as great as this one? And you just sit down and don't show any appreciation." So people began throwing money to us on the floor. After he put me back on stage he collected all the money and brought it to the band. That was Fela!

From that day on my day would never be complete if I didn't see him and he would not go out without seeing me. We became very close even though he was about twenty years old and quite a few years older than me. I would spend a lot of time at his house, but I never met his mother until one day I went there and she was washing clothes.

Fela had told his mother a lot about me and she said that how is it possible that I look so much like her children. Like we're related. She also said that I'm too young for my mother to have allowed me to leave Ghana and stay in Nigeria, so from that time I should consider her my mother, call her "Ma," and when I need consolation, food, or whatever, I should always go there.

Fela and I used to hang around in the night and roamed the whole of Lagos. You know it was then a very peaceful place and we used to walk to the Marina from Surulere. We were so free. We bought food from the women who cook on the roadside and we visited friends. We walked over Carter Bridge to go into Lagos [Island] itself to get to the Marina and the real ghettos around the lagoons where the people were so friendly. Even the traffic in Lagos was exciting as it was then 80 percent full of bicycles. Even Fela had a bike. When we came back in the night to sleep I sometimes stayed with Fela and sometimes at my place, as some mornings we started rehearsals early.

At this time one incident occurred that I've never told anyone before, as I'm a bit embarrassed when I'm talking about it. This was one Saturday night when we [The Downbeats] were playing at our normal place, and after finishing singing women were coming after me too aggressively. Fela was watching. He staved them off and said: "Leave him alone, don't you know he's a small boy? Don't you have any shame?" I don't know how one Yoruba lady talked Fela into this but all I saw was that the lady was following Fela. Her name was Dukpe. So Fela called me and told me: "Joe, Dukpe is going to teach you something tonight as she's going to sleep with you. I've told her everything, she knows you are a kid and knows how to deal with you." I said that Fela I can't do this.

We got to my room that I shared with quite a few people and I don't know how Fela managed it, but my roommates did not come in. Fela said goodnight and as he was going to close the door this lady just appeared in the room. Fela locked the door from outside and was laughing and saying that now we'll see what will happen in the morning. Well, I need not continue on that story any more but this is to show how much Fela and I loved each other, like brothers; innocent young guys with talent.

Then another incident occurred the day he went to Britain [in August 1958]. Fela had a very beautiful bike, but even at that age he drove recklessly. His mother had bought a little German Opel car and all of a sudden Fela came to me with his left hand bandaged. He had run his mother's car into a ditch and so he was going to inform her. I went to the house with Fela and his mother complained that Fela was giving her hell, so he's going to London today to study. Fela said he wasn't going to any *oyinbo* [whiteman] country, so as we were parting he said that I should come back as we were meant to be going out that night. His mother told me: "Don't waste your time to come as you won't find him here, he'll be gone." So this woman tied her headgear and over-cloth, took Fela's passport with £90, and somehow this stubborn Fela wound up on an airplane to London. And that's how we parted in the first phase of our friendship. In London he went to stay with one of his brothers who was training to become a doctor, as his mother also wanted Fela to be a doctor. From what I understand he entered medical school briefly but then went on to a music school in London.

What was Fela like when you first met?

You know Fela is a very brilliant chap, very intelligent, and very well rounded up in knowledge of many subjects. And Fela read a lot. He was also then very shy—we were both shy—but it was when we got together that we became terrible and could do anything. At that time he had finished one phase of his education [at Abeokuta Grammar School] and was waiting to go to university. He was an aspiring musician pianist for the second band of [Victor Olaiya's] Cool Cats highlife group.

What was Fela's relationship with his mother like?

Beautiful, very beautiful. You would think the mother only had Fela as a child, and for some time this is what I thought, only to learn later that there was an older and younger brother. Fela was the one who gave more challenges and trials of motherly patience and endurance. You should have seen the mother then. She was middle-aged, very strong, very determined, very forthright, very courageous, and very outspoken. I remember in the presence of Fela the mother told me not to follow him but rather show him how to be a good boy, and Fela just walked away making annoyed sounds. I could say that the love that he has for his mother, which later on showed, would be because they are very much alike in character. Both spoke their minds—from the little I saw of her she had values she adhered to. Like the value of a woman being able to do many other things besides the usual feminine classifications we give to women.

At that time Fela's father had died and so the mother was twice of a father and once a mother—all rolled into one. If you go to the house you will see that she kept the house under rigid control. She wouldn't follow any ideology, any saying, or any people blindly. I wouldn't say she was always against the norm but I know she could not be swayed easily. She knew the world situation and politics, especially in Nigeria. She stood by her guns on principles that even go contrary to tradition and custom. Also she was a big freedom fighter and agitator—not only in words, but in action. On top of all that she was very affectionate, because if I look at how concerned she was about me then I can imagine how fortunate Fela and all her children were.

What about Fela's father?

He had died but what I heard was that he was a trumpeter and also a reverend minister, and as such he used to hide his trumpet in his *agbada* [Nigerian attire] to go and play, as church congregations frowned upon their minister playing in clubs and social gatherings. They would take it as degrading to the pulpit. If it had been Fela's mum she would have blown the trumpet in church. That was the type of determination she had, that eventually rubbed off on Fela. I guess through Fela's father having been a musician Fela got to know quite a bit about music.

You saw Fela again when he returned from London in 1963?

Yes, I was in Lagos with the Uhurus and luckily there was Fela at a place called the Paradise in Ibadan. He came looking for me, and when we started playing he came in on his trumpet. It was when Fela came back from music school in London that he came out with the trumpet. Maybe his father also taught him, I don't know. But when I first saw him in Lagos I never saw him with a trumpet. And I've never, up to today, heard any trumpeter that great. He was just fresh from tutelage and had been taught classical music at the conservatory. And he applied that to jazz. So his jazz was classic as well as innovative. Fela had all the qualities of a great trumpet player—the embouchure, the intonation, the dexterity, the fingering. It was just after this time that he formed his Koola Lobitos highlife band and you can see from his early works that Fela was a jazz fanatic.

I believe that you met Fela when he was in the United States in 1969?

Yes, I went to New York in 1964 to study civil engineering. While there I followed up Fela's progress and I got his Koola Lobitos recordings. Also Fela would send people to me, and some of them would stay with me, because if he's a friend of Fela he's my friend and guest as well.

Then I was told that Fela was coming to the US to perform, and I met him in New York with his Koola Lobitos. Animashaun was on baritone sax, Tony Allen on drums and Tunde on trumpet. They played one night at the New York Sheraton Ballroom in a show organized by the African American community and a group of Nigerians for Nigerian National Day or some significant African day.

Then Fela left for California to tour, but wound up living there for a long time. That is where he gained his extreme African consciousness, blackmanism, and Afrocentrism. And he translated all this into his Afrobeat music.

I think this happens to all of us. It happened to me. My American friends, especially African Americans, found me to be too British. I had two Christian names and they didn't see anything African about me as my values were too British, my dressing was too British, and my music was too conservative. So you start to form and evolve your own identity. And that is what Fela might have gone through when he was in California.

Tell me what you think about Afrobeat.

Its ingredients are a unique combination of highlife, jazz instrumentation, African percussion, and typical Nigerian movements. I can say with pride and love that myself and the other Ghanaian musicians in the Downbeats might have been the first link with Ghana and highlife for Fela. The way we did things was curious to Fela. The way we would take pains to create things, how we blended and performed our music. That was the foundation of Fela's Afrobeat—I'm talking of highlife. You see at the time in Lagos there was only the *apala* and juju of I. K. Dairo and Haruna Ishola, which were mainly an aggregate of percussive instruments. So Fela got easily attracted to highlife, since his interest was in horns.

Afrobeat is a very sensitive music because Fela created it at a stage of his life when he required a lot of sympathy. He was always in difficulty for being outspoken and people would not leave him alone. So he found solace in the Afrobeat, as that was the only time Fela feels free, when he's playing on stage.

Afrobeat was unique as he made his girls sing chorus for him. Because they are a bunch of dancers and not singers their voices could not stand a very good [complicated] sequence. So because of the ordinary nature of the chorus singing, Afrobeat became the music for the average man and woman in the street. If you take away the girls who sang the choruses you would be left with Fela as an avant-garde jazz-influenced African musician.

Fela always had a message and he made sure it was clearly heard. Here you have him come with a horn segment and it would disappear, then the guitar was there as if it's monotonous—but it's preparing you for what Fela was going to say. And when he starts singing everything holds up behind him. Everything stands still, goes on the bed and lies below him so he can express himself.

Fela was also influenced by his own traditional music, which is always held together by the steady metronomic figures of the cowbells and clips [claves] that maintain the measure. Also, if you listen to indigenous Yoruba ensembles and you have good ears, you will hear [something like] the string bass in it. You see, the Yoruba speaking or talking drums come in different sizes. They have, for instance, a big one they call *yalo,* the mother of the talking drums. Others are bigger or smaller. And they always provide the tonality under the whole percussion. So it was easy for Fela to take this and transpose it onto bass [guitar]. That gave a solid rock to his music.

Afrobeat is a beautiful legacy and great gift that Fela has bestowed not on just Nigeria and Ghana, but on Africa and the whole world at large.

FELA IN GHANA

Fela's early Afrobeat hits in both Nigeria and Ghana were the singles "Mister Who Are You" and "Chop and Quench" ("Jeun Koku"), and the albums *Open and Close* and *Rofo Rofo* [Rough Rough] *Fight*. According to Bayo Martins, the song "Mister Who Are You" is a complaint against "bigmanism" and pomposity and aimed at the then Lagos State governor. "Jeun Koko" was "directed at those sit-tight politicians and soldiers in office, refusing to let go, while squandering the purse of the nation."

During the 1970s, Fela, now with his Africa 70 instead of the older Koola Lobitos, continued to visit Ghana. Indeed, at one point he even thought of building a house in Ghana. I first saw him in 1972 when he was touring Ghana and played for the students at the University of Ghana cafeteria at Legon, where I was a final-year student studying sociology and archaeology. By then Fela was playing electric piano and tenor saxophone instead of the trumpet he had been using with the Koola Lobitos.

A favorite song of the time was "Gentleman," in which Fela states he would rather be a natural and original African man than one dressed in a suit and tie and affecting refined manners. Another was "Lady" (on the flip side of "Sakara Oloje"), poking fun at refined Nigerian women and sung in pidgin English.

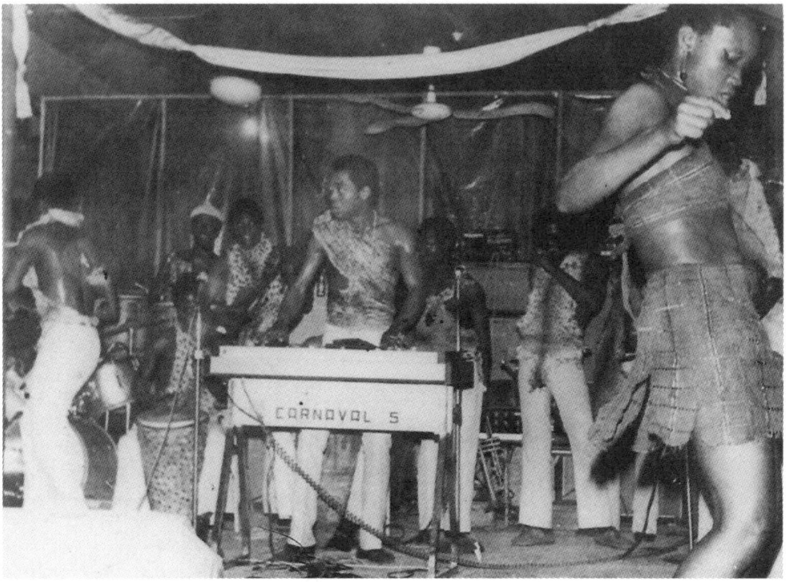

Fela plays, circa 1972.

On that trip Fela also played at the officers' mess at State House for Colonel Ignatious Acheampong, who had just taken over the country in a coup against the civilian government of Prime Minister Busia, who had suddenly devalued the local currency. At that time Acheampong was still seen as a progressive, and as a result Fela dedicated his new 1971 album *Open and Close* to him, and indeed on the inside cover of the album is a photo of Fela and Colonel Acheampong.

As Faisal Helwani explains, it was in Ghana in 1972 that Fela began his habit of lecturing or "yabbis" his audiences:

> I organized lectures at the University of Ghana and the African Youth Command at Tema. At Legon he was talking about Pan-Africanism, patriotism, "blackism," and the black land of the Nile, not about day-to-day politics. And you know the Legon university students—anyone who will

come and stand and talk more than thirty minutes, they will walk out and leave you. But Fela lectured them for three hours and they were still there. Some of today's ministers were among the students he lectured.

Then Nana Kofi Omane and I organized two Fela lectures for the African Youth Command in Tema. Nana was a lawyer for the Tema Development Corporation and an executive of the African Youth Command set up while [now] General Kutu Acheampong was in power to bring back Nkrumahism. In fact, as early as 1971, I and Nana, who had an organization called the Black Brothers International, organized a celebration on Nkrumah's birthday at the Orion Cinema, Accra. It was packed out, and it was the first time since the anti-Nkrumah coup of 1966 that anyone had identified publicly with Nkrumah.

After the 1972 lectures, Fela got invitations from Nigerian universities like Ibadan to talk on the wrongs and corruption of society and how big men donkey the ordinary people. That's when he became more political. Fela did this before Bob Marley. Marley did it more intellectually, Fela did it more directly.

Another important interaction between Fela and Faisal occurred in 1973 when the exiled South African trumpeter Hugh Masekela traveled around Africa for musical inspiration. He met Fela in Lagos, and Fela told him to go to Faisal's newly opened (1971) Napoleon Club in Accra to join the club's just formed resident band, Hedzoleh (Freedom). So it was with this Afro-rock group (led by Stanley Todd and with Okyerema Asante on percussion) that Hugh Masekela went back to Lagos in December 1973 to record the album *Introducing Hedzoleh* at the EMI studio.

However, as Faisal wrote in an article for the *Ghanaian Mirror* of February 7, 1975, things did not go very well in this collaborative enterprise:

I founded, created, financed, managed, produced and arranged them for recordings. On top I organised the Masekela-Hedzoleh tour of the United

Left to right: Faisal Helwani, Hugh Masekela, and Stanley Todd in Accra, 1973.

Fela (*seated center*) next to Faisal Helwani (*standing*) with J. K. Braimah (*seated right*) and Alex Oduro (*seated left*) in Accra, around 1976, prior to the shooting of "The Black President" film. Photo courtesy of Samy Redjeb, Analog Africa

> States. In all I broke through the universal market with Hedzoleh within the short period of one-and-a-half years. Hugh Masekela showed up in Accra [after he had been] introduced to me by Fela Ransome-Kuti, my friend. At the time Hedzoleh was already a champion band of Ghana and they had won a contract for the sound track of the film *Contact.*

As mentioned in the introduction, in early 1976 Fela made several trips to Accra to play at Faisal Helwani's Napoleon Club jazz jam-session nights, alongside the highlife stalwarts like E. T. Mensah, Stan Plange, Jerry Hansen, and King Bruce, while Fela also played and did his political "yabbis," entitled "Who No Know Go Know," for the university students. The Africa 70 also performed for General Acheampong at the officers' mess at State House in Accra. At this time the Ghanaian military government of Acheampong was still relatively friendly to Fela, as it was still perceived as a radical government that had refused to pay debts to the World Bank and International Monetary Fund and was rather propagating Ghanaian self-reliance through initiatives like Operation Feed Yourself. Fela himself, on the other hand, was angry about the assassination of the radical Nigerian military leader General Murtala Mohammed, whom he admired, in a Lagos "go-slow" or traffic jam. He believed, for instance, that Murtala would have legalized marijuana.

Fela returned to Accra in June 1976 with J. K. Braimah and the Ghanaian poet and scriptwriter Alex Oduro to discuss with Faisal Helwani "The Black President" film that was based on the biography of Fela and his musical career in Ghana and Nigeria. As usual Fela came by car, which he always drove himself, as he never trusted anyone else's driving. Then in December 1976, Fela came yet again with his eight-track mobile recording studio and a huge entourage of musicians, actors, women, and Kalakuta people to begin shooting the Ghanaian portions of the film. This included historical scenes of slaves in the dungeon at El Mina Castle and shots of the Star Hotel where Fela reenacted scenes of his Koola Lobitos band that often played in Ghana in the 1960s.

4

STAN PLANGE REMEMBERS

Guitarist Stan Plange met Fela in the late 1950s when Stan was playing with Chief Billy Friday's Downbeat highlife dance band in Lagos. Stan had first joined the Nigerian Downbeats group in 1957 when the band had been resident in Ghana, and then had briefly been with Ray Ellis's Comets and Eddie Quansah's Stargazers before going to join the Downbeats again in Lagos in 1958. He left the Downbeats in 1962 and returned to Ghana to play for the reformed Stargazers and then the Broadway Dance Band. Broadway was renamed Uhuru in 1963 when Stan became its leader. He left the band in 1972 when he set up his Obibini Record Company. Stan is currently the director of the Ghana Television dance band. This interview was recorded at Stan Plange's house in Osu, Accra, on August 18, 1998.[1]

When did you first meet Fela?

I first knew Fela when I was in Nigeria playing for Downbeats from 1958 to 1962—I was also then the treasurer of the Nigerian Union of Musicians. By that time [1958] Fela was just leaving high school in Abeokuta, but he used to come to Lagos to play with highlife bands like Victor Olaiya's

[Cool Cats]. He played trumpet but was playing very badly. Fela was never very good on trumpet but was much better on the keyboards, especially jazz piano. But in those days there were no keyboards [for local dance bands]; we knew of the organ only in church.

It was at that time that Fela got into a good friendship with Joe Mensah, who was playing in the same band as me. The Downbeats was made up mainly of Ghanaians, but the leader was an Ibo Nigerian called Chief Billy Friday. Fela used to come to our shows and at that time he doesn't drink. He was a very clean musician and even condemned people who smoked and drank. Fela was a very good musician and I must admit very disciplined at that time. This was before he became successful.

Then Fela went to Britain and came back, and the first time I met him again was in 1963 when the Uhurus were playing at a dance at the University of Ibadan. Every year they have a dance called Havana Night—a big thing—so many bands come playing at different places around the campus. That time Fela came to join with us on stage, playing trumpet and wearing a suit. That was the first and only time I saw Fela in suit.

How did Fela first come to Ghana?

It was through Zeal Onyia [a famous Nigerian trumpeter] that Fela first came to Ghana. In 1966 or 1967 Zeal wanted to bring Fela and his Koola Lobitos group to Ghana, so Fela first came alone in his small Opel Rekord car. Zeal brought him to Uhuru House [in Asylum Down, Accra] and told me to take care of Fela. I've known Zeal for a long time, even when he was in Ghana in the 1950s [with E. T. Mensah's Tempos band]. So we went around to book clubs, but Fela wasn't known in Ghana then at all and didn't have any recordings.

Anyway Fela went back with Zeal and came back with his band, which was playing highlife but in a very jazz mood. We got the Koola Lobitos to play at Ringway Hotel, Accra, when Ignace de Souza's Black Santiagos

The Uhuru band on tour in Togo, 1968. Mac Tontoh is standing on the far right.

was the resident band. The Uhurus also played there [as did other bands like the Ramblers and Geraldo Pino's Heartbeats]. Fela also played at a couple of other places, but it wasn't successful financially. He was sharing the gate with the club owners. His boys were staying at Ringway Hotel. Fela was staying with me at Uhuru House, but he had been wasting all his gate money on their accommodation, so I suggested that Fela bring his boys to stay with mine, because Uhuru was a big band and Fela's was just a small combo.

It was after that trip that Faisal Helwani began bringing Fela to Ghana and was promoting him through his F Promotions. Fela so loved Ghana that any time he stays in Nigeria he rushed back down to Ghana for a holiday, and then would stay with me. I could guess that he used to come five or six times a year. Even when I'm not in he will leave his trumpet at my front door, as whether he was with his group or not Fela was always with his trumpet.

I haven't seen a musician who rehearses so much as Fela. I suspect it was because he didn't have a very good embouchure, so if he doesn't play his trumpet for one day he finds it very difficult to get a sound out of it. Immediately I come home and see the trumpet I know Fela is in and so I will open the door, put the trumpet inside and keep the key under the doormat. But once Fela is in I can't stay in the house because he would bring women. He goes to see one woman off before he's coming with another. So when he came I used to go to my parents' or girlfriend's place to sleep, Fela's own [interest in women] is like a disease. There's no day that he doesn't have a girl, different, different girls.

Around 1967 or 1968 Fela took your Uhurus on tours of Nigeria?

Yes, we went twice, but the first time it wasn't promoted by Fela but by Chubby Checker [the famous African American king of twist]. You see immediately after the 1966 coup here we toured Ghana with Chubby, and I remember how he regretted that Nkrumah had been overthrown because black Americans regard him highly. Anyway, a year later Chubby was meant to be going to Nigeria but at the last minute his group couldn't come. So Chubby came down to Ghana and wanted us to back him in Nigeria. Our first night we played at Onikan Stadium in Lagos and Fela was there. I remember that he didn't like the arrangement of one of the songs we were playing. Fela said he didn't believe I did the arrangement.

After the Lagos show an Ibo promoter wanted us to tour the east, as he wanted to get into favor with Ojukwu's government, as by that time [1967] the Nigerian Civil War was starting and Ojukwu [Lt. Col. Emeka Ojukwu] was preparing to break [Biafra] away from Nigeria. So on that trip we saw them preparing every night with sticks as guns, and we played in Nsukka the day before the federal government attacked the town.

It was a little later that Fela himself promoted the Uhurus in Nigeria. He was able to organize that trip because we had engagements already at the Yaba College of Technology and Nsukka University. So he took

Uhuru on tour in Uganda, 1968. Stan Plange and Faisal Helwani are standing third and fourth from the left in the back row.

advantage of that, and we did two shows for him in Lagos, one at the Glover Memorial Hall and the other at Lisabi Hall. We stayed at a hotel near Yaba side and shared the gate with Fela.

At the student-organized show at Yaba College we played "Yeshe Yeshe" [one of Fela's highlifes]. Fela was sitting behind us on the bandstand and just jumped and grabbed the microphone from our singer Eddie Entreh, as he was so much moved because we were playing as a big band.

All of a sudden I heard that Fela had gone to America and he was there for such a long time that there were rumors that he had got stranded, his boys had left, and even that Fela had been arrested and jailed for dabbling in narcotics. He was there for months. When he came back he told me he hadn't been in prison but he had had it tough—but had the help of one American girl, Sandra. That was when he got involved in the Black Power thing and that changed his life when he came back completely.

He was smoking cigarettes and grass [Indian hemp] and I haven't seen any experiment that that boy hasn't done with grass. He would put it in brandy for it to ferment for some time and would then drink the brandy. He would even chew the grass and would always smoke some before he goes on stage. I remember one time I was there Fela told me: "Stan, I've got some cake, will you take it?" So I said yes as he also likes cakes and anytime I'm leaving Ghana for Nigeria I used to buy Ghanaian bread and cake for him from a confectionery in Osu RE [Osu Royal Engineers, a suburb] in Accra. So they cut this cake and when I took it I realized that they had used cannabis in preparing it. So I spat it out and Fela started laughing at me. Fela went deeply into smoking Indian hemp openly.

It was after his trip to America that Fela really began his Afrobeat. His first hit as single was "Jeun Koku" ("Chop and Quench") followed by "Who Are You." You see Fela is one of the few musicians who are credited with having invented a beat. He based it on highlife and a James Brown type of soul. I think he got the soul idea when James Brown toured Nigeria in the late 1960s.

It was immediately after a show [in Accra] that Fela invented Afrobeat. So I think it was a fusion of soul and highlife, as already Fela was playing highlife in a jazzy form. Fela was also particular in his earlier Afrobeats with his bass line, trying to get it [the bass guitar] to go like the patterns of the big African drums. He was also one of the first here to introduce piano and organ to dance music.

Personally I didn't like the later Afrobeats he recorded when he became more political and made songs attacking the government. He wasn't minding the music then, and I thought personally that they weren't very good recordings. I preferred his earlier Afrobeats like "Jeun Koku," "Who Are You," "Lady," "Yellow Fever," and "Swegbe." "Swegbe," for instance, is about someone who pretends to know how to do something, as part of the song says that a carpenter not knowing carpentry work is "Swegbe." It's a word that Fela coined and means "not the real thing." The opposite, "pa-wo," is somebody who really knows his work and is genuine.

I believe that you brought Fela and his Africa 70 band to Ghana in the early 1970s?

Yes, I promoted him twice to Ghana in 1971 and 1972. The first show was at the Lebanon Club in Tudu, Accra. The minister of education, Mr. R. R. Amponsah, the minister of information, Mr. Brodie-Mends, and the Nigerian high commissioner were there. Then Fela played a number and all of them felt so embarrassed.

The song is called "Na Poi"—it's a bit filthy, and there are portions [where] Fela sings "when men take women lock door, what thing they do? Na poi"—sex and all this sort of thing. When Fela was playing it the Nigerian high commissioner bent his head and didn't raise it until the show had closed. So at the end of the show Mr. Amponsah called me and asked me to bring Fela to his office the following day, before the next engagement in Takoradi. So I sent Fela there, and Mr. Amponsah pleaded with him to take that song out of the program, and Fela promised he would.

Our next show at the Atlantic Hotel in Takoradi had a very full attendance. So many people were standing on the chairs and tables to see Fela's band and his half-naked girls that they broke over one hundred of them. After the show the manager of the hotel seized Fela's instruments and we had to pay for the damage. It was that night that the anti-Busia military coup was announced [by Colonel Acheampong], and the following day we were meant to be going to Kumasi to play at the City Hotel. So the show couldn't come on. However, as the first two shows had very good crowds the money we made was substantial. After that I brought Fela and his group to Ghana once again.

Fela always used to travel by road then and on these two [1971 and

1972] trips he had a VW bus that carried the instruments. He also had two Opel cars, Fela drove one and his drummer, Tony Allen, drove the other. J. K. Braimah also came. He was a longtime friend of Fela's and was the band's road manager. He also attended primary school here in Ghana, so he knows the country well.

Fela told me a story of what happened once after playing here at one of the trips I organized. He was going back to Nigeria, and when he got to Lomé [the capital of Togo] he began driving on a one-way street. He was stopped by one man who looked scruffy and told Fela in very bad English that this is one-way and you shouldn't go. So Fela said: "So what, are you police?" The man said yes, and that he was a gendarme. Fela said no, as he was convinced the man couldn't be a policeman, as he wasn't wearing a uniform. So the man said that [if] I'm not a gendarme let us go to the police station. So they went there as Fela was so sure that he was going to report that the man was impersonating a policeman.

Immediately they got there the man gave Fela a big slap and told him to go behind the counter-back, as "I be gendarme" and all the other police said, "Oh yes, you be gendarme." You see Fela was a rebel and when he wants something he will just do it.

After that [the two 1971–72 promotions] anytime I used to go to Nigeria Fela put me in a hotel, as we were close. Just to give you an example of my relationship with Fela there was a time in the early 1970s when Remi [Fela's wife] was sick and needed convalescence. I was at Fela's Afro-Spot club in Yaba [originally called Kakadu], and Fela told me that "I'm sending Remi, the children, and their English grandmother [Remi's mother] to you in Ghana to look after them." So I housed them at the Star Hotel in Accra, although Fela paid the bills. I used to go and pick up Remi and the three children and take them to Flagstaff House, the zoo, and places. They stayed two weeks. Remi was very nice, and in a way I would say that Fela didn't deserve that woman, as she was so patient and understanding with his womanizing.

Was it Fela who introduced the South African trumpeter Hugh Masekela to Faisal Helwani and his band Hedzoleh?

Yes, I took both Uhuru and Hedzoleh to record in December 1973. Hedzoleh recorded an album [called *Introducing Hedzoleh*] with Hugh. You see, I was the A&R [artist and repertoire] man for EMI at the time. In fact it was Fela who introduced me to the EMI management, as he was then recording for them. Mike Wells was the managing director, and then Mr. Plumley came in. But Fela fell out with Plumley. There was a time I was passing through Nigeria and met Fela at Lagos airport. I asked him what he was doing, and he said he was coming to stop Plumley going to London, as he owed Fela. Fela said he'd been at Plumley's house but Plumley had been dodging him. So Fela stopped Plumley from going to England that day. There was a lot of crowd there with Fela. They were all arrested and taken to the Apapa police station where Plumley gave an undertaking or check—and Fela was paid. That's the type of man Fela is—if he wants something he will go all out, using legal or illegal means to get what he wants.

PART TWO CONFRONTATION

5

THE KALAKUTA IS BORN

On April 30, 1974, the police raided Fela's house, opposite the old Africa Shrine at the Empire Hotel, Mushin, and he was charged with possessing Indian hemp. In fact, he did have some on him, but he quickly swallowed it. Hemp was a term, incidentally, that Fela himself hated as he claimed that cannabis was not Indian. According to him it had been around in Africa for centuries, so he called it Nigerian natural grass, or NNG.

After the raid he was imprisoned for a while at the police CID headquarters at Alagbon Close. It was because the police examined his stools for traces of marijuana that he wrote the song about his "expensive shit" that was so interesting that doctors had to examine it with microscopes. As the note on the album cover says: "The men in uniform alleged I had swallowed a quantity of Indian Hemp. My shit was sent to lab for test. Result negative—which brings us to Expensive Shit."

In fact he was never prosecuted, as the other prisoners would keep switching their buckets of feces with his, so the police could never find any evidence.

During this time at Alagbon Close he was locked in a cell the prisoners jokingly called the "Kalakuta Republic" (*kalakuta* is Swahili for "rascal") and scratched this name on the cell wall. Because of Fela's popularity

Fela yabbing to Lagosians outside the Africa Shrine on November 26, 1974, after his court acquittal.

with the downtrodden Lagosian underclass, or "sufferheads," he was elected "president" of this "republic" by his jail mates. On his release he promptly named his house the Kalakuta Republic and brought out two albums whose lyrics dealt with his brush with the law. One was the above-mentioned *Expensive Shit* and the other *Alagbon Close.*

On November 23, the same year, Fela's house was attacked for the second time, this time because he was harboring a young runaway truant girl called Folake Oladende, who wanted to join his band. Her father was the inspector general of police for Lagos. The police officer claimed his daughter was only fourteen, and so under age. She claimed she was seventeen. After several fruitless attempts to get her back, the exasperated inspector general sent in the riot police, complete with metal helmets, shields, and tear-gas grenades.

By coincidence I was staying at the Africa Shrine that day, having just come to Lagos with two of Faisal Helwani's bands, Basa-Basa and Bunzus, to record at the new eight-track EMI studio in Lagos. What follows is a journalistic account I made of that memorable eleven-day trip, written on my return to Ghana.

THE 23 NOVEMBER RAID

After a sixteen-hour journey to Lagos, a session at Victor Olaiya's Papingo nightclub at the Stadium Hotel, and finally sleep at the Empire Hotel (Africa Shrine) Mushin, we were woken up on our first morning (23 November) by the roar of an angry crowd.

From our hotel balcony we could see about sixty riot police axing down Fela's front door, just a hundred yards away. Fela's people fought back, so then came the tear gas, and we Ghanaian musicians were down-wind!

We discovered later that he had refused to allow the police to make a routine search of his place and consequently suffered injuries to his head that needed nine stitches for his trouble.

According to the *Nigerian Daily Times* of 27 November: "Afrobeat King, Fela Ransome-Kuti, stepped into freedom from confinement again yesterday when the police granted him bail following his arrest after last Saturday's police raid on his home." The very same day he was released he had to appear in court, and the *Times* continued its report: "Fela was this morning discharged and acquitted by an Apapa Chief Magistrate's Court on a three-count charge of unlawful possession of Indian hemp."

That day we saw a happier demonstration from our balcony than the one on Saturday—after the court case a huge crowd followed Fela's cavalcade to the Shrine, causing a massive go-slow of traffic.

The same night Fela played alongside Basa-Basa and the Bunzus, with one arm in a sling and wearing a skullcap that he humorously called a "pope's hat."

For the days Fela had been away his lawyer had sung the vocals and subsequently became known as "Feelings Lawyer," as he made such a good substitute.

Faisal most certainly did the right thing when he decided to lodge us at the Shrine, the centre of the modern West African music scene. There we met Johnny Haastrup of Moro-Mono, who told us he was thinking of bringing his band to Ghana for a tour. Berkely Jones of BLO was around briefly and mentioned that he had recruited a new bass player. Big Joe Olodele, who used to be with the Black Santiagos in Ghana, is now with the Granadians—and Albert Jones from the Heartbeats '72 was down from his base in Kano. And we had live Juju every night from the Lido nightclub opposite the hotel.

Our bands went down very well at the Papingo, where we played four nights alongside the resident All Stars (ex–Cool Cats). We then spent two days in the recording studio where Faisal and Fela were co-producing the session, and Faisal jammed on organ for some numbers. On 30 November we all departed, including the midget Kojo Tawiah Brown who came as our mascot, leaving Fela and Faisal to mix the recordings.

We were meant to play at the Cultural Centre in Cotonou, Dahomey [now the Republic of Benin], on our way back home, but we arrived the day the "People's Revolution" was declared in Dahomey and found Cotonou deserted; everyone had gone to Abomé. We did, however, play the following night at the Centre Communitaire in Lomé, Togo.

We all learned a lot from our short stay in Nigeria. Fela is the top musician there, much more popular than foreign artists such as James Brown, or Jimmy Cliff, who was barely able to pull in a crowd of 6,000 at the 60,000-capacity football stadium at Surulere on 28 November. A lesson for Ghanaian pop fans, I think!

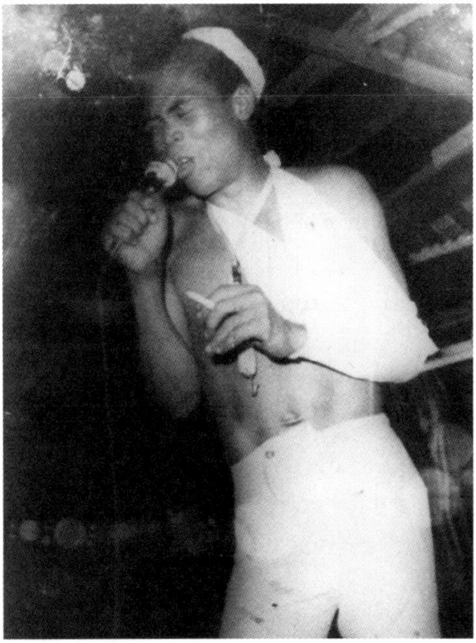

Bandaged but unbowed, Fela (*left*) performs in what he called a "pope's" or "alhaji's hat" after returning from his court victory.

The entrance of the Africa Shrine (*below*) in Mushin in 1974.

Five days after the November 23 attack Fela was released from jail and so was able to help Faisal coproduce the albums by Basa-Basa and the Bunzu Soundz. Fela also took over from Feelings Lawyer (Wole Kuboye) and played some of his current songs. One I recall was "Everything Scatter," which praised African heroes such as Kwame Nkrumah of Ghana, Sékou Touré of Guinea, and, more controversially, General Idi Amin of Uganda. Fela insisted Amin was a heroic figure, settling scores with the Indian traders in his country and getting Europeans to carry him around in a palanquin. Another song that Fela was playing at this time was "Confusion," released the following year, which is about the problems created for West African countries having multiple languages and currencies.

In 1976 Fela used his technique of turning confrontation with the authorities into music when he released for EMI his album *Kalakuta Show,* which describes the police attack on him on November 23, 1974.

6

"J. B." TALKS ABOUT FELA

Daniel Koranteng, better known as "J. B.," was one of Fela's conga players between 1971 and early 1975. He is half Ga, half Fanti, and was born in the Accra Police Depot in 1948. I interviewed him at the music department of the University of Ghana, Legon, on May 11, 1999. As he explains, although he did not start playing congas for Fela until April 1971, he danced for him much earlier.

How did you meet Fela?

Fela came to Ghana in 1967, and at that time I was playing drums for a traditional Ga kpanlogo group called Play and Laugh and was the soul dancer for the Bugulu Dance Group of Accra Newtown. I was a fantastic soul dancer, and so was called J. B., or James Brown. The dance group played at the Pan African Hotel, Grand Hotel, Tip Toe Gardens, Lido—and anywhere where there were bands that could play soul; like the El Pollos, Barbecues, Uhurus, Geraldo Pino's Heartbeats [a Sierra Leonean band] and the Black Santiagos led by Ignace de Souza from the Benin Republic. Fela and his Koola Lobitos band came with a beautiful Nigerian lady dancer called Dele and they all stayed at the Pan African Hotel. Fela

Fela with Africa 70. Daniel "J. B." Koranteng is standing second from right.

normally played side by side with the Uhurus, and as the Bugulu dancers used to perform with them we also performed with Dele. I loved the way Fela held his trumpet, he turned it sideways and played Yoruba highlife like "Ashe Love" in a jazzy way.

When was the next time you met Fela?

It was in Lagos. You see there was an Al Hadji who lived in Accra Newtown who heard in 1969 that Geraldo Pino and later the El Pollos were making it in Nigeria with the James Brown thing. The Al Hadji was managing a soul group called the Triffis led by Lindy Lee [Lord Lindon], and he wanted to take me as well. Later, in December 1969, when we were in the north of Nigeria, we heard that thousands of Nigerians were being repatriated from Ghana [during President Busia's infamous Aliens' Compliance Order]. So we changed our name to the Big Beats [that later recorded the famous Ghanaian Afrobeat song "Kyenkyemma," which means "decrepit" or "old-fashioned"].

I then joined a Lagos soul group called the Immortals, playing jazz drums that sometimes played at the Kakadu Nightclub in Yaba, which Fela renamed the Afro-Spot when he came back from the United States in 1969.[1] So Fela asked me to dance with Dele for the Nigeria 70 on a permanent basis and paid me five pounds a week. Six months later two black American music students came to the Afro-Spot to feature on conga drums with Fela's band, then called Nigeria 70. It was marvelous. The following day Fela asked me that "Do you know anyone who can play congas because I want to infuse these two congas into my Afrobeat." I told him that I played congas myself. Fela said I should go and look for another person, and I got Friday Jombo [or Jumbo], who played congas with Peter King's Voices of Africa band. The first time we played double rhythm congas for Fela was Tuesday, April 9, 1971, and it was also the first ladies' night [women got in free] at the Afro-Spot.

Three months later we toured England and recorded at the Abbey Road multitrack studio *Fela Live with Ginger Baker,* with Ginger Baker and Tony Allen doing drum solos. We played in clubs in London like the West End, Countdown, and Speakeasy and then went to Wales and Kessington where Ginger Baker comes from. We also met Paul and Linda McCartney and the other members of the Beatles who also recorded at Abbey Road.

Was there not some trouble between Fela and Paul McCartney?

This was the following year [actually in August 1973] when Paul McCartney and his new band Wings came to Nigeria and visited Fela at his new Afro-Spot club in Surulere—before he used the name Africa Shrine. Some of Fela's musicians were taken by McCartney to help record the

Wings album [*Band on the Run*] without Fela's permission.[2] They employed the horns-men, guitarists, and bass player. Fela is a jealous man and told [backstage]—I believe it was McCartney at the Afro-Spot: "Man you can't do that to me, do you want to spoil my band, you should have taken permission from me."[3]

I believe it was in 1972 that you toured Ghana with Fela?

Yes, we went there in February 1972 when Colonel Acheampong took over from the civilian Busia government. We were actually in Accra when the military coup took place. On that tour we were playing "Open and Close," "Who Are You," "Fight Finish," "Chop and Quench," and "Je-Je" and we performed at the Apollo Theatre, Tip Toe Gardens, and the university campus in Accra; and also in Takoradi, Cape Coast, and Kumasi. We also played at the officers' mess at State House for Colonel Acheampong. He was very happy to see me, a Ghanaian, playing in Fela's group. It was on that Ghanaian tour that Fela got the idea for his "Shakara" and "Lady" tunes. He went to lodge at the Presidential Hotel in Accra and asked the receptionist: "Woman, how do I book my lodging?" She said: "Please, I'm not a woman, I'm a lady." She was bluffing. So Fela composed the two songs when he got back to Nigeria.

Were you the only Ghanaian musician in Fela's band at that time?

No. There was Peter Kadana from the north of Ghana who played guitar and later changed his name to Rescole. Then there was Henry Kofi, who was half Ghanaian and half Nigerian and played the triple lead congas. And the drummer Tony Allen, who is half Nigerian and half Ghanaian Ewe. Also a bit later the Ghanaian Nicholas Addo replaced Friday Jombo on the rhythm conga.

When was it that Fela began to get into trouble with the authorities?

It was from the end of 1973 when Fela had changed the name of his club to the Africa Shrine (still in Surulere). There was a judge's daughter who came to the afternoon jump when she was on school holidays and followed Fela and wouldn't go home. Then there was a police commissioner's daughter who came to the Shrine and also went to live at Fela's house [his mother's house in Mushin later called the Kalakuta]. So the parents of these girls sent some brothers to call their sisters. Fela beat one of the brothers and put out a burning cigarette on his skin. Fela told them that if you know your sister is missing go to the police and report—don't come here. So the parents sent policemen and policewomen with dogs to arrest anyone they see at Fela's house. This was in April 1974.

I had gone there to collect money to repair my conga drum. The police first sent two officers inside the house and told Fela they were coming to search for Indian hemp and the two missing girls. Fela told them that before you come into my house I will first search you as you may be coming in with drugs to put in my house to put me into trouble. So Fela searched the two officers up and down and found a talisman in one of the policeman's pockets.

Fela asked him what he is doing with a talisman and the officer said we use it for protection. So after a long argument Fela said you can all come in—by which time everything had been put in order and the two girls had gone through the back door and jumped the fence. So the police couldn't catch either of them but rather arrested we who had come innocently, and the musicians and girl dancers living there—fifty-two of us in all—and took us to CID headquarters at Alagbon Close.

They also arrested Fela, saying that he was smoking Indian hemp and took him to a cell at Alagbon Close where they keep all the political detainees, eminent personalities, veteran soldiers, and military officers who had been arrested during the [Biafran] civil war. This area of the prison is called "XX Timbuctu" and has only one door and no proper windows. So the moment Fela entered, these people shouted: "Fela, Fela you are going to be our president in this prison." That is how his name the Black President started. And the actual corner of this large cell where they put Fela is called Kalakuta.

You were also arrested. So what happened then?

We fifty-two were in the cells for a week and the torture and beatings in prison were too much. As I'm talking to you now I have weak teeth. Hitting me with gun, kicking me with boot, calling me a Ghanaian. Fela's mother bailed Fela, and Beko [his brother] bailed Fela's girlfriend, but as a Ghanaian I didn't have anyone to bail me. However, later on one of the gatemen of the Shrine told the court clerk that that man you want to take to Ikoyi Prison is my in-law. So he bailed me too and we all started going to Court Two at Bode Thomas in Surulere for four months. Then they changed the judge and took me, Fela, and the others to another court in Apapa.

I made the mistake of telling the court that my father was a Ghanaian policeman, thinking I would be let free as a policeman's son. Not knowing it was worsening things as the CID was saying I had three charges against me. That I was a Ghanaian who was bringing Ghanaian girls to Fela, that I had originally come into the country illegally, and that I had a false Nigerian passport. But it wasn't true, as I had first come to Ghana on a band group-passport. Fortunately the two CID men who went to Ghana to investigate about me at police headquarters in Accra couldn't get documented evidence on my father, as he had retired as a pensioner and couldn't be located. So I was saved, as during the fourth month of the case, when the court was charged, the new judge couldn't find my file.

"Feelings Lawyer" [Wole Kuboye—one of Fela's lawyers] said as there is no evidence that this man is a Ghanaian, he's a Nigerian.

So I was discharged and acquitted, and when I jumped and shouted the judge said, "contempt of court." So "People's Lawyer" (another of Fela's lawyers) told me to keep quiet while the judge read the acquittal verdict again. When I got outside Fela and the others were waiting and I shouted "Fela, Fela I'm free" and did somersaults and rolled on the ground. Fela said: "Yes, you are the first to win and now all of us are going to win our cases."

What happened after your release?

I went on tour with Fela [then still out on bail] to Ilorin University in Kwara State and the police came and found Indian hemp in one of the saxophones as we were coming home. Then when we got back the police started looking for Fela, still in connection with the two girls. The band also went to Cameroons around this time and was also chased there by the Nigerian police.

Were you arrested during the second attack on his house that year in November 1974?

I had gone to the Ghana High Commission that day to a friend working there who normally gives us Ghanaian *kenkey* [fermented corn dough] and I was teargassed near the Shrine [by then the Empire Hotel] near Fela's house [by then called Kalakuta]. I dropped the *kenkey* but wasn't arrested. The police, however, did arrest two other Ghanaians—the conga player Nicholas Addo and my junior brother who was driving Fela's mother's car, called Aryee. After that Fela started dodging in hotels and so we were not playing for some time as Fela was being charged again with abducting girls.

We musicians were feeling hungry. I didn't want to leave him as I loved him and his music but in early 1975 I joined a new juju-music group called the Juju Rock Stars and became a session musician at the EMI studio in Apapa. After that I joined Sonny Okosun's band and featured in his *Papa's Land* album. Then I was recruited to the University of Lagos cultural group by Igo Chico [a former saxophone player of Fela's] and we played at the 1977 FESTAC black arts festival. I then met the university musicologist Joy Nwosu and worked with the Lagos University Cultural Centre Performing arts group until I recently retired.

What is Afrobeat?

Many bands played funky Afro, Afro-soul and Afro-highlife before I left Ghana [in 1969]: Uhuru, Broadway, the Black Santiagos, and later Osibisa. And in Nigeria there was Chris Ajilo, Segun Bucknor, Orlando Julius—and of course Fela and his distinct beat. The name Afrobeat was made in 1969 when Fela met Stan Plange of the Uhurus and the Nigerian/Ghanaian promoter Raymond Aziz in Accra. Fela told them he wanted to change the name of his music from jazz-highlife to something else. So Stan and others said: "Fela you used to raise your shirt collar like an 'Afro' guy so call your music Afrobeat." At that time Fela was passing through Ghana from America where he had been arrested. You see in America he was moving with an Afro-American mayor or politician's daughter called Daniels [Sandra Daniels Iszadore].

Later the family, who didn't like Fela, said Fela had raped her, and put him in jail. He was bailed by Duke Lumumba, an Ashanti trumpet player who owned a recording studio in the US where Fela recorded. Duke told Fela he didn't think these people would leave him. He said: "I want you to escape, so when I bail you, you'll fly to Ghana—and I will arrange for your musicians to also go to Ghana with their instruments so you can join them there and fly together to Nigeria." So Fela left America with Duke Lumumba and came with only $10 in his pocket. That's why Fela couldn't go to America for many years.

7

THE KALAKUTA REPUBLIC

The following is a diary I kept from January 2 through January 28, 1977, when I was acting in Fela's film, "The Black President." I have expanded the original somewhat by adding comments in brackets or in small print indentations.

Sunday, 2 January 1977

Arrived at Kalakuta, Faisal, his Lebanese friend Victor Azzi [a chef], and the Ghana Film [Corporation] crew already here. Fela in his usual pants. All happy to see me. Then Fela dramatically told me that I had to do my part well or my children would not be allowed to stay in Africa. I was surprised by this bit of melodrama, as the two parts in the film for whites, me as Inspector Reynolds and Albert [another Lebanese friend of Faisal] as the governor of the Elmina slave castle had been picked by Faisal and Fela as insiders.

Except for a small swimming pool, things much the same at the Kalakuta as before. The monkey at the gate, the donkey in the yard, and the big shaggy Alsatian dog Wokolo ("go and find prick") still around. The yellow waiting room with its plush lounge chairs, bear rug, and photos of

Sitting, left to right, Victor Azzi, John Collins, and Fela's bodyguard Segun.

Fela and friends still the same as 1975. But there is a new painting I hadn't noticed before of a group of police attacking the Kalakuta with tear gas and axes and people on the roof throwing rocks and things down on them. This must be the original painting (by Ghariokwu Lemi) they used on the cover of the *Kalakuta Show* album.

The tiny cushioned "session" room and Fela's special chair where he held court also as before. He still hasn't put a door on the adjoining toilet, just the same thin piece of cloth. So presumably he still sometimes holds his sessions and court while shitting and farting for all to hear. When I first saw him at the Kalakuta in 1974 he didn't even bother with the cloth partition so I guess it is some sort of concession to the fact that lots of foreign visitors and journalists are beginning to visit him, who may be upset.

They've forgotten their own history. Some old European kings, like Louis XIV of France, also held court for their more intimate retainers while sitting on a toilet-cum-throne. Some people's greatest thoughts come whilst they're on the toilet. Look at Luther and his Protestant Vision—it all occurred in a privy while having a mighty crap after being constipated for several days. The Ghana Film crew did some shots at the Kalakuta, and Jackie [Faisal's Ghanaian Mr. Fixit] took me here to the Crossroads Hotel, just a few yards from the Kalakuta.

Monday, 3 January 1977

Saw a weird sight at the traffic lights at the crossroads near the Hotel. Either the lights weren't working or no one was minding them, so a group of policemen carrying whips were trying to control the traffic. At one point a policeman got so infuriated that he began whipping the cars. One poor guy was on a motorbike—so to try to dodge a lashing he accelerated off right into the flow of moving traffic, managing somehow to get across. He presumably preferred taking his chances in a crash rather than a whipping.

Victor told me after that Fela's YAP [Young African Pioneers organization] had just distributed half a million broadsheets that condemned the giving of horsewhips to traffic police.[1] At the Kalakuta, Fela told us that it was a particularly stupid thing to do with the FESTAC coming up.[2] What would black American visitors think of seeing these whippings—it would be like scenes from South Africa, but this time blacks whipping blacks? It would freak the Americans out.

Fela's now saying that he will do more broadsheets, he's even bought a press and is going to stand for President. Whether this is due to the popular support for YAP or is something to do with the film The Black

President, I'm not sure. The line between reality and art often gets blurred at the Kalakuta—reality becomes dramatised and dramas real.

In the afternoon there was an argument as one of the dancers hit one of the bandsmen. Fela shouted "court" but the dancer ignored him. Everyone worked himself or herself into a frenzy of excitement and Fela and some others chased her to the front of the house. Someone slapped her and forced her into the session or courtroom where she was slapped again and fell on me. She was then taken out to the backyard where everyone surrounded her and the bandsmen. Everyone was shouting as they fought, but every time the bandsmen hit the dancer hard Fela said stop, he should only slap her.

After the fight Fela called all the dancers and told them not to trouble the bandsmen again or he would allow them to beat them. The rules of the house are that bandsmen cannot touch the dancers, whatever they do or say, but the dancers were taking advantage of this rule—until today. Then Fela asked if any of the other girls wanted to fight a bandsman. One promptly volunteered and was slapped and fell to her knees for forgiveness. The dancer who caused the original trouble was also made to kneel and beg for forgiveness from Fela. To everyone's enjoyment she was told to clean the toilets.

All this happened in the backyard where the Kalakuta's little wooden Kala-Kosa jail is situated. Actually it's only a symbolic jail locked with string, but if you don't do your penance in it you have to quit the Kalakuta altogether. The whole incident reminds me of something that happened in the "punishment" back-yard two years ago. A bald-headed dancer who had been moaning and shouting for hours in the Kala-Kosa was taken out in the yard and surrounded by the Kalakuta residents. She began screaming about at Fela and he, J. K. Braimah, and the others began chanting back and clapping their hands rhythmically. Suddenly this abusive call-and-response gelled into a song. Then the whole thing broke up, the girl

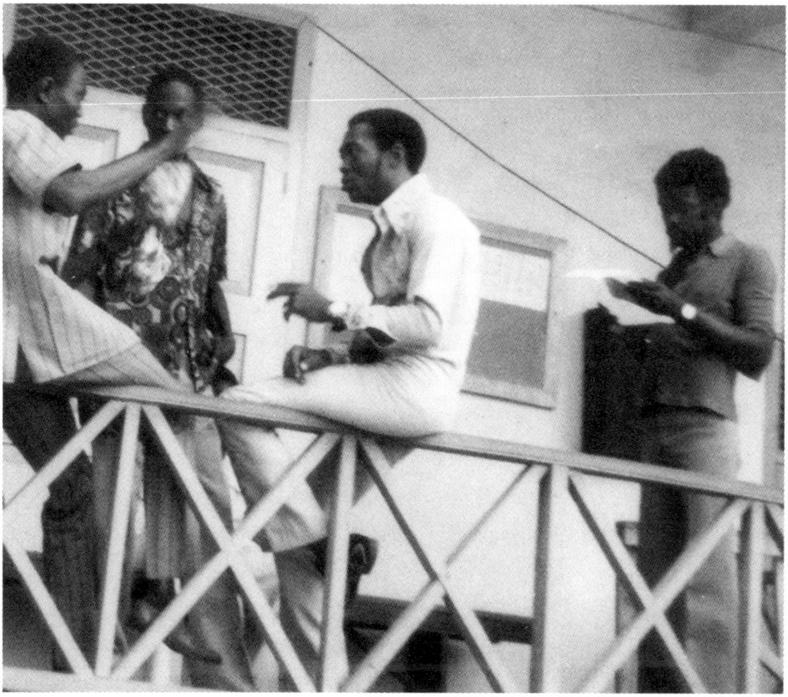

In Abeokuta: Fela (*seated*) in conversation with A. J. Moreson (*middle*), a friend (*far left*), and Alex Oduro (*right*).

became quiet and was left free, and the Kalakuta people went their own separate ways talking excitedly as if they had just seen a stimulating film.

Still the same exciting vibes at the Kalakuta: great music, intense rages, showmanship, violent palavers, bluffing, ego-tripping, unexpected happenings, radicalism, decadence, friendly fierceness—and what Jackie calls a "bunch of half-naked Bohemians."

Faisal and Victor also at the Crossroads with me. All my food and lodgings paid for and getting 28 naira a day. Going to Abeokuta tomorrow to do my part. Gave my passport to one of Jackie's Ghanaian boys, Nii

Papoti, to get it stamped. Says no problem, as he knows some immigration officials. So should be able to leave by Friday.

Tuesday, 4 January 1977

Now at Abeokuta, staying at a hotel near the famous Abeokuta Rock. Faisal's gone to Rank in London to deposit some of the films already shot. The 23-member Ghana Film crew came up in a convoy of three trucks, dolly, and a 60-kilowatt generator. I came in Fela's VW with J. K., Feelings Lawyer [Wole Kuboye], Alex Oduro, Fela's three children, Victor, and an Afro-American called A. J. Moreson and some of the Kalakuta artists and house people. Fela drove—he always does—he never allows anyone to drive him on a long journey. Fela in a good mood to be going to his hometown and joking around on the road by allowing cars, especially Mercedes saloons, to come behind us and try to overtake. As soon as they were overtaking he put his foot on the accelerator and it became a neck-and-neck race at 80 or 90 miles an hour.

This went on until a vehicle came in the opposite direction and the big-man in the Mercedes saw Fela's gleeful manic look and the name of the band painted in psychedelic colours on the side of the bus—and would drop back, as Fela never gave way. He did this about ten times on the journey. The first few times I was petrified. Towards the end I was as exhilarated as everyone else. Being with Fela was giving me the feeling of being with an immortal. No wonder he uses the name "Anikulapo," which means a dare-devil who keeps death in his pocket.

In the morning went to Fela's old school, the Abeokuta Grammar School, to see the Principal about arranging mine and Feelings' scene. The Principal kept us waiting and when we finally saw him he said the scene was too controversial and he would have to get permission from the Ministry of Education. Fela was furious, as he had given a 1,500 naira donation to the school. He threatened to collect the money back and do the scene at his mother's private school, a huge campus-like place that we then went to.

Afterward we went to his mother's house [Mrs. Funmilayo Ransome-Kuti] to discuss the plan, but she didn't like the idea of collecting the money back and said she would try and sort things out with the Ministry by phone. At this point Fela thought that one of his minders had insulted his mother—I don't know what it was all about. But suddenly Fela began kicking the guy viciously with his pointed shoes into a corner until his mother stopped him.

After this she phoned up the Minister. She talked to him like he was a small boy, as she is a prominent political figure herself. Anyway, she got the Ministry to at least allow us to shoot the part of the scene where Feelings and I enter and leave the school office. The more sensitive bit that the Ministry thought would embarrass the British government we'll do in Lagos. One of Fela's girlfriends gave his mother a necklace.

Fela and most of the others went back to the grammar school to inform the Principal, and the three children and me stayed with his mother. We hit it off immediately; I find her a very pleasant and penetrating women. She showed me some photos of when she was young. Very beautiful and still very striking with her graying short Afro haircut and impeccable English. She was very inquisitive about me and how I came to fall in with Fela. I told her I had been a musician at Faisal's Napoleon Club, had met Fela through Faisal and had stayed at Fela's Shrine twice already.

I also told her I was a science school-teacher in Ghana and she asked me to talk about this to the three children, Femi and his two sisters, Sola and Yeni. So I sat for a while with them and a large number of dogs in an upstairs room. Sola is 14, and Femi and Yeni, who are older, told me they were born in England. I quizzed them on what they knew of chemistry and physics.

In the afternoon Fela and all of us went around his old school, which has an old colonial church- or cathedral-like structure. Fela got mad when he noticed that one of the pictures in the assembly room wasn't hung properly. It was askew—and he went into a long diatribe about Africans never doing anything one hundred percent, but always half-baked, and this was hindering the development of the continent.

This was all because one picture was not hung right. Fela also told us about his dad, who had been the principal of the school when he was a pupil in the 1940s. He said his dad was like an English Victorian, really strict. He also said that his grandfather [Reverend Josiah Ransome-Kuti] was a composer and a preacher who had been responsible for spreading Christianity amongst the Yoruba—and he wanted to undo this and return to "blackism."

Some of Fela's ideas on Christianity are well captured in the following quote from the FESTAC edition of the Lagos *Indigo* magazine:

I can say that my religion is Modern African Reality. If I am to believe that God is a spirit as the Bible says, then I also believe in witches and wizards because they all perform wonders. I don't believe in God as a spirit. I believe God is a human being because I have been exposed to many things that made me think of God as a human being.

I [also] believe that Jesus was a man—a man of high intelligence. And how can one person be father, son and holy ghost at the same time. Christians are messing us up today. They say human beings were made in the image and likeness of God. Who told them that? Who saw them? That is why I believe in flying saucers. I think God is just an advanced and well-developed human being and I think Jesus was put on earth [i.e., by flying saucers] not by the Virgin Mary.

Wednesday, 5 January 1977

No shooting today, so this morning went to the Abeokuta Rock [Olumo Rock] with Lyday [dancer], Segun [one of Fela's bodyguards] and Oghene Kologbo [Africa 70 guitarist]. It's a rock hill that the town's inhabitants used to flee up in times of war. It's a natural fortress, and there's a place where only one person can pass up at a time. If there are people above you stopping you it's impossible to pass. There's a huge white cross on top of it.[3]

No water at the hotel, and it's a peculiar place. To prevent robberies all the air conditioners are inside the hallway that leads to our rooms. With all the heat being pumped out it's hell going through the hallway and the rooms are not cool—as all the air conditioners do is pump in and out each other's heat.

Another heavy session with A. J., who told me point blank he doesn't like whites and it's a great privilege for me to be here. He's been in Nigeria for one year. He told me that he had been involved in the Detroit riots and that he had been imprisoned and got off hard-labour by working as a clerk in the prison library. Through that he had read all the greats like DuBois, Padmore, and Nkrumah and was able to help his brothers. He's a musician.

In the afternoon went with Fela, Victor, and some Kalakuta people to Mrs. Ransome-Kuti's. She asked me to continue my private classes with Femi, Yeni, and Sola, and before I had had time to start Fela burst into the room. I think someone had told him about yesterday. He ordered me to stop and told his kids about the uselessness of school, especially science, math and English. His mother disapproved of his attitude and winking at me she chastised him and said she wanted her grandchildren educated even if he didn't. She said that I should continue, which I did, and Fela left. I think because I'm playing the part of a colonial education officer he actually thinks I'm a colonialist. Despite Fela's father being an educationalist, Fela himself did not believe in sending his own children to schools, sentiments expressed in his 1976 release "Mr. Follow Follow." This song advises people to open their own eyes and ears and "no follow book-o" as books are where rats, cockroaches, and darkness are found.

A lot of playing-acting, bickering and skin-pain go on at the Kalakuta. Went roaming around the town with J. K., Victor and a couple of the dancers. J. K.'s a lovely guy; he's been with Fela since the Highlife Rakers days.

Thursday, 6 January 1977

Morning. Still don't know when we're going to shoot. Waiting for official permission from the Ministry of Information. Evening: Finally got permission to shoot. Fela spent morning condemning a government proposal to ban local private cars during FESTAC, to ease Lagos's notorious traffic go-slows.

Quite a bunch of Kalakuta people here. Fela, in pants as always, spends a lot of time practising his sax. He has two bodyguards: Oyo [also a driver] and tall bouncy Shegun. Then there's Sonny who holds his purse and Tunde who is one of his valets. There's also Steve, his personal PRO, Nepa [Nigerian Electrical Power Authority], his electrician, and Feelings, his lawyer.

The Africa 70 musicians are friendly, especially Kologbo and drummer Tony Allen. The women are rather snooty and stand-offish—always complaining that they find Abeokuta dull and boring. I've only got to know the dancer Lyday, who is an open and thoughtful person, and Shi-Shi, who is always looking sad. Then there's tall Emelia (her Ga name is Naa Limley Lampty) who is quite haughty as she's Fela's number one girlfriend—but she's Ghanaian and I know her from when I was playing with the Bunzus at the Napoleon Club in Accra.[4]

Strange conversation with A. J. an hour ago. He told me he was an African mystic and had had four previous lives. Think he was trying to freak me. I giggled in disbelief and then surprised him when I told him I had been living in Africa since 1952, had a Ghanaian stepmother and was running a band in Ghana. Because of the black and white matter that he constantly talks to everyone about we have a prickly sort of relationship.

Also I've heard he was understudying my part as Inspector Reynolds and that if I hadn't come he would have acted the role of the white colonial education officer—quite how I don't know. So he's a bit annoyed with my

Fela's electrician Nepa with "The Black President" film mobile generator.

coming anyway. In spite of all this we're both musicians and we've both been thrown together, so quite enjoy getting together chatting about the weird and nutty goings-on in this place.

For instance, this morning on the balcony of the Abeokuta Rock Hotel Fela was blasting one of the dancers for having abused bandsmen. So she was told to kneel down in front of the guy, hold his prick and kiss his arse. She did kneel, but that was all, as at the last moment Fela turned the thing into a joke.

Friday, 7 January 1977

Me, Feelings and Fela did our scene this morning. Or just the outside shots, as the Ministry of Education only gave the school permission for that. Also the part where I'm actually being beaten by Feelings [i.e., playing Fela's dad] was cut due to Ministry instructions.

Anyway, I don't think that actually happened in reality—it's a bit of poetic license by the scriptwriter Alex Oduro. So I finally got into my colonial outfit that one of Fela's valets was looking after and went to Fela's old school. Fela himself was dressed as a schoolboy pretending to be a prefect. Because the confrontation scene in the school office will be done in Lagos when we get back, the shots were quite short. All I had to do was to walk into the office, run out chased by Feelings waving a cane, and then knock Fela down in my flight. In fact I really knocked Fela hard and he glared to me a bit after. But that's what he told me to do—he wanted the thing realistic. I just hadn't taken into account that despite Fela's huge charismatic persona he's quite lightly built.

After he had dusted himself off and got his wind back Fela was very pleased with the shot.[5] Everyone was, except the school principal, who was furious as the Ministry had told him no cane was to appear in the scene. Fela and Feelings tricked him. Before getting out of costume, me, Fela and J. K. Braimah had some photos taken in the school compound.

Afterwards we went to Mrs. Ransome-Kuti's house, and as we were going in, Ojo who was driving carelessly, damaged the car slightly. Fela went mad and told the six or seven people with us to beat him. Everyone converged on the hapless Ojo and got in two punches each before Fela stopped them. Sola commented that he was very lucky. After Fela and the others left I stayed and chatted with his mother again. In spite of her being a prominent Nigerian nationalist who had led tax riots against the British in the 1940s, she told me she quite liked the British for being gentlemanly. So whereas I have problems with Fela as he sees me as an

English gentleman, which is my role anyway in the film, it's the opposite with his mum. I told her that I'm only half English as my dad is from Ireland—which was a British colony. I told her about my dad having helped set up the University of Ghana's Philosophy Department in 1952 and now, on his Ghanaian pension, he's gone into farming.

After lunch talked to Feelings. When I told him that Lyday was the only woman with us who was quiet and friendly he told me it was because she quietly drinks half a bottle of whisky a day. He told me she can really do crazy things. Once at Lagos airport when Fela was travelling to Zaire, Lyday dropped her pants and pissed straight onto the carpet of immigration control. The officials raised hell and then she started to abuse them, saying that the toilets had been full up and there was a long queue waiting outside. She yelled at them that a modern airport should have more toilets. She caused so much trouble that Fela's departure was almost delayed.

Feelings [Wole Kuboye] is quite a character, big physically and a lawyer with an artistic streak and great voice. Anytime Fela's in a scrape and Feelings can't get him out of jail, Feelings himself sings Fela's part on stage. He did this when I was staying at the African Shrine in November 1974. After the Kalakuta was tear-gassed, Fela was locked up for a few days and Feelings took over. He knows all of Fela's songs, and his voice is identical. Feelings also told me about the time that Fela got stuck in the United States in 1969. The musicians' union there wouldn't let him play, and he didn't have enough money to get out of the country. It was then that the Afro-American singer Sandra Iszadore Daniels helped him and introduced him to the Black Panthers, which had such a profound influence on Fela.

Saturday, 8 January 1977

Spent the evening with "Alhaji" (J. K. Braimah), A. J. and some of the Kalakuta people being driven around in the VW by Fela in one of his magic mystery roamings of the town. Ended up in a disco so went to bed late. Before we went out, Fela's older sister (Dolu) came around to the hotel to visit. She's a strong, masculine-looking woman with some front teeth missing. She was quite drunk and noisy and Fela didn't seem to mind her much. He was playing his saxophone against her booming voice in some sort of anti-dialogue.

> Fela's elder sister is called Oludolupo or Dolu Ransome-Kuti and is the mother of Frances Kuboye, who was a dentist and married the jazz bassist and nightclub owner Tunde Kuboye. Frances was Fela's favorite niece; sadly she died of a heart attack at the age of forty-eight, the day after Fela himself died. Oludolupo lives in Abeokuta and was a trained nurse. She became the matriarch of the family when Fela's mother, Funmilayo, died in 1978. It was Oludolupo, "Aunty Dolu," who later nursed Fela when he lay dying.

It's ironical that both Fela's mother and sister are such powerful liberated women. He worships his mother in fact. But Fela himself seems to like very submissive (but volatile) women.

Just struck me odd that my name in the film, Inspector Reynolds, is the name of my grandparents' family. But far from being colonialist they were working-class Bristolians living in the slums of Bedminster. On my dad's side however (the Irish branch of MacNaughtons) there is a colonial connection. My grandfather was an educationalist in the old British Indian Empire. Whatever the case, my playacting yesterday seems to have purged my colonial past as far as Fela is concerned. Seems much more relaxed with me now.

At midday went to say goodbye to Mrs. Ransome-Kuti. She knows about the terrible shortages in Ghana, in fact she quizzed me on the situation yesterday. So she's bought me a huge plastic bag of commodities: soap, Omo detergent, toothpaste and so on. Got back to the hotel to find out that poor Ojo had been beaten again. Seems he had bought inferior palmwine to Fela who also suspected him of stealing. So one of the bodyguards had to give Ojo ten dirty slaps.

Going back to Lagos any moment now—in time for tonight's show. Huge argument for the last one-and-a-half hours between Ekow [Alex Oduro] and A. J. over the black American comedian Sammy Davis Junior. Ekow saying that even though he's an Uncle Tom he's been giving monies to the black cause. A. J. said his image is derogatory to the black man, so the money he gives to the Panthers is nothing—just a dash. Both appeal to Fela, who came down slightly on A. J.'s side. Actually, in spite of Fela's blackism philosophy he's not a racist. On the way up here in the Volkswagen, A. J. had actually said to Fela that no whites should be allowed to live in Africa. Fela's reply was that's crazy—some whites help the cause and he even has white friends—he mentioned Faisal for instance.

Back in Lagos at the Crossroads Hotel with Victor Azzi. Several incidents on the way down, besides Fela's usual dicing with death driving. First poor old Ojo was kicked around by Fela when we had to stop for a flat-tyre as we drove off. Fela said it was Ojo's job to look after these things.

Then as we were passing out of Abeokuta a traffic policeman on a pedestal was unfortunate enough to make a rather vague signal to Fela. He had already gone past when the policeman shouted at him and Fela became so furious that he reversed the VW at speed, right up to the policeman, so their faces were inches from one another. Fela called him foolish and asked whether he was going to be arrested. He also shouted at the amazed policeman that all police are corrupt. The surprised man could only splutter a few words before Fela, who was smoking NNG [Nigerian Natural Grass], blew a huge puff into the policeman's face and speeded off. I last saw the bullied man waving his arms about and screaming something about not being god. He or Fela I don't know.

Fela is notorious in Nigeria for his open smoking of marijuana. Two years ago he was arrested and, as the police thought he had swallowed

Fela's van with one of its car repair "fitters," Ekow.

the evidence, he was purged and his feces analyzed. No trace found but this special scientific treatment led Fela to compose "Expensive Shit."

This incident with the policeman put Fela into a good humor until we drew up at a petrol station halfway to Lagos. Fela got out to stretch his legs and for some reason called the petrol attendant a monkey—who made a grab for Fela's testicles. Segun jumped out of the van and pushed the boy away—who dashed into the building and came out brandishing a crowbar. By this time the other attendants had seen the name Africa 70 on the bus and told the boy it was only Fela's way of joking and he should cool down. Fela meanwhile had smartly jumped back into the driving seat and said that he hadn't meant any insult. Everyone laughed as we drove out—except the young petrol attendant who was left fuming and clutching his iron bar.

Just seen Nii Papoti, who still hasn't been able to get my passport sorted out. He is a Ghanaian, tall, glasses, owlish looking—been with Fela for twelve years. Told me while I was away one of the Kalakuta girls had attacked him with a glass-covered ludo game-board. It shattered and he had to have stitches.

Going to Fela's Comprehensive Show tonight—this always begins with Fela and a huge cavalcade of people crossing the road between the Kalakuta and the African Shrine [Empire Hotel]. First Fela pours a libation at the shrine near the Hotel's entrance dedicated to Kwame Nkrumah. Then he joins the band, which has already been doing an hour or two of warm-up.[6]

Sunday, 9 January 1977

Spent whole night at the show. Much the same band format as in 1974 and 1975. The stage is T-shaped and Fela is out front with his electric piano, flanked by maracas and clips players. The band is stretched out behind him: two trumpeters, tenor and baritone saxes [including Lekan

Animashaun], three guitarists, two seated conga drummers, and trap-drum wizard Tony Allen.

In between him and the band are six beautiful women chorus singers. He is strict with his musicians, and if any makes a mistake or loses concentration he fines them on the spot. In 1974 I actually saw him throw a microphone at a musician during a rehearsal. So everyone has their eyes glued on him. One new guitarist was so nervous he spent the whole night chewing his lips.

As he plays, four sexy dancers perform on the same shrouded podiums that Fela used previously. One is at each corner of the dance-floor and the dancers are silhouetted onto the lace material by coloured lights. Fela controls them with four foot pedals that can turn the podiums' lights off—which means the dancer should get off, as Fela thinks she's tiring. Last night he actually beat one of the dancers for not looking nice enough, when he was taking a break in the dressing room. Then, all steamed up, he went out to play.

Fela's Afrobeat is a unique combination of styles. The dance-band highlife influence of Victor Olaiya, E. T. Mensah and Ambrose Campbell is there, especially in some of the dance movements, the use of punctuating horn sections and Tony Allen's brilliant web of off-beats. In fact, yesterday I spent an hour at the corner of the stage just watching him drum. Jazz is there of course, Coltrane, Miles Davis, Charlie Parker, and also Ghana's Guy Warren [now Kofi Ghanaba] who was playing Afro-Jazz 10 years before Fela's Koola Lobitos. In fact I've been told that Zeal Onyia, when he was with Nigerian Broadcasting, complained about Fela borrowing Ghanaba's Afro-Jazz records from the gramophone library and not returning them.

Then there's the Brazilian influence. Just listen to "Water No Get Enemy" or the clips beat of any typical Afrobeat. Not surprising, really, when one remembers that large numbers of Brazilian ex-slaves settled in Lagos in the last century and brought the samba with them. Traditional

African features of Afrobeat are found in the pentatonic scales that Fela usually sings and solos in, the call-and-response between voices and horns, and the use of the modal harmonic structure of Afrobeat that is based on the movement between two chords, usually a tone apart. Most certainly soul music of James Brown and so on has been an influence, first brought here live in the late sixties from Sierra Leone by Geraldo Pino's Heartbeats. But I think it was James Brown's radical "Black and Proud" lyrics that influenced Fela more than his music. Because soul uses African-derived call-and-response, modal chords, and pentatonic [i.e., blues] scales, some people say Fela copied soul. I think it would be true to say that these musical features of soul rather reinforced Afrobeat's utilisation of traditional resources.

In between songs last night Fela "yabbis" about three matters. He said something about my role in The Black President. How a white actor was willing to come down to help, but was blocked by the Ministry of Education and the Principal of Abeokuta Grammar School. He went on to condemn colonial education, including the use of teaching of English, maths and science—just as he did at his mum's house a few days ago. He also condemned the government's latest attempt to deal with the traffic for FESTAC. Instead of a complete ban on private cars the government has rather decided to let people only drive on alternate days—depending on whether your car licence plate ends in an even or odd number. Fela said what will happen is that the rich will buy two cars, one with an odd and one with an even plate.

This afternoon went to the YAP offices with Nii Papoti to type out my newest application for a passport stamp. There was court this evening, and Yemi, the boss of the male Kalakuta house people, was given twelve lashes of a wire flex on Fela's orders. He was accused of stealing while we had been away. He ran out of the house and was pulled back to receive the whipping. I was surprised as usually a wrongdoer had the option of forgoing a punishment by walking out of the house and never coming back.

Monday, 10 January 1977

Spent whole day with Nii Papoti in town trying to get my passport sorted out. Roads clear today due to government's new directives concerning private cars. Also rubbish being removed and kiosks being pulled down as part of a big face-lifting operation for FESTAC. We couldn't get the re-entry permit so I could go back to Ghana for a few days, sort out things with my school, and then come back to finish my scene. So Fela decided I would do my part tomorrow at his brother's Junction Clinic, which is located inside the Kalakuta.[7]

We wouldn't wait to try and get permission from the Ministry to do the inside shots—but rather do them in Beko's clinic made up like a school office. Fela had Papoti beaten for messing up my passport matter.

Black President film dialogue between Inspector Reynolds [John Collins] and Mr. Ransome-Kuti [Wole "Feelings Lawyer" Kuboye] shot at Dr. Beko's clinic later edited into the Abeokuta shots:

MR. RANSOME-KUTI [Feelings Lawyer]: Now Mister? Inspector Reynolds. *(who is on the other side of desk)* What can I do for you, Inspector?

INSPECTOR REYNOLDS: On routine inspection, Mr Kuti.

Mr. Ransome-Kuti: No.

INSPECTOR REYNOLDS: I wouldn't take much of your time.

MR. RANSOME-KUTI: No.

INSPECTOR REYNOLDS: But surely Mr Kuti, I mean I cannot understand . . . I don't think you have a plausible explanation for your actions.

Mr. Ransome-Kuti: No.

INSPECTOR REYNOLDS *(furiously)*: I will not take any more insults from a black!

Mr. Ransome-Kuti grabs a cane and raises it.

INSPECTOR REYNOLDS: Man, you're mad! You must be off your rocker. *(is chased out of the room by Mr. Ransome-Kuti waving the cane)*

John Collins with Fela on the set of "The Black President" film.

Tuesday, 11 January 1977

Felt feverish this morning so Beko dosed me up with chloroquine. Amazing guy, he's basically running a free clinic for the poor people of Mushin [area of Lagos]. Did my part with Feelings earlier this evening in Beko's office. But before this happened Fela's valet, who had been looking after my costume, was slapped on Fela's instructions, as he had allowed my solar topee helmet to be crushed. I tried to argue with Fela that there was no problem as I could fix it. Fela told me to keep out of it, as it was a house matter. I stuffed paper into the flattened helmet and got it more or less back to its original shape.

Because of the malaria I'm about to go to bed early. Fela and company have gone off to Feelings Lawyer's house to film a small jazz combo in the backyard. J. K.'s involved, so I think it's meant to be of Fela's early Highlife Rakers band. A. J. is on bass and a Cameroonian guy on electric piano. Now I've finished my part I hope to be going back home to Ghana on Thursday.

Wednesday, 12 January 1977

Every morning since we came back from Abeokuta I have to join a line of Kalakuta people collecting their daily allowance from Fela's purse-man, Sonny. I get 28 naira a day. Getting over malaria but weak. Saw my friend Ignace de Souza from last year when I was in Benin City. He's a Dahomean bandleader I met at Victor Uwaifo's club. He's come to greet Fela.[8]

Ashela, one of the Basa-Basa musicians, came around today, wanted to see Faisal. Ashela was down and depressed as he had been beaten by some area boys and even had his glasses stolen. He said that because of the 1969 Ghanaian Aliens Order (when Ghana suddenly expelled hundreds of thousands of resident Nigerians) some people here don't like Ghanaians at all. I lent him five naira.

Thursday, 13 January 1977

Morning: expecting to go today. Fela's given up on Nii Papoti so J. K.'s gone to immigration to collect my passport. Evening: J. K. couldn't get passport, he'll go tomorrow.

This morning when Fela was asleep one of the Kalakuta women was shouting herself hoarse in the back-yard, complaining bitterly about something. Then someone poured water on her from an upstairs balcony and she began screaming so loud that Fela was awoken. He ordered her to sweep up the backyard and she became so annoyed that she began sweeping maniacally, scattering water on everyone around. We all disappeared until she finished. Kologbo came around with an English guy who's the chief cook at the Double "O" Hotel. They're both karate experts and go around looking for scrapes.

Friday, 14 January 1977

Faisal back from London—took another bunch of reels to the Rank film deposit. Fela planning to sue the police who attacked the Kalakuta in November 1974. No passport and now no sign of J. K.

Saturday, 15 January 1977

Fela was filmed at the Shrine last night. Opening ceremony of FESTAC today. Watched opening ceremony on TV. Fela has given instructions that none of his people should have anything to do with FESTAC.

Sunday, 16 January 1977

Some FESTAC visitors and performers beginning to visit Fela. The Ghanaian Afro-rock group Osibisa were here today—as was the Ivorian musician François Lougah. Fela very apologetic to me over the delay in my going. Heard that Kologbo had a fight with a soldier, but when he was taken to the army head-quarters the chief there, who knew him, let him go.

Monday, 17 January 1977

Still no J. K. and no passport.

Tuesday, 18 January 1977

Attempted coup in the Republic of Benin today. Still no J. K. and no passport. An apologetic Fela gave me a 40-naira dash and said that J. K. and

Nii Papoti had now given my passport to the Lagos Inspector Chief of Police, whom they knew. Fela thinks the delay might be because the IGP is up to his ears in FESTAC business. He told me J. K.'s dodging us because of this and also because he borrowed 250 naira from Victor, which he has gambled away.

This evening Steve, the Kalakuta PRO, told me of a joke story Fela had told him. An Afro-American saxophonist had come to Africa to play to the animals in the jungle—and they had all gathered around him. Then the tiger ate him and when the other animals asked why, the tiger had said because he didn't hear anything. A rather tasteless sort of joke I thought.

Wednesday, 19 January 1977

Fela rehearsed three numbers in the backyard this morning—insulted the bass guitarist for being slow. Fela uses the tonic sol-fa system for explaining notes to his musicians. Mrs. Ransome-Kuti watching all the antics from a balcony above. J. K. finally appeared and very apologetic about the delay. Today the part of The Black President film where the police attack the Kalakuta in 1974 was filmed. Fela got some of his people to dress up as police-men and make the mock attack.

This filming reminds me of the whole incident vividly, as I was around when it occurred on that early Saturday morning of November 23, 1974. I had come by road the day before with members of Faisal's Basa-Basa and Bunzus Soundz band that were, like his earlier Hedzoleh Sounds, experimenting with Afro-fusion music. I was playing the harmonica with the Bunzus—and we were all coming to play at the African Shrine and record at Nigeria's first multi-track studio, the EMI one at Apapa. Faisal and Fela were the co-producers. We got in on Friday staying at the Africa Shrine (Empire Hotel) diagonally opposite the Kalakuta Republic. We all woke up early in the morning complaining of nausea and thought we had all eaten some rotten food the night before. Then we opened the shutters and saw the whole road full of tear-gas—that's what was making us sick—and scores of riot police in blue shirts, tin hats and wicker basket shields were attacking Fela's heavy concrete and barbed-wire fence with axes. Fela and his people were on the flat roof of the two-storey Kalakuta throwing down anything and everything they could lay their hands on. In the end Fela was able to temporarily escape by putting a plank across to the top of an adjacent building. The police ransacked the Kalakuta and beat anyone they saw around.

Fela finally gave himself up and spent three days in jail. So Feelings Lawyer had to take over on stage as the show had to go on. The whole incident was over a young truant girl who had run away from home to become one of Fela's dancers. Unfortunately, she was the daughter of the Inspector General of Police of Lagos who before the attack had on several times politely sent policemen around to Fela to collect the girl. She didn't want to go and Fela wouldn't let them through the gate—even though they informed him that she was under age—fourteen years old rather than the seventeen she claimed.

After Fela was released he came back from the court to the Kalakuta with a cavalcade of vehicles and 10,000 supporters, causing a major traffic go-slow in Lagos that day. On top of a car outside the Shrine he blasted the government to the huge crowd—and again blasted them at his show that night. He actually performed with his arm in a sling and a bandage on his head which he humorously called his "Pope's cap." He immortalised the whole incident in his 1976 album *Kalakuta Show*—as usual turning his violent confrontations with authority into music.

Thursday, 20 January 1977

Rusty Dusty, the manager of the Surulere Night Club and T Fire Band, was at Kalakuta today. Very nice intelligent guy. Noticed I was reading a book by Colin Wilson on the occult. Said Fela also had a copy of the book in his library. In fact Fela has hundreds of books on Africa, mysticism and music in his private library. I told Dusty I'd never seen the place but had actually contributed to it. Last year I gave Fela an album of old photos of Ghanaian bands that I had been collecting over the years. Alex Oduro was there at the time and he condemned the first photo, from around 1900, which showed a white officer at the head of a Gold Coast Territorial Army regimental brass-band consisting of uniformed but shoeless Ghanaians. Alex said it was a colonial picture—which it was—and should be rejected. Fela rather loved it as he said it represented a part of African history. In fact he became so engrossed in the photo album that I dashed it to him, as it was a spare copy.

Friday, 21 January 1977

Yesterday one of the Kalakuta women disgraced one of our Ghana Film crew—a middle-aged bearded man. He sat down in one of the television chairs in the yellow waiting-room that one of the women had vacated. She wanted it back and he tried to argue. All the young women present mocked him and called him an old man. Me and Kwese just looked on and wondered about their behavior.[9]

Some French reporters from the French Afro-culture magazine *Mammy Water* in today to see Fela. This evening and an increasingly apologetic J. K. took me and Victor to the Gondola nightclub where they were shooting some scenes. J. K. had to pretend he was a young man so he wore a ridiculous unkempt and bedraggled Afro-wig. It didn't look real at all. It looked like a mop.

It took five hours to shoot the three or four minutes of action. Musings on the behavior of the sixty members of the Kalakuta household. Melodramatic, neurotic, cathartic, very involved and immediate, direct, little forethought or meditation, mixture of bluff and bullshit—only those who take will receive. When not arguing everyone bouncing around with joy—even after a beating. All huddled together at the Kalakuta and interacting to the fullest extreme. Everyone supremely self-confident, but lots of friction and skin-pain between them. Much stupidity and hurt, but much of it dramatic over- statement. Everyone's a born actor. As Shakespeare said: "All the world's a stage."

Saturday, 22 January 1977

Faisal's back from London. Fela's run out of money so he's going to Decca to record so he can get an advance on royalties. They've spent 50,000 naira extra due to delays in the film. Fela didn't bother to get permission from the Port Authorities, Ministry of Education, etc., before shooting. So that's what's holding them up. Faisal complaining about Kalakuta disorganisation and how in his contract with Fela he made a clause that makes Fela pay any extra bread after a certain date. Film was meant to have been finished two weeks ago.

On TV for FESTAC the Trinidadian band Mighty Canary, which contains a member of parliament; a steel band from Guyana called the Invaders led by a Minister; and Osibisa, who had problems with poor equipment. Best so far was a traditional dance group from Tanzania.

Before tonight's Comprehensive Show an American gospel singing group led by a fat grey-haired Afro-American women came to visit Fela. They were in for FESTAC. She completely freaked out when she saw a cripple who does an acrobatic floor-show and odd jobs for Fela. He has two withered forearms that come to points like very long fingers and he offered the old lady his hand to shake. She nearly fainted and hurriedly left, leaning on two of her people. I've seen this guy do this to unsuspecting people on several occasions. Fela gets a great laugh out of their shock, of course.

Sunday, 23 January 1977

Comprehensive show started last night with Fela's musical machine slowly put together and warming up. Songs always begin with the clips (claves) and maracas, followed by the bass and percussion and then horns—all fitting together in the end like a jigsaw puzzle of sound. Then the trumpeter Tunde Williams plays some pentatonic solos with the female chorus—and after 20 minutes or so Fela comes on stage.

As soon as he's ready he nods to a young man waiting on the wings of the stage, who gracefully leaps in to clip the sax on Fela. Fela waits patiently, not moving a muscle, until the microphone is adjusted and everything is set. Then one, two, three the band really takes off for up to an hour of solid groove. All his sins are forgiven by those who are held spell-bound by his musical magic.

Yesterday he played "Upside Down," a song about the disorganised state of things in Africa. He composed it with the black American vocalist Iszadore Daniels. And "Yellow Fever," which pokes fun at Nigerian women who use skin-lightening creams. Both these he recorded last year, so I was surprised to hear them live, as Fela usually doesn't play a song he's recorded. Maybe it was because of the FESTAC visitors being around.

In his in-between song "yabbis" he blasted Muslims, as he saw an Alhadji in the audience. He said that with 160,000 Nigerian Muslims going on the Hadj and taking 1,000 naira each with them they were draining Nigeria of cash. Last night he also blasted FESTAC and called the organisers rogues. He said that on the first day of FESTAC the 200 specially bought buses were collected by their drivers and completely disappeared. He's even bringing out a YAP brochure on the subject.[10]

Lyday told me that at last week's filmed show he also blasted the Pope and that the Italians should drop the Catholic Church being a state religion. Fela is the original adolescent rebel who always wants to confront authority and likes-dabbling-in-politics artist.

Last night the crowd was so great that the Shrine was packed tight. Fela is really popular—anywhere he goes in public he goes with a huge entourage and people shout his name. Even when he crosses the short distance across the road from the Kalakuta to the Shrine to start a show.

I saw a striking example of this at the Surulere Football Stadium in late 1974, during the Jimmy Cliff show. Towards the end of this famous Jamaican's reggae session Fela and his entourage arrived in a cavalcade of cars. When Fela entered the stadium some of the crowd spotted him, gave him the Black Power salute and carried him on their shoulders down to the grass field where the stage was situated.

When everyone realised he was around the whole audience deserted the stage area and charged en masse around the field with Fela on their shoulders. Jimmy Cliff, realising the audience had gone, shrugged his shoulders and mumbled something into the mike about now that Fela's here we might as well close the show. So the show ended like that.

Monday, 24 January 1977

Fela's electrician Nepa wounded in the arm by a bayonet. Happened in an incident I saw the beginning of when coming back to the Crossroads Hotel from the Shrine, after last Saturday's comprehensive show. There was an accident between a car and a motorbike and all the car people began to beat the bike rider—then some of the soldiers from the nearby barracks came. I didn't see the rest but somehow Nepa got involved.

Spent most of the day in the Hotel with Faisal, the Ghanaian crew, Victor, Ashela, Jackie, and E. T. Mensah, who is currently doing a second album of his old 1950s' highlife hits for Faisal.[11]

Nii Papoti came to report that still no success with the IGP over my passport—and now also Victor's. Said the reason for the delay was that Fela was protecting a West Indian that Immigration wanted out of the country. Therefore Immigration and the IGP were holding my and Victor's passports until further notice. Yesterday at the Kalakuta, Nii Papoti got beaten by J. K., who was vexed over him asking for 100 naira from Fela, Faisal and Victor to get the passports—with no results. Accused him of chopping the previous money.

Tuesday, 25 January 1977

Nii Papoti meant to come around early this morning to take me to the IGP. Didn't turn up. Jackie very annoyed. Rusty Dusty came around jokingly arguing with Faisal as usual. Amoah Azangeo turned up today. He's the Fra-Fra calabash player who plays with Faisal's Basa-Basa Sounds. Amoah's chief up in the north of Ghana is quite famous, as he appeared jamming with Harris and McCann's modern jazz group in the film of the Soul to Soul concert that was held in Accra's Black Star Square in March 1971.

A funny incident concerning Amoah occurred when we [the Basa-Basa and Bunzus bands] were doing the recording session at EMI here in 1974. Because it was the first time we had all gone into a multi-track studio Faisal wanted Amoah to do his singing and calabash playing for Basa-Basa separately. He tried singing without the calabash—it didn't work. He tried playing (really a sort of complex juggling) the calabash alone—it didn't work. Faisal got more and more frustrated until Fela (who was co-producer) told him he should use two microphones and let Amoah do things naturally. Which is how it was done.

Heard today more about the West Indian who is blocking our passports. He's a Trinidadian whom Immigration wants to see for some reason. He was brought in on Fela's FESTAC quota of seventeen visitors and journalists he's allowed to bring into the country. Unless Fela produces the guy, Immigration won't give him our passports.

This evening went to Bobby Benson's Caban Bamboo with Faisal, Victor, Feelings Lawyer and two Afro-American women. First Bobby Benson's son, Tony, played—mainly soul and funk. Then Bobby did a crazy floorshow singing and humming silly songs.

Didn't see Fela today. He needs more bread so was at the Decca studio the whole day recording a new song, "Sorrow, Tears and Blood." Saw

Yemi, his chief Kalakuta house-hold boss. Really quite a tough, brutal-looking guy. He went off to buy another car for Fela with the advance on royalties that Fela's getting.

Wednesday, 26 January 1977

Good music last night at Caban Bamboo—especially the Northern Pyramids from Kaduna, who play Hausa Afrobeat. Some members of the South African Ipi Tombi cultural group who were present got up and sang a couple of soft melodic songs. Then a magician in dreadlocks and looking like a criminal stuck cigarettes into his ears and nose. Lot of people around. Faisal was announced to the audience by Bobby Benson and had to take a bow. Fela still not around. Still doing his recording. E. T. Mensah and the Osibisa guys here this morning. Osibisa not happy about the FESTAC equipment, so sending to London for their PA system. Faisal told us that the problem was that the amps that the FESTAC organisers had brought were American 110-volt types. And they forgot to bring the step-down transformers.

I met the Osibisa conga player Kofi Ayivor and had an interesting chat with him. Told me it was ET who had trained him in music as a young boy. He also told me that he used to live in Temple House where I'm now living. It's in James Town, Accra, and he was there when the daughter of the famous Ghanaian lawyer Hutton-Mills, who built the house in 1890, was still alive. The daughter herself was a concert pianist. We were both musicians. Me and Kofi were struck by the coincidence. Temple House seems to like musicians. Rusty Dusty came in later, condemning Faisal as usual. So Faisal accused him of promoting foreign music like reggae in his club and band. Dusty had actually come to find out about the shots tomorrow at his Surulere Nightclub—which was where Fela's original Africa Shrine [the Afro-Spot] was.

Thursday, 27 January 1977

Went to Kalakuta with Faisal and Victor. A lot of arguments going on among the household. Nii Papoti again blasted by J. K. over the passport matter. About twenty people were dressing up in police uniforms for the Surulere shot which was going to reconstruct a police raid on the place. Me and Victor went in the bus with these baton-holding "police." Our crazy driver, when we were turning right, cut the corner too sharp, nearly pushing a car that was trying to overtake on the inside onto the pavement. Unwisely, the car driver jumped out of his car and ran across the corner—as we were in a go-slow—and began to hit our driver. As we moved off all our mock policemen put their batons outside the window and hit the poor man in turn. So we left him lying on the ground. He must have been mad to single-handedly attempt to fight a busload of police.

At the nightclub Dusty was busy putting up posters. Bas, one of Fela's seven girl-friends, was there waiting for Fela. While waiting had a drink. Victor told me that before one of the mock police-attack scenes of The Black President film, Fela got some of the "police" and some of the crowd being raided to step forward and slap each other. This made everyone so annoyed that a real fight happened. So Fela got a realistic riot scene. Method acting's got nothing on Fela's technique. Fela never showed up, so tonight's scene wasn't filmed. If it had been maybe I would have seen another "real" riot.

From Surulere me, Faisal, Victor and J. K. went to the Caban Bamboo again—resident band not very good but a nice "fetish" act by a dancer called Rose and an orgasmic one by a singer and sexy dancer to a Congo song. Papoti finally got my passport!

Friday, 28 January 1977

This morning said goodbye to Fela, who thanked me for doing my part. Faisal and Victor stayed on. Me, Jackie and Ashela came back to Ghana this morning by road. On way to my flat at Temple House passed my School (Ghana International School) and found out a rumour had gone around that I had been killed in Nigeria. I had told my head mistress, Mrs. Acquah, that I was only going for five days. Ended up as nearly a month!

8

THE BLACK PRESIDENT

On February 16, 1977 Faisal left Nigeria, and he deposited Fela's "Black President" film in 128 cans of 35 mm film in the vaults of Rank-Xerox in London. The film was complete except for some of the sound track that was left at Fela's small recording studio at the Kalakuta. At eleven o'clock on the morning of February 18 the crew of Ghana Film completed packing its equipment and left by road for Ghana. Later that day the infamous attack by soldiers that destroyed the old Kalakuta took place.

From piecing together the stories from various Kalakuta people after the event, what happened was that around the time the Ghana Film Corporation crew were leaving, one of Fela's drivers accidentally knocked down a lance corporal driving a motorbike. Some soldiers then came to the Kalakuta to see Fela to ask him to let them have the culprit so he could be charged with careless driving. Fela refused. A little later some officers came to make the same request. Fela in pants standing above them on the balcony of the Kalakuta and surrounded by a group of scantily dressed women holding umbrellas above him abused them by playing his recently released 1976 "Zombie" on his saxophone. The officers left in a furious mood after questioning Fela's right to call his house a "republic" and surround it with an electric fence. They said that as far as they were concerned there was only one republic, and that was the Nigerian one.

Fela talking into a microphone at a Brixton show in London, 1983. Photo Jak Kilby

At three o'clock in the afternoon, one thousand, mainly Hausa, soldiers broke through the Kalakuta's electric fence, set fire to the house, and prevented the fire brigade putting out the fire—so destroying Fela's library, the recording studio, the sound track of "The Black President" film as well as Dr. Beko Ransome-Kuti's Junction Clinic. All sixty inmates of the house at the time were beaten up and sent to jail, and the house animals were killed. Seventy-seven-year-old Mrs. Funmilayo Ransome-Kuti was made to watch all this in a chair on the second story, and was then tossed out of the window by an unknown soldier, which fractured her leg.

One of Fela's bodyguards, Segun, was wounded in the stomach with a bayonet and dirty water was poured into his wound. The African American A. J. Moreson was clubbed on the head with an axe and lost his memory for months. A French magician and snake charmer who just happened to be visiting had his finger cut off by a soldier. Ekow's testicles were stomped on. Bas had her stomach jumped on, Lyday was cut and had to have twenty-one stitches, and one woman had her breasts flattened with a stone. Dr. Beko Ransome-Kuti's arm was broken.

Fela himself was beaten unconscious and hospitalized with a broken jaw. In fact the soldiers had wanted to kill Fela, but the brigadier in charge pulled a gun on his own troops to prevent this. Later Fela was charged with using the word "republic" for his Kalakuta residence in defiance of the Nigerian constitution. After he recovered, Fela counteracted by attempting to claim five million naira in damages from the commander of the Albati Barracks unit at Idioro that undertook the operation, and the army chief of staff, General Theophilus Danjuma.

Faisal's Account

Although Faisal Helwani left two days before that attack, it is worth presenting his views on the incident:

Here is a situation where a small boy and newly employed is driving carelessly and knocks down a soldier in uniform driving an army bike, and then comes to the Kalakuta to hide. In any country in the world the driver of that car must be arrested to explain things. So the lower-ranks soldiers came first to ask Fela to give them this boy so he could be reported at a police station. Fela said no. And no to the officers who came later when he played "Zombie" on his horn on his veranda. So you see why it was a brutal attack. It was like a war.

That same boy who Fela risked everything for, less than two months later, stole Fela's and some of the Kalakuta people's passports and sold them to a passport contractor for five naira a passport, and ran away. Fela used to sacrifice so much for some of his household who didn't deserve anything. I once told Fela: "Imagine if all Nigerians did like you and drivers knocked down people and didn't report. How would Nigeria be?"

What I liked about Fela was his Pan-African message, calling on the women not to bleach [their skin] and change their culture, calling on Africans to be proud so that they don't have an inferiority complex, calling on the people to fight for their rights, opposing corruption in society. This is all fine. But these boys who can go out and misbehave in town and he gives them protection is wrong. So I would not put Fela's doom at the military doormat, I would put it at some of the people around him.

Fela spent a month in hospital and jail—and then Lagos State government probed the incident and in April 1977 came to the verdict that the destruction of the Kalakuta Republic was done by an "unknown soldier" and at the same time closed down the Africa Shrine.

The Afrodisia Connection

While all this was happening, Faisal Helwani in Ghana was unable to do anything in connection with "The Black President"—and so rather began his *Afrodisia Hour* every Friday on Ghana Radio and an Afrodisia Night at the Tip-Toe Gardens in Accra, which featured the bands he intended to record. These were the Uhurus and E. T. Mensah's Tempos dance bands, the Adzo and Abladei Ga cultural troupes, the Voices of South Labone choral group, the Old Fanti guitarist Kwaa Mensah, my own Bokoor highlife guitar band, the West Indian Black Angels singing duets and Faisal's Napoleon Club bands, the Bunzu Soundz, Basa-Basa, and New Hedzoleh.

Faisal then signed a contract with Fela's recording company, Decca West Africa (Afrodisia), to release several Ghanaian albums, and in June 1977 Faisal took some of these groups to Lagos to record at the Decca Studios. While there he arranged for Fela to come to Ghana to begin rerecording the burnt sound track of "The Black President" at the Ghana Film dubbing studio in Accra and also do some shows. In fact this idea appealed to Fela, as after the destruction of the Kalakuta Republic the Lagos State government had made it almost impossible for him to play anywhere in Nigeria.

As a consequence Fela and his usual large entourage came to Ghana for a month in October, and some of the scripted parts of the film (like mine and Feelings Lawyer's portion) were successfully dubbed. But it was impossible to synchronize the scenes of the Africa 70 band playing in the dubbing studio to the relevant parts of the band playing on film.

It was likewise almost impossible to redub the improvised parts of the film, such as the riot scenes, where the actors and actresses had ad-libbed the lines and so had forgotten what they had said. Rushes of the film were shown to us at the Ghana Film preview theatre, including grotesque scenes of Fela having sexual intercourse with one of his woman friends, which we all, except Fela, thought should be cut.

Mrs. Funmilayo Ransome-Kuti had come along on this trip, although she was quite frail and completely white-haired, due to the injuries she had sustained when thrown out of a second-floor Kalakuta window during the army attack the previous year. She was quite vague and confused and did not recognize me at all.

Fela Live in Ghana

While in Ghana Fela and his groups did several live shows. On October 2, 1977, they played "Opposite People" at the Apollo Theatre in Accra, and Fela yabbied about how four-seater Volkswagen vehicles with comfortable seats were being converted in Africa to lorries with fourteen hard seats. The next day at the Regal Cinema they played a song critical of the Nigerian government called "VIP" (Vagabonds in Power). That night they also played "Shuffering and Shmiling" in which Fela blasts Islam and Christianity as being non-African, irrelevant to the ordinary Nigerian, and sidelining legitimate anger and rebellion.

Rift with Abiola

In November 1977 John Booth, the English codirector of Decca West Africa (Afrodisia) was sacked by Chief Moshood Abiola, who by then had a 40 percent share in the company. Abiola cancelled Decca's contract with Fela and also put a freeze on Faisal's twelve Afrodisia productions, as Abiola decided that some of these were seditious.[1] This subsequently led to a long-running conflict between Fela and Abiola that by the middle of 1978 resulted in Fela and his entourage occupying the Decca studios in Lagos for six weeks. He slept in the managing director's office while his entourage camped on the premises. Unfortunately, some of Fela's people broke into the Decca warehouse and stole equipment. This weakened Fela's position and meant he lost the court case against Decca and Abiola. Things were not helped when Fela had his people dump fourteen barrels of human feces outside Abiola's villa. Because of Faisal Helwani's friendship with Fela, Abiola also canceled the Ghanaian productions that were still in the pipeline.

However, we are getting ahead of the story—and back in February 1978 Fela and his large crew came back to Ghana to continue again the difficult task of redubbing the soundtrack of "The Black President." In fact, during

1978 Fela was continually going back and forth between Accra and Lagos in connection with the film.

On his February trip he stayed at the Hotel President in Adabraka, Accra, and got into a confrontation with a Syrian trader who had a shop nearby. The Syrian had told local women hawkers not to stand outside his shop to sell. But one persisted and so the annoyed shopkeeper threw a bucket of water at her. Fela became so inflamed when he heard the noise and was told what was going on that he went out on the street and abused the Syrian man. Some of Fela's people also went to the local police station to complain of the man's behavior, but they ended up squabbling with the police. This case went to court and the judge said the shop owner had every right to remove these squatters. So Fela was charged with a breach of the peace but released on bail—although he was also beaten up by a group of irate friends of the Syrian man who went to Fela's hotel room to deal with him.

Around this time eleven of Fela's entourage were arrested at the hotel for possessing Indian hemp. Fela's previous lawyer, Nana Akuffo-Addo, was too busy at the time to take on the case, so another Ghanaian lawyer, George Gardner, took it on and won the case on a technicality. Because of this he became Fela's lawyer until 1981.

In 1978 things began to get difficult for Fela with the Ghanaian military authorities, as he had been playing "Zombie" and giving more and more political lectures at student rallies. He also met the twelve activist leaders of Ghana's three universities and generally encouraged them in the groundswell that was emerging among them and their student supporters against the Acheampong/Akuffo regime. Conversely the military government was suppressing student radicals and demonstrations.

Student Activism

Faisal describes the situation at the time:

> I didn't then or don't now talk government politics. But then I was connected with Fela when Acheampong was hunting the political youth. Also, I had been helping the students and their Student Representative Council and sponsored their delegates to go to Cairo for the All African Students Union conference.
>
> Then, no one [in authority] had any sympathy for the students and wouldn't give them anything at the time. At the Napoleon Club I used to have a restaurant, and when the students had an African function I would sponsor their dinner and make donations. So when Fela came I also arranged lectures for him as I knew the student leadership. I also used to do free shows, some with Fela, at the Legon campus to entertain students.

It was also during this period, according to Carlos Moore, that Fela called a meeting of the leaders of Ghana's four universities (Legon, Cape Coast, Kumasi, and Wiineba) and lectured them on a number of topics. That Africa is not "non-aligned" but rather is the "center of the world," that the West is being ruled by unnatural and unbalanced leaders, and that Africans should embrace "naturalology" rather than a technology that has led to a "progressive loss of respect for life, for nature, for the environment."[2]

Marriages of Convenience

It was in the context of the increasing discontent with the Ghanaian military government and its dictatorial reaction to opposition that Fela's famous 1978 multiple marriage took place. Fela arrived at Kotoka Airport in Accra with his usual large group, including twenty-seven women singers and dancers. The Ghanaian authorities wanted to harass him, so these women were forbidden entry by immigration. Fela went straight back to Nigeria and on February 20 married them all in the customary manner in Nigeria, with some of the women's families present. The ceremony took place in a Lagos hotel and was officiated by a priest of the Yoruba divination Ifa ("destiny") cult.

Ghana recognizes traditional polygamous marriages, so Fela was able to return to Accra with them as his official wives. So his well-publicized group marriage to twenty-seven women was not intended to provide him a harem, but was rather a ploy to get all his people back into Ghana and to continue redubbing the film.

Acheampong Cracks Down

Even though Fela had played for Ghana's military ruler Colonel (later General) Acheampong in 1972 during the the early part of his rule, by 1978 Fela's antimilitarism had become such a thorn in the side of the Ghanaian military government that, as Faisal explains, Fela was completely banned from entering Ghana.

> Normally, when Fela worked for two or three weeks on the film he goes back to Lagos for a weekend and comes back. But this time he came he was not allowed to enter from the airport and was asked to go back on the same plane. Me too, a week later, when I sent my passport to the Nigerian Embassy in Accra they stamped visa rejected on five different pages.
>
> So I had to complain to my [the Ghanaian] Ministry of Foreign Affairs and a new passport was issued to me. Even General Acheampong and the director of military intelligence called me to the Castle to find out whether the banning of Fela entering will affect my financial interests in "The Black President" film. They asked me how much I would be losing so that they could compensate me. I told them I didn't want anything. So Fela was not

> allowed to enter Ghana, and I was not allowed to enter Nigeria for about four or five years. And within that period too, we were economically harassed, so we went broke. We didn't have the money to complete the redubbing of the film.

Rawlings Opens the Door

However, when Flight Lieutenant Jerry John Rawlings and his Armed Forces Revolutionary Council overthrew the unpopular Acheampong-Akuffo regime in mid-1979, the government ban on Fela was relaxed. Again Faisal explains.

> When Rawlings came to power one of the first things he did was lift the ban on Fela. In fact he even invited Fela to come to Ghana, for Rawlings had been in touch with Fela before he made his AFRC revolution in 1979. Although many people knew Fela smoked ganja and thought his private life may not be appreciated, Rawlings was listening to his ideas and recognized the power of his music in creating awareness. In fact, before the AFRC time Jerry [Rawlings] had been in touch with Fela through correspondence. Fela even met Kojo Tsikata [Rawlings's right-hand man]. You see, Fela wanted to do a people's political party in Nigeria called the Movement of the People (MOP). Jerry and Tsikata wanted to do something similar here and so were writing to Fela, and Fela was writing to them.

The Rise and Problems of MOP

MOP was a mass political party that preached Nkrumahism and African socialism. Fela got his Ghanaian lawyer, George Gardner, to set this up officially in 1978 in order for Fela to be able to stand for president of Nigeria in the elections the following year, when General Obasanjo gave back power to the civilians. But MOP was disqualified, as all political parties had to have branches in all of Nigeria's then twenty-six states, which MOP did not. Also, because of the burning of "The Black President" soundtrack, Fela was almost bankrupt and could not afford to set up multiple MOP branches.

On September 10, 1979, the day before Obasanjo handed over power to civilian rule under Shehu Shagari's Second Republic, Fela deposited a coffin at the door of Obasanjo's residence at Dodon Barracks in Lagos. The coffin was meant to symbolize the coffin of his late mother, Mrs. Funmilayo Ransome-Kuti, who had died on April 13, 1978, from injuries received in the 1977 army attack on the old Kalakuta Republic, when Obasanjo had been head of state. In 1981 Fela went on to release an album called *Coffin for Head of State* directed at President Obansanjo and his deputy Umaru Musa Yar'Adua for corruption and "killing my mama."

9

AMSTERDAM AND AFTER

The last time I met Fela was in the summer of 1981, when he was on a European tour. He was playing at an open-air annual festival in the Amsterdam Woods on a very rainy day. At the time the new songs that he and his newly named Egypt 80 band were playing were "Movement of the People No 1," "Gimme Shit I Give You Shit," and "Custom Check Point."

I talked to J. K. Braimah backstage, and he told me that after Fela had been kicked out of Ghana in 1978, he had become recognized by the international jazz community and had again played at the Berlin Jazz Festival in October 1978, taking with him a huge entourage of seventy musicians, dancers, road managers, and friends.

It was after this trip that his drummer, Tony Allen (Oladipo)—who had been with Fela since the Koola Lobitos was formed in the mid 1960s—left him and moved on to a solo career.

In the following interview with Jak Kilby (Muhsin) in 1985 Tony Allen explains why he left Fela in 1979:

> He owned everything. He won't even like you to bring your instruments, if you have one yourself he won't allow you to use it on stage. He wants you to use his instruments, so if you are leaving you leave his instruments there.

> Then somebody will come and move into that place. It's just a dictatorship ideology. I don't see myself belonging to such an organisation. Like in Fela's band, Fela thinks he's paying the musicians, but they always stay on the same money. If they make millions, he's going to have the millions, not any of the members. The money was paying for Fela's politics. He's into politics, I'm not. I don't want to play politics and I don't want to be a politician. To me he's just talking now. Fela does not sing. He has good musicianship, [but] he's kind of losing it bit by bit, by going into politics.[1]

Then, in 1980, Fela had played in Milan at the invitation of the Italian Communist Party and had been busted and jailed for five days by the police when five kilograms of Indian hemp had been found in the advance luggage. Later in the year he embarked on a tour of Kano, Zaria, and other northern Nigerian towns with the African American musician Roy Ayers, but on the way back their buses had been stoned by crowds angry over the anti-Islamic lyrics of some of Fela's songs. Nevertheless, the two musicians had managed to produce a joint album with two songs on it. On one side was "2000 Got to Be Black" by Roy Ayers, and on the other "Africa, Center of the World" by Fela.

After the Amsterdam show I visited the hotel with some Dutch journalist friends and met Fela in his usual fighting mood. He was vexed with the British for having cancelled the UK segment of the tour because of visa problems. He was also complaining about the US multinational telecommunications company ITT, whose vast Nigerian operations were run by Chief Moshood Abiola, who, as former head of Decca West Africa (Afrodisia), had been sued by Fela for breach of recording contract, and whose studio Fela had occupied for a month and a half. In fact, on this European tour Fela had brought with him hundreds of copies of his just-released record album *International Thief Thief* (ITT) that played on the letters ITT to condemn ITT's director, Chief Abiola, as a "useless chief" of "low mentality."

Tapping magical powers: Fela shakes hands with Professor Hindu prior to a UK show in November 1983. Photo Jak Kilby

Oddly enough, and in spite of Fela's vitriolic attack on Chief Abiola in "ITT," the two of them had a public rapprochement a few years later. Much later, in the mid-1990s, Abiola stood for the elections later annulled by the dictator General Sani Abacha, who put Abiola in prison.

At the meeting at his Amsterdam hotel during the 1981 European tour, Fela also complained about the psychological warfare that American organizations like ITT and the CIA waged against developing nations in terms of language. He did not see why the terms "Third World," "undeveloped," or even worse, "Non-aligned countries," should be used, as they all implied inferiority. Fela's annoyance with these terms took musical form in his 1982 song "Original Sufferhead," released on the Arista label.

I asked Fela about how his three children were, as I hadn't seen them for four years. He told me that Sola was actually sitting right next to him.

I simply had not recognized her. In four short years she had changed from a fourteen-year-old schoolgirl into a beautiful young woman.

A press conference was arranged by us for Fela during his Amsterdam stay, and one thing that perplexed the Dutch journalists was how Fela could be so progressive on the one hand, and yet have a harem of twenty-seven wives on the other. One woman journalist accused him of having no respect for women at all. Fela's response to this was that men and women have different specific duties to perform in life. He would, for instance, never enter a woman's kitchen, which was their sole domain. As he put it, in Africa categories like old and new, day and night, male and female are distinct and never mixed up and that "nature is clear with no confusion." He added that unisex might be fine for Europe but not for Africa. This explanation did not satisfy the journalists, who considered Fela to be a male chauvinist—which indeed he was.

In the early 1980s Fela had changed the name of his band from Africa 70 to Egypt 80, and based himself at the new Africa Shrine at Pebble Street, Ikeja, Lagos. During the 1980s, Fela became decidedly more famous. Indeed, a biography by Carlos Moore entitled *Fela, Fela: This Bitch of a Life* was published in 1982.The same year a French documentary film was made about him called *Music Is the Weapon*. And in 1983–84 the Egypt 80 toured Europe.

In 1984 Fela shot again into the international limelight when he was arrested at Murtala Mohammed Airport in Lagos on spurious currency charges and became a prisoner of conscience for Amnesty International when he was given a long prison sentence. The arrest occurred at the airport when he was arriving from one international tour and was about to embark on another. He was accompanied by Professor Hindu (Kwaku Addaie), one of two Ghanaian stage magicians and fakirs (the other being Professor Peller) that Fela had acquired to act as his spiritual gurus and keep him in touch with his dead mother. Professor Hindu is famous throughout Ghanaian towns and villages for his magical concert-stage performances and for the burying of an entranced accomplice, who is dug out of the earth alive the next day. It was when he performed the same act at the Africa Shrine in 1981 that Fela became convinced of Hindu's powers. Indeed through the influence of these Ghanaian magician "professors" Fela and some of his wives or "queens" became possessed by spirits that put them in touch with the deceased Funmilayo Ransome-Kuti. According to Carlos Moore, this "spiritual saga" was part of an existential crisis that Fela went through triggered by the death of his mother.[2]

In 1984 Fela did not want to go through the tedium of having to declare his £2,600 foreign exchange twice (i.e., coming in and going out of Nigeria), as he was literally in transit and the money was the band's float for the next, Los Angeles, trip. Professor Hindu assured the gullible Fela that he could make the money vanish if he was given it.

Prisoner Number E1106

Unfortunately, Hindu's magic did not work, and the money was discovered on him by immigration control. Fela created such an immediate fracas that things could not be smoothed over on the spot. The matter was taken to the top airport authorities and Fela was consequently arrested, becoming prisoner number E1106. At first he was sent to a prison in Lagos, but he was so popular with the prisoners there that he was sent to Maiduguri, in the far north of Nigeria, where the anti-Islamic sentiments of some of his songs led to rough treatment.

Partly because of international pressure he was released after serving only twenty months of his five-year sentence and subsequently went to the United States to do a show on behalf of Amnesty International, which had collected 100,000 signatures on a petition for his release. At that show he played alongside the big British and American rock, folk, and funk artists Peter Gabriel, U2, Sting, Joan Baez, Lou Reed, and the Neville Brothers.

Although pressure from Amnesty International helped in Fela's release, the actual event that triggered it was that the judge, Justice Gregory Okoro-Idogu, whose court handed out the prison sentence, went to Maidugari almost two years later and, according to Fela, came to beg forgiveness. This created such a scandal in the press that Fela was released early and the judge was sacked from his post. The Ghanaian musician Stan Plange, who visited Fela just after his release, relates the incident:

> Fela was jailed by the government over money, and he managed to come out by blackmailing the government. You see there had been a change in government, and he blackmailed the new Babingida government by saying that the judge who convicted him went to the prison to apologize to him, saying it wasn't his [the judge's] intention but the [previous] government had told him he should convict Fela.
>
> The judge later published his version of things, saying that he went to Maiduguri to visit a relative [in the prison hospital] and when he was coming out he was told that Fela was in a room he was passing, so why don't you just say hello to him. Stupidly, the judge agreed, and so the government had to release Fela. I visited Fela then [after the release], at the house and clinic of his brother Beko, in Anthony Village. At the time Fela's band was playing at the Africa Shrine in Ikeja, but Fela wasn't playing, as he was fresh out of prison. His son Femi was then leading the group.

During Fela's imprisonment his son Femi had kept the forty-strong Egypt 80 going, later forming his own band called Positive Force. Fela himself was weakened by his prison experience but in 1986 undertook another tour, with Rikki Stein as promoter. He also quarreled with the American Celluloid record-label producer Bill Laswell, for what Fela considered had been an overly hi-tech mix of "Army Arrangement," recorded before Fela's imprisonment but mixed during his two years in jail.

In 1987 Fela and his group played in Burkina Faso and met its radical young leader Captain Thomas Sankara, who had personally invited Fela to play in his country. This visit was cut short by Fela developing skin eruptions which were, in fact, the very first signs of the AIDS disease that he always denied he had—but nevertheless was to later kill him. Fela was much impressed by the revolutionary president of Burkina Faso, who was, sadly, assassinated a few months later in October 1987. Fela commemorated this event in his 1992 song "Underground System," which was about the international web of intrigue that has led to the downfall of key African leaders like Nkrumah, Lumumba, and Sankara.[3]

In February 1988 Fela and his Egypt 80 played at a Reggae Sunsplash organized by the Liberian music producer Keith Wilson and Synergy Africa that was held at the Samuel Doe Sports Stadium and featured the Jamaican artists Peter Tosh, Burning Spear, Yellowman, U-Roy, Sly Dunbar, Robbie Shakespeare, and Judy Mowatt—as well as the Nigerian juju-music star Sunny Adé.[4]

During 1988 Fela and his band undertook more world tours and released his famous album *Beasts of No Nation* criticizing apartheid, US president Ronald Reagan, and Britain's Margaret Thatcher.

But in 1993 Fela was again charged with a crime. This time, the cause was the death at the Africa Shrine of one of his band technicians, whose body was found near the Kalakuta house. There was no evidence that Fela was connected with the crime, and he was released.

In 1994 Fela made his last brief trip to Ghana when he was invited by hotel manager and music promoter Smart Binete. As described by Binete in chapter 13, Fela and his Egypt 80 band performed at three venues in Accra and Kumasi.

In 1996 the Abacha government arrested Fela and thirty members of his band for marijuana possession, and the Shrine was closed down. Then in early 1997 the National Drug Law Enforcement Agency (NDLEA) of Nigeria sent operatives in full combat gear, under the command of Major General Musa Bamaiyi, to raid the new Kalakuta Republic at 7 Gbemisola Street,

Ikeja, and a hundred people were arrested on Indian hemp charges. Fela was subsequently paraded in chains before press and television reporters by the Lagos State commissioner of police at the Ikeja High Court. He was released after five days, and in April 1997 filed a court case against the NDLEA boss for illegal detention, violation of his rights to a private family life, and contravening his right to personal dignity by displaying him, in public, in chains.

Fela's Last Days

By the end of July 1997 Fela became very sick and was nursed at the Kalakuta house by his older sister, Oludolupo Ransome-Kuti, a retired nurse. In the weeks that followed there were several false newspaper and radio rumors that Fela was dead. He died, though, on Saturday, August 2, at 5:30 p.m. at the hospital on Victoria Island, Lagos. His death was officially announced by the family through his older brother, Professor Olikoye Ransome-Kuti, who gave a press conference at the Africa Shrine. There, Professor Ransome-Kuti not only stated that Fela had died of AIDS, but warned the journalists and crowd present that 10 percent of them were probably HIV positive.

Tens of thousands of Nigerians filed past Fela's glass coffin at his funeral on August 12. Lagos almost stopped work for that day. It was the biggest funeral the country had ever seen, bigger than for any head of state. At one point busloads of angry university students turned up demanding Fela's body. They did not want it to be buried in a cemetery, but to be placed in a mausoleum, which they would construct at the University of Lagos campus.

Things were only settled when Fela's youngest daughter, Sola, told them that the family had received permission from the Lagos City Council to bury Fela in the garden of his Kalakuta Republic in Ikeja, which would become a monument to him. Sadly, Sola herself died a few weeks later from misdiagnosed cancer.

The following is the Ghanaian musician Stan Plange's account of the huge wake keeping and funeral for Fela:

> There was a rumor in Ghana that Fela was dead, and so I went to ring Zeal Onyia to ask him whether it was true. He said it wasn't true, but Fela was very sick and his family had come for him and nobody knew where he had been sent. Then on Saturday [August 2] I heard on the BBC that Fela was dead. The following week I left for the funeral by road and arrived in Lagos at midnight and went to Zeal Onyia's house at FESTAC, as my sister-in-law stays there; Zeal was in London.
>
> The following morning I went straight to Tafawa Balewa Square where Fela was being laid in state. I went to sit on a raised dais with Fela's family and Faisal. There was a canopy on one side of the square and Fela's and other bands were playing on the other side. Fela was in a glass coffin and people had formed queues to look at him. I saw an old man lying in state because he had deteriorated so much in his last days. I saw his hands were wrinkled. I'm older than Fela by a year or so, so I didn't like what I saw. The last time I met him after coming out of prison [in 1986] I saw that he was having some sort of light skin pigmentation. You know he has a very light complexion and was getting lighter. He was so proud of it and said: "Oh Stan, see how my skin de shine because of the African things I've been using."
>
> At one point at Tafawa Balewa Square a mass of students came in with trucks and said they wanted to carry the corpse away, as the students said he was for them. The family would not allow this. Then in the afternoon I saw people looking up at the sun and we saw the full moon also appear. This was around 1:00 p.m. I don't know if this used to happen but people started interpreting it in a different way [as a mystical sign or miracle]. Later that day the body was moved to the Kalakuta house.
>
> The following day I could not go to his house where he was being buried in the yard. The burial was meant to be at 1:00 a.m., so I left Zeal's house at nine but I could not enter as the human traffic was so thick for

about a mile around the house that there was no way to get there without being pickpocketed in the crowd. I could not fight through that crowd. I understand that Faisal had to pay some strong people to take him there. Honestly speaking I haven't seen a funeral like that. I was in Lagos when Awolowo died and had a state burial at Tafawa Balewa Square, which is a huge place. Fela's funeral was bigger.

Ghana's Grand Send-Off

In Ghana, the country that Fela had loved and visited so much and where his highlife and Afrobeat music had always been popular, there were two wake keepings for him. On Monday, August 11, the musicians' union of Ghana (MUSIGA) held a vigil at the Centre for National Culture (the old Arts Council) in Accra, with music played by Nana Ampadu and his African Brothers, the singer and MUSIGA president Joe Mensah, Jewel Ackah and his Butterfly Six, the Fanti singer Papa Yankson, A. B. Crentsil and Ahenfo, Ebo Taylor, and others.

At the same venue on Sunday, August 17, a wake was held for Fela by the Copyright Protection Committee, organized by Faisal Helwani and Stan Plange, who had both just returned from Fela's funeral with Femi Kuti. That night Femi played some of his dad's numbers such as "Palava" and "No Agreement" backed by the Ghana Broadcasting Band under its leader Stan Plange. Other musicians that played included the Kumapim Royals, Kofi Sammy and his Okukuseku group, Professor Abraham, and master drummers Okyerema Asante and Mustapha Tetty Addy.

A Royal Eulogy

A eulogy and funeral speech in honor of Fela was given by Nana Kofi Omane, the chief of Akyem Nkwantanan, who had helped organize student and African Youth Command lectures for Fela in the 1970s in Tema and Accra. Nana Omane had the following to say about Fela:

> Fela used his music for socio-political and cultural commentary, critique and appreciation. His courage or fearlessness was without bounds, uncircumscribed, as he hit the high and the low, the gentleman and the lady, the powerful establishment or the apparently untouchable. Even though Fela was controversial that was the spice to social and political dynamism. Fela did not hate anybody, he only hated wrongs. He did not abhor men who wore European clothes. But if wearing a suit on a hot day in tropical Africa is what would turn a man into a gentleman, then he would not be a gentleman at all.
>
> Fela abhorred the imposition of western values and institutions on indigenous African systems. He trumpeted that colonialism in Africa was a clash of cultures where Africans were defeated, leading to the social and cultural crises in which we find ourselves. Fela's mortal remains have been interred in the bowels of the earth in Lagos but his memory lives on while his soul is in transition.[5]

Although Fela died, his Afrobeat music continued to live on in Nigeria in the bands of Kola Ogunkoya, the saxophone player Kayode Olajide, Dede Mabiaku, the masked performer Lagbaja, and Positive Force, Femi Kuti's band. Positive Force was formed by Femi after 1986 when he quit his father's band. Father and son were not on speaking terms again until they came together in 1990 on the birthday celebration of Fela's late mother and Femi's grandmother.

Thereafter, Positive Force played at the Shrine and became so successful that in 1999 Femi won the Kora All Africa Music Award as top male African bandleader. The following year he won the World Music Award at Monte Carlo. Fela's old band, Egypt 80, also continued operating, jointly led by Fela's youngest son, Seun Anikulapo-Kuti, and Fela's veteran baritone sax player, Lekan Animashaun. In Ghana some of Fela's songs, such as "Shuffering and Shmiling," "No Agreement," and "Upside Down" have been orchestrated by both Nana Danso Abiam's Pan African Orchestra, and PAO Youth Orchestra, based at the National Theatre, Accra.

Both are large outfits with forty-plus players, utilizing African percussion and melodic instruments, such as hand pianos, kora harp lutes, bamboo flutes, xylophones, and one-string fiddles and organized in symphonic-like sections led by a conductor. The Pan African Orchestra is taking Afrobeat closer to the classical or art-music style, which Fela often considered to be the direction in which his music was moving.

Local rap artists are now also using Afrobeat as a resource. Nigeria has its UK born female rapper and emcee, Weird MC (Adesola Adesimbo Idowu), who chants over old remixes of Fela's tunes, and in 1999 Ghana's Nana King had a vernacular rap ("hip-life" in Ghana) hit called "Champion," based on loops from Fela's song "Lady." This topic is further discussed in chapters 18 and 19.

PART THREE RETROSPECT

10

MAC TONTOH ON FELA

Mac Tontoh, together with his saxophonist brother Teddy Osei and drummer Sol Amarfio, were founding members of the London based Osibisa band that pioneered Afro-rock in the early 1970s and had a large number of international hits in Europe and the United States. But it was earlier, when Mac was playing trumpet for the famous Ghanaian highlife Uhurus dance band, that he first met Fela. At first he developed a close friendship with Fela both in Ghana and Nigeria, but later on and as the Osibisa band shot to international fame the relationship turned rather prickly: a topic that Mac dwells on at some length in this interview. After twenty-five years of touring with the Osibisa supergroup Mac returned to Ghana to settle. After a few years he established his current band called Osibisa Kete that combines a battery of traditional Akan and other Ghanaian drums with Mac's trumpet. Mac also became an executive member of the Ghanaian musicians' union (MUSIGA), and in 2001 was appointed to the board of the National Commission on Culture, Ghana's equivalent to a cultural ministry. This interview was done on October 6, 2001, at Mac's house in Dzowulu, Accra. Sadly, Mac died at age sixty-nine in August 2010 at Korle Bu Hospital, Accra.

Mac Tontoh (*in middle waving a trumpet*) and members of the Osibisa Kete band.

How did you first meet Fela?

Before I even met Fela I did already admire him as we used to tune in to an NBC [Nigerian Broadcasting Corporation] radio program on jazz hosted by Benson Odanije on which Fela used to feature with his jazz trumpet. At that time I was the trumpeter for Stan Plange's Uhurus dance band that was based at Uhuru House in Asylum Down, Accra. So one time the Uhurus went to Kumasi to play, and, as I had malaria, I couldn't go. This was in 1966 just before Nkrumah was overthrown. So I was at

Uhuru House when Fela and his manager [and music journalist], Benson Odonije, came in two Peugeot Caravan cars with the eight-piece Koola Lobitos group and some very old instruments. Fela and Benson told me that Zeal Onyia [a famous Nigerian trumpeter] had advised them to come to Ghana and come and see Stan Plange, as Stan had lived in Nigeria for a long time, and Zeal used to come and do TV and radio shows with us Uhurus. Also Fela used to worship the Uhuru band. Zeal realized that as Nigerians already had Victor Olaiya and all the old highlife stuff they couldn't understand what Fela was doing [i.e., by jazzing it up]. So Zeal told Fela you're wasting your time here, go to Ghana, and what you are doing, Ghanaians will love it because they are more versatile in listening.

So one afternoon he appeared, no letter and no information, they just drove to Ghana and I received them. Then I tried to get them a hotel in the Accra hotels but they didn't have enough money—so I put them in Uhuru House, as all the Uhuru boys were in Kumasi, so the place was empty except for me. When the next Monday the group came back we put them all up. Stan accommodated Fela and I accommodated Odonije and four of the musicians in my own room. So I had to take them to Tip-Toe and Metropole nightclubs and other places to give them gigs, and also went to see my friend Kobina Taylor at Ghana Broadcasting TV to get Fela on the air. The Koola Lobitos, they had their first gig at Ringway Hotel in Accra and at that time it was a swinging place for jazz and highlife, and Ignace de Sousa's Black Santiagos was the resident band. So they gave them a spot. And "boom" the Ghanaians loved Fela's highlife sound, especially the jazz part of it. And the Koola Lobitos had some very good players, Fela was a great trumpeter, then there was Isaac who was a brilliant alto player, Tony Allen was on drums, there was another second trumpeter called Eddie, Animashaun was on baritone sax, Isaaca was on congas, and the guitar player was Johnson who was a scholar in a firm. And they were getting followers. There was a hit song of Fela's called "Yeshe Yeshe" he used to play then that even Uhurus adapted and played. A lot of the bands in Accra would play Fela's jazz style. They would play their highlife and then what Fela brought. So Fela became popular in Ghana before Nigerians got to know him. That was the first time in Ghana and Fela loved it and would go to Nigeria and then back every two or three weeks.

Fela also loved Ghana as he thought Ghanaians were gentle. Once me, Benson Odanije, and Fela were walking from the Tip-Toe club one afternoon to the Ebony restaurant to eat and we saw people in a long queue. When Fela asked what was going on I told him they were waiting for a tro tro [bus] to go to Nima. Then Fela said, "Jesus, in Nigeria they will be scattered and wait until the bus comes and then will fight and whoever is strongest will get in." Then in the restaurant there was also a quiet queue so Fela said, "man we should get Nkrumah to Nigeria to straighten up Nigeria." He even used to say this later in Nigeria.

What was Fela like during those days?

Fela at that time was very sharp and was very gentleman with his white shirt with chest open and collar raised up and tight tight trousers. He wasn't even smoking or drinking, and I remember I used to buy a crate of Fanti for him and he would finish it the same day. Fela was very neat, and the girls were following him, as he was so handsome. He was so gentle and didn't talk much. He loved Ghanaian women, not prostitutes but the home girls. Even I remember that some of the guys used to smoke ganja but they had to hide it from Fela.

I believe that the Uhuru band also used to play with the Koola Lobitos in Lagos.

Yeah, from those years [i.e., 1966–69] when Uhuru used to go Nigeria to play we would play side by side with Fela's band. So as he and I were friends by then, anytime I go to Lagos I stay with Fela at his mother's house, Fela's Jamaican wife, and the kids. So they look after me and Fela and I would go out to jazz clubs in Lagos. Fela's mother was very supportive of him. I remember one time Fela wanted to put on some trousers but they were too tight and they split, and we were going to a jazz club. So his mother removed Fela's trousers and quickly did the sewing for him. His mother was always supportive of Fela and always liked whatever he was doing. In Lagos the Uhurus and Koola Lobitos used to play side by side at the Empire Hotel (opposite his mother's house) and a club called the Green Onion or something like that. Sometimes, weekends, I would just go to Nigeria myself personally and take a car from Accra to go and see Fela and play jazz in Lagos. I would go straight to Fela's house, as I knew I was welcome and had a bed there. And his mother would always make me "dodo," as she knew I liked fried plantain.

There was a time when you didn't see Fela for a couple of years.

This was when Fela went to America and I went to Germany and Europe to further my career. Fela and the Koola Lobitos in 1969 stayed in Los Angeles and stayed with Duker or Duke Lumumba a hot Ghanaian trumpeter then, who died recently. He was a Fanti and his real name was Kwerku Baidoo, and his family name was Duker. He then had a contract with Capitol Records and released a big African-jazz record album called *Lumumba,* so everyone knew. At that time, except for Hugh Masekela, he was the only popular African musician around. Duker had played in Ghana from the late fifties with many highlife bands, like the Modinaires, Star Gazers, and the Blue Jewels in Kumasi that had included my brother Teddy Osei, and then Broadway dance band that later became Uhuru. In fact it was when Duker left Uhurus for America that the Uhurus came for me to join them as a young trumpeter.

Anyway, Duker and Fela became friends in Los Angeles. And then, through Duker, Fela met an African American girl called Sandra Jean

Smith [Sandra Iszadore] who was associated with the Black Power movement. And so Fela became influenced by the ideas of the Soldad Brothers and Angela Davis. So after he met Sandra, Fela became militant and changed the name Koola Lobitos, as he realized that the name was for Spanish people: and he changed it to Africa 70 [actually at first Nigeria 70]. It was also in Los Angeles that Fela started smoking ganja. So Fela really changed from Los Angeles.

When did you first meet up with Fela again?

That was in 1971 when I heard Fela was in town [i.e., London], as he had come alone to see Ginger Baker and arrange the visit of Africa 70 when they recorded at Abbey Road Studios later that year. So Fela called on me, as at that time Osibisa was coming up and was popular in London, even without our first record having been released. I took him to see our manager of Bronze Record and to see jazz-rock groups like Coliseum and Uriah Heap. Fela was around for two weeks. Then I saw one article in the *Sounds* music magazine that interviewed Fela, and Fela was saying that what Osibisa was doing was bullshit. That's when I realized that Fela had really changed, because for him to say this about us was strange when I had been taking him around and helping him. Then in 1972 Osibisa played with Fela at a show organized by the Igbo businessman Mr. Nzerebe at National Stadium in Lagos. And we had sixty thousand at the stadium and Fela opened the show for us. When we started it was the first time Fela had seen us play, and he didn't like it as the whole place went berserk over us. So he rushed his people home so they wouldn't listen to us. So our friendship was becoming diminished as Fela took Osibisa as rivals. But we were doing different things and appealing to different people. Even we were based in England. Not in Africa. But he didn't see it that way. But still I used to visit him from time to time when I visited Nigeria. But after that, anytime I met him it was as if he hasn't seen me, and he would just call me "Mac Mac," so I started calling him "Fela Fela."

Did you ever meet Sandra Smith Iszadore?

Yes, that was when Osibisa went to Los Angeles in 1972 to play and sign up with MCA. I met one guy there who was Fela's Nigerian friend called Emmanuel. So Emma gave me Sandra's number, and she came and showed us around town. She became my girlfriend. Then after we had finished that tour she came and stayed with me in London. What happened is that Osibisa had gone to tour Japan and when we got back to London my junior brother told me at the airport that I had a visitor at my and Teddy's house in Kingsbury. And when I got back, there she was with all her luggages. She had changed my room, and I couldn't see my clothes, and she had hung her family pictures around my room. She was very pretty, and she stayed with me for four months. But she was very domineering and wanted things her way. She had her own agenda and wanted me to leave Osibisa and help her sing. So I became fed up, although she was a nice woman, cooking and everything. Then I went with Osibisa again to America and left her in my house, and when I came back from America my room was empty, as Sandra had gone to live with a Jamaican drummer called Conrad Iszadore in Fulham. Conrad was a friend and used to come to my house with Wendel Richardson [Osibisa guitarist] and the Jamaican bass player Fuzzy Samuels, who played with Crosby, Stills & Nash. So when I heard where she was I gathered her passport and ticket that I had been keeping for her and took it to her in Fulham. But I kept in contact with them until they went to America.

I believe you were quite shocked when you first went back to visit Fela's house having not seen the place since 1969.

That was in 1973. We were hearing in London that Fela had ten cars and swimming pool and women around—as if it's some great place. So when me and Teddy went to visit him in 1973 we saw broken cars around and we saw this girl pissing around the edge of the pool. Then I went into a room and saw rats. And as soon as we sat down he wasn't looking at us all, but he called for some ready rolled stuff [i.e., marijuana] and started to throw them about at people, even though by that time we had stopped smoking. And there were a lot of *kobolos* [ruffian] boys around. I even advised Fela why don't you move from Lagos to the outskirts of Lagos and build a neat shrine, but Fela wasn't interested. He was even saying that Victor Olaiya [the old-time highlife musician that Fela had played with as a youngster] was deceiving Nigerian musicians and not doing the right thing, as Olaiya was just imitating the E. T. Mensah style of Ghanaian highlife. I was shocked, as with the Koola Lobitos he had university guys and student followers, but when he changed to Africa 70 and changed his lyrics he attracted all the riffraff and street boys.

Around that time I was at the Kalakuta with a friend and we were sitting with Fela and he suddenly said he wanted to have a bath. So about three or four girls came straight away with sponges and they stripped him in front of us and held his hand and led him, like a king, to the bathroom, a very dirty bathroom. And Fela had led a clean life with the mother. The same house I mean. So the four girls locked him in the bathroom. Then six other girls came and started knocking on the bathroom door saying they wanted to be fucked too, and complained that they hadn't had sex with him for so many days. And we spent about thirty minutes waiting for him. Finally he came out with the girls and with his trousers in a mess. Then as soon as he had sat down with us another three girls complained he hadn't had sex with them, so they went into the bathroom and started raping him. It was too much for me, as I had known Fela as a mild and gentle man. And I remember Fela's older brother used to come to the house and advise him about his life—but Fela didn't listen.

Mac, I remember that you and I met at the old Kalakuta in 1977 during the FESTAC Black Arts Festival that Fela was then blasting. Tell me about that time.

We were playing at FESTAC and on one day myself, Teddy Osei, and Sol [Amarfio] went there to watch Fela playing at the Shrine at the Empire Hotel. We were standing at the back listening when and some of Fela's Young African Pioneer boys came up to us. One of the YAP boys said that they had an office at the place and wanted some donations for it. So we said OK, no problem, we would donate. And then another young YAP guy came up to us and said, "Osibisa is bullshit," and then another one came and joined him and they wanted to rough us up. So we kept quiet as we were getting agitated. Fortunately a YAP guy came who was a Ghanaian, and when he saw us he spoke to us politely in Twi. And then Duker Lumumba's younger brother Ebo, who was then Fela's manager, also came, and the two Ghanaians rescued us. So from the back of the club we then went to watch the show from the audience side. And when Fela saw us, man, he stopped playing and began his yabbis and began really abusing FESTAC and its participants. He said that zombies are organizing FESTAC and had brought all these stupid bands that didn't know anything and why wouldn't they leave things for him to organize properly. He also said that now at the Shrine it's happening more than at the FESTAC. He went on and on, although he didn't mention our band by name. So we left.

I believe that you had another problem with Fela's people the following year.

Yeah, that was in 1978 or '79 [probably 1980] when I went personally to Nigeria to do some business [to collect Osibisa royalties] and I heard that Fela and Roy Ayers were playing at the Lagos "FESTAC" National Theatre. Even I had booked a hotel at Ikeja that was close to Fela's new Kalakuta

House. So I went to the gig and visited them in the dressing room. But I only knew a few of the old band members. Fela and the musicians were smoking grass and had a Bible from which they would tear papers for rolling. As it was night, I was afraid of taking a taxi alone, so as my hotel was near Fela's place I decided to wait and go with them in their bus. So late in the night Fela was going to drive the bus in his underpants and was shouting for everyone to get in. But when I got into the bus one boy would say, "Oga you're in my seat-o" and would push, and when I took another seat another young boy would say it was his seat. So they threw me out. And Fela was watching all this and when he saw me out of the bus he just sparked the engine and went. I was shocked. I was stranded and saw a policeman and started talking to him like a friend so that I'm safe. Then I saw a car coming and it was a guy called Bayo Martins [a Nigerian percussionist] who was leaving the show very late. So I told him my story and we went to my hotel and gathered all my things and he took me to his house to stay.

You once got messed up in Berlin because of the behavior of Fela and his Kalakuta crew.

We used to go to play in Berlin a lot at symphonic music halls and always stayed at a certain big four- or five-star hotel. And I could say that in our band we were gentlemen and we never messed up hotels: so any hotel would be glad to have us even. Then this promoter brought Fela to Berlin and to the same hotel. And because of our good record at the hotel they were glad to receive Fela and his band. But Fela's people were rolling and smoking [marijuana] at the reception area. They would come there naked with towels. And because of the dirt and blood on their bedsheets the cleaners even refused to clean their room. In the end they had to throw them out from the hotel. Later Fela's promoter told us that the management had called him and asked him if Fela's band was from the same Africa as us, and the promoter said yes, but the management didn't believe him. And our brother's band misbehaving even went against us; the next time we went to Berlin they told us that hotel was full.

When was the last time you actually saw Fela?

That was in 1981 when he came to London and I had just come back from an Osibisa tour of India. At that time Alex Oduro and J. K. Braimah were with him so, as they were friends of mine, I thought I would visit Fela and all of them at the Russell Hotel in Russell Square. There I met them with Fela, Femi [his son], some recording-company people, and many fans. When the people saw me they were happy and asked me how was the Indian tour. You know what Fela did, he just look at me and said, "Mac Mac how's your trumpet." He didn't ask me how I was, just my trumpet. So I said that my trumpet was fine. Then he asked, "What band are you playing with now." Then everyone was quiet and I didn't answer. Then some of the people around said its Osibisa of course. Then Fela asked "Is the band still around?" Then I sat down and didn't look at Fela but turned to Femi, whom I had known since he was a kid, and joked with him that my son is a young up-and-coming drummer and maybe one day Fela's son and Mac Tontoh's son will jam up together and create a sensation. But Fela wouldn't mind my attempt to be friendly. It was so strange and everyone was looking. Then one lady who was coming to engage Fela at her club, the Iroko Country Club where Ginger Johnson and Osibisa used to play, said, "But this is Mac Tontoh." Fela still said nothing. Then J. K. gave me a sign to leave and told me outside that he didn't like what Fela was doing and told me that Fela was annoyed that I was taking the attention and he told me not to go back in the room. In fact his old friends, when they hear Fela bullshitting me get shocked, because they remember what I and Stan Plange did for Fela in Ghana here. That time in London was the last time I saw Fela physically.

What is the difference between your Afro-rock and Fela's Afrobeat?

Although we all came out from highlife there is a vast difference. To begin with Fela's lyrics were different from ours. Ours was not militancy it was about philosophy and joy to the world: like "We are going, heaven knows where we are going" and "welcome home," while Fela's was "Expensive Shit" and "Zombie." Now come to the music, we were using many indigenous drums from every part of Africa, and Fela was using less drums. Also he was using this juju music and Afrobeat and playing jazz with it, but we were combining African music with rock 'n' roll and jazz. Even our live shows were different from Fela's. With Fela people didn't dance too much as his was a one-man show. But we got people to physically express their energy. You see when we first came out the Europeans didn't dance. It was "hippy" time, and the audiences would just sit down and shake their heads. So we encouraged them to get up and move, because we also were all moving on stage. We weren't standing still like Fela. Also Fela did all the things on stage and commanded his musicians to play solo, stop, or this or that. But with us everyone was a leader, as it was a collective group and we were all moving spontaneously. So our audiences began to move to our music and then began dancing.

Any last word about Fela and the contribution he made?

I always talk good of Fela as Fela brought something to Africa. He even helped Osibisa by being around, for at that time we were the only African group touring around the world, and it was tiring. But you can never get too big when you are alone, for as you are here today, tomorrow you are in New Zealand. Then if you leave New Zealand another African group should come and take over, so the African thing will stick there. But we had been alone and then when Fela came on the international scene it was good for us. So Fela didn't need to be jealous of us, as we in Osibisa used to admire him and always talked better about him in any interviews because we thought he was a brother and was doing what we are doing—and the more the merrier. We loved what he was doing and any time we used to have parties we always used to play records by Fela because we thought he was doing a great service to Africa.

FRANK TALK ABOUT FELA

Frank Siisi-Yoyo was born in Cape Coast and began his drumming career with the group at St. John's Secondary School in Takoradi. He spent almost twenty years years on and off with Fela and was personally trained in Afrobeat drumming by Fela's original drummer, Tony Allen. Frank now plays at the Bassline Club in Accra with the Fabija band and at the Hoops Nightclub in Bubuashie with the keyboard players Ernest Honey and Kiki Djan. But his main band is Fabija, and the members include Ben Ago, who formerly played with a reggae group in Nigeria called the Alex O band; Jackson, who was the trumpeter for the Grass Roots band; and a Cameroonian saxophonist called Professor Fats, who, like Frank, was formerly with Fela. This interview took place at the School of Performing Arts at the University of Ghana, Legon, on June 5, 2000. Frank is currently a much sought after session musician.

How did you first meet Fela?

It was through Fela's drummer Mr. Tony Allen. You see, my family was based in Yaba, as my aunt worked there for the W. Y. Biney Shipping Agents. So when I used to get school vacation from Ghana I used to go to my aunt in Yaba and she had one Ghana girl in the house called Sister Efua who was a friend to Tony Allen. That was around 1977 or just before. So my cousin Efua used to take me to the old Shrine [Empire Hotel]—that is near the [old] Kalakuta in Yaba that later got burnt. So me and my sister go to Mr. Tony Allen who used to rehearse Afrobeat rhythms from eight in the morning to twelve in the afternoon. He alone. So I would be sitting there and he would show me the cowbell. That time I was young but I knew how to play the drums small. Sometimes I would try his drums, and one day he saw me playing and came [and] said I'm good, and so he started training me.

Then unexpectedly they have to transfer my aunt back to Ghana, and I came back here and was playing with the Sappers military band and from them I went and played with Blay Ambolley's Zantoba Mark Three Band in 1978.

That same year Fela came to Ghana and were based at Penta Hotel, Osu [in Accra], and he had a problem with the management, so Mr. Faisal Helwani took him to the President Hotel and there too trouble came. All the time Fela is an innocent soul as it was people around Fela who created problems for him. Fela hated bad. Only he liked smoking his marijuana. He was a positive soul and liked to put people together. Fela hated discrimination and tribalism and he believed in truth and reality.

For instance we went to Abeokuta for some festival. This is where Obasanjo and the late Abiola came from—and Fela too came from. They are from the same family, they live in the same area and went to the same school. The picture [i.e., school photograph] was there at Fela's room and you could see Abiola, Fela, and Obasanjo. You can see that at that time Fela used to wear shoes, and Abiola and Obasanjo don't. Fela was the most brilliant student in the school and was its prefect, so Fela had control of the two of them when they were youths. So Abiola and Obasanjo respect Fela. But because of their corruption they like cheating.

That's why Fela don't agree with them, as he wants each man to get his own benefit and rights.

A lot of time they invite Fela to come to visit them as they want to give him money they want to build house for him, but Fela would not go because as he knew that that money is not clean money. Fela made his own money by playing music and he use it for others, as Fela is not a cheater.

That time in 1978 is when Fela was in Ghana I still followed my master Tony Allen all the time. Sometimes he come and sleep in my house—his mother is an Ewe woman who used to sell beans and oil in Accra. His daddy is a Nigerian, for as you know during that time there were Nigerians staying in Ghana. Tony Allen used to play drums for Koola Lobitos in Ghana [in the late sixties], and the Koola Lobitos was popular here in Ghana before Nigeria. So Tony Allen is the oldest musician with Fela.

I believe that Fela fell out with the Ghanaian government during that stay in 1978.

This was during President Acheampong's regime. Fela was playing at the Orion Cinema [near Nkrumah Circle in Accra] with Sidiku Buari and a lot of musicians, and Fela took the mike and abused the government of Ghana and Acheampong himself. So the government became wild with him and gave Fela forty-eight hours to leave Ghana. And Acheampong too was a best friend of Fela. Half of Fela's family comes from Acheampong's area, and half of Acheampong's family comes from Abeokuta—his family house is there. You know some of Acheampong's family were missionaries—with Adamu Atta. He was a minister in Nigeria.

His name sounds like a Ghanaian one.

Yes, his family is from Abeokuta, but like Acheampong's, it is linked on both sides, Ghana and Nigeria.

But I thought Acheampong himself was an Ashanti.

Yes, he was Ashanti and his home place is Akim Oda in Ashanti

Then how did he get connected with Abeokuta?

Because his dad was a missionary and traveled to Abeokuta and had a house there. Fela used to take us every year to Abeokuta for a festival, and he used to show us around and show us the different houses and which man stay there before. Because when he was young he liked history

I seem to remember back in the seventies a controversy about Acheampong's Nigerian ancestry and even his family name Kutu.

In Nigeria it was Kuti—but they make it Kutu in Ghana.

Did Fela himself ever visit Ghana as a boy?

Yes, when Fela was about fifteen or sixteen he visited Akim Oda Old Town and was playing for the Methodist church there. He was in the choir and used to play piano for the church. He used to come with his dad, who actually got sick in Akim Oda before he died. The father was in Akim Oda working as an elder of the Methodist church before the Nigerian Civil War and used to go up and down to there from Abeokuta. Sometimes he used to take Fela. That's why Fela had friends there. During Busia's time [president of Ghana from 1969 to 1972] when they made the Aliens Order they sack half of them [i.e., the Nigerians] in Akim Oda. That's what brought the problem for the chief of Akim Oda as he was half Nigerian—his mother was Ghanaian and father a Nigerian. And that brought the problem of removing him. Fela grew up with him too.

Did Fela spend a lot of time in Akim Oda?

No, as Fela didn't want to use his dad's background too much as Fela believed in African culture but his dad believed in orthodox things. So Fela was not together with the dad. He even he told us that when he came to Ghana he didn't all the time stay with the dad.

So what happened when Fela was expelled from Ghana by Acheampong?

My master Tony Allen says I should follow them back, although my parents didn't like the idea. When I went with them, that is, in 1978, I was not playing the drums. My master was playing but he kept training me and sometimes if he doesn't play he gave me the chance.

But then didn't Tony Allen leave Fela?

That was in 1979 after Tony Allen came from America and he left Fela to form his own group in Paris. The problem [with this] was that when Tony stop with Fela the band's rhythms would lose—because the feel that Tony Allen uses is hard for any drummer.

But why exactly did Tony leave Fela?

Tony was the leader of the band but there was a problem between Fela and him over a recording, as Tony wanted to claim his rights from Fela. The thing started from abroad [i.e., the United States] so when they came back Tony decided to stop with Fela. So he formed his group Afro Waves in Nigeria and then went to America and later Paris.

So how did Fela manage without a top-rate drummer?

At that time Ginger Baker was in Nigeria with the ARC studio, and he had one Cameroon drummer whose name is Jojo, and Ginger introduced him to Fela. Jojo had played with Manu Dibango—and Manu Dibango was a best friend to Fela. Jojo was the best drummer at that time in Nigeria—a hard-hitting jazz drummer. So he was able to play with Fela. But when Fela went to America in 1982 Jojo stopped with Fela and stayed there. In fact, a lot of Fela's people drop there, like our Ghanaian saxist Acheampong. So when Fela came back he decided to take two drummers so that if he was traveling one would stay and one would go—as Fela depended on drummers.

Not any drummer can go and play with Fela unless you train for years before you can understand the rhythm because Afrobeat rhythm is a hard-concentration rhythm. So at that time [i.e., 1982] I and Ateba—he was a Cameroonian—played for Fela. He's dead now, and it was when he came from France he sick and he die. Ateba start and I close the show.

But later you left Fela's band for a while?

Yes, it was when Majek Fashek formed his [reggae] band and he needed a drummer and at that time I wanted to go inside Rastafarian dread. But Fela don't like me to be dread and he told me that if I like to be dread I had to go. You see Fela is a [sort of] Rasta, but he don't like that sort of hair, or wigs and things. So he told me if I want to be Rasta I could not play with him.

Why didn't Fela like dreadlock hair?

I don't know. But you will never see a dread-man playing for Fela. He said it was an idol. It was the same with Colombo [i.e., Kologbo] who was on guitar. When Fela came back in 1982 from America, Colombo also drop as he always liked to play solo for guitar, which Fela didn't like. But Columbo also wanted to make Rasta, and as I mentioned Fela don't like Rasta. Colombo's in Germany now and is a dread.

What happened to you when you became a Rasta and joined Majeck Fashek's band?

I played with Majeck Fashek and then became a session drummer for a while. But later I heard Fela was still have problem with drummers, so in 1986 I have to decide to go and cut my dread back and go and play with Baba [i.e., Fela] again. That time I was the lead drummer although I used to train some other guys. Fela was renting a house in Ikeja just at the back of the New Shrine on Pebble Street for me and the keyboardist Keje. Fela liked Keje past all the musicians, as he was such a funny guy. I played with Fela up until he died, and then I came back to Ghana. So in all I played with him over sixteen years [i.e., from 1982 to 1997].

Besides yourself and Acheampong, how many other Ghanaians played with Fela?

After 1986 there were three of us. That is, Charles from Takoradi on bass—but later he dropped out in Germany and we get another Ghanaian, Biski Chase, also on bass. And then there was one of my friends, Tiaku, who played the sax who replaced Acheampong. Then there was Professor Hindu, who was a best friend to Fela. He wasn't a musician but used to come perform some magical acts for Shrine.

Did you travel abroad with Fela?

Yes I went to Brazil with Fela. That is the festival Kisomba 84 and we went and stood for Nigeria. Then after I came back from Majek Fashek we went to Italy and Japan.

Who were some of the famous musicians who visited Fela and the Shrine in the years you were with him?

Because of Fela I was able to know Hugh Masekela and Peter Tosh. Peter Tosh stayed in Fela's house for three days and it was after Peter Tosh went back to Jamaica from Nigeria that they [an armed robber] shot him. I also met Manu Dibango, the Third World reggae group, and I was able to shake hands with [the] Commodores at the Children of Africa show.

What about Fela's relationship with his sons?

At one time Femi want to take school fees from Fela. As you know Femi don't smoke and don't drink—only he get the father spirit. So when he came to Fela's K.K. [i.e., the new three-story Kalakuta house near the Airport Hotel at Ikeja—now a mausoleum for Fela] the father was making love with some girls. You know, like to make love with plenty girls.

So Fela was busy and he told the bodyguard Aniboro—he only get one eye as soldiers spoil his eye and Fela take him to Europe to fix another [false] eye for him. Aniboro is one of the oldest bodyguards for Fela and is about nine feet tall. Anyway, Aniboro tells Femi make he wait. But Femi didn't understand and so he went and stand for front of the house and started to abuse the bouncer and say, "You fool, my father de pay you and I want to see my father, can you stop me?" And Aniboro vex and slapped Femi. So Femi too slap the bouncer even though at that time Femi was a young boy. So the bouncer go tell Fela, "You see the thing your pikin [child] dey do." And Fela laugh and supports his pikin and tells the bouncer that what his son do is good as "like father like son."

Then Seun, the small pikin of Fela, said he won't go to school. Fela tell him, "No school, no problem, put your dress for house [your house clothes rather than school uniform], and if you don't want to go to school that is your own problem, do anything you want." So [in the end] Seun go carry his house dress. He resemble Fela and do and act everything like Fela. Only Seun's not red, he's black and doesn't have Fela's fair color—because his mummy is black.

How did Fela strike you as a person?

He respect positive laws but he also applied the negative at time. Because it's like the keyboard, you cannot make white alone you have to apply the black notes. But Fela used to practice occult. He had the books. Sometimes when we were playing music it was like some spirit with us there. For every Saturday's incantation he killed chickens and he drink blood. So when Fela dey stage it's not he himself there because when Baba feel shout—like the spirit come everybody.

When Abiola win the government after he had stood for election he wanted to use Fela to gain popularity—as they are more or less brothers So Abiola invite Fela to his house for a big party, and Fela have to go as they are family—even though Fela had yabbied Abiola in his song "ITT" [International Thief Thief]. And it's true, Abiola duped the country for that money—everybody knows it. So when we were going Fela went and bought a big white ram. And you see when Abiola was standing there his face is like the ram. Then Fela presented the ram to Abiola for his congratulations and they give Fela mike. Fela say, "Well, ladies and gentlemen, I want to say only one thing before I leave, I beg look this ram that stand here. This and Abiola they no be the same?" Abiola no feel laugh and he vex[ed]. But true the ram, dey resemble Abiola.

Then one day we go play for Calabar Stadium. Then that day one of the police IG [inspector general] he started to beat people when Fela came on stage as plenty crowd wanted to see Fela. Then Fela take mike and told the police that even though he doesn't have power if they are not careful he will tell the whole stadium to beat the police. So people dey yab Fela and say, "We will die for you finish, so sing for us." Fela make quiet and became busy with fixing his sax. Then people shout, "Baba play our music or we will take our money."

But Fela didn't mind them as he vexed and took a spanner and continued to repair his sax. So the crowd went and beat the gate people. Fela and we all escape from the other side. But these people knew the road we would follow to Lagos, and even though it was night they went and put huge timber trees on the road. And when we were traveling in the big bus for us musicians and the five-ton car for the instruments they block us. Then they come from the bush with guns. We don't know whether these are armed robbers or what, but they say they want their money, so make we bring Fela come. So Fela say, "You de craze, why don't you go to Lagos to meet us. Now roadside to come me talk. Me I no be roadside guy like you." The armed robbers or fans began to laugh and say, "OK, Fela you will play for us in the bush now and if you no play we will beat you and your people."

So right there we have to fix the generator and small-small instruments and play for about an hour. Then Fela like it and became happy because they go bring smoke and then Fela get wife there too. So Fela tell us was make we stay there. It was a village on the Lagos road near Calabar at the bridge past Omukpa. So we have to stay in that village for one day and they cook food and everything for us there. This happened about a year before he died.

Tell me about his death.

When Fela was coming to die we saw it because when the government came out [freed] Fela for Aso Rock prison [where he was imprisoned on a marijuana charge] they inject Fela. The barber who used to clip him told us that Fela's hair was all removing and coming out with the meat. Fela lose appetite. Fela can't eat all the time. Baba is weak, and so his brother went to see the minister of health that they should treat him. But Fela do occult and so told them no—and said they should leave everything to god. Because of the occult, if he goes to the hospital and doctors give him medicine or injection, he say he will not take them. When Fela enter inside the occult his life became confuse.

In K.K. [Kalakuta] house you know man like to yab [talk heatedly] with one another. So after Fela came out of Aso Rock we yab him [i.e., Fela] that you this man who is the black president of Africa now AIDS catch you. Then Fela go laugh and he say AIDS na [is] a small thing. Near the day when he die I see him and he smoke and smoke. Then he call all the girls and tell them he come die. And he no feel make love with them, as he tire.

That day, Saturday, he was supposed to play at Shrine and he only play one hour, then he drop the sax and tell everyone from the stage he's going to come [go]. So people think he's going house and will come back. But Fela no come as he takes some girls to his car. He told the girls he could no feel fuck but they force him and hold his prick. "Make you wake up," the girls cry for the prick. Fela de look them and says I'm going. And that night he smoke though they [i.e., the doctors] tell him not to smoke. And he cough and cough. The following day they rush him to the Methodist hospital in Abeokuta.

You said that that some people killed Fela by injecting him at Aso Rock. What do you mean?

You know these people kill him—Abacha dem—they inject him at Aso Rock in Abuja [Nigeria's capital city] where the president used to stay. It has security and they have prison there and that's where they lodge the big-big people when they do bad. The political guys, that's where they lock them. They took Fela there from the prison cells at Pachin in Jos

Plateau State where it's cold. He was there for some months and he was seriously sick and had a cough. And so they have to release him to Aso Rock as the Nigeria whole go say if they no remove Fela something will happen [i.e., he will die]. So they transfer him.

He told us all afterwards that they gave him something to drink and he became weak and there one doctor injected him. Fela says he wants his own doctor and anyway they no get right as he is an occultist man. Fela even showed us the marks. You see that time Fela write some music so that when he come out from prison he will release it so that everyone will know the secret. Because as soon as he enter Aso Rock he know all the secrets of Nigeria. He also wanted to sue the government. So when Fela came out of Aso Rock his brain was slow and Fela don't do thing like he did before—like every morning he wake up he used to take him sax and smoke. But Fela became dull and he no play again for stage except for the one hour on that Saturday.

How long was he in the two prisons altogether?

Five months and that time we just play without Fela. And Seun, the small one, used to play just like the father. But Femi was afraid to play for Shrine because the day the soldiers came to scatter the Shrine [i.e., the earlier marijuana bust that led to the imprisonment], it was Femi's instruments that were there, not Fela's. Femi was playing when they attacked the place so they seized all his equipment.

Tell me about the marijuana case that got him locked up in Jos and then Abuja in the first place.

All the time Fela himself was innocent. One guy went and stole something from the Airport Hotel so he run and enter inside the Shrine. So the police and mobile force chased the boy to the Shrine and it became like fight. Then they brought reinforcement. But Fela was not at the Shrine he was at his K.K. house. So they went there and catch Fela there with the marijuana. And all the girls there sells marijuana.

You were at Fela's funeral. Can you describe it?

Like from K.K. house, before they will take Fela to Methodist church at Oba Olande where Fela's mother used to go, the streets were full of people. So we have to carry Fela's coffin and walk with it. And the church too was crowded. This man who he die, Abacha, he came give speeches at Tafa Belewa Square. That's where they lay Fela's body from one o'clock. So people look at the body until five before they carry the body and put it inside car. Then people followed the car till they take him back to K.K. house. So they buried him in the house. Femi's now working on it to make it a place whereby you can go and look. Because they mummy [i.e., mummify] the body so he's still like that. Even recently I see him. Some glass dey there so you can see Baba.

12

OBIBA PLAYS IT AGAIN

Obiba Sly Collins played percussion and bass with Fela between 1980 and 1984. Obiba ("someone's son") was born in Bekwai, Ashanti, in 1961 and played with Konadu's guitar band in 1977–78 and then went on to join Kofi Sammy's Okukseku in 1979, a Ghanaian guitar band that was then resident in eastern Nigeria. After Obiba left Fela he joined a number of Nigerian artists and bands, including the Blue Diamonds run by the Ghanaian Techi Menson, Alex Zitte (a "lovers rock" band also run by a Ghanaian), reggae star Ras Kinomo, Danny Wilson, the Terracota band, the top Nigerian producer Lemmy Jackson, and the South African singer Yvonne Chaka Chaka. Obiba also ran three bands himself in Nigeria called Kazz, the Preachers, and Goldfinger. He returrned to Ghana in 1998 and released his *Odo Fantastic* CD there in September 2001 at the premises of the Alliance Française. I interviewed Obiba on October 1, 2001, at the offices of his Nigerian manager Fransesca Nielson of Universal Entertainment in Dworulu, Accra.

How did you first meet Fela?

About 1977–78 when I was playing band with Konadu, when Fela came to play in Ghana and Konadu was one of the biggest bands in Ghana here.

Obiba Sly Collins, who played bass and percussion with Fela in the early 1980s.

So at a show in Accra, Konadu was playing one highlife that Fela loves and so Fela begins to play his saxophone. But Konadu pushed him on the stage. I was annoyed even though I didn't dream I was going to play later with Fela. That day Fela warned Konadu never to step in Nigeria.

I actually joined Fela from Okukuseku who was a close friend of Fela. So there was a time in 1980 I went to the Shrine and Fela was rehearsing, and Fela had some of these big African drums. So I started beating the real *adowa* feel for the music they were playing. You see I had learnt drumming, as my mother was the Queen Mother of Ashanti Nnwonkoro folk music in Ashanti Bonwire, the kente-cloth town. So I learnt my percussion from my mother's band.

So Fela asked me where I was from and I said I was a Ghanaian and he said you aren't going anywhere. So I stayed at his Kalakuta in Ikeja, first playing percussion and then learning to play piano and bass guitar. I just love the bass.

What was it like staying at the Kalakuta?

There were forty-six people living in the house including musicians and dancers. And I saw many people living with Fela even who weren't musicians. Baba (Lekan Animashaun) was the leader of Fela's Egypt 80, and the drummer was Alu Ade. All of Fela's wives had their own rooms one by one and there was an Ashanti girl called Seewa staying there who Fela loved very much.

I was together with some Ghanaian boys staying in one room at Kalakuta. Fela liked Ghanaians and called them to stay free if they don't have a home. Acheampong was a saxophonist, Charles was the second bassist, as Fela always liked to have two musicians, and one guy who was a trap drummer was called Tunde, but he was a Ghanaian. That time they call me Kekere, which means "smallest," as I was about nineteen years old at the time. Fela never let me use my English names Sly or Collins, he always called me Kekere or by my Ghanaian name, Obiba.

The house had rugs and was very neat and everybody staying there was equal there, so we all could use the kitchen. We musicians were getting about 150 naira monthly, big money at the time, and three times normal government service salary. Any day you go show there was also an allowance for you, and sometimes, if you are lucky your allowance can be more than your salary. Fela didn't like to play outside shows too much and when I was with him he played at Lekan Beach, at Port Harcourt, and at TBS [Tafawa Belewa Square].

Also people used to come to watch the rehearsals at the Shrine as a rehearsal too was show. The only thing was the audience couldn't bring tape recorder and couldn't take pictures. But we never took a day off as Fela never had a holiday but he would sleep in the morning and we would rehearse in the afternoon. Although on Sunday afternoons he would sometimes let other bands play, as Fela believed in encouraging African youths and told them as he couldn't give them money he could give them space. Femi sometimes played there but later he left. Majek Fashek's band and the Justice band also played there on Sundays. They were reggae bands and their musicians were dreads.

But I thought Fela didn't like dreadlocks.

It's true he didn't like dreadlocks and he didn't like men who used jelly curls as he said they were for Africans who are lost in the diaspora. However, if you smoked he liked you, so he liked very much the drummer for Majek Fashek who had dreadlocks and a young guy called Charlie Boy who had jelly curls. But he would insult Charlie and say, "Look the thing you do your hair, you craze, you don lost your culture."

Did you ever record with Fela?

I recorded for him as a percussionist once in 1982. That was the day we recorded a second version of "Fefenefe" that he had done originally in 1976 [actually in 1973, CRLP 502]. It is an Ashanti proverb that says that it is nice the way a woman who is running holds her breast, not that the breast will fall, but just to cover herself and respect herself.

What about the drugs at the Kalakuta?

What Fela hated is cocaine. If he catches you he will detain you in his own cell at the Shrine. It was just like a police cell with iron bars and [a sort of] police who wear uniform and carry sticks and are strong. The kind of beating you will receive you won't go back to cocaine. Fela of course did smoke Indian hemp, and it was because of this that police in uniform came to Shrine. But Fela hated to see uniforms because of the way they [i.e., soldiers] killed his mother. So he tells his boys to beat the policeman up and then they will come back in trucks. I was there in 1983 when they raid us and take us to Alagbon [police headquarters]. They took everybody, even with the fans, and for one week they discipline us brutal. It was from that day I first thought to leave the band because I saw every time problem, problem. In the prison Fela just kept insulting the police and told everyone to shit here and shit there and everyone began to act like mad people and shout, "Baba don come." He go use one Yoruba word, "Ofu se lu," and his people will reply, "Aya kata," which means, "If you want to know you will know, but then you will fall to the ground." He actually sings these words in one of his songs called "Basket Mouth" or "Big Mouth" that was recorded by Decca [in 1977] when Chief Abiola was chairman.

But by the time you were with him hadn't he fallen out with Chief Abiola?

According to Fela he did many recording for the Decca Afrodisia label, so he asked for Abiola for his royalties, but Abiola did not mind him as he said he was no longer the chairman. But Fela said that as he was the chairman at that time he is still supposed to pay for Fela's sweat. But Abiola still refused because he said that Fela had sung a song against him called "ITT" [International Thief Thief] and insulted him. So now why is Fela asking for money? So Fela decided to carry shit go throw it at Abiola's house. They carried it in two of those big trucks [used for draining septic tanks] and Fela followed in his own van and paid the workers not to throw it away, as he had a special place to throw it. So they sprayed the house with the hosepipes on the trucks. It went on the wall, over the wall and all the house. So Abiola couldn't come out of the house.

Were there a lot of rituals going on at the Shrine when you were there?

Sometimes Fela would baptize all his musician with the "spirit of music." He would give us palm wine and touch our heads before a show. And that day it would be different and I would play very well. One day he called me and asked me did I know that music is a spirit. If you want to play music be open [here Obiba put his hands out palm up] not closed [Obiba puts his palms down]. Those musicians who he sees have a bad spirit he has to baptize, and when we were going to stage he would tell us that if you know you are quarreling with any of the other musicians remove it now, before we go to the stage, or the spirit catch you and fire will burn your head.

And Fela had some special day that when we are coming to perform we are first going to our ancestors. And the ancestors are no more than Fela's mother and Kwame Nkrumah. He will chew kola nut for himself and blow it out on heads of some statues of his mother and Nkrumah. And he also had two pictures of them with curtains around. That's the "Shrine." And we had some special days like Thursdays and Saturdays when we worship at that place for about an hour—just before the show. At that time he doesn't play any foreign instrument. African only percussion. Sometimes he tears the necks off chickens. We will drum, sing, and dance to traditional music. Sometimes I sing some Twi there. And that time you will see the man is in a different mood. Me I believe Fela was a spiritual person.

Tell me more about Fela's love of Kwame Nkrumah.

Once he when we playing on stage he asked me did I know the meaning of Ghana and I said I only know it was called Gold Coast before. He said you don't know the name of Ghana, and he then spoke into the microphone and yabbied the audience that the meaning of Ghana is "God Has

Appointed Nkrumah Already—before President Busia, before Acheampong, before Rawlings."

Another head of state he loved was Thomas Sankara of Burkina Faso, as he was a small boy president and Fela loved the way the boy was stubborn. Even before Fela died, if you go to his house you could see Sankara's picture there. Sankara had even visited Fela too—it was not a long time before they killed him [i.e., when President Sankara was assassinated in a palace coup].

Can you recall any other notable visitors to Fela's house or club?

Hugh Masekela from South Africa and the musicians of the Third World band came. And I do remember there was one time in 1982 I was in the house when President Shagari's vice president, Ekwueme, came to visit Fela, and Fela that time was completely naked in the Kalakuta as he was having fun with his girls. So when we said Baba you hear the siren, Fela go shout and say, "Who is making noise in my house tell them make stop." The vice president had come with one Lagos oba [chief] and they got down from their vehicle. So Fela came out to meet them and as he was completely naked the two men were ashamed. The Yoruba man told Fela he is not correct asked him to go into the house and dress. So Fela said he would go and put on a woman's sexy pant just to cover himself. After that the two men came in and sat down and Fela was smoking a stick of Indian hemp as big as a mineral bottle in their presence. I don't know what they came to discuss as they excused us and we left them.

I believe the Ghanaian concert-party conjurer, Professor Hindu, was another frequenter at Fela's place.

That began when Professor Hindu started to come to Lagos, and he became very friendly to Fela. Hindu first came to perform at the Shrine when he killed a person on stage and later woke the person up. Hindu slaughtered the women he brought with him with a knife and then butchered her and put the pieces in a pot. This pot was kept in a room at the Shrine and then Hindu would wake the woman up on the third day. So Fela just liked Hindu as Fela believed in all this African spiritual system. Hindu even gave a good-luck necklace to Fela that Fela used to hook his saxophone around his neck. Sometimes Hindu stays at a hotel and other times at Fela's house in Ikeja [Kalakuta].

Tell me about your rehearsal and how Fela composed his songs.

He wouldn't write anything down, he would just use keyboard and percussion [i.e., clips, maracas, and congas] when he composes. Then he would ask us what would you like to play now. He would like to test us. So if you are a sensible person you will play something to match what he is playing. But he wouldn't tell us what to play. Then if he liked it he would say wait and tell us to only play that one. He would do this first with bass. And Fela didn't like when playing bass I should only use two strings. He told me to always use all four so that the sound will be full. After getting the rhythm going on the percussion and bass he will leave his piano and from there tell the trap drummer, the tenor, and guitar where to come in. And if you no play well he will shout and say you never get music spirit to compose to create your own, you are a fool and don't know anything. Then he will take the instrument from your hand and will show how to play and strike for you: even the guitar, as he could play this too, but not too strong. From there he will take his saxophone and the arrangement will come When he teaches you something and then teaches you it the second time—the third time he will shout on you, slap you, or throw the mike on you.

Any new song the words are already in his head. Maybe he sees something that vex him which give him an idea. Fela sometimes composed on stage and sometimes when he wanted to sing it again he would forget. Then he will compose a different thing from what we rehearsed. But the rhythm and the arrangement will be the same.

Why is it that at his shows people didn't usually dance?

The reason is that when Fela is playing he always want to create something on stage so your attention will go to him. Sometime he would even come on stage with lightning in a pot—a pot of flaming palm oil—as part of the show. Or make like he was having sex with one of the dancers. Also he won't give you chance to dance because he can just stop the music anytime and talk. And the crowd loved to watch Fela open his mouth and yab. He mainly yabbis the Nigerian bigmen who stole the people's money. He would start with late Obananjos deputy Yai Adua and say he had a neck like an ostrich. And then he will also yab Obasanjo, his own brother from the same village (Abeokuta), as the man with big fat stomach. Fela would also call out Margaret Thatcher's and Botha's name.

What do you think are Fela's main contributions to you now that you are back in Ghana?

If you listen to Afrobeat you will hear that Fela got it from highlife, to which he added some jazz touches. So I am also planning to blend highlife, as because right now we don't have any international artists in this country.

I learnt a lot of things from him, and in my country the music is dying and I know Fela picked a lot of things from our highlife. So I have decided to bring the rhythm he is playing and fuse highlife into it. So my music is Afrobeat highlife. I've just recorded one Afrobeat highlife called "Wiawase" (The world), and the meaning is that the world doesn't belong to anyone, but only to God, so why are we hating, cheating, and oppressing one another; it's better we come together and build a peaceful world. But some of Fela's character I am trying to dodge. Fela had money already as his family got money. My family doesn't have money, so if I start trouble now I will be finished.

13

SMART BINETE SORTS IT OUT

Smart Binete is from the Delta State of Nigeria, but his family has been in Ghana since 1948. Smart began running the Ghana branch of Balkan Airlines in 1986, which he has now expanded into a travel and tour company. He completed his SECAPS Hotel in 1993, and his extended family in Nigeria has hotels in Benin City and Lagos. Smart has known Fela since the early 1960s, organized that last trip by Fela to Ghana in the early 1990s, and one of his family properties in Lagos was Fela's Africa Shrine for many years. The following interview was done at SECAPS Hotel, Accra, on September 2, 1999.

Because of your managing Balkan Airlines that passes between Lagos and Ghana you've been able to bring a number of Nigerian artists to Ghana.

I have brought Majek Fashek, the Mandators, Evi Edna Egholi, of course, the bigman himself, Fela.

I believe the last time he came to Ghana was through you. How did you manage this?

You see Fela is a personal friend and a family friend. So one day in 1990 I went to see him in Lagos and asked him why don't you come and play in Ghana—and he said OK. I made arrangements for three shows over the Christmas holidays of 1990–91. Two at the football stadium and Star Hotel in Accra and the last one in the Kumasi Stadium. He was here for ten days with about sixty people and they were staying at the Penta Hotel in Osu and then went up to Kumasi in a bus.

The shows were full of problems with equipment. We had a guy in Lagos who was supposed to give us band equipment. We paid him and he said he was taking them to the Murtala Muhammed Airport and that we should go ahead. But when we got to Accra there was no equipment. So it was a real disaster, and we had to start running around Accra grabbing whatever we can—a drum from here, that from there. By the time we were through the Accra Stadium show started about 3:00 a.m.

The one at the Star Hotel went very well, and we had members of the PNDC government present. That was the time Fela already had the record "Zombie" out, which was criticizing the soldiers, and you can imagine what it was with the government officials there. It was a military government but they took [it] in good faith and stood up and danced. The other song he was playing on that tour was "United Nations" that goes "Who is united in the united nations so they should stop calling themselves the united nations."

The Kumasi show was another disaster, as there was no light at the stadium, the electricity corporation wanted us to pay money for it in advance. Also the stage was not ready, so we had to postpone the show for that night and it was set for the next day. Unfortunately for us the next day the rain fell. So we had to put it to the third day. It was hell so I had to put Fela in my open-top Mercedes car and take him around Kumasi so everyone could see him in town, as they did not believe Fela had come to Ghana.

How did you get to know Fela?

Fela is my friend since we were together in London in the 1960s when he was studying music there. Then when he came back to Nigeria in 1962–63 we used to hang around together, and actually his girlfriend used to live in my family house in Lagos. Then I went back to London, and when I came back I met Fela again at my brother's Octopus Hotel in Surulere. Fela was then staying there because of the destruction of his Kalakuta Republic, and my brother Bayo decided to help him out. This was in 1977 after FESTAC.

That is also how we gave Fela the New Shrine that is at Ikeja, as it is our family property and is very close to another of our hotels, the Binete Hotel. Then when Fela turned to drugs and the whole trouble they wanted him out of the area, but my old man said, "Don't let me hassle Fela, because if I do he'll make a record about me, so let him stay." So that's how he continued to stay even after my old man died. But then when Fela himself died we thought there was no need for the club to remain there and that's why now the Africa Shrine reverted back to the Binete's just a few months ago.

You've known Fela for a long time. What type of character do you think he is?

People don't understand Fela. He's a nice person. He is just himself, he knows who he is. I also know Fela is a kind man, that I can tell you. Fela didn't go out much he's always indoors, and if you have a problem and don't have anywhere to stay Fela will say, "Okay, any space you see available in the yard take it over, that's yours." So that's why when you go to Fela's house the place is full of mattresses and blankets, everybody is welcome.

But he has a no-nonsense rule that you must follow. No fighting, no messing around with the chicks in the house, as they're all his wives. But if you need money he will take care of you. They live like a family. So you see, anytime the police come for Fela they come with lorries and armored cars. They don't come in one or twos because people love Fela and they will defend him any day.

So he was a kind man, and I'll tell you what happened when he came to Ghana in 1990. Because of the first bad show at the football stadium, he told me "Don't worry, I'll do the next show for you." So I didn't pay him for that [i.e., the Star Hotel show] because he saw that the things that went wrong with the equipment not coming from Lagos wasn't my fault.

Did Fela have any problems when he was in Ghana in 1990?

At the Penta Hotel he had only his shorts on with his balls hanging out and he stood at the balcony overlooking the main road—and people just laughed as they knew that that was Fela. He just didn't put clothes on. You go to Fela's house any time of day or night and he doesn't wear trousers he doesn't wear nothing, just his underpants. That is Fela's signature.

14

ANKU CHECKS OUT THE BEAT

Dr. Willie Anku is a percussionist and violin player who knew Fela in the late 1970s. Since 1997 he has been head of the Music Department at the University of Ghana at Legon. He was originally a music-diploma student of the Legon Music Department before going to Montana University in 1974 to do a master's in music education. He subsequently came back to Legon for five years as a lecturer in the Music Department and then did a master of arts at Pittsburgh University, followed up with a PhD there under Ghana's leading ethnomusicologist, Professor J. H. K. Nketia. Dr. Anku's doctoral specialty was Ewe and Akan drumming, and I was able to help him with some of his analytical recordings in the early 1980s. He has also analyzed some of Fela's songs, including "Shuffering and Shmiling," discussed and presented in this chapter. After obtaining his doctorate, Dr. Anku taught in California for three years before returning to Ghana in 1997. The following interview took place in Dr. Anku's Music Department office on August 28, 1999. Anku later became a professor and director of the University of Ghana School of Performing Arts, and it was a great shock to all of us when this great scholar was killed in a car accident on February 1, 2010.

How did you first meet Fela?

I met him first through Faisal Helwani, when Fela came here to Accra to film [i.e., redub "The Black President"] in 1978. At that time myself and Mr. Amoah recorded some background violins at Faisal's studio for his Edikanfo band led by Osei Tutu. I got to know him better, as I had a friend staying with me at Legon called Tommy Anan, and his African American girlfriend, Nella, got Fela to come to spend a whole day with us to eat, talk about all sorts of things, and then come to one of our drama productions here. I also made a number of visits to his room at the Hotel President in Accra that he had transformed into a Kalakuta Republic, wearing only pants, with all his women and the clock reversed. You see Fela was going by Kalakuta time even in Ghana, as he would sleep at very odd hours sometimes getting up at eleven in the night. We visitors and friends would sit down and Fela would come with his saxophone. He would talk and talk and then go and play saxophone for perhaps ten minutes and then he would break and talk to us again.

What was the research project you did on Fela's music?

It was one of the assignments I did for my PhD final comprehensive exam at the University of Pittsburgh. I analyzed two pieces of music; one was a jazz composition entitled "Jungle Trio" by Jeff Louna and the other was a portion of Fela's "Shuffering and Shmiling."

I discovered so many interesting things about Fela's style that makes it so unique. First of all he never uses the usual chord progressions of the Western popular idiom as he built his chords from the pentatonic five-tone scale. And here I think Fela is exploring very well the Yoruba tradition scale.

And then also, and probably the main feature of his music, was the way he used call-and-response. This, as we all know, is a dominant feature of African music, but I have never heard anyone who has used it in such a creative manner.

What grabbed me was that in addition to the usual call-and-response between chorus and solo voice he added other layers at the same time, such as between the voices and horn section and guitars and drum; but not in the same structural framework as the original call-and-response, but above and overlapping it and coming in at different times. He added as much as four layers of call-and-response, which was very intriguing, as I hadn't seen anything like that before. For example [pointing to score], he has a solo voice here and a keyboard response, then he has the chorus above that and then horns—which is really the climax of the song. This creates a polytonal structure, or megastructure of call-and-response, which I think is an important contribution to composers who are looking for new ways of writing African music. So far as I know no one has done this as well as Fela.

His horn solos are based on a polyphonic arrangement of the other instruments. He takes the same melody or tonality as these and plays a fifth above them, which harmonizes very well with what is below. He's not thinking in terms of chords (to structure a solo) but in terms of the polyphonic parts.

The drumming is also a different layer of events above which all the other musical structures are built. If you have a well-constructed ostinato [repetition] background of drums, bell, bass, and guitar you create a strong groove, and this is one of the richest techniques we have in African music. His arrangements are based on these ostinatos, as Fela creates a loop that goes on for a long time and then when he wants it to go somewhere else he gives a signal. I don't think his orchestra counted bars up to say six or whatever times and then moved to a new section of the song. Fela does one section until he's satisfied and then he moves to the next stage and they all know what the next stage is. So the music can

"Shuffering and Shmiling" score, transcribed by Willie Anku.

For the complete score, see page 303.

go on and on and Fela can move to any section that he wants, as each one is self-contained.

So the concept of ostinato in the background and his genius for layered call-and-responses is what made his music so rich and distinctive. His use of flattened thirds and sevenths is also modeled on our established African traditions. He was sincere to the African music structure, as he didn't go after existing Western models. He stayed within the African context even though he was using Western instruments.

15

NANA DANSO ORCHESTRATES

As mentioned in a chapter 9, the Pan African Orchestra was established in 1988 and uses solely African instruments, but these are organized into symphonic-like sections. Moreover it is led by a conductor and is presented in an art, rather than dance music, context. In 1994, after performing at the World Music and Dance (WOMAD) festival in Britain, the orchestra recorded at Peter Gabriel's Real World Studio in the west of England. In 1995 the resulting CD entitled *Opus One* went to the top of the international New World music charts for six weeks, and several extracts were used as signature tunes for radio and television series, for instance the BBC program *One World*. The orchestra was formed and is led by Nana Danso Abiam, who was trained at a French music conservatory, later becoming director of Ghana's National Symphony Orchestra. During the late 1990s the Pan African Orchestra began orchestrating some of Fela's Afrobeats, and Nana Danso intends to continue on this path. To discuss this whole question of Fela's music and influence on this important contemporary Ghanaian musician-composer, I interviewed Nana Danso at the Music Department of the School of Performing Arts at the University of Ghana campus at Legon on March 17, 2000.

How and when did you first come across Fela's music?

As you know, Fela was quite popular here in Ghana from in the sixties when he had put together the Koola Lobitos. And then in the seventies he was also very popular here, and many local groups were actually performing his Afrobeat items. I had a lot of respect for Fela as in Ghana at that time in the pop music scene most of the influences were predominantly from European sources. I remember the Beatles and Rolling Stones. But many of the creative guys were looking for ways of departing from that style of music and ways toward Africanization and yet looking forward. I think Fela was one of the main musicians who showed the possibilities.

How did you meet him?

That was in Lagos in 1973. I had actually put a small Ghanaian rock group together called Edzayawa ["Pot of Fire"] in Lomé, and we decided to go to Nigeria on an adventure. I had two particular people in mind to see. One was Tony Benson and the other was Fela Kuti. And so when we got to Lagos I went to Tony's, as we didn't have any place to stay. We started playing at his Caban Bamboo nightclub [actually his father's, the famous dance-band highlife musician Bobby Benson]. That was when I went to visit Fela and told him we had a small group in town and that we would like to play at the Shrine in Surulere. So he agreed, and I remember in our discussions he was actually trying some chords on his electronic piano. We were talking and he was going about these chords. So we performed from time to time and I remember we would start the evening and then Johnny Haastrup [of the Mono Mono Afro-rock band] would take over and Fela would finish.

Why has the Pan African Orchestra decided to take some of Fela's material? As a modern composer what is great and distinctive about Fela's music?

Fela was a composer who was able to use musical raw material from his immediate society and very successfully incorporate that into his instrumentation, which was an eye-opener that showed other possibilities in African music orchestration. By this I mean that he would, for example, utilize concepts from, say, the *dundun*, the hourglass drum of the Yoruba people, and I see his bass guitar patterns relying very much on this. I mean the *dundun* is also a melodic instrument as well as a drum, and its notes sometimes stretch over an octave.

But I think his greatest innovation is his departure from the major and minor modes and to the Dorian mode. As you are aware, the Dorian mode is very similar to the minor mode, especially the first half of it. The Dorian mode is quite widespread and is used all over Africa. In Guinea, Senegambia, parts of Uganda, and in the Mandinke kora [harp lute] cultures. I'm sure even in certain parts of Nigeria. And Fela being a Pan-Africanist adopted this into his music. This immediately changed the texture of his music.

You see the first tetrachord [i.e., four-note half] of the Dorian scale is similar to the natural [cf. the harmonic and melodic] minor scale, as it is made up of intervals of a tone, semitone, and a tone. For instance, in the key of C minor, C to D being a tone, D to E♭ being a semitone, and E♭ to F being a tone—which also forms the first half of the Dorian scale. Then the second half of the Dorian is the same spacing as the first half; that is, a tone from G to A, a semitone from A to B♭, and a tone from B♭ to C. However, in the normal minor mode the second tetrachord is G to A♭, then to B♭, and then to C [i.e., semitone, tone, tone].

This Dorian scale is used by Fela for his singing, his soloing on the sax or keyboard, or when his trumpeter plays. Moreover, most of his basic sounds, the bass, and all the various ostinato lines, like the tenor lines on the guitar—which I see as having been derived from the *molo* [Yoruba lute]—refer continuously to the root all the time. It is not based on the Western conception of tension being created by chords moving from one degree to the next and then to another [i.e., harmonic progressions]. The various ostinatos rather refer back to one tonal center all the time.

You mean it rotates back and forward from a tonal center?

Exactly.

Is this is why Fela's rhythm instruments use two chords, for instance his guitarist continually strikes two minor or major chords, mainly minor ones, but they are a tone apart?

Yes.

Let me ask you a specific point. I've realized as a rhythm guitarist playing Afrobeat, if suppose I'm playing in A minor and therefore rotating between an A minor and a B minor chord, I've noticed that when I come to play Afrobeat solos I'll pitch a fifth above the A minor, which is E minor.

That is what exactly gives you the A Dorian mode, but by emphasizing the first half you get something very similar to an ordinary minor scale, but when playing the whole Dorian scale it sometimes creates a confusion—especially for analysts—as it gives a bitonal flavor.

Let me explain again what I was saying before. With an ordinary minor, say, A minor, the notes A–B–C–D make up the first half [i.e., tetrachord] of the minor chord. The other half is E–F–G–A. And these different halves have the different intervals. Whereas with the Dorian the second half is

E–F#–G–A, and so the two halves are identical. If you identify the song as in a minor scale from root A and then you begin to hear an F# in the sax playing, not as a passing note but as part of the scale, you then begin to get the impression that Fela is using a bitonal scale or two gravitational centers.

So this creates the optical, or rather auditory illusion, that Fela is using two different scales; that is the scale of A minor if you take the first half of the A Dorian scale and E minor if you take its second half?

Exactly, but in reality he isn't. You are actually just playing in A Dorian. And although E minor is a fifth above A, it is equivalent to, or rather has the same relative scale, as A Dorian.

So actually because most of the notes of the minor and Dorian scales are identical, when I think I'm striking an A minor chord I'm actually striking some of the A Dorian notes.

Yes, and what Fela does is let the bass and rhythm guitar sounds spell out part of the Dorian mode [which corresponds to the A minor triadic chord A–C–E]. But the solos play the whole Dorian scale, which gives the impression it is being played a fifth above [i.e., E minor] and so playing in a different scale from the guitars. However, when you see it from the Dorian point of view you do not see it as bitonal at all. Everything is A Dorian.

To help the reader understand what Nana Danso is saying about the Dorian nature of Fela's Afrobeat music I am providing a series of diagrams that deal with different types of scales, or what in the past were known as "modes." The Western diatonic scales (modes) are composed of seven "natural" notes (i.e., heptatonic) that are spaced out on twelve

A wheel divided into the twelve semitones or half steps of the diatonic scale showing all of the notes (intervals) in the C major, D Dorian, A minor, and A Dorian scales that respectively begin on the notes C, D, A, and A.

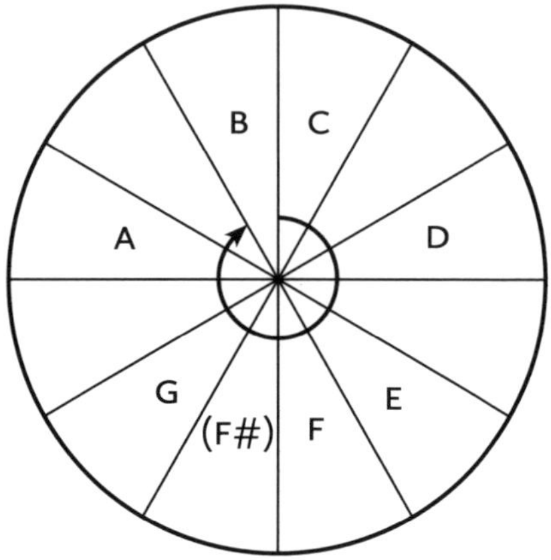

melodic intervals called half or semitones. Some of the seven notes are separated by whole tones (T), and others by semitones (S). As after the seventh note the first note of the scale/mode is repeated again but at a higher octave—the whole schema can be pictured in circular form—as in the following figure.

In the above representation the spacing of tones and semitones of the seven notes starting at C is known as a major scale. But starting (clockwise) on the circle from D it becomes the D Dorian scale—and starting from A it becomes the A minor scale.[1] We are here particularly interested in the minor and Dorian scales whose sequence of whole tones (T) and semitones (S) are depicted here:

A minor: T (A–B) S (B–C) T (C–D) T (D–E) S (E–F) T (F–G) T (G–A)
D Dorian: T (D–E) S (E–F) T (F–G) T (G–A) T (A–B) S (B–C) T (C–D)

Now let us take a specific example that Nana Danso uses, this being the key of A. In this case the spacing of the A minor is exactly as in the minor above—as it starts on the note A. However, A Dorian is different from the one above and its interval spacing is as follows:

A Dorian: T (A–B) S (B–C) T (C–D) T (D–E) T (E–F#) S (F#–G) T (G–A)

As can be seen from the above, the first four notes (i.e., tetrachord) in both A minor and A Dorian (i.e., the notes A–B–C–D) are identical, whereas the second tetrachords are slightly different: namely, the notes E–F–G–A for A minor, and E–F#–G–A for A Dorian. However, it is this overall similarity between these two scales that creates the ambiguity between them referred to by Nana Danso.

Furthermore, it was mentioned that the minor scale a fifth above the orian (in this case A) could be used for soloing. The minor scale a fifth above the A Dorian is E minor (begins on the fifth note above A)—and its spacing is shown below.

E minor: T (E–F#) S (F#–G) T (G–A) T (A–B) S (B–C) T (C–D) T (D–E)

A careful look by the reader at the above scale of E minor (E–F#–G–A–B–C–D–E) and A Dorian (A–B–C–D–E–F#–G–A) will show that they are identical, except for the fact that they start at different points on the same cycle. Thus in a Dorian scale one can easily play and improvise melodies a fifth above it.[2]

Which songs of Fela's are you orchestrating?

So far we've worked on "Shuffering and Shmiling," "Upside Down," "Water No Get Enemy," and "No Agreement." These are predominantly instrumental arrangements, but in "No Agreement" we have a vocal section.

And these songs all use the Dorian/minor ambiguity?

Yes. For instance, in "No Agreement" Fela maintains the first part of the Dorian scale and, as previously discussed, your impression is that it is based on the minor scale or key. Also, as just mentioned, the only times you see it go beyond the minor is when Fela departs melodically, either on a solo or from his voice. And then he spells out the exact [Dorian] scale by extending the minor scale. The same applies to "Water No Get Enemy."

You've mentioned at length Fela's use of the Dorian scale.
What about his harmonies?

Fela's departure from the major and natural minor approach accounts [for] why his music is qualitatively different from other African pop styles such as highlife and soukous, as his harmonic structures no longer rely on the tonic-subdominant-dominant [I–IV–V] and related triad chords of the diatonic scale. However, Fela sometimes is unable to harmonize, especially when it comes to harmonies based on heptatonic [i.e., seven-note] scales. However, although he uses the Dorian he makes use of the pentatonic [i.e., five-note scale] within the Dorian's seven notes, as he puts most of the predominance on these five pentatonic notes. Let me take the example of his song "Water No Get Enemy" [see following diagram].

Whenever Fela wants to use all seven notes as in "Water No Get Enemy" you see that the harmonies of his different horns rely on unison, because one has to be very careful harmonizing in the Dorian mode. As I mentioned, sometimes he gets around this by just picking out the five pentatonic—or six hexatonic notes within the Dorian scale. Say, if he's playing in A, he would use the pentachord A–C–D–E–G or hexachord A–B–C–D–E–G. Although these five or six notes are common to both A natural minor and A Dorian, they both avoid the note F, which would pinpoint the scale as A minor. As a result, Fela's musical explorations in the pentatonic and hexatonic scales tend to send out bitonal signals [i.e.,

In Water No Get Enemy, for example, Fela's woodwind and brass sections take the lead in the introductory passage. The lead saxophones and trumpet play the following melody:

The melody is repeated several times with other accompanying melodic instruments (guitar, bass, keyboards) exploring sounds within the D minor hexachord. Then comes the main body of the piece, whose lead lines are as follows:

Although the introductory passage suggests the D minor hexachord as being the functional tonality of the piece the introduction of the sound B natural immediately rules out this suggestion. The scale type DEFGABCD can only be D Dorian and not D minor as it has been misconstrued by some performers of Fela's music.

A portion of Fela's song "Water No Get Enemy" transcribed by Nana Danso Abiam.

the A Dorian and A minor scales—or even A minor's relative major, the scale of C major].

When he does harmonize the horns you are saying that he focuses on the pentatonic or hexatonic scale within the Dorian. Is a pentatonic chord based on triads or what?

I've devised a new system for harmonizing pentatonic sounds. I don't actually use the exact harmonic structures that Fela utilizes, but I've applied it to his music and it works perfectly. Because this system originates from ethnic societies I look at it from that point of view. So when it comes to referring to intervals of thirds and fifths of the Western seven-note heptatonic [diatonic] scale I'm very careful. You know that within the pentatonic scale on a xylophone we have five sounds after which we have an octave. I see these five sounds as fundamental. So it is five sounds to the octave, nothing else. Sometimes if we are not careful we relate to it from the point of view of the Western diatonic scale and imagine other sounds that may be missing within the pentatonic scale. No, I want to look at it as it is.

As far as I'm concerned every consecutive step [up or down] in the above pentatonic scale [A–C–D–E–G] is an interval of a second [e.g., the interval E–G], every pentatonic third is a third—whether a large third or a small third. Although in the West the interval may be described as a fourth. If, for example, we take another similar pentatonic scale but start it on C instead of A, it would be something like C–D–E–G–A. Here yes, the interval of C to E is considered as a third both from the pentatonic and the Western diatonic point of view [in Western musical language, a major third]. However, the D to G or E to A from a diatonic point of view is a perfect fourth. So in the pentatonic system the C–E third is seen as a small third and the other two as large ones. But they are all thirds. So the harmonic structure I use in the Pan African Orchestra is based on this concept of pentatonic triads [i.e., two consecutive pentatonic thirds such as C–E–A or D–G–C, etc.]. And these apply to Fela's music, as his music, although it is melodically Dorian, it is mainly harmonically [i.e., chord-wise] pentatonic.

What about some other features of Fela's Afrobeat, for instance, his use of polyphony?

Yes I look at this from the [traditional] heterophonic [multiple voice] point of view, as Fela's music is made up of many layers. For instance, the idea of incorporating many basic ostinato [repeated] lines such as the bass, which, as I mentioned before, is based on the *dundun*. Even though he uses Western instruments he is therefore able to distribute the sounds of these traditional drums. And then there is the contrapuntal effect produced even just by the various drums he utilizes. Basically his rhythm section of hand drums, trap drums, light percussion, bass, and guitars are all built on layers of ostinato cycles.

Another important feature of Fela's music is his use of dynamics [i.e., moving between loud and soft sounds]. You know, African music is sometimes described by Europeans as wild music. You start wild—it never ends—and then you finish "kpaah." You don't explore very loud and very soft, the various dynamics. But Fela does.

Which traditional African instruments of your orchestra do you transfer his instruments onto?

We play the bass-guitar line on a five-pronged *premprensua* [local giant hand piano] and Fela's snare rhythm on the *gome* drum [a large frame drum also known as the goombay or gumbe]. The motifs I pick from, say, the keyboard we play on the *atenteben* [bamboo] flutes, while my two *gonje* players [local one-stringed fiddles] sometimes take up the lines of the rhythm guitars.

I believe you have scored and adapted some pieces of Fela's music for your orchestra?

These are "Shuffering and Shmiling" and "No Agreement," but I leave room for improvisation. The songs are all purely instrumental and are scored for my orchestra's sections: eight flute parts, two xylophones, two *gonjes,* and then various percussion instruments and drums.

Are you going to include more of Fela's songs in your orchestra's repertoire?

We are working on some of his very early songs like "Lady," "Don't Gag Me," and "Zombie." We do change Fela's arrangements, however. What I do is pick concepts from him. I listen to the all the different motifs from the drums and the melodic motifs that come above all of these rhythmic ones. I listen to what he plays on the keyboard, which may, for instance, come from the keyboard just playing some simple lines.

You were trained in a music conservatory, and, as you know, many classically trained musicians do not like popular music. Also your Pan African Orchestra has a conductor and is organized into sections rather like a Western symphonic orchestra. Nevertheless, yours seems now to be making a breakthrough into popular music by using ideas from Fela.

The music that we make is comes from the masses of the people, and it is based on the musical concepts of the societies we've been exploring. In our case, although we present our music within a so-called art-music context it gets across very well to the people because it is easily identifiable, as it is like local raw material being processed and being presented back in another form. Fela's Afrobeat is also an African resource, and I look at him technically, not what he did or didn't do in his personal life. And I see what he achieved was far ahead of its time. We cannot allow this development to just die. And I can tell you that it is styles like Fela's that will in the future become the basis of the conservatories that will develop in Africa.

Toward the end of his career Fela was talking of the creation of a classical style of Afrobeat for listening to as well as dancing. With his long compositions, big-band instrumentation, and complex arrangements he himself seemed to be moving in the direction of creating a classical style. What do you think?

Well, Fela has always described his music as classical despite the fact that he presented his music within a popular music context with people dancing and doing other activities, so full attention is not paid to his music. That's the only difference I see. When music is presented as classical art music it is meant to imply absolute silence whilst the composer explores various areas and you cannot imagine dancing.

Of course, in traditional Africa there are genres that are not meant to be danced to, for instance the quiet philosophical music of the Akan ***seprewa*** *harp lute. It seems almost that Fela's music fits everywhere. It has an art ingredient, an indigenous ingredient, and a jazz and popular one.*

Exactly, that is the big challenge for composers. They should be able to get across to a wide audience whatever style of music they make.

Any last words on Fela's contribution?

Although Fela's music speaks within the Yoruba and Nigerian musical language he is also a Pan-Africanist and was looking for ideas from all over. He also has a jazz background and was looking at things scientifically as he was thinking of music theoretically. Although his instrumentation is predominantly Western he has therefore succeeded in finding a new idiom that is totally African within the Afro-jazz arena. That is why his music deserves more attention than it has been given.

Right now, as we talk, I don't see any modern composer in a popular music vein in Africa making use of the Dorian as Fela has. Moreover, he explores other scales within the Dorian mode such as the pentatonic and hexatonic ones, which are widespread in Africa—they are found within every single West African country. So Fela for me is an idol. I see the future of African music in his works. I see him as a person who needs to be researched. Where he got all his concepts and from where they are based.

16

SOME EARLY AFRO-FUSION PIONEERS

In this chapter I will focus on three musicians who pioneered Afro-fusion music. These are the Nigerians Orlando Julius and Segun Bucknor, who were contemporaries of Fela, and the Ghanaian Guy Warren (Kofi Ghanaba), who began experimenting with Afro-jazz as early as the late 1950s.

Segun Bucknor was one of several musicians in Nigeria during the late sixties blending highlife, jazz, and soul into Afro-soul—and thus paving the way for Afrobeat. There was Orlando Juilus whom I will discuss later—and also Bobby Benson's son, Tony Benson, who played jazz and soul music in the late 1960s at his father's Caban Bamboo club in Lagos. Meanwhile, in Benin City Victor Uwaifo was experimenting for several years with his own version of soul music he called "Mutaba." Another early soul man in Nigeria was the resident Sierra Leonian singer Geraldo Pino who fronted the Heartbeats (which included Francis Fuster) and who had spread live soul music in West Africa, ending up permanently in Nigeria in 1968. When Francis Fuster formed Baranta in Lagos, Pino left for Kano where he teamed up with a Ghanaian group called the Plastic Jims[1] who, after leaving Pino, renamed themselves the Big Beats, a band that went on to have a big Afrobeat hit in Ghana in 1971 called "Kyen Kyema Osi Akwan" (The oldsters are blocking our path).

Ghana had several bands and artists around this time experimenting with Afro-soul and also Afro-rock (pioneered by Osibisa in 1970). One of the earliest was Ricky Telfer's Magic Aliens formed in 1967,[2] followed in the early to mid-seventies by Oscar Sulley Braima,[3] Prince Ali, Stanley Todd's El Pollos (with singer Elvis J. Brown), Tommy Darling's Wantu Wazuri, Sawaaba Sounds, Alfred "Kari" Bannerman's Boombaya, Kris Bediako, Nana Ampadu's African Brothers (his "Afro-hili" sound) and the Zonglo Biiz, whose bass player, George McBruce, later joined Fela's band for a while.

Segun Bucknor

It was in Nigeria, however, that Afro-soul first really began to take off in West Africa. I interviewed Segun Bucknor at his house in Yaba, Lagos, on December 21, the day before I talked to Fela on my 1975 Nigerian trip.

Segun told me that he began his musical career as a member of the Hot Four schoolboy pop band in 1964, and then in 1968, after a two-year trip to the States, he teamed up with the Nelson Cole brothers to form the Soul Assembly. By 1969 Segun was fusing soul with African music and so changed the name of the group to Segun Bucknor and the Revolution and released a string of pioneering Afro-soul hits, such as "Pocket Your Bigmanism" and "Poor Man No Get Brother" that combined highlife, soul, and jazz. The following are some extracts of the interview I did with him.

I first asked Segun about the early pop and soul bands in Nigeria.

> They were school bands, and the first one was the Blue Knights. Then the first serious rock 'n' roll band we saw was called the Cyclops; they were just out of school and were formed in 1964. The beginnings of pop and rock 'n' roll was at the United States Information Service, as they had an amplifier and PA system. We used to go there on weekends, but there were

"Sir" Afro-Fifi performs at the Shrine, circa 1974–75. This Ghanaian acrobat-dancer-juggler-fire-eater stayed with Fela and played at the Africa Shrine for two years.

no permanent groups, as we would just team up and give ourselves a name. Soul groups like the Hykkers International and Tony Benson's Strangers came later, around 1968. Around 1964 to 1968 you had people who, even if they were not schooled in music, had the innate talent. They could listen to a record, pick it, play it, and sometimes do it better with their own innovations. The Hykkers' guitarist was very good, and so was Berkely of BLO [the initials stood for its three founding members: Berkely Jones, Laolu Akins, and Mike Odumosu]. Then around 1970 to 1971 there came an urge, not just to play what you hear on records, but for compositions. I will say modestly that this trend has been around since 1969 when I started my own band, and we were doing our own songs. Then you had band boys coming up with their own beautiful compositions: the Hykkers, Ofo, Johnny Haastrup of Mono Mono, Sonny Okosun, Wings, and Ofo and the Black Company. For you to thrive here in Nigeria you have to be very prolific and good at your compositions, even though you have to play a few pop numbers for the nightclub clientele.

I asked Segun about what he was trying to do with his Revolution band.

After the [Soul] Assembly, I changed the name to Revolution because I was experimenting with pop music but using the real basic African beat, the African jungle beat. We sounded like a current group called Ofege, which uses a similar basic West African 6/8 beat called "kon-kon." It's like what Santana did with Latin music and pop. Before Santana there were Latin American groups that were making it, but not that big. But since Santana came out with a rock-Latin beat, older Latin American musicians are coming up, like Mongo Santamaria who is a [Cuban] bongos player and is now enjoying some success. You know Latin America's and our music is virtually the same. It's all in 6/8 time, but when you play Latin American music you have to double the tempo.[4]

Orlando Julius

Another veteran Afro-fusion pioneer is the Nigerian saxophonist Orlando Julius Ekemode. Orlando began his career during the late 1950s with Nigerian highlife bands like Eddie Okonta's and the Flamingo Dandies, and went onto form his own jazz-influenced Modern Aces highlife band in 1963 that was based at the Independence Hotel in Ibadan. There Orlando began to rub shoulders with a number of younger Nigerian artists who, by the mid-sixties, were experimenting with highlife combined with soul and funk music. One was Fela, and some others were the ex–Bobby Benson saxophonist Eric "Showboy" Akaeze, Bola Johnson of the Easy Life Top Beats, and Tunji Oyelana of the Benders Band. In 1966 That year Orlando's Modern Aces released the album *Super Afro-Soul,* and the following year changed the name of his band to the "Afro-Sounders," which released songs like "Ijo Soul Ololufe," "Psychedelic Afro Shop," and "James Brown Rides On." Julius met James Brown and his bassist Bootsie Collins when the J. B.'s played in Nigeria in December 1970. Orlando even gave James Brown a copy of his soulish Afro-Sounders album.

In 1972, Orlando relocated his Afro-Sounders band to Lagos and then in 1974 he went to the States and joined the Afro-fusion band Umoja, formed by Stanley and Frankie Todd[5] after the breakup in the US of Faisal Helwani's Hedzoleh Soundz. It was Umoja that in 1975 released the classic Afro-fusion album *The Boy's Doing It* for which Orlando (under the name O. J. Ekomode) and Hugh Masekela cowrote the hit track "Ashiko." Orlando also played and recorded with Hugh Masekela's Ojah band as well as with the Crusaders, Isaac Hayes, Gil Scot Heron, and Gladys Knight. He, together with his African American wife and singer Layoya Aduke, returned to Nigeria in 1998 where he formed the Nigerian All Stars band and set up a recording studio in Surulere. I got to know him when he and his wife settled in Accra in 2003 for a couple of years where they became involved with the local jazz scene and operated a studio, before going back to Nigeria. Orlando also appeared alongside other Nigerian artists who were active in the 1960s and '70s (like Fatai Rolling Dollar and Victor Olaiya) on the 2011–12 documentary *Stadium Hotel* released by NEPA Films.[6]

Kofi Ghanaba

When talking of Afro-fusion pioneers one cannot forget to mention the ace Ghanaian drummer Kofi Ghanaba whose late-1950s and early-1960s Afro-jazz style influenced the young Tony Allen and predated the Afro-fusion music of Fela by a decade. Kofi Ghanaba (formerly known as Guy Warren) was born in Accra in 1923 and was the trap drummer during the late 1940s in E. T. Mensah's famous Tempos highlife band. Ghanaba was also a journalist for various Ghanaian nationalist newspapers (like the *Gold Coast Independent*) and a staunch supporter of Nkrumah. He went to the US in 1955 to join the Gene Esposito Band and also played with a variety of American jazzmen, such as Charlie Parker (just prior to his death), Miles Davis, Thelonious Monk, and Billy Strayhorn. However, by 1956 Ghanaba had a creative crisis that forced him to move from jazz to Afro-jazz. As he once explained to me at his house in Accra way back in August 1973:

> It was a personal decision I made in my room in Chicago. I said to myself, "Guy, you can never play like Gene Krupa, Max Roach, or Louis Bellson. They have a different culture, and can never play like you." I had to make a choice between being an imitation of Buddy Rich or playing something they couldn't play. I could play jazz well, but I possessed something that nobody else had. So I started to play African music with a little bit of jazz thrown in, not jazz with a little African thrown in.

So it was in Chicago in 1956 that Ghanaba met in a vision what he calls his "muse" and consequently became "decolonized," "found" himself, and decided to become the African musician who "reintroduced African music to Americans."[7] As a result, between 1956 and 1963 he released a string of Afro-jazz albums in the States and Britain on the Decca, Victor, Fiesta, HMV, and EMI labels. In rough chronological order these include *Africa Speaks, America Answers* (with Red Saunders), *Themes for African Drums, African Soundz, African Rhythms,* and in 1963, *Emergent Drums, Afro-Jazz,* and *Third Phase.* By the 1960s Ghanaba was playing a highly Africanized drum set he had invented that used twin foot pedals with African drums. This is what his jazz drummer friend, the late Max Roach, said about Ghanaba in a 1973 letter:

> I would like to record that Ghanaba was so far ahead of what we were doing that none of us understood what he was saying—that in order for Afro-American music to be stronger, it must cross-fertilise with its African origin. . . . We ignored him. Seventeen years later Black music in America turned to African for inspiration and rejuvenation.

Ghanaba died in 2008 but was actively playing right into his mideighties. I will leave the reader to draw his or her own conclusion about the similarities between Ghanaba and Fela—who both began as highlife musicians, both had major problems with their fathers but idealized their mothers, both were jazz fanatics, both were political Nkrumahists and Pan Africanists, and both "found" themselves by turning to their African roots after going to the United States. In Ghanaba's case the trigger was a female spirit or muse, in Fela's it was his African American lover Sandra Iszadore.

INTERVIEW WITH FELA

The following is an interview I did with Fela when I was in Lagos for a few days in December of 1975, en route to Benin City to tour and work with the Nigerian highlife musician Victor Uwaifo. On that Nigerian trip I stayed at the Africa Shrine/Empire Hotel with members of the Ghanaian Basa-Basa band who were Fela's resident support band at the time. I interviewed Fela at his old Kalakuta Republic; it was a year after the police attack, and he was in the process of turning the whole event into a new song, later released as "Kalakuta Show" (EMI 1976) with melodramatic artistic sleeve designs by Lemi Ghariokwu of police with wooden batons and cane shields attacking the Kalakuta Republic house. This interview was originally published as chapter 16 in my *Music Makers of West Africa* (Washington, DC: Three Continents Press; and Pueblo, CO: Passeggiata Press, 1985).

What first brought you into music?

It was in the family; my mother, my father, and also my grandfather were musicians. My grandfather [the Reverend J. J. Ransome-Kuti] was playing traditional music on the piano from the 1920s and '30s, and he did some records for EMI in England. It was religious music, and he used African folksongs and united them to Christian songs to spread Christianity in the Yoruba area of West Africa. He was a preacher and was responsible for making Christianity in the Yoruba country here—which I think is very bad, so I have to undo what he has done

You mean that is what is motivating you?

I wouldn't say that I am purposely antagonizing my grandfather, but I would say his mistakes are colonial, and we are trying to get the colonial thing out.

Kofi Ghanaba [a.k.a. Guy Warren, the pioneering Ghanaian Afro-jazz percussionist] said a similar thing to me once. He said his father was doing the colonial thing and he had to undo it.[1] What were the early musical influences on you?

At the very early age I was influenced by Victor Olaiya.[2] I used to sing for him before I went to England. But these types of band were all colonial. And they had the influence of hymns somewhere or another in their music. It is the Christian influence, which cannot really work in African music.

Yes, I remember last year at the Napoleon Club[3] you told me that highlife was Black Victorian music. But [yet] you did play highlife with the Koola Lobitos, though influenced by jazz.

Yes, I was influenced by Miles Davis, Coltrane, and Thad Jones. I was very much into modern jazz at the time.

I also remember at the Napoleon you said you went to America in 1969, and it was there you found your mistakes.

I wouldn't say mistakes but shortcomings.

You mean in terms of direction?

I mean in terms of direction and music both. Africans are confused people you know, because of colonialism, so it is difficult for an African man to really find himself. You see—probably half his life he has thought like an Englishman or a Russian; it depends on where he has got his education. We are all fucked up, so we have to get this influence out of our system. It is this influence I call a shortcoming, because you cannot as an African be influenced by English culture and play African music. It can't work.

Are you saying it destroys authentic creativity?

It destroys authentic creativity.

So in the Koola Lobitos you were trying to bring highlife toward black American jazz?

At the beginning my musical appreciation was very limited, but later I got opened to many black artists. And I saw that in Africa we were not open, as at that time they only let us hear what they wanted us to hear. When you played the radio it was controlled by the government, and the white man played us what he wants. So we didn't know anything about black music. In England, I was exposed to all these things, but in Africa they cut us off. It was after I was exposed that I started using jazz as a stepping-stone to African music. Later, when I got to America, I was exposed to African history, which I was not even exposed to here. It was then that I really began to see that I had not played African music. I had been using jazz to play African music, when really I should be using African music to play jazz. So it was America that brought me back to myself.

Where did you get your rhythms for Afrobeat from?

I always tell my friends that if we say Africa is the home of rhythm and music, which will have to be accepted sooner or later, it is because Africans have been playing music for millions of years. If Africa is the home of music then anything that comes from the head of an African artist must depict Africa: that's the true African artist. Now, if I had been an Asian or Chinese artist then I would have to think and write if I wanted to play African music. But as an African artist it comes to me naturally, spontaneously; and that is the essence of finding oneself.[4]

But you are more than an African artist, you are a political African artist.

Oh yes, yes. The political part of it is a necessity. I don't see how an African music today can be about what doesn't affect our lives now. Our music should not be about love, it should be about reality and what we are up to now. You see, if you want love in Africa, we have so many women you don't need it [i.e., romantic love songs]. Even our music before was for purposes like religion, work, and politics. And so Afrobeat is an occasion for politics because that is the occasion we are in now—people suffering.

You call your house the Kalakuta Republic. Could you tell me where you got this name?

It was when I was in the police cell at the CID headquarters in Lagos.[5] The name of the cell I was in was named "Kalakuta Republic" by the prisoners.

I found out that when I went [later] to East Africa that *kalakuta* is a Swahili word that means "rascal." So, if rascality is going to get us what we want we will use it. Because we are dealing with corrupt people we have to be "rascally" with them.

Could you tell me your plans for the future?

I want to have a press, as my plan is to extend my communication system so I can reach as many people as I can. Across Africa at first, as I'm not interested in Europe right now.

Will you be involved in the Black Arts Festival [i.e., FESTAC '77]?

Oh yes, I'm very cool with this government [i.e., of Murtala Muhammed[6]]. We feel that we are going to progress now because this government sees the sense of having a change. So we are with them and we will support the festival.[7]

18

AFTERTHOUGHTS AND UPDATES

I began writing this book in 1998 after receiving a very positive response to the diary I had kept when I worked with Fela in 1977, and published just after Fela's death in the Nigerian *Glendora* magazine.[1] It was then that I decided to go ahead and write a full book that would be based on my personal knowledge of Fela—as well as that of other Ghanaian musician and promoters who played and worked with Fela over the years. In fact, the original working title of the book was "Fela through Ghanaian Eyes."

The bulk of this book was written by 2002, and a version of it was published in 2009 by the Dutch Royal Tropical Museum in Amsterdam. This is a good opportunity to update the book and look at the way Afrobeat continues to flourish in Africa and spread internationally.

Deaths within the Kalakuta Family and Circle

This chapter begins on a rather sad note: the deaths that have occurred since 2002 of some members of Fela's family and some of his Nigerian and Ghanaian friends and musicians. In 2006 both Fela's elder sister, Dolupo, and his younger brother, Beko, died. Oludolupo (Dolupo)

Ransome-Kuti, the eldest and only female child of the Reverend Ransome-Kuti's four children, died in January 2006. She was a strong-willed and outspoken woman who had a prickly relationship with Fela, but being a trained nurse it was she who looked after him when he lay sick and dying. Dr. Beko Ransome-Kuti died in February 2006 at sixty-five years. The militant medical doctor was cofounder of the Campaign for Democracy (CD) and was jailed in 1995 during the corrupt Abacha military regime on trumped-up charges. Beko was, until his death, one of the leaders of the pro-National Conference Organisation (PRONACO).

Another Fela person of note was the musicologist Bayo Martins, who died in Germany in 2003 and who was at one point the trap drummer of Fela's Koola Lobitos.[2] Moreover, during the 1970s and together with Fela and Bobby Benson, Bayo was an executive of the Musicians' Foundation of Nigeria. I knew Bayo well and recall the time he came to Accra in 1988 to play at the Du Bois Centre with fellow percussionists Guy Warren and Remi Kabaka[3] for the "Focus on Nigeria" event, when the Nigerian high commissioner presented Nigerian cultural and archival materials to the Centre.

The Ghanaian highlife singer Joe Mensah died in 2002. In more recent years Joe was president of Ghana's copyright collecting body (COSGA), and at the time of his death was president of the Ghanaian musicians' union, MUSIGA.

The most recent loss to the Fela clan is his longtime Ghanaian-Lebanese friend and promoter, Faisal Helwani, who died in 2008. Faisal's last big musical project was the talent hunt he began in 2005 when hundreds of youngsters were auditioned and some recorded at his Bibini Studio at the Napoleon Club. Faisal's musical daughter, Yasmin, made her first recordings in this studio, while his sons Sami, Waseem, and Bassam were trained there as recording engineers.

I should also mention the death of Sola Anikulapo-Kuti, Fela's youngest daughter, who died of cancer at the age of thirty-three just a few weeks

Thirteen-year-old Sola Anikulapo-Kuti in Abeokuta in 1977.

after her father's death in August 1997. As mentioned in chapter 7, I had got friendly with Fela's three children (Femi, Yeni, and Sola) in Abeokuta in 1977 when I was playing a part in "The Black President," and really appreciated Sola's quick and vital intelligence.

A few years later in 1981, when Fela and the Egypt 80 were playing at the Amsterdam Woods in Holland, I met her again, when I took a group of Dutch journalists to meet Fela at his hotel. At the hotel I asked Fela how Sola was, and he looked a bit perplexed by my question as she was sitting right in front of me. He pointed her out sitting among his dancers. As noted previously, I had not recognized her, as she had transformed from a small wiry girl into a beautiful young woman in the space of just four years.

Femi Kuti on saxophone. Photo © by Bugs Steffen

Fela Lives On: Femi, Seun, and Tony Allen

Fela's legacy is thriving and, in fact, expanding as the years pass by, with more and more African, European, American, and Asian artists, bands, sound systems, and dance-floor DJs utilizing the Afrobeat groove. But let us begin by looking at the recent activities of Fela's drummer Tony Allen and Fela's two saxophone-playing sons, Femi and the younger Seun.

Tony Allen joined Fela's Koola Lobitos at age twenty-five in 1965, after having played with Nigerian highlife bands like Victor Olaiya's Cool Cats (which the young Fela had also played with), Agu Norris's Heatwaves, and the Western Toppers. Tony stayed with Fela for almost fifteen years, and, as mentioned earlier in the book, he made a unique contribution to Afrobeat drumming. After leaving Fela's Africa 70 band in 1979, Tony formed the Mighty Rockers (or Iroqos) in Nigeria. However, he did play on Fela and Roy Ayers's 1981 album *Africa, Center of the World.* Then in 1984 he released *N.E.P.A.* in London and relocated to Paris where he was a session man with artists such as Randy Weston and Grace Jones—and also released his own Afrobeat albums such as *No Discrimination, Afrobeat Express,* and *No Accommodation in Lagos.*

In more recent years he has added more albums to his portfolio, such as *Lagos No Shaking, Tony Allen Live, Black Voices,* and *Eager Hands and Restless Feet,* as well as the 1997 *Funky Juju* (with the Parliament-Funkadelic vocalist Gary Cooper), and around 2000 the *Psycho On Da Bus* project. In 2002 Tony released *Homecooking,* which featured the British vocalist Damon Albarn (formerly of Gorrillaz and Blur) and in 2005 Tony Allen and his manager Samuel Kayode released *Lagos No Shaking.* By 2007 Tony had joined Damon Albarn, bassist Paul Simonon (ex-Clash) and guitarist Simon Tong (ex-Verve) in a supergroup called The Good, the Bad and the Queen. This group toured the UK in 2008 with Salif Keita and the Senegalese rapper of Positive Live Soul, Awadi. Tony Allen also collaborated with a whole host of other international artists, from Brazil to Sweden, Ethiopia to London.

In 2009 Allen released his album *Secret Agent* and also *Inspiration Information Volume 4* (on the UK Strut label) in which he collaborated with the Finnish saxophonist Jimi Tenor. In November 2010 he came with some of the musicians who played on it to perform at the Alliance Française in Accra. Tony Allen was both playing drums and singing in a group that included the guitarist Claude DiBongue, the French keyboard player Fixi, and percussionist Ekow Savage Alabi. Tony's manager was the young Nigerian promoter Kole Israel Payne. I had a chance to catch up with Tony after the show and asked him why he was now singing. He explained that any time he got a singer that person would then decide that he was the star of the band. Naturally, Tony did not like this, and so for live shows was forced to sing and drum at the same time—a very difficult feat for any musician. In 2012 Tony released the album *Rocket Juice and the Moon* on the UK Honest John label.

Femi Kuti was born in 1962, and I first met him in 1977 in Abeokuta when I was involved in "The Black President" film, and again in 1997 when he came to Ghana for a musical wake keeping for his father held at the Ghana Arts Council and organized by Faisal Helwani and Stan Plange. By then Femi had already formed his Positive Force band (in 1987), made six European tours (1988–94), released two albums, and had gone on his first US tour (1995). In 1998 he formed the student-based Movement Against Second Slavery (MASS) to push for social change, and the following year he released *Shoki Shoki* on the MCA label that included the hit song "Beng Beng Beng" that was banned by Nigerian radio for being too sexually explicit. Femi Kuti rebuilt the New Africa Shrine in 2000 in the Agidingbi area of Ikeja in Lagos and in 2002 was made a UNICEF "goodwill ambassador" for campaigning against AIDS, the illness that killed his father at the age of fifty-eight. Femi has continued making records and touring Europe and North America. In 2000 he was featured on one of the songs by Common (Lonnie Rashid) on this Chicago rapper's top-selling album *Like Water for Chocolate.*

In 2001 Femi released *Fight to Win* in which he collaborated with Common, Mos Def, Jaguar Wright, D'Angelo, and Macy Gray. In 2004 Positive Force released *Live at the Shrine,* and in 2007 Femi released his *Definitive Collection* double CD (Wrasse Records) and then went on the UK "African Soul Rebels" tour that featured his Positive Force band as well Ba Cissoko and Akli D. Femi's next CD, released by Wrasse Records in October 2008,

Poster for a performance by Seun Kuti and Egypt 80 in New York.

was *Day by Day*. Then in 2012 he released *Africa for Africans*, followed in 2013 by *No Place for My Dream* (Knitting Factory label). In June 2013 Femi played with the rapper Common at the New York Central Park Summer Stage. Femi also makes occasional trips to play in Ghana, including one in September 2013 when he played in Accra at the State House Banquet Hall for the Kasapreko African Legends Night, alongside the highlife musicians Amakye Dede and George Darko. The orchestration of Femi Kuti's Positive Force band is similar to his father's, and although he draws on his father's Afrobeat style and occasionally plays one of Fela's songs, Femi has moved on to incorporate elements from rock music and hiphop into his Afrobeat compositions.

Fela's younger son, Seun Kuti, on the other hand, sticks closer to his father's style of Afrobeat music for his own compositions, and indeed took over the running of Fela's Egypt 80 band after his father died in 1997. Seun was born in 1982, and from the age of nine he began singing in the chorus of Egypt 80. He also learned to play guitar, piano, and later, saxophone. When Seun took over the running of the eighteen-strong Egypt 80, it included stalwarts like baritone saxophonist Lekan Animashaun, trumpeter Tunde Williams, and pianist Dele Sosimi. He and the band toured Switzerland in 1992, and Seun also found time to study at the Liverpool Institute of Performing Arts (set up by Sir Paul McCartney in 1996). In 2008 Seun and the Egypt 80 toured Europe and the US to promote his maiden album *Many Things* (on the Disorient label) that includes the "Mosquito Song" featuring Tony Allen and Manu Dibango. For this tour, Lekan Animashaun was replaced by Adedimeji Fagbemi. Of interest here is that the then American presidential candidate Barack Obama had to personally intervene to allow the Egypt 80 members to obtain their US visas. There is some sibling rivalry between Seun and Femi, but nevertheless both play at the Africa Shrine; at one point Femi's Positive Force played on Tuesdays, Thursdays, and Sundays, while Seun's Egypt 80 played on the last Saturday of every month.

I met Seun in 2009 when he came to Accra to play at the Alliance Française with his Egypt 80 band that included Lekan Animashaun, who is, sadly, now deceased. The Egypt 80's manager for this event was the French promoter Martin Meissonier. Seun's performance was part of the High Vibes Festival, which involved a symposium in which I spoke together with Fela's old manager Benson Idonije on early Ghanaian and Nigerian highlife. The following day I went to the Wangara Hotela where the Nigerians were staying in Accra to present Seun with the Dutch version of my *Fela: Kalakuta Notes* book, and also interview Benson Idonije on Nigerian jazz, a portion of which appears in chapter 1 concerning the jazz influence on the young Fela.

Seun has released a number of albums since 2007 including *Think Africa, Many Things,* and in 2011 *From Africa with Fury,* recorded in the UK with the

Yeni Kuti dancing on stage. Photo © by Bugs Steffen

producers John Reynolds and Brian Eno. In 2012 he became involved in the countrywide Occupy Nigeria Protest against President Goodluck Jonathon's decision to remove fuel subsidies. When Seun is on stage he and his band play in the typical bitonal Afrobeat mode; and although taller and bigger than his late father, Seun has a strong resemblance in physique and mannerisms to Fela. Although Seun composes his own Afrobeats, like his older brother Femi he occasionally plays some of Fela's old compositions

Afrobeat Stars Today

A number of Afrobeat performers have been influenced by Fela's music in Africa. In Nigeria, Fela-inspired artists and bands include Dede Mabiaku (Underground Sound band) and Bodun Ajayi (Black Beats band) who both look, dress, sing, and play sax like Fela. Dede made several trips to Ghana in the mid-2000s to record (with engineer Panji Anoff) and performed at the Alliance Française in Accra. Bodun's band has played from time to time at the Union Bank Sports Complex in Surulere, Lagos. Amala is a contemporary Afrobeat musician who holds an art diploma from the Yaba College of Technology and plays a faster sax style than Fela. Coming from the poor Ajegunle neighborhood of Lagos, his lyrics, like Fela's, dwell on the suffering of ghetto people. Kola Ogunkoya has gradually combined Afrobeat and highlife into what he calls his "Gbedu" style. Although based in Lagos, he spent some years in the United States where he released a double album CD entitled *Foreign Mentality* and *Shayo High-Life Music.*

An artist who has been blending folk materials with percussive Afrobeat is Olaitan Adeniji (a.k.a. Heavywind). Also of note is the jazz pianist Duro Ikujenyo and his Sound of Aquarius band that at one point operated out of the Jazzhole Club in Lagos. In the late 1970s Duro had been a secretary for Fela's Young African Pioneers (YAP), a researcher for

Movement of the People (MOP), and a member of Africa 80, supplying piano licks for songs like "Unknown Soldier," "Original Sufferhead," "International Thief Thief," and "Coffin for Head of State." Another jazzist who is fusing traditional jazz with Afrobeat horn arrangements is Biodun "Batik" Adebiyi. Yet another Afro-jazzist is the saxophonist Kayode Olajide, who formed his Weavers in Lagos in 1993, and collaborated with Tony Allen for the Weavers' 2002 *Iba* release. The masked singer and saxophonist Lagbaja (Bisade Ologunde), operates his Motherlan' amphitheatre in Lagos and is still going strong with his blend of Afrobeat and highlife that he calls "higherlife."

Other Nigerian Afrobeat-inspired artists are Baba Ken and the Afro Grooves, Najim Lasisi (ex–Sunny Adé), and the pianist Funsho Ogundipe, who formed his jazzy Afrobeat Ayetoro band in the mid 1990s. Ayetoro later released its *Afrobeat Chronicles Volume 3* CD, partly recorded in Ghana at Panji Anoff's Pidgin Studio and included the Ghanaians Frank Siisi-Yoyo as well as trumpeter Long John, and tenor saxophonist Kofi Karikari. Dele Sosimi (ex–Egypt 80 and Femi's Positive Force) is still going strong but is now based in London, while the bassist Ken Okulolo (ex–Sonny Adé's African Beats) and guitarist Soji Odukogbe (ex–Fela's Egypt 80) are in the States with the Kotoja Afrobeat band formed in 1986 with the guitarist/percussionist/vocalist Danjuma Adamu and others, Adamu himself having played in Nigeria with Orlando Julius, Fela Kuti, and Sunny Adé.

Some up-and-coming Afrobeat-influenced bands and artists from Lagos are Konikima "Kilimanjaro" Ndaro and his I.Q. Band, Alariwo of Africa (Rotomi Martins), the Afro-juju musician Shankar the Amuludun (Ogunbadewa Ayodele Peters), and saxophonist Amala, who, in 2003, recorded in Lagos with French musician Bruno Blum. And from Abuja comes the Alkebu-Lan band led by Segun Damisa (ex–Sunny Adé and Femi Kuti musician), and the ten-piece Dovie Sounds run by keyboard player "Baba 2010" (Mena Okon Dovie).[4] Other Nigerian musicians who play Afrobeat are the veteran guitarist Bright Chimezie, Kunle Adeniran

(Kunniran Band), and Charlie Boy Oputa, who at one point was president of the Performing Rights Association of Nigeria, PMAN. Some Nigerian or "naija" hip-hoppers also draw on Afrobeat, like the female rapper Weird MC (Sola Idowu), Lord of Ajasa, Tony Tetuila (Anthony Olanrewaju Awotoye), the US-based Wale Oyijide, and the German-based Nigerian woman Nneka, while in Britain there are MC Breis and also the Anglo-Yoruba rapper JJC (Abdul Bello), and the 419 Squad.

In Ghana there are a number of performers and bands that are influenced by Afrobeat or include Afrobeats in their repertoires. One group includes local Afro-fusion bands such as Smart Arpeh Pozo's Bawasaba, Nii Noi Nortey's jazz-oriented Musiki w'Afrika, the late Mac Tontoh's Osibisa Kete Warriors, Lash Laryea's Amartey Hedzolleh, and Kojo Esa's and Cliff Asante's Takashi Band. Some of Ghana's northern musicians who sing in the Frafra language and use the local Sahalean *koliko* or *kologo* lute (ancestor of the American banjo) have also been influenced by Afrobeat. One is the late Captain Yaba. Another is Atongo Zimba who currently resides in the UK. Incidentally, as a young man, Atongo did opening acts for Fela at the Africa Shrine; he also opened for Osibisa, Manu Dibango, Hugh Masekela, and Angelique Kidjo. The current star of this northern Ghanaian stringed instrument is King Ayisoba, who combines local rap, Afrobeat, and traditional music. He won the 2007 Ghana Music Awards and released the album *Modern Ghanaians* (recorded and produced by Panji Anoff) that includes the hit song "I Want to See You, My Father."

In the reggae vein is Rocky Dawuni, whose "Afro Roots" style combines reggae and Afrobeat. Rocky currently resides in Santa Monica where he hosts programs at the Zanzibar Club with Afrobeat/funk and electro-dub DJs like Jeremy Sole. Another Ghanaian reggae band that used to play in an Afrobeat vein is Native Spirit. Sadly, their German keyboardist, Chris Luhn, died in 2006.

From the highlife side comes Gyedu Blay Ambolley, still going strong since the 1970s with his "simwigwado" funky highlife style. His voice is remarkably similar to Fela's, and his Fanti rhyming slang anticipated the current wave of local Ghanaian rappers or "hiplifers." Another veteran highlifer influenced by Afrobeat is Ebo Taylor, who is currently on a series of world tours playing funky highlife and Afrobeat. Other Ghanaian highlife bands that include Afrobeat numbers are Desmond Ababio's Alpha Waves, Ackah Blay's Abiza dance band, and the Local Dimension run by John Collins and Aaron Bebe Sukura.

Mention must also be made of the guitar bands that follow the late Alhaji K. Frimpong's style of minor-mode highlife[5] that has a lilt and groove remarkably similar to Fela's Afrobeat. It is this style of highlife that some of Ghana's local hiplifers (Ghana's local hip-hop and rap artists) draw upon. But some local rappers also occasionally use Fela's music itself. One is Nana King, whose 1999 hit "Champion" used a loop from Fela's song "Lady." The same year the "godfather" of Ghanaian hiplife, Reggie Rockstone, released his song "Eye Mo De Anaa" (It's sweet for all), which samples Fela's 1972 song "Shakara." Then in 2004 the Ghanaian hiplifer Tic Tac (with Nigerian Tony Tetuila) released "Fefe Naa Efe" (It's really beautiful) that sampled Fela's 1973 song of that name. Incidentally, this song by Fela (on his 1973 *Gentleman* album) is partly in the Ghanaian Akan language and is the song about the beautiful way that women hold their breasts while running. Ghana also boasts the hip-hop/Afrobeat poet DK Osei Emmanuel Dickson.

A number of Ghanaian neo-traditional groups (that use predominantly African instruments) also include Afrobeat (and Afro-rock) numbers in their repertoires. One such was Nana Danso Abiam's Pan Africa Orchestra that, as already mentioned in the book, has done orchestral renditions of "Shuffering and Shmiling" and "No Agreement." More recently Fela's songs and his style of music are sometimes featured in performances by Asebre Quaye's Sanekoye band, Dela Botri's Hewale Sounds, and Nii Tettey Tetteh's Kusun Ensemble.

Before dealing with the international Afrobeat scene I will give a list of just a few of the Afrobeat-inspired bands and artists that hail from other African countries. Sierra Leone (the Refugee All Stars); Cameroon (Ihims, the Negrissim hip-hop band); Liberia (DJ Jeremiah, Z Plus); Togo (Yawo's Afrobeat Band); Republic of Benin (the Gangbe Brass Band that released an Afrobeat tribute in 2000 called *Remember Fela*); Uganda (Kingdom Dancers, Sarah Ndagire, Milly Namukasa, Charles Mipakuko, Bobbin Kasule); Kenya (Mwanbu, Big Matata, Victor Sila, Robert Kamanzi); Senegal (rappers Baay Bia and 5Kiem); Ethiopia (Ejigayehu "Gigi" Shibabaw, who recorded with Tony Allen for the American producer Bill Laswell); Zimbabwe (Gandanga Music, the Zimbabwe Spirit); South Africa (the township funk of DJ Mujava, the South African Jam Band, the trumpeter Hugh Masekela[6]).

Afrobeat Goes Global

Here we move on to the impact that Fela has made outside of Africa, starting with North America, where there has been such an efflorescence of Afrobeat bands and Afrobeat-inspired performers since his death in 1997. But before discussing the contemporary scene a few words must be said about the influence this Nigerian music style had on a number of African American jazz, soul, and funk musicians during the 1980s and early 1990s.

As already mentioned, Roy Ayers actually toured with Fela in 1980 and played on Fela's 1980 *Music of Many Colors* (Nigerian Phonodisc label). According to Michael Veal, this soul-jazz vibraphone player later performed with Fela and his Egypt 80 in the States in 1986 and 1991: the first show being filmed and released in 1987 as the commercial video *Fela and Roy Ayers* (Family One Productions). As mentioned earlier as well, James Brown played in Lagos in 1970, and, according to Michael Veal, Brown's bass player, Bootsie Collins, was so impressed by the music he heard at the Afro-Spot that Fela's music influenced later songs of his like "Jamaica" released by his Sweat Band in 1980. Moreover, Veal mentions that one of James Brown's 1960s arrangers, Pee Wee Ellis, released *Africa, Center of the World* in 1996 using the same title that Fela used for his 1980 album. Veal also mentions that the 1983 "Nubian Nut" song of the funk artist George Clinton includes choruses from Fela's "Mr. Follow Follow." Likewise, the Art Ensemble of Chicago (with trumpeter Lester Bowie) recorded a version of "Zombie" on their 1987 album *Ancient to the Future*. Then the saxophonist Branford Marsalis also sampled "Beasts of No Nation" for his 1994 hip-hop project *Buckshot leFonque* album, while the fusion band Hotel X did an instrumental version of Fela's "Black Man's Cry" on their 1995 record *Ladder*.

In the last few years Afrobeat and Afro-funk have became very big in North America with the younger generation. In Canada there are the Afrobeat outfits Mr. Something Something, Ikwunga the Afrobeat Poet, and Femi Abosede's Culture (all in Toronto); Afrodizz and Follow Follow (both in Montreal); Five Alarm Funk (Vancouver); the Souljazz Orchestra (Ottawa); and the Afro Musia band of the Angolan musician Edo King Matwawana (in Nova Scotia). From the United States come bands like Superkali and the Superpowers (both from Seattle), the Afromotives (North Carolina), the Chicago Afrobeat Ensemble, and the Baltimore Afrobeat Society. In Portland, Oregon, there was the Afro-fusion Kukrudu band of the late Ghanaian master drummer Obo Addy and also the Afro-juju Jujuba band of Najim Lasisi. From San Francisco come the Albinos and the (female-led) Aphrodisia big bands. Another is Kotoja, the brainchild of the veteran Nigerian singer-bassist Baba Ken Okulolo supported by ex–Egypt 80 guitarist Soji Odukogbe and two Ghanaian musicians.[7] As mentioned earlier, Danjuma Adamu helped found this Bay Area group, as well another Afrobeat group called Ntu Shamala, before forming his current Onola band.

Yet another San Francisco–based band is the Afrofunk Experience run by Victor Sila from Kenya. Also from California comes Afrobeat Down, formed in 2002 and which sometimes works with the famous

Sandra Iszadore, who so influenced Fela's political views in 1969.[8] Fela's legendary trumpeter Baba Tunde Williams is also now living in California where he occasionally plays with the New York Antibalas when they are gigging there. New Jersey is where the famous Nigerian Afrobeat/rock Lijadu Sisters are now resident. When I met them in Lagos way back in the midseventies these Yoruba identical twins told me they were related to Fela's family. They also told me that in 1972 they had been part of Salt, a band formed by British rock drummer Ginger Baker.[9] These singers (Kehinde and Taiwo) still regularly perform, and some of their 1970s hits are being released in the States as Afro-house mixes.

Afrobeat is also alive and well in Boston, which has its local Afrobeat Society and the Afrobeat/hip-hop/reggae band Soulfege run by the Ghanaian Derrick Ashong. From Washington, DC, comes Chopteeth, which includes ex-members of the Temptations, Four Tops, and Gladys Knight and the Pips.

But it is New York that seems to be the center of the American Afrobeat scene, with bands and artists like the Kokolo Afrobeat Orchestra, the twelve-piece Budo, Foly Kolade's Asiko Afrobeat Ensemble, Akoye (with Beninoise singer Kaleta), Yerba Buena, Amayo's Fu-Arkist-Ra, Femme Nameless, and the Zozo Afrobeat Band. This thirteen-piece band is led by the guitarist-percussionist Kaleta (Leon Ligan-Majek) from the Benin Republic, who from 1979 played with Sunny Adé, Shina Peters, Oliver de Coque, then Fela in 1984, and finally Femi Kuti's Positive Force—until he moved to the States where he joined the Akota band and then formed his Zozo big band.

Very important in New York is the Brooklyn-based Antibalas that includes ex-members of King Chango, the Daktaris, and Soul Providers. Furthermore, there are Afrobeat clubs in New York such as the Globesonic and Jump 'n' Funk that feature DJs Rich Medina, Trevor Schoonmaker, and ZGM. American hip-hop bands influenced by Fela include Red Hot collective, the DJ Chief Xcel (Xavier Mosley), and also the rapper Mos Def

(Dante Terrel Smith), who sampled Fela's "Fear Not for Man" in a 1999 release. In fact, a number of American rappers and hip-hoppers have recently sampled Fela's music. According to Joseph Patel,[10] these include Timbaland (Timothy Mosley) and the Blackalicious rap duo, who both sampled Fela's "Colonial Mindstate." Some others are Common (Lonnie Rashid Lynn), who sampled Fela's "Water No Get Enemy," and Nas (Nassir Jones), who sampled portions of "Teacher Don't Teach Me Nonsense" for his 2002 "Warrior Song."

Afrobeat has also caught on in Europe. In France the 1980s Ghetto Blasters formed by Egypt 80's ex-percussionists Nicholas Avom and Udoh Essiet has reemerged. It was initially formed in Nigeria in 1983 and then relocated to Paris where the musicians lived and rehearsed on a houseboat on the river Seine (I once visited them there in the mid-1980s). The band broke up in 1997 but was reformed in 2003 when it released the album *River Niger.* Other French-based African groups and artists are Les Nubians, the late Segun Damisa's Afrobeat Crusaders, Chief Udoh Essiet (one-time conga player for Fela), and Frank Biyongi's Franco-Cameroonian band Massak. Another is Fanga, the brainchild of the Burkina Faso rapper Yves "Korbo" Khoung and hip-hop programmer Serge Amiano Fanga. Other French Afrobeat outfits include Café Crème & les Frères Smith, Black Pyramid, Fifi Rafiatou's (a Togolese) Keteke group and the Zouk/Afrobeat band Shawa. Some artists influenced by Fela are Bob Sinclair, the T Boys, the reggae artist Bruno Blum, the rapper Kaysha (Edward Mokolo from the Democratic Republic of the Congo), DJ Floro's (Republic Afrobeat), and Kutiman. Tony Allen and his Afrobeat Messengers band also resides in Paris, as does the Cameroonian jazz-fusion saxophonist Manu Dibango, whose 1972 smash hit "Soul Makossa" became an essential ingredient in the early Afro-soul mix.

From Scandinavia comes Okes Masima, Afro Moses and his Ojah Band,[11] Maluka and the Rhythm Funk Masters, and the Danish woman singer Gudrun Holck, who spent four years in West Africa. Also important is the Swedish alto saxophonist Sofi Hellborg, who for her latest Afrobeat release *Drumming Calling* collaborated with Tony Allen and the Swedish rapper Timbuctu. Sofi got her training in African music with the 1980s London highlife band Orchestra Jazira and then spent fourteen years in Paris working with the Guineaian Kora player Mory Kante.

From Germany comes the half Nigerian Afro-hip-hopper Adé Bantu Odukoya, as well as Oghene Kologbo (Fela's ex-guitarist), the Afrobeat Academy, the Poets of Rhythm, the Cologne-based Schälsick Brass Band, the ten-piece Frankfurt RAS band, the Berlin-based Rhythm Taxi, and the Whitfield Brothers. Spain has Gecko Turrier's Afromero and also the young Pablo Diaz Reixa from the Spanish Canary Islands who samples rock, dub, and Afrobeat for his Barcelona-based El Guincho studio band. Belgium has its Belgian Afrobeat Association, and in Holland there are the Mdungu and Yusu Nuweku's (a Ghanaian) Zulwannsago Afrobeat bands both based in Amsterdam, as well as the recently formed Jungle by Night. This outfit was formed by Pieter van Exter, Bo Flor, Pyke Pasman, and with the other six members of this music collective went on to release their first album *Hidden*.[12] Much older is the Cool Collective, a Dutch jazz big band that was formed back in the mid-1990s, but in 2005 began working and recording (their *Trippin* double CD) with Tony Allen. Then there is the eight-piece Sinas Funk big band that was formed in 2006 and that in 2008 released its *Global Explorations* CD of dance-floor music that included Afrobeat tracks.

British pop musicians have been influenced by Afrobeat since the 1970s, the first being Ginger Baker in 1971. Brian Eno became a Fela fan and also visited Ghana in 1980 (he stayed with me and Faisal Helwani). Fela's influence is evident in Eno's 1981 album *My Life in the Bush of Ghosts* that he did with David Byrne. The late Ian Dury of "Blockheads" fame was also an avid collector of Fela's records, as I discovered when I met him in London in the mid-1980s and taught him to play a Ghanaian *televi/asratoa* percussion instrument.

In recent years there have been a number of British acts under the Afrobeat spell. First and foremost there are a number of African-based (mainly Nigerian) bands and artists in the UK, like Tunday Akintan's Afro Soul People, Inemo Samiana's (a Nigerian singer-guitarist) Afrobeat Experience, and the half Nigerian and British vocalist Wunmi, granddaughter of Nigeria's highlife veteran Victor Olaiya. Then there is the Lagos-born saxophonist Bukky Leo, who went to the UK in the 1980s where he became an "acid-jazz" pioneer, and in late 1990s formed his Afrobeat band, Black Egypt, that in 2008 was playing at Ronnie Scott's club in London. Another British-born Nigerian is the pianist Juwan Ogungbe, who runs the African Connection band. The previously mentioned Egypt 80 keyboardist Dele Sosimi settled in the UK in 1995 where he now simultaneously runs two Afrobeat bands; the fourteen-piece Afrobeat Orchestra and six-piece Gbedu Resurrection. He also occasionally teams up with the Nigerian Afrobeat poet Ikwunga. The Nigerian pianist Funsho Ogundipe who, as previously mentioned, runs his Ayetoro band in Lagos, is simultaneously running another version of Ayetoro in London with a group of Nigerian, Ghanaian, and British musicians. Also in the UK is Tunday Akintan, a saxophonist from Lagos who studied pop and jazz at Goldsmith College in London, after which he created a fusion of Afrobeat, juju, and fuji he calls "Yorubeat." The ten-piece Yaaba Funk is a south-London Afrobeat and highlife band composed of British and Ghanaians, such as the percussionist Nana Tsiboe, guitarist Alfred "Kari" Bannerman, and singer Richmond Kwame Kwessie.

Tony Allen, as usual, comes into the picture. Ty, a Black British hip-hopper (of Nigerian descent) is working with Tony Allen, while Tony's manager, Samuel Kayode, is running Awa Clash with Barbara Snow, which plays a combination of Latin music, funk, and Afrobeat.

There are numerous British bands and artists who are influenced by Afrobeat. One is the nine-piece Leeds-based Ariya Astrobeat Arkestra that released their debut album of that name in 2010 followed by *Towards*

Other Worlds in 2012. Other UK bands and artists influenced by Afrobeat include Franz Ferdinand, Vampire Weekend (actually an American group popular in Britain), Baka Beyond (Afro-Celtic), Juju Juice, the Oxford Quintet Foals, Orange Juice, and Damon Albarn. Since Albarn's trip to West Africa in 2002 his eclectic Honest John's record label (and West London record shop) now produces and sells classic Afrobeats. Also London-based are the DJs (Ghanaian born) Rita Ray and Max Reinhardt, who have for some years been running a techno-music dance club called the Shrine, named after Fela's Shrine. Other London clubs that feature Afrobeat are the Afro Chill Out, the Limpopo Club, and Jamm. In Brighton the electronic/house DJ Fatboy Slim had been lifting Fela horn sections from songs like "Roforofo Fight" for his massive seaside shows. Then there are the Afro-dub recordings emanating from Glyn "Bigga" Bush's Dorset-based Lion Head label. Mention must also be made of Abdul Bello, known as "Skilzz," of the Big Brovaz hip-hop/R & B band and as "JJC" of the south-London 419 Squad. The latter is composed of seven Anglo-Yorubu rappers (Nigerian and Nigerian descent) influenced by hip-hop, Fela's Afrobeat, and Shina Peters "Afro-juju." Abdul Bello comes from Kano but settled in Britain as a youth—which is why he uses the name "'JJC" (Johnny Just Come), a West African pidgin-English expression (like "Johnny Just Drop," "Been To" and "Burger") for Africans who have lived abroad.

In other parts of the world Afrobeat spreads and flourishes. Australia has its bands Drum Talk and Blue King Brown, as well as the fourteen-piece Stride Band that in 2010 teamed up with the Ghanaian musician Afro Moses to cover versions of Fela's songs like "Zombie." Japan has its Afrorocks and Fresh Jumbe, while Colombia's own local South American Afro-Colombian and cumbia music scene is being enriched with local renditions of Afrobeat coming from the Tribez Band, the Buena Vibra Sound System, the Cumbia Moderna de Soledad, and Palenque Records. Still in South America and according to Sterns' Robert Urbanus,

Fela's music has been influencing the music of Brazilian bands and artists like Nação Zumbi, Instituto, DJ Dolores, the Mamelo Sound System, and Monjolo, while Tony Allen has recently recorded in Brazil with Pupillo (Nação Zumbi's drummer) and the female vocalist Ceu.

Incidentally, the famous Afro-Brazilian singer-guitarist Gilberto Gil met Fela at the Africa Shrine in 1977 when he performed at the FESTAC 77 Black Arts Festival. Like Fela and his Afrobeat, Gil had been involved in creating a radical popular music style of the late sixties and early seventies known as "tropicalia." Like Fela, Giberto Gil was locked up (for a year in 1969) by the military government of the times (1964–1985). However, unlike Fela, who failed in his attempt to become Nigerian president (i.e., the "Black President"), Gil moved on to become Brazil's minister of culture for a time, after Lula da Silva was elected as president of Brazil in 2002.

New Releases

Since Fela's death in 1997, many of Fela's two hundred songs recorded with the Koola Lobitos, Africa 70, and Egypt 80 bands have been released by international record companies and distributors. These include Polygram, Universal, Amazon, Shanachie, Celluloid, Mercury, Capital, Sterns, Ioda, and Calabash Music—as well as Wrasse Records, which between 2000 and 2002 rereleased half of Fela's total repertoire on CD.

However, I will concentrate on an even more recent phenomenon: the growing number of small companies that are rereleasing any sort of Afro-fusion music recorded in Africa on vinyl records made in the 1970s and 80s, exactly the time when Fela was evolving his Afrobeat sound. This current crop of releases of vintage Afro-fusion music (i.e., Afro-jazz, Afro-soul, Afro-funk, Afro-rock, and Afrobeat) from Africa is catering to the growing number of world music fans. Furthermore, the music is also being sampled and electronically remixed by the MCs and rappers of hip-hop, ragga, and the dance-floor DJs of house, garage, trance, jungle, and drum 'n' bass music. For just as an earlier generation of dance fans utilized the old soul and funk music of James Brown and George Clinton in their remixes—so contemporary dance fans are now turning to the equally old grooves of the Afro-fusion music of Africa itself.

To provide some idea of the current ferment concerning the discovery and rerelease of old Afro-fusion and Afrobeat music I will use some examples of British and other European labels, as I am more familiar with this area—and I will begin with some recently rediscovered Nigerian music. The British Strut record label has in the last few years put a number of CDs of this old material on the market. In 2001 came their triple-CD compilation *Nigeria 70* that contained songs by Fela and other 1970s Nigerian Afrobeat/soul/funk artists, such as Orlando Julius, the Great Pyramids, Bongos Ukwue, Sunny Adé, Shina Williams, the Lijadu Sisters, Gaspar Lawal, Victor Uwaifo, and Afro-rock bands such as Jake Solo's Funkees[13] and Johnny Haastrup's Mono Mono (formed in 1971). Moreover, this CD package also contains interviews with Femi Kuti, Steve Rhodes, Sonny Okosuns, J. K. Braimah, Ginger Baker, Eddy Grant, John Collins, and the writer Wole Soyinka, who is related to Fela. Around this time Strut also produced CDs of songs by some individual 1970s Nigerian Afro-fusion artists like Tony Allen (2000), BLO (2001), and Segun Bucknor's "Poorman No Get Brother" (2002). Then in 2007 the prolific Strut label produced *Lagos Jump* that contained tracks by the Afro-jazz musician Peter King, the highlife of Victor Uwaifo's Melody Maestros and the Peacocks, and the Afro-juju bands of Shina Peters and Dele Abiodun.

Some international CD rereleases also extended their range to include Afro-fusion music from other African countries. Again taking the example of Strut, in 1999–2000 they released a double-volume CD entitled *Club Africa* that consisted of Afro-funk/jazz/beat songs from the Nigerian artists Ginger Johnson, Babatunde Olatunji,[14] the Nkengas band, as well as the Cameroonian Manu Dibango and South Africa's Hugh Masekela, Miriam Makeba, and Letta Mbulu. *Club Africa* also included songs by the

Americans Roy Ayers (who had worked with Fela), Plunky's Oneness of Juju,[15] and the Daktaris (a 1990s Brooklyn-based American Afro-soul/beat band). In 2001 the UK based Shrine label (of Rita Ray and Max Reinhardt) released its *Afro-Digital* CD of dance-floor Afrobeat for what it called "Afro-House/Garage/Hip-Hop/Dub" remixes of the works of Tony Allen and Femi Kuti, as well as Senegal's Vivianne N'Dour; French-born Francois K; Cheikha Rimitti, the "queen" of Algerian Rai music; and Cape Verde's veteran female singer Cesaria Evora. Then in 2002 the British Rough Guide book publishing company released its *Rough Guide to the Music of Nigeria & Ghana* that included an Afrobeat by Tony Allen, and funky highlifes by Ghana's C. K. Mann, Amanzeba Nat Brew, and the late Captain Yaba (Azongo Nyaaba) from northern Ghana. The Captain Yaba track was a rerelease of a song from an earlier 1996 album called *Yaba Funk* (released by RetroAfric, UK) in which Yaba plays the two-stringed African *koliko/kologo* lute, backed by the Ninkribi band led by none other than Sierra Leonean percussionist Francis Fuster (ex-Heartbeats and Baranta), with Osei Tutu (ex-Edikanfo) on muted trumpet.

A number of international rereleases of classic Ghanaian Afro-fusion music have also come onto the international world-music and dance-club market in the last few years. In 2002 Duncan Brooker's Kona Records in the UK released *Afro-Rock* that included 1970s Afrobeats and minor highlifes by K. Frimpong's Cubano Fiesta, Nkansa's Yaanom band, John Collins's Bokoor, and Yiadom Boakye's Mercury Dance Band—as well as Sierra Leone's Geraldo Pino and some tracks from central and eastern Africa. The same year the British label RetroAfric released a CD of a 1969–70 recording done in London by Ghana's Afro-jazz pioneer Kofi Ghanaba (Guy Warren). Then came Miles Cleret's Soundway label based in Brighton, which between 2002 and 2004 released two CDs entitled *Ghana Soundz: Afro-Beat, Funk and Fusion in '70s Ghana*. These two CDs included remastered vinyl recordings by Marijata (ex–Sweet Bean musicians Kofi "Electric" Addison, Bob Fiscian, and Nat Osmanu), keyboardist

Honny, Ebo Taylor's Apagya Show Band, Joe Mensah and the Uhuru band, A. B. Crentsil's Sweet Talks, Kwadwo Donkor's Ogyatanaa, Oscar Sulley Braima, Bob Pinado,[16] and Chester Adam's Uppers International with vocals by the late Christy Azuma.

In other European countries there are also record labels that specialize in rereleasing 1960s to 1980s West African music, including Afrobeat. One is the German company Analog Africa that in 2008 reissued some tracks of the Orchestra Polyrhythmic de Cotonu[17] on a double CD entitled *The Voudoun Effect 1972–75: Funk and Sato from Obscure Benin and Togo Labels.* LC Music of Belgium distributed Fela's complete back catalogue as well as Femi's new "Day by Day," while Spanish-based Vampisoul has *Fela Ransome Kuti: Lagos Baby,* a compilation of Fela's early 1963–69 recordings. Specialist labels in France that disseminate Afrobeat and Afro-funk include Comet, which releases Tony Allen's current works, as well as older 1970s Afro music from Africa and the Antilles. Others are Buda, which has rereleased old Ethiopian Afro-funk, and Superclasse, which has produced two editions of its *Afrojazzfunk Round.* In the case of Holland there is Rob Biering's Hippo Records that in 2005 released *Savannah Breeze* by the northern Ghanaian Frafra lute player Atongo Zimba, which includes a remix of the 1978 Bokoor band Afrobeat "Onukpa Shwarpo."[18] Also based in Amsterdam is the Otrabanda label (run by Scott Rollins) that issued two CDs of old Ghanaian Afro-fusion records. First in 2004 came *Rhythmology,* a collection of Afro-rock songs from the ace Ghanaian percussionist Kofi Ayivor who, from the late 1950s to 1980s played with many artists, including E. T. Mensah's famous Tempos highlife band, Alexis Korner's Blues Band, Mac Tontoh and Teddy Osei's Osibisa Afro-rock band, the West Indian reggae-men Eddie Grant and Jimmy Cliff, the black British funk band Hi-Tension, and the Nigerian artists Jake Solo, Mike Odumosu,[19] and singer Dora Ifudu.[20]

Otrabanda followed this CD with its 2007 *Bokoor Beats,* a collection of highlifes and Afrobeats from John Collins's 1970s Bokoor Band and his

1980–1990s Bokoor Recording Studio in Accra. Songs included a classic guitar-band highlife from T. O. Jazz and some funky highlifes from the Mangwana Stars and Oyikwan Internationals (both formed by ex-members of F. Kenya's guitar band). *Bokoor Beats* also includes four Afrobeats by John Collins's 1970s Bokoor Band ("Onukpa Shwarpo," "Yea Yea Ku Yea," "Maya Gari," and "There Is Time") as well as the Afrobeat "Egbe Enyo" recorded at Bokoor Studio in 1992 by Blekete and the Big Beats, led jointly by Jigga Mofy and by the late Lord "Akakpo" Lindon, leader of the early 1970s Nigerian-Ghanaian Big Beats Afrobeat band.[21]

In 2012 and with the permission of the Fela Anikulapo-Kuti estate and assistance of Fela's one-time British manager, Rikki Stein, the Knitting Factory Record Label of New York released a twenty-six-CD box set entitled *The Complete Works of Fela Anikulapo-Kuti*. It included forty-six of Fela's albums and an accompanying booklet and sleeve notes written by the British journalist Chris May. In addition the box contained a DVD called *A Slice of Fela* that included shots of him playing taken from various films made of him over the years—as well as a discussion of the *Fela!* Broadway musical by Fela's first biographer, the Cuban Carlos Moore, and the director of the musical, Bill T. Jones.

I should add that in Nigeria few years ago a special CD box set dedicated to Fela (with fifteen albums on five CDs) that included a twenty-four-page biography on him was released by Femi Esho's Evergreen Musical Company in Lagos—again authorized by the Fela estate.

Exhibitions, Festivals, Books, Films, and "Felabrations"

There are various ways that Fela has been celebrated in Europe, the United States, and Nigeria since his death—and I will mention just some of these in chronological order. In 2003 "The Black President Exhibition" was opened at the New York Museum for Contemporary Art, which featured concerts, symposia, films, and the works of thirty-nine international artists (including Fela's record-sleeve artist Lemi Ghariokwu). This exhibition then went on tour of the US and then to Britain, where it was lodged at the London Barbican in October 2004, with music being provided by Blur (Damon Albarn), Baaba Maal, and Femi Kuti's Positive Force.

In 2006 Dan Ollman released his sixty-five-minute documentary *Suffering and Smiling* (with dialogue in English and Yoruba) that highlights governmental injustices and corruption in Nigeria by focusing in on Femi and fellow Afrobeat musicians at the Africa Shrine who continue Fela's support of the country's disenfranchised "sufferheads."

In September 2008 a New York off-Broadway musical on Fela was staged, written by Jim Lewis and Bill T. Jones and featuring Aaron Johnson and the Antibalas band. This was so successful that it was extended for another month. In 2010 this show then became a Broadway show after getting backing from Jay-Z, Will Smith and Jada Pinkett-Smith; the musical traveled across America and then to Europe, and it garnered many Tony nominations and awards. In 2011 the London production of *Fela!* was made into a film, and the same year the Broadway show went to Lagos. There it played to packed houses at the New Africa Shrine and the Eko Centre on Victoria Island. In 2013 the show was again touring across the United States with plans for it going to Russia.

In 2008 an Afrobeat celebratory tour of Germany and Belgium was organized by Adé Bantu, who put together a show of performers and DJs influenced by Fela. These include the guitarist Oghene Kologbo, the German-Nigerian singer Don Abi (Adiodun Odukoya), DJ Eric Soul (Afrogroove, London), DJ Frenchman (Gobalplayers & Funkhauseuropa), and the Firedance Crew from Nigeria. Adé Bantu later went home and started a series of monthly performances called "Afropolitan Vibes" at Freedom Park in Lagos that features the twelve-piece Bantu Collective and fellow Nigerian "AlterNative" stars like Aduke & Siji.

A number of books on Fela have recently come out. In 2007 Mabinuori Kayode Idowu released his book in Italian called *Fela Kuti: Lotta Continua,* and in 2009 an early version of my *Kalakuta Notes* book was published by KIT in the Netherlands. Then in 2010 Carlos Moore republished his original 1982 British-published version of *Fela: This Bitch of a Life* in Nigeria with Cassava Republic Press—and as part of his Nigerian launch of the book he also came to Ghana. In fact, we teamed up, as both Carlos's book and the 2009 version of my own *Fela: Kalatuta Notes* were launched together in Ghana at the Nubuke Foundation in Accra on November 4. On this Nigerian/Ghanaian trip Carlos was accompanied by an Afro-Brazilian film crew and his Brazilian wife and daughter, Ayeola and Rosana, as they believe they are of Ghanaian extraction and so wanted to film their ancestral homeland. Then in 2012 the Nigerian author Uwa Erhabor published *Kalakuta Diaries* based on his personal experiences as a friend and aid to Fela. A book on Tony Allen by Michael Veal was published recently, while Fela's longtime friend and one-time manager, the journalist Benson Idonije, is writing a book on him called *Dis Fela Self* (forthcoming from FESTAC Books, Lagos) that, as he puts it, will be from a "participant observer perspective."

Back in 2009 the Grenadian filmmaker Steve McQueen was working on a biopic on Fela for Focus Features, but has since handed the project over to the Nigerian producer Andrew Dosunmu. The film is based on Veal's 2000 book *Fela: The Life and Times of an African Musical Icon,* and the screenplay is by the Nigerian author Chris Abani and James Schamus. There are rumors that the British-Nigerian actor Chiwetel Ejiofor—well known for his role in McQueen's 2013 film *Twelve Years a Slave*—will play Fela.

Back to "The Black President" Film

"The Black President" was made way back in 1976–77. The soundtrack was largely destroyed in the army attack on the Kalakuta Republic on February 18, 1977. Fortunately the audio of some of the scripted dialogue portions (including my part) were redubbed at the Ghana Film Industry

Corporation studio in Accra in 1977–78. Since then the hundred or more reels of 35 mm film were languishing in the Rank Xerox vaults in London—and these include the audio redubs done in Ghana in 1977–78, as well as the audio portions of the earlier shots filmed in Ghana in 1976. The real loss to the film, when Fela's Kalakuta recording studio went up in flames in 1977, was that it contained the soundtrack of Fela's live musical performances as well as the unscripted portions of the film shot in Lagos. At that time, and owing to the prevailing technology, it was impossible to replace the original and destroyed live audio recordings of the film with correctly synchronized music from some of Fela's music available on record. Another problem was that many parts of the film shot in Lagos (for example, the spontaneous reenactments of riots, confrontations, police attacks, and so on) were unscripted and so no one could remember exactly what was said. This is why only the few scripted portions were redubbed at the Ghana Films studio in the late 1970s. It is these two problems, of how to synchronize the live-performance scenes and the redubbing of unscripted dialogues, that seem to have been the major stumbling block (besides financial ones) in continuing the editing of the film. And so the reels sat in film vaults gathering rent for thirty years.

Today, however, with digital technology, it would easily be possible for the filmed portions of Fela playing various songs to have audio tracks dubbed in from his commercially produced records and correctly synchronized with the footage. Furthermore, a spoken commentary could be done over the improvised dialogues that took place during the many realistic and often chaotic recreations of violent scenes shot in Lagos. So, although it might not be possible to turn "The Black President" into a feature film as Fela intended (the film was never completed), it might be possible, if all the original partners and stakeholders are brought together, to release the film as a drama-documentary on Fela; or as there is such a lot of footage, as a series of such documentaries. This would have the added bonus that this would be a special type of drama-documentary or reconstruction that would actually include the very people that the story is about, including, of course, Fela himself. As far as I can recall the stakeholders in this film would involve the following people (or their estates) coming together.

1. The majority production share belonged to Fela—and therefore this now belongs to Femi, Yeni, Seun, and other members of the Fela estate.

2. The late Faisal Helwani held a small but substantial share (20 percent) in the film, as he helped cofinance it (especially the Ghanaian segments), and hired the Ghana Film Corporation crew to film in Nigeria. His share would now be in the hands of the Helwani family in Ghana.

3. The Ghanaian poet Alex Oduro was the film's scriptwriter and had a stake in the film.

4. Fela's lifelong friend J. K. Braimah also had a small stake in the film. He now lives in London, and when I spoke to him a few years ago he told me he had some rushes of the film.

With all the growing interest in Afrobeat at home and abroad, I feel that a release of "The Black President"—even as a drama-documentary—would be much appreciated by fans and admirers of Fela and his Afrobeat music. If the above stakeholders could come to an agreement and the right financiers could be found, this could happen.

19

FELABRATIONS AT HOME AND ABROAD

How the Felabration Started

Yeni Anikulapo-Kuti is the force behind the annual Felabration that celebrates Fela's birthday on October 15 and which has taken place every year (except 1999) since 1998. With the assistance of her brothers, family, friends, as well as private sponsors, and in more recent years the Lagos State government, Felabration has greatly expanded.

It now involves weeklong activities and performances by her brothers Femi Kuti and his Positive Force and Seun Kuti and his Egypt 80 and many others at the New Africa Shrine and various locations in Lagos. But there is also an array of diverse activities. In Ikeja, these include debates at secondary schools, photo exhibitions, book readings, and a Fela street-carnival parade involving musicians, dancers, masqueraders, and gymnasts performing atop flatbed trucks. In Lagos, there are discussion panels, performances, and exhibitions in the parks, clubs, and art galleries in the city.

Recent Felabrations have also included what are called "Fela Debates," which cover a range of topics on culture and politics that touch on Fela's life and enduring contribution to society. Some of the past lecture speakers have been Fela's cousin Wole Soyinka; the writers Michael Veal and

Carlos Moore; Dr. Femi Falana; Mr. Donald Duke, former governor of Cross Rivers State; the publisher Ben Murray Bruce; the Nigerian author Mabinouri Idowu; the academic Dipo Fashina; and former Lagos attorney general Yemi Osinbajo.

African Artists at Felabrations

Many artists—mainly African—have played at the Felabrations in Lagos, and some of these who appeared before the 2013 event are mentioned here. Some of the internationally recognized African artists who appeared are the South African trumpeter Hugh Masekela and the late reggae star Lucky Dube, the Congolese singer Awilo Longomba, the French-based musical sisters Les Nubians, the Senegalese guitarist–kora player Baba Maal, as well as Nigeria's Sunny Adé, Tony Allen, and Lagbaja.

From outside of Nigeria have come the Togolese musician King Mensah,[1] the Gangbe band of the Republic of Benin, and from Ghana the VIP hiplife group, the reggae-man Rocky Dawuni, and the R & B–influenced Afropop diva Efya (Jane Awindor).

Naturally most of the Felabration acts have been Nigerian, and over 160 local bands and dance troupes have performed up until the 2012 Felabration,[2] including the veteran artists Biodun "Batik" Adebiyi, the late palm-wine guitarist Fatai Rolling Dollar, playwright-poet-singer Jimi Solanke, singer Don Jazzy, and Paul Play Dairo who sings highlife, juju, and R & B and is the son of a legendary juju music pioneer I. K. Dairo. Then there is Femi Eso's Evergreen Band, a dance band that has collaborated with artists such as Victor Olaiya (All Stars), Sunny Adé, Ebenezer Obey, and Yeni and Femi Kuti.

From the reggae and dance-hall front is General Pype from Ogun State and the singer-songwriter and guitarist Keziah Jones (Olufemi Sanyaolu), who plays what he calls "Blufunk," a fusion of blues, funk, and Yoruba music.

Felabrations have featured a whole host of young Afro hip-hop and naija (Nigerian) rap artists, for instance, Tuface (or 2face) Idibia (Innocent Ujah Idibia) who had been a member of the pioneering local hip-hop group The Plantashun Boiz[3]; the female rapper Weird MC, 9ice (Abolore Akande), and D'Banj (Dapo Daniel Ayebanjo), who in 2004 was one of the Mo Hits musicians, a collection of Afro hip-hop artists established by Don Jazzy. Two other young Afro hip-hoppers, both from Abia states, are the singer-rapper Nigga Raw (Okechukwu Ukeje) and rapper Ruggedman (Michael Ugochukwu Stephens). Also featured on the New Africa Shrine Felabration stage was the solo rapper and hip-hop artist Eedris Abdulkareem, whose 2004 album critical of government corruption, *Jaga Jaga,* was banned from the radio. Later Eedris made a video called *Fela* in which Femi was featured.

Women performers have been well represented at past Felabrations, such as guitarist and singer Asa, who draws on R & B, soul, and reggae; the singer Yinka Davies; Nigerian-German hip-hop and soul singer and songwriter Nneka (Lucia Egbuna); and Tiwatope "Tiwa" Savage, a Nigerian singer-songwriter from Lagos who performs contemporary urban R & B and soul.

Some of these women, who do local renditions of "contemporary R & B/urban"[4] and neo-soul, fall into the category of the increasingly prevalent Afropop style, or "Afrobeats." Another example of an Afrobeats artist is the male singer Olu Maintain (Olumide Edwards Adegbolu), who was influenced by Bobby Brown and his "new jack swing."[5]

Felabrations in the United States

There have also been Felabrations held in many parts of the world. In 2010, for example, there were thirteen Felabrations across the United States[6]: the Chicago Afrobeat Project (with DJs Tone B Nimble and King Scratch); a Fela tribute by Ikebe Shakedown from the Fela Undustrial Complex at the

Knitting Factory in Brooklyn, New York; Lunchbox Theory at the Bossa Lounge in Washington, DC, (with DJ Underdog and A Special Fela Tribute Band); the Uhuru Afrika program at the Brewery in Boston presented by Adam Gibbons, KC Hallett the "Fela Edit King," Max Pela, and master percussionist Sidy Maiga; and the Jazztronica in Austin, Texas, with DJ Chicken George, El John Selector, and Northstar Groovement. On the West Coast, there was AfroBeat Down at the Worldbeat Cultural Center in San Diego, California; Afro Funk at the Zanzibar Club in Los Angeles with resident DJs Jeremy Sole, Glenn Red, and host Rocky Dawuni; and the Yoruba Dance Sessions at Oakland's AfroTechHouse with Carlos Mena and DJ Cecil.

In 2010 and 2012 Felabrations were held at the Shrine world-music venue in New York that featured the thirteen-member Zozo big band. In October 2012 the Chicago Shrine featured the American actor and hip-hop recording artist Mos Def (Yasiin Bey), who appeared with the Hypnotic Brass Ensemble.

Felabration 2013

The fifteenth Felabration took place on October 14–20, 2013. Theo Lawson was the chairman of its organizing committee with other members being Yeni Kuti, Olufemi Odebunmi Femi Falana, Nike Ransome–Kuti (Dr. Beko Ransome-Kuti's daughter), and Femi Eso/Esho of the Evergreen Musical Company and Evergreen dance band. Others involved included Fela's niece Yemisi Ransome-Kuti, Fela's sons Femi and Seun and youngest daughter Motun, not forgetting the tireless and dedicated organizer Jumoke Coker.

There were events at the Mydrim Gallery in Ikoyi, Terra Kulture on Victoria Island, and the Centre for Contemporary Art in Sabo, Yaba. Other Felabration spots included the Jazzhole in Ikoyi, started by Kunle Tejuoso in the early 1990s, which also operates a record label for both contemporary and veteran artists.[7]

The 2013 Secondary Schools Debate took place at the newly opened Freedom Park in Lagos. Oriwu Senior Secondary School won for the second year in a row. The topic for debate was "Should Heroes Be Celebrated in Their Lifetimes?" Freedom Park itself is built on the location of the old British colonial prison, and as one of the Felabration organizers, Theo Lawson, was also the architect who designed and now manages this park, it is not surprising that many Felabration events took place there in 2013.

After the secondary school debate, there was a week of activities at this venue, including films on Fela, a panel discussion followed by performances by Gboyega Oyedele's Afrologic, Emeka Keazor's Ikenga band, and Seun Olota's group Fusion. Other Freedom Park musical events included a reggae night, a highlife night, and an Afropolitan night that celebrated both Fela Kuti and the Pan Africanist Thomas Sankara and featured Adé Bantu's band, Funsho Ogundipe's Ayetoro, Jimi Solanke, and female artist Oyemi. The Freedom Park program closed on a Saturday with performances by Seun Kuti, Bob and Rita Marley's son Kymani Marley, and the Gangbe Brass Band from the Republic of Benin.

The 2013 Fela Debate

The Fela Debate was the fifth such debate since 2009. It was held at the NECA House auditorium on Hakeen Balogun Street in Ikeja, just opposite the New Africa Shrine. The place was packed with about three to four hundred people, including about a hundred students in school uniform and many journalists and TV film crews. Some of the people I noted in the audience and demonstrating Afrobeat's wide fan base were Fela's album cover artist Lemi Ghariokwu, the highlife promoter and preserver Femi Eso, Taiwo Oluwafunso of the Nigerian Panafest event, Fela's ex-keyboardist Duro Ikujenyo, and the social and political activists Olajide Bello, Afrikaman Desmond Offong, and others who are mentioned below.

The topic of debate was "Movement of the People: The Fela and Bob Marley Perspective." Though these two artists never met, this symposium examined their respective roles in raising consciousness among people through their songs and through their cultural-political initiatives, such as Fela's Movement of the People (MOP) and Marley's Movement of Jah People.

Fela set up MOP when he wanted to stand for Nigerian president, and the song "Movement of the People" was released on his 1984 *Live in Amsterdam* album. Marley released his hit album *Exodus* in 1977, a year after his involvement with local Jamaican politics resulted in gunmen attacking his home in Kingston. During the December 1976 assault he was shot and wounded, and left Jamaica for two years in London. The lyrics "movement of jah people" urged mass migration back to the African motherland.

The moderator of the Fela Debate was Fela's cousin Yemisi Ransome-Kuti who is a patron of the arts and director of the Nigeria Network of Non-Governmental Organisations. The speakers included Eleanor Wint, myself, and Vivian Goldman. Wint, who is the administrative coordinator of the Rita Marley Foundation in Ghana, was standing in for Rita Marley, who wasn't able to attend due to illness. In the early 2000s Marley partially relocated to Ghana where she assisted children of the Konkonuru School, became a Queen Mother in the Aburi area, and in 2013 was made an honorary citizen of Ghana.

In my talk I began by saying that, although from the 1970s both Fela and Bob Marley used the popular music styles of Afrobeat and reggae to mobilize the masses, Nkrumah was doing the same thing as far back as the 1950s, but using highlife music instead. Fela was also an avowed Nkrumahist and this is reflected in Nkrumah being a central figure in Fela's shrine dedicated to Pan African heroes.[8]

Vivian Goldman, a New York–based British journalist and author of *Bob Marley: Soul Rebel, Natural Mystic* (1981), knew both Bob Marley and Fela and noted that both used music to create a community and that both

Yemisi Ransome-Kuti and John Collins at the 2013 Felabration debate in Lagos.

had sought spiritual powers, through either Rastafarianism or through traditional African religion. In terms of differences, she noted that Fela was from an elite background and liked to be ostentatious and the center of attraction, whereas Marley was from a poor family and had a quiet unassuming manner. She played snippets of Marley's "Ambushed in the Night" and Fela's "Sorrow, Tears and Blood," both of which demonstrate their concern with African unity and a premonition of physical attacks on them.

Shola Olorunyomi, a poet, bass guitarist, and scholar from the Institute of African Studies at the University of Ibadan, was the next to speak. He stated that Afrobeat is primarily a cultural and political musical practice and its aesthetic is one of cultural politics. It is not just a rhythm, but a rhythm of "alterity" (or alternative perspectives). He called on Nigerian youth to shun their ethnic pride as these divisions are being used by those who want to undermine Africa. He pointed out that Fela's commune was an assemblage of peoples of different cultures, as Fela's preferences were not tribal or ethnic—but continental. Also, both Fela and Bob Marley confronted in their music and lifestyle the divisive and ethnic narrative that is currently tearing Africa to pieces.

Some concluding remarks were provided by Femi Kuti, who advised the audience not to forget the legacy of Fela and that they must fight government corruption peaceably, for the MOP does not use guns and violence. He ended by saying that Nigeria does not need an "Arab Spring," as it has failed in Libya, Egypt, and Syria. There followed a lively discussion between the audience and panel and contributions from the floor.

Isa Aremu, vice president of the Nigeria Labour Congress, said that the Nigerian labor movement should honor Fela and his music, as these were the epitome of the fight for peoples' well-being in Nigeria and Africa. He suggested that African leaders look at the works of Fela and Marley, as these artists were not interested in the development of specific ethnic groups but the whole continent and black people in general. Depo Towobola pointed out that he had been with Fela during some of his confrontations with the police and said that not just the Lagos State government but the federal government of the whole of Nigeria should honor Fela with a posthumous award, as he was a person more popular than any Nigerian president, past or present. Lekan Arogundade got up to declare that Nigeria needs the MOP, since it needs an alternative political party that will reflect the wishes and desires of people.

Freedom Park and the "Post-Fela" Panel Discussion

On a guided tour of Freedom Park, its principal architect, Theo Lawson, told me that the Lagos State government was at a loss for many years about what to do with this space on Victoria Island that had once been a colonial British prison and hanging ground. Theo's idea for a cultural park has been fully realized, as right in the middle of one of the busiest parts of Lagos there is now a space that includes parks and gardens, the Wole Soyinka Art Gallery, the Kongi's Harvest Art Gallery, a museum, seminar rooms, restaurants, bars, statues of Nigeria's three founding fathers, an amphitheater, and a stage. In fact, when Theo pointed out to us the permanent stage, he told us it is situated where the gallows once were. He also took us through rows of six-foot-by-four-foot unroofed cement boxes that replicated the size of the original prison cells.

Following the tour, I stayed on at the park to wait for the "Post-Fela" discussion panel that was to take place in the afternoon, and I had a chance to interact with people beginning to congregate there for the panel and the later music show at the amphitheater. Some I already knew, as they sometimes come to Ghana, like the musicians Adé Bantu, Funsho Ogundipe, and later on I met the music promoter Fidelis Akpom, who had been a journalist with the Nigerian *Glendora Art Journal* for which I had occasionally written. I also met Frank Halim and his wife, who are publishers—and Segun Bucknor, but not the one I interviewed way back in 1974, but rather, his cousin. Then there was Pascal Ott whom I had met when he was with French Embassy's Cultural Section in Accra in the mid-2000s and before that with the French Cultural Centre in Lagos when he had helped with many jazz, Afrobeat, and highlife music festivals. I also met two of his friends, Olu Amada, a lecturer at Yaba College, and the Washington, DC-based sculptor Victor Ekpuk.

The "Post-Fela" panel discussion took place Kongi's Harvest Art Gallery in the afternoon, and its theme was "Fela and Those Who've Come After: Interrogating the Post-Fela African Classical Music Movement." The moderator was the culture advocate Jahman Oladejo Anikulapo, one-time media editor of the *Lagos Guardian* newspaper and editor of the *Sunday Guardian* and currently executive director of the IREP International Documentary Film Forum in Lagos

Around one hundred people attended the panel, and as I was the special guest I opened up the discussion for the Nigerian panelists by briefly running through some current Ghanaian artists who are influenced by Afrobeat. These include the funky highlifers and Afro-funk men Ebo Taylor and Gyedu Blay Ambolley, the neo-traditional artists Atongo Zimba, Nana Danso (Pan African Orchestra), and Dela Botri (Hewale Sounds), current Afro-fusion men like Afro Moses, Kofo Essa (Takashi), and Smart Arpeh (Bawasaba), and the hiplifers Nana King, Reggae Rockstone, and Tic Tac who have sampled Fela's songs. Then the seven panel members spoke, and I will present them and what they said in the order they appeared.

First came Audu Kaikori, who cofounded the Guild of Artists and Poets in Abuja in 2000, established his 2002 Chocolate City Music Company in 2002, and co-organized the first International Nigerian Music summit in 2007. Not surprisingly, he talked about the Nigerian music industry and also about the younger generation of Nigerians who have been influenced by the omnipresence of Fela's music. He went on to discuss the difference between the word "Afrobeat" for Fela's music and the new word "Afrobeats" for the electronic contemporary urban music of the youth. I should add that Audu is a radical who in 2010 took part in the "Enough Is Enough" campaign that marched to the Government Assembly Offices in Abuja over the breakdown of basic social infrastructures and nearly got shot by policemen.

The vocalist, keyboardist, and reeds player Seun Olota of the Fusion band came next. He had studied creative arts (including jazz and classical music) and mass media at the University of Lagos (UNILAG) and began his solo music career in 1998 by forming the Janveer and then the Dotcom band, as well as being a sideman for Jimi Solanke, Fatai Rolling Dollar, Victor Olaiya's granddaughter Wunmi, and the jazzists Tunde and Fran Kuboye. I should mention here that the singer Fran Kuboye was Fela's cousin, and like Fela's daughter Sola, died just a few weeks after Fela.[9] Seun Olota's music falls into the category of what is sometimes called "nurban" (i.e., Nigerian urban) or what he himself also calls "Yurban" (i.e., Yoruba urban)—and he mentioned that it has been influenced by Fela's music. He concluded by pointing out that some songs of Fela's were influenced by Yoruba *apala* music and used traditional 6/8 polyrhythms.[10]

The third speaker was Adé Bantu Odukoya who was discussed in chapter 18. He currently runs his twelve-piece Bantu Collective at the weekly "Afropolitan Vibes" program at Freedom Park. Adé said that, although he had started out as a rapper, Fela has been a strong Africanizing influence on him. Adé went onto to speak of his dislike of the new word "Afrobeats" as he thought it a name invented by white journalists and is disrespectful of the politics behind Fela's Afrobeat. I responded that the label "world music" was likewise also invented by British music journalists and independent record-label owners who met in 1987 to find a substitute word for the "Afro" popular music that was then beginning to explode onto the international market. I pointed out that myself and the Ghanaian Charles Easmon had objected to the term "world music" at one of the London meetings where the word was coined, since by removing the prefix "Afro" it downplayed the African significance of this breakthrough phenomenon. However, others at the Freedom Park meeting decided that names are irrelevant—as long as the music itself provides an avenue for African music.

Then came the tall and lanky keyboard player and leader of the Ayetoro band, Funsho Ogundipe, (also discussed in chapter 18) who pointed out that Fela never stood still and that he constantly moved on stylistically: from highlife to jazz, to R & B, to Afrobeat, and finally in the 1980s to what he called "African classical music." Funsho went on to explain that Fela's approach influenced him because Fela was always operating in the present.

Gboyega Oyedele was formerly the radio DJ "Eddie Gee" and then in 1997 joined the Jazzhole record label and worked with Fatai Rolling Dollar, Olaitan "Heavywind" Adeniji, and the guitarist Keziah Jones—before forming his own Afrologic band in 2002 that combined soul, funk, jazz, Afrobeat, and ethnic grooves. In 2009 this electronic band did a remix of

Fela's "Viva Afrika" as the theme song for Felabration 2009. The influence of Fela on this musician goes back further, as Gboyega was running a band in the early 1990s called African Society that sampled two of Fela's songs, namely, "Power Show" and "Why Blackman de Suffer" for which he obtained permission from both Fela and Beko and which were released in 1997. He told us that Afrologic was currently creating songs that sampled works of John Coltrane, Fela, and Bob Marley—and he played us one entitled "Movement of the People." Gboyega concluded by saying that Fela was also able to infuse various genres into his art and music.

The fifth speaker was Emeka Keazor, a solicitor and multi-instrumentalist who has helped put together the supergroup band of veteran musicians called the Ikenga ("endeavor" in Igbo) that plays Afro-funk, Afro-jazz, highlife, and juju music. This group evolved from the Rhythm Project group that was formed in 1995 and played at the Elders Forums in Lagos. In 2013 the Ikengas supported the reunion of the old Nigerian Funkees band in Brighton, UK, and are about to release their first album entitled *Soul*. Emkea spoke of the important role that J. K. Braimah had for Fela—as it was he who introduced Fela to highlife music and got the young Fela onto the professional stage for the first time with Victor Olaiya and his Cool Cats. Emeka also pointed out that music is never static and is always changing.

The last Nigerian speaker was the art journalist Basil Okafor, who was also the artist who did the painting of Mrs. Funmilayo Anikulapo-Kuti that is displayed at the New Africa Shrine. He told us of the time that Fela played in Liberia's capital Monrovia, for the Reggae Sunsplash in 1988 when he refused to call Master Sergeant Doe "President." Basil also told the audience that twenty-five years ago he had done an eight-hour interview with Fela that he hopes soon to publish. He concluded by saying that Fela was a great artist and poet who saw far ahead and that the use by Fela of the name "Anikulapo" (one who has death in his pouch) and so never dies was apt—as his works of art will live forever.

As guest speaker I was invited to give a closing presentation in which I focused on the panel's interest in names of music genres and who coins them. As there had been some discussion on when and where the word "Afrobeat" had been invented, I first pointed out that the general consensus was it was coined by Fela in 1968 when he was in Ghana—and that he renamed his music "African classical music" in the 1980s when his compositions became longer and more complex. I then moved on to the current debate about the difference between Afrobeat and the fact the youth in Nigeria and Ghana now call their current local electronic pop "Afrobeats" and that this new name, like the term "world music," seems to have been invented by music journalists. Still on the topic of musical names I said something on the origin of the word "highlife" way back in the 1920s. For some the name implies that highlife was invented by the high-class Ghanaian ballroom musicians and audiences. But this was not so, as it was rather the poor who gathered outside the exclusive elite dancing clubs who coined the word "highlife" when they first heard their own local street songs being orchestrated by high-class dance orchestras. So although the name "highlife" was coined in the context of the rich, the music itself was a street music created much earlier by poor folk living in southern Ghanaian towns.[11]

Bands That Played at the 2013 Felabration

At the 2013 Felabration, Femi's Positive Force played at the New Africa Shrine, Seun's Egypt 80 played at Freedom Park, and the Jamaican reggae guest Kymani Marley played at both of these venues. Some of the big bands that played at the Shrine were the Evergreen Band and D'Afrikanaas, a fourteen-piece band formed by the trumpeter Lufem in 2009. They play a combination of highlife, Afrobeat, folk music, salsa, and jazz that they call "Afroblend" and played onstage with Femi Kuti. Yoruba fuji[12] music was presented by King Asiu Marshall, Wasiu Ayinde (KWAM 1), and

Pasuma (Wasiu Alabi Ajibola Odetola) from Mushin, while juju music was supplied by the Afro-Juju group of the guitarist Sir Shina Peters.[13] Rock music was provided by the Fadabasi band led by the guitarist of that name that plays what they call "trado-rock," which draws on the traditional percussion and music of the Akwa Ibom State in Nigeria's southeastern Delta River area. Three of the artists who played at the Shrine had passed through the now-defunct Don Jazzy's Mo'hits collective. One was the Jos-born rapper Mr. Incredible or M.I. (Jude Lemfani Abaga) who, after returning from studying in the United States, began releasing singles in 2007. Another was Wande Coal who joined the Mo'hits All Stars in 2006 and began releasing Afro hip-hop and R & B records in 2007. Third there was Kay Switch (Kehinde Oladotun Oyebanjo) who, like his older brother, D'Banj, began his career with Don Jazzy's music collective.[14]

Several other Afro hip-hop and naija rap stars played at the Africa Shrine with some, like Weird MC, Tuface Idibia, and Olamide Adedeji having played at previous Felabrations. Newer faces were the rappers Jimmy Jatt (Jimmy Adewale Amu) from Lagos Island, the eighteen-year-old Skales (Raoul John Njeng-Njeng) who appeared onstage with Femi Kuti, and Vector (Olanrewaju David Ogunmefun) who was accompanied by Lady Seyi Shay.

Then a whole host of up-and-coming young Afropop and Afrobeats musicians performed, some of whom had played at previous Felabrations. One was the singer Wizkid (Ayo Balogun), who almost caused a riot when he threw naira notes into the audience. Another was the Sound Sultan (Olanrewaju Fasasi) who calls his style of R & B "Jagbanjantis." This rapper, singer-songwriter, actor, and comedian is often referred to as the "Naija Ninja" because of his stage energy, and he was accompanied by Femi Kuti on sax.

Other new Afrobeats and Afropop artists were Seun Tizzle (Seun Morihanfen) a rapper turned singer who came back from a UK tour to play for Felabration, and Kenny Saint Brown, the younger sister of Kenny

Ogungbe (a.k.a. Kenny Saint Brown of Kennies Music) who began her career as a gospel singer. Some others were Iynaya the R & B man from Calabar, Davido (David Adedeji Adeleke), singer-songwriter Dammy Krane (Oyindamola Johnson Emmanuel), Lace, and also Orezi (Esegine Allen) who was accompanied by two erotic women dancers.

One of the very last Felabration performances, on the early morning of Sunday, October 21, was by Burna Boy (Damini Ogulu) from Port Harcourt who sings Afrobeats with a Jamaican ragga/dance-hall influence. He played some of his own hit singles as well as those of Fela, and this singer stripped down to his underpants during the performance at the New Africa Shrine claiming this was a tribute to Fela who often played bare-chested and in tight pants.

There were also five acts from Ghana organized by the Ghanaian music promoter and recording engineer and owner of Pidgin Music, Panji Anoff, who came to Lagos with over thirty musicians. They played during the last few days of the Felabratory shows at the New Africa Shrine. There was the singer and guitarist Knii (or Khini) Lante who plays reggae and Afropop and came with a ten-piece band. Then there were the Afropop and Afro-hip-hop Fokn Bois that consists of Wanluv the Kubolor (a Ghanaian-Hungarian gypsy called Emmanuel Owusu Bonsu) and Mensa (Mensah Ansah), who have been making waves in Ghana since their 2007 "Konkonsa" (Gossip) hit on their *Green Card* album and their starring roles in the 2010 pidgin music movie *Coz of Moni*. Also with the Ghanaian contingent was the freestyle rapper Yaa Pono who combines highlife, hip-hop, and dance-hall and has had seven releases since 2007. Even younger is the twenty-two-year-old Lady Jaywah who sings neo-soul, reggae, highlife, and hiplife and has fronted Funsho Ogundipe's Ayetoro Afrobeat band. Completing the Ghanaian lineup was the Afro Harmony band that consists of guitar, bass, drums, and keyboards and can play everything from highlife to swing and Latin music to Afropop.

Felabrations 2013 Abroad

On October 14, 2013, a Felabration took place at the New York Brooklyn Bowl that featured the Zozo band led by Leon Kaleta who, as mentioned in chapter 18, had played with both Fela's Egypt 80 and Femi Kuti's Positive Force. Accompanying Zozo on stage was the bass guitarist Kayode Kuti who had played with Fela (on the *Opposite People* album) and then with Seun Kuti's Egypt 80—until he formed his own Black Notes band.

In New York a few days earlier there was a tribute to Fela on NBC's *Late Show with Jimmy Fallon*. My Morning Jacket played their version of "Trouble Sleep and Yanga Wake Am" (i.e., "Palava") that they had recorded for the Red Hot Foundation album *Red Hot + Fela* that was being released on the Knitting Factory record label. The band was joined by guitarist and singer Brittany Howard of the Alabama Shakes, Merrill Gaubus of Tune Yard, and the horn section of the New York–based Afrobeat band Antibalas: Stuart Bogie, Kyp Malone, and Tunde Adebimbe. The Red Hot Foundation was created in 1989 to fight AIDS though using pop culture, and, over the years, has involved four hundred musicians and producers and released fifteen albums. A 2002 album called *Red Hot + Riot* was also dedicated to Fela and included a contribution by the American hip-hop recording artist Common (Lonnie Rashid Lynn) who, as mentioned in chapter 18, shared the platform with Femi Kuti's Positive Force in June 2013 at New York's "Central Park Summer Stage."

The current *Red Hot + Fela* itself is a collection of tracks and Fela remixes assembled by different musicians including "Trouble Sleep" by the artists mentioned above. Africans who contributed are the South African rapper and Afro-futurist composer Spoek Mathambo; Fela's ex-drummer Tony Allen; the Beninoise Afro-rock and funk singer Angelique Kidjo; the Belgium-based Congolese rap artist Baloji, who combines funk, urban and ragga; and a Kenyan group formed in 2008 called Just a Band that plays house, funk, and disco. Others who contributed to the *Red Hot +*

Fela album were the American–Sierra Leonian Sahr Ngaujah who played the part of Fela in the Broadway musical *Fela!* and the Los Angeles–based female R & B trio Kings, who provided a slow version of "Go Slow."

Shortly after, there was another Felabration at the New York Brooklyn Bowl during which the *Red Hot + Fela* album was officially launched by the Okayafrica organization as part of the 2013 annual New York music festival of CMJ Music Holdings. Bands and artists that appeared were the Sierra Leonian hip-hop group Bayah and the Dry Eye Crew (formed in Freetown in 2000) who were joined by Abena Koomson on vocals. They were followed by the Fela Band, which consists of some of the musicians and cast of the *Fela!* Broadway show (e.g., Antibalas and Sarh Njaugah) and also the DJ Ahmir Questlove Thompson, the drummer for the Roots hip-hop/neo-soul band.[15]

On the West Coast there was a Felabration at the New Parish venue in Oakland, California, on October 19 that featured two bands. One was the eighteen-piece Lagos Roots Afrobeat Ensemble formed in 2010 by the ex–Sunny Adé and Nigerian All Stars drummer Geoffrey Omadhebo—and which includes Fela's longtime trumpeter Babatunde Williams. The other group that played at this Bay Area Felabration was the multicultural Onola band led by ex–Fela musician Danjuma Adamu who, as mentioned in chapter 18, had previously been involved with several California-based Afrobeat bands.[16] Still on the West Coast, but in Canada, there was a Felabration in Vancouver, British Columbia, on October 18–19, 2013, that featured the multicultural Kara Kata Band and the Afrobeat/hip-hopper Charity ig Idemudia.

Turning to Felabrations in Europe, in the UK BBC television did a special *Focus on Africa* program on Fela on October 19. This included brief clips on Fela by leading musicians such as the jazz guitarist George Benson who called Fela "Africa's James Brown"; while the British rock musician Brian Eno[17] waved one of Fela's early '70s albums around and said his sound was "revolutionary." On the other hand, Paul McCartney of the Beatles recalled a riff he had heard at the Africa Shrine in 1973[18] from a song he called "Shakara Women" that he particularly liked—and played it on a keyboard for the program. Three others were also interviewed in more detail about the importance of Fela. One was Rikki Stein, Fela's one-time manager who had recently and together with the Knitting Factory record company[19] released a forty-six-album box set of Fela's music. Another was Afrikan Boy (Olu Shola Ajose), the British-born Nigerian hip-hop emcee who had just released the single "Hit Em Up" that sampled an old 1965 Fela recording. Also on the TV panel was Egypt 80's ex-keyboardist Dele Sosimi, who was introduced as the "Afrobeat Ambassador" in the UK and who said that in December 2013 he would perform for a Felabration in London with his Afrobeat Orchestra.

Other European Felabrations included a Spanish one on October 10 at L'Ateneu de Nou Barris in Barcelona, an Irish one in Dublin on October 25 called the Afrobeat Collection (when an album by Ajo Arkestra was released), and an event held at Amsterdam's famous Paradiso. This Dutch Felabration was held on October 11, with performances by the youthful Jungle by Night Afrobeat band and by the veteran highlife guitarist Ebo Taylor with his Konkoma Afro-funk/Afrobeat band. This event followed a 2012 Felabraton at the very same venue that also featured Jungle by Night, as well as Tony Allen with the Kabu Kabu band.

Going further east there was a Japanese Felabration at the Raw Tracks Club in Osaka on October 12, 2013, that featured the Japanese dance band Afrobeat Eat Osaka (A.E.O.), while a little earlier in May an Australian tribute to Fela was presented by Afro Moses and his Ojah Band at the Rhythm Hut at Gosford in New South Wales.

The New Kalakuta Museum

The Fela Anikulpao Kuti family recently obtained funding from the Lagos State government to convert the Kalakuta Republic on Gbemisola Street,

The granite tomb of Fela and a clear shot of the mosaic wall inscription.

Ikeja, into a museum, which was designed by the architect Theo Lawson and is managed by Fela's youngest daughter, Motun. Fela's tomb is in the courtyard in front of the museum. The tomb is a massive triangular piece of granite lying on a square base with a mosaic on the wall at the back of it consisting of pieces of stone, wood, iron, and glass, with the simple inscription "Fela 1938–1997." According to Theo, the tomb's triangular pyramidal shape is because of Fela's interest in ancient Egypt, and the mosaic materials are related to aspects of Fela's origin and character: stone to symbolize his birthplace at Abeokuta with its famous Olumo Rock, iron for Fela's strength, wood for his naturalistic beliefs, and glass for his radiance and clarity.

The building's ground floor has a space for an elevator and contains a large room that will become a coffee shop—and another for Fela souvenirs and memorabilia. Painted on the walls are large-sized versions of some of Fela's album covers and various of his sayings, such as "Who no know go know" and "If a man wants to enslave you forever he will never tell you the truth about your forefathers."

There is a series of stairs that spiral up to the top of the building, where there is a huge skylight. On the walls of the flights of stairs are photos of Fela as a child, as a young man, with his parents, their Abeokuta house, Fela's brothers Beko and Olokoye, and Fela's children and grandchildren—as well as pictures of Fela and his bands playing music.

The second floor contains Fela's bathroom and his bedroom that can be clearly seen, as one of the walls has been replaced with glass. It is a small carpeted and simple room containing Fela's mattress-like bed, a guitar, a saxophone, a table full of books, a small fridge and many of Fela's shirts hanging on coat racks. Another room on this floor contains Fela's pants on hangers, dozens of his shoes and three mannequins wearing some of Fela's clothes, including a thick winter fur overcoat. The adjacent room contains dozens of newspapers (like the *Nigeria Times*) with stories about Fela's activities and exploits going back to the 1970s, and these are opened out on racks for the public to browse. Another room is dedicated to Fela's political party, the Movement of the People, that he formed in 1978. The MOP manifesto and its four-year development plan for the 1979 elections is spread out for the public to read—and in the middle of all these documents is an old typewriter that probably represents his printing press. Still going up, another gallerylike room contains artistic paintings of Fela and several huge, hand-carved drums.

There is yet another room on the same floor with photos of Fela at the piano, with his car, and a number of color shots of scenes from "The Black President" film made in 1976–77.

When we got to the floor that led onto the roof we were greeted by a huge six-foot-wide black-and-white photo of Fela with some of his wives. On the partly covered roof garden of the building there were some

Felabration and media people sitting at tables listening to the Afrobeat blaring from some speakers.

This top floor will be the kitchenette of the premises and also provide an open-air space for live bands. Looking over the wall around the garden from the top-floor balcony one could see an adjacent plot below that was being cleared as a car park and had been bought with some of the money received from the Lagos State government.

The exit of the lift (yet to be installed) was also on this top floor, and when the place is officially opened to visitors next year (2014) the tour will begin with visitors first taking a lift up to the top of the building and then doing their sightseeing as they wend their way down the various flights of stairs. When the museum opens there will be five rooms that will be available for lodging guests.

CHRONOLOGY

1938 Fela is born on October 15 in the Yoruba town of Abeokuta Ransome-Kuti. His grandfather was the composer Rev. J. J. Ransome Kuti. Fela's schoolteacher father was Rev. Oludotun Ransome-Kuti. His mother, Funmilayo Ransome-Kuti, was a nationalist and women's rights activist. Fela's siblings were his older sister, Dulopa, and his older and younger brothers, Olikoye and Bekolari.

1947–48 Fela's mother, Funmilayo, successfully led a number of mass demonstrations of local market women who opposed the British-instigated plan of taxing them via the *alake* (king) of Abeokuta.

1953 Fela completes his primary education and for four years attends the Abeokuta Secondary School. He becomes friends with J. K. Braimah who, in his free time, sang with Victor Olaiya's highlife group the Cool Cats in Lagos—sometimes accompanied by Fela.

1956 Fela finishes school, goes to live in Lagos with his mother, works at a government office, and joins Olaiya's band as a singer.

1957 Fela meets Nkrumah when the Ghanaian leader makes a trip by boat to Lagos and meets Fela's mother.

1958 Fela is befriended by the ex–Uhuru band Ghanaian singer Joe Mensah, then in Nigeria with Bill Friday's Downbeat band.

1958 Fela goes to London for music studies and at one point (with J. K. Braimah) stays at the flat of his cousin Wole Soyinke.

1960 Nigeria becomes independent in October and is dominated by three political blocks representing the northern (Hausa, Fulani) western (Yoruba) and eastern (Igbo, Efik) peoples. An alliance of the northern and eastern block wins the elections—and Abubakar Tafawa Balewa becomes the first prime minister, with Nnamdi Azikiwe as the governor-general.

1962 Fela forms the Highlife Rakers/Koola Lobitos in London, which includes J. K. Braimah and Bayo Martins.

1963 Fela returns to Nigeria to form a jazz quintet and then re-forms the Koola Lobitos, which plays "highlife-jazz," while he is working at the Nigerian Broadcasting Corporation.

1964–68 Fela and the Koola Lobitos's first recording of jazzy highlife and later proto-Afrobeat.

1965 Fela leaves the Nigerian Broadcasting Corporation and reorganizes the Koola Lobitos. The highlife/jazz drummer Tony Allen joins. They play at the Kakadu nightclub in Lagos, with Fela on trumpet.

1966 (January) Military coup by young Igbo officers in which the prime minister and other government officials are assassinated. The coup quickly results in General Ironsi coming to power—who tried to de-federalize Nigeria and create a unitary government. Despite General Yacubu Gowon ousting him and restoring the federal system, the country had become destabilized—leading to civil war.

1966 (February) President Nkrumah of Ghana overthrown by military when on a trip to China attempting to broker a peace deal for the Vietnam War, in a Western-orchestrated coup. Nkrumah exiled in

Guinea, while the National Liberation Council (NLC) military government of General Kotoka and General Afrifa rules Ghana—until elections in late 1969, when the civilian government of Dr. Kofi Busia takes over.

1966 Sierra Leonian band Geraldo Pino's Heartbeats, which specializes in soul music, moves to Accra in 1966 and then in 1968 settles in Lagos.

1967–68 Multiple tours of Ghana by the Koola Lobitos organized by the Nigerian Raymond Aziz and the Ghanaian Faisal Helwani. This was the period of the National Liberation Council military government that overthrew Nkrumah. Fela was much impressed by the Accra-based Uhuru highlife big band led by Stan Plange (which included trumpeter Mac Tontoh, cofounder of the Osibisa Afro-rock group).

1967 Massacres of Igbos in northern Nigeria. Civil war breaks out when oil-rich southeastern Nigeria attempts to form the breakaway Biafra under Colonel Emeka Ojukwu—and with financial and military assistance from France.

(Late 1960s) Experimentations in Afro-soul music by Fela, Segun Bucknor, and Orlando Julius.

1968 Fela invites the Ghanaian Uhuru band to Nigeria to play alongside the Koola Lobitos in Lagos and Nsukka.

Fela renames his regular place at the Kakadu the "Afro-Spot" and on a Ghanaian trip coins the name "Afrobeat."

1969 (June to March 1970) The Koola Lobitos spends ten months in the United States, and with help of Ghanaian Duke Lumumba records a pro-federal-government song. Through the African American Sandra Iszadore, Fela becomes politically radicalized. Plays at Los Angeles clubs and records his first real Afrobeats.

1970 (January) The federal government wins the Nigerian Civil War but a million people die, and the southeastern Igbo areas are devastated.

(March) On returning to Lagos Fela reopens the Afro-Spot at the Kakadu but already in the United States had changed the name of his band to Nigeria 70, with Fela playing keyboards and trumpet.

Fela releases his first big Afrobeat hits "Mister Who Are You" and in 1971, "Jeun Ko'ku."

Fela introduces occasional hand drums to the Africa 70 ensemble and then in April 1971 employs two permanent hand drummers (one was the Ghanaian Daniel "J. B." Koranteng).

(December) James Brown a plays in Lagos and Ibadan.

1971 (January) Stan Plange of the Uhuru band and Faisal Helwani organize a Ghanaian tour for the Africa 70, but this is cut after performances in Accra and Takoradi due to the civilian government of Dr. Busia being overthrown by Colonel Ignatius Kutu Acheampong's military coup on January 13.

Fela moves from the Kakadu Club to the bigger Surulere nightclub, which he calls the "Afro-Spot" and then the "Africa Shrine."

1972 (April 27) Nkrumah dies in Guinea where he had been made honorary joint president by the country's president Sékou Touré. Nkrumah's body transferred to Ghana and buried in his hometown of Nkroful in the Western Region by the military regime of Colonel Acheampong that, at the time, was still in a relatively radical stage.

1972 (February) Africa 70 tours Ghana, plays for the pro-Nkrumahist Colonel Acheampong, and Fela yabbis students in Tema and Accra. Fela drops trumpet and starts to play tenor saxophone.

1973 (August/September) Paul and Linda McCartney and their band Wings come to Lagos to record their *Band on the Run* album at EMI. They visit the Africa Shrine then still in Surulere.

1973 Visits to Fela by Hugh Masekela—who later records in Nigeria with the Ghanaian band Hedzoleh Sounds. The Africa Shrine is relocated to the Empire Hotel in Mushin, Surulere, near Fela's house.

1973–74 Several West African tours (including the Cameroons) by Africa 70.

1974 Jimmy Cliff plays at Surulere Football Stadium. Fela's presence stops the show.

1974 (April) Fela arrested for possession of Indian hemp. In jail at Alagbon Close he discovers the name Kalakuta (Rascal's) Republic from fellow prisoners and uses it for his house. He composed "Alagbon Close" and "Expensive Shit" that dwell on this arrest.

Album cover designer Ghariokwu Lemi begins working with Fela.

(November 23) Fela's Kalakuta Republic (his mother's family house) attacked and tear-gassed by riot police, which results in Fela's song "Kalakuta Show." The Ghanaian bands Basa-Basa and Bunzus (including John Collins) were the resident support bands at the Africa Shrine at that time. On November 26 Fela wins the court case where he was charged with possessing Indian hemp.

1975 Fela changes his name from Ransome-Kuti to Anikulapo-Kuti.

(June) Faisal Helwani's three Ghanaian bands Basa-Basa, the Bunzus, and New Hedzoleh are in Lagos to record albums at the sixteen-track A.R.C. studio, partly owned by Ginger Baker. Fela jams with them on some of the songs.

(July) Nigeria's third military government installed when General Murtala Muhammed overthrows Gowan in a bloodless coup, Fela is much in favor of this head of state who was against corruption and, who Fela believed, wanted to legalize marijuana.

(December) John Collins visits and interviews Fela. The Ghanaian band Basa-Basa was then Fela's support band.

1976 (February) General Murtala Muhammed is assassinated in an abortive coup and so his chief of staff, General Olusegun Obasanjo, takes over. Nigeria is divided into nineteen states. The Obansjo regime lasted until 1979 when he arranged for elections. Fela is furious about the killing of the radical Murtala Muhammed, whom he admired.

Fela made several trips to Accra to play at Faisal Helwani's Napoleon Club jazz jam sessions. Also plays and "yabbis" the university students. Begins planning "The Black President" film that starts with shots of El Mina Castle and the Star Hotel in Accra.

Sandra Iszadore records the album *Upside Down* with Fela. Fela's controversial *Zombie* album that lampoons the military mentality is released. Fela establishes his Young African Pioneer (YAP) that disseminates news through broadsheets printed by Fela's own press.

(October/November) The famous Ghanaian trumpeter E. T. Mensah plays at the Africa Shrine, as he was taken there for a month by Faisal Helwani to record at the ARC Studio in Lagos an album of the Tempos' old hits called *The King of Highlife Is Back.*

1977 (January) John Collins, Faisal Helwani, and the Ghana Film crew were in Nigeria to film "The Black President" in Lagos and Abeokuta. At this time Fela's younger brother Beko Ransome-Kuti was running his Junction Clinic at the Kalakuta Republic and was also the general secretary of radical Nigerian Medical Association.

(January/early February) The Nigerian FESTAC black arts festival takes place with thousands of visitors from sixty-two countries. Fela quarreled with the organizers for embezzlement of funds and broadcast his views through his YAP News. Fela refused to participate—but many FESTAC musicians visited him and the Africa Shrine, like Stevie Wonder, Osibisa, Gilberto Gil, Francois Lougah, Sun Ra.

(February 18) Soldiers attack Fela's Kalakuta Shrine, beat, wound, and arrest inmates including Fela's mother, Funmilayo. They burn the property including Fela's Afrikana library and the sound track of "The Black President" film.

(April) Lagos State government probe into the destruction of the Kalakuta by fire concludes it was caused by an "unknown soldier."

1977–78 Multiple trips to Ghana by Fela to play at concerts in Accra and re-dub the portions of the burnt sound track of "The Black President" at the Ghana Film Studio in Accra. The Ghanaian military leader, Colonel Acheampong, was becoming increasingly corrupt and becomes nervous about Fela and his song "Zombie."

1978 (February) Fela marries twenty-seven women of his musical dance group on February 28 in Lagos. He does this to bypass Ghanaian immigration authorities as Ghana, like Nigeria, recognizes customary marriage. Nevertheless, after this trip the increasingly corrupt Colonel Acheampong made it impossible for Fela to come.

1978 (April) Fela's mother dies from injuries sustained in the 1977 soldiers' attack on the Kalakuta Republic. For six weeks Fela and entourage occupy the premises of Decca/Afrodisia in Lagos run by Chief Abiola for unpaid royalties.

(September/October) Fela and seventy musicians, dancers, road managers, cooks, and friends fly to Germany, and the Africa 70 plays at Berlin Jazz Festival. Songs performed include "Power Show."

Tony Allen leaves the Africa 70 after the German trip—and other drummers take over. One of these was the Ghanaian Frank Siisi-Yoyo.

Fela sets up the Movement of the People (MOP) political party with the help of the Ghanaian lawyer George Gardner. This party preaches Nkrumahism and African socialism—but is disqualified by the Nigerian federal electoral commission from participating in the 1979 elections.

1979 Acheampong is executed for *kalabule* (corruption) in 1979 after Flight Lieutenant Jerry John Rawlings' first coup. Rawlings' Armed Forces

Revolutionary Council lifts the ban on Fela but, despite the new government's friendlier attitude, Fela does not visit the country.

Fela moves to a new Kalakuta Republic house and opens a new Africa Shrine, both in Ikeja.

The elections organized by Obasanjo lead to a return to civilian rule with Nigeria's Second Republic under President Ahaji Shehu Shagari. At this time Nigeria was going through an oil boom. This resulted in millions of records a year being pressed by Nigerian companies like Chief Abiola's Afrodisia/Decca Company in Lagos, Haruna Ishola's Phonodisc record factory near Ibadan, and Prince Tabansi's Rogers All Stars record plant in Onitsha.

(September) Just before Obasanjo hands over power to Shagari's Second Republic, Fela deposited a coffin at the door of Obasanjo's residence in Lagos. This symbolized the coffin of his late mother, Funmilayo Ransome-Kuti, who had died in April 1978 from injuries received in the 1977 army attack on the old Kalakuta Republic, when Obasanjo was head of state.

1980 Roy Ayers performs and records with Fela, but they have problems playing in northern Nigeria due to the anti-Muslim sentiments of some of Fela's songs.

Fela renames his band Egypt 80.

1981 Egypt 80 play at the Amsterdam Woods in Holland during the summer and then in October go on an Italian tour sponsored by the Italian Communist Party. At Naples airport Fela is busted for smuggling marijuana. On this trip Fela is accompanied by his Ghanaian lawyer George Gardner and the framed charges are dropped.

Fela meets the Ghanaian magician Professor Hindu who puts him in spiritual touch with his dead mother.

1982 French documentary on Fela released called *Music Is the Weapon,* directed by Stephane Tchal-Gadjieff and Jean Jacques Flori.

1983 The civilian president Shagari is reelected for a second time, but was accused of widespread vote rigging and so, in 1984, there was a military coup led by General Buhari.

1983–84 Egypt 80 tours Europe including a show at Britain's Glastonbury Festival.

1984 Under the Buhari regime Fela arrested at Lagos airport for currency violations and given five years in prison.

1985 A peaceful military coup by General Babingida who, from 1986, introduced IMF and World Bank–directed economic structural-adjustment policies. Consequently there was austerity and the purchasing power of the naira currency dramatically dropped. Fela's older brother, Professor Olikoye Ransome-Kuti, becomes minister of health

The American producer Bill Laswell releases on the New York Celluloid label a hi-tech remix of the album *Army Arrangement* that Fela had recorded before going to prison (Fela never liked this mix). Amnesty International takes up Fela's imprisonment case.

1986 Fela released from prison after only eighteen months. Fela moves to new house in Ikeja and his son, Femi, leaves Africa 80 to form his own Positive Force band. Fela tours the UK and United States promoted by Rikki Stein. Similar tours were undertaken during the summers of 1989 and 1991.

1987 Fela and Egypt 80 perform in Burkina Faso at the invitation of its president, Captain Thomas Sankara.

1988 Fela and his Egypt 80 played in Liberia at the Reggae Sunsplash '88 held in Monrovia alongside follow Nigerian Sunny Adé and the Jamaican artists Peter Tosh, Burning Spear, and others.

1990–91 Fela's last tour of Ghana took place organized by the Ghana-based Nigerian hotel manager and music promoter Smart Binete. At this time the military Peoples National Defence Council government of J. J. Rawlings is in its tenth year of power—but the following year the country returned to civilian rule.

1993 General Babingida's government (and the short-lived extension of Ernest Shonekanof) is overthrown by Defense Minister Sani Abacha, who introduced draconian laws against civil rights, and arrested Chief Abiola (president elect), General Obansajo, General Shehu Musa Yar'Adua, and trade-union leaders. The Abacha regime also hanged the Ogoni writer Ken Saro-Wiwa and eight other activists who were campaigning against the multinational oil companies in the Ogoni area of southeastern Nigeria.

1993–97 The Abacha regime increased the persecution of Fela, who was repeatedly arrested for drug and other offenses. This military government in 1995 also imprisoned Fela's brother Dr. Beko Ransome-Kuti, who was then chairman of the Nigerian Campaign for Democracy.

1997 (July) Fela falls sick with AIDS and dies on August 2 in Lagos. A huge funeral took place in Lagos, and Femi Kuti attended two wake keepings for Fela in Ghana. Fela's youngest daughter, Sola, died shortly after her father.

1998 Abacha dies of a heart attack and is replaced by General Abubakar who releases political detainees and holds elections in 1999. Obansajo wins, so there was a return to civilian rule and the Fourth Republic was created—after sixteen years of military dictatorship. Dr. Beko Ransome-Kuti is released from prison. Obansajo is reelected again for a second term in 2007—then a new election ushers in the government of Uumaru Yar'Adua and Goodluck Jonathan.

(October) The first annual "Felabration" in Lagos is organized by Fela's children in honor of their father's birthday.

NOTES

Introduction

1. See the *Catalogue of Zonophone West Africa Records by Native Artists* (Middlesex, UK: EMI Hayes, 1929), 33–34.

2. (London: Rex Collings Ltd, 1981).

3. See Michael Veal, *Fela: The Life and Times of an African Musical Icon.* (Philadelphia, PA: Temple University Press, 2000), 33; also Carlos Moore, *Fela: This Bitch of a Life* (Abuja, Nigeria: Cassava Republic Press, 2010); originally published as *Fela, Fela: This Bitch of a Life* (London: Allison & Busby, 1982).

4. See Veal, *Fela,* 33.

5. See Ajayi Thomas, *History of Juju Music* (New York: Thomas Organization, 1992); Chris Waterman, *Juju: A Social History and Ethnography of an African Popular Music* (Chicago: University of Chicago Press, 1990); Afolabi Alaja-Browne "Juju Music: A Study of its Social History and Style," PhD dissertation, University of Pittsburgh, 1985.

6. See my 1974 interview with Yebuah Mensah of the 1930 Accra Rhythmic orchestras in my *E. T. Mensah: The King of Highlife* (Accra, Ghana: Anansesem Press, 1996); and also my *Highlife Giants: West African Dance-band Pioneers* (Abuja, Nigeria: Cassava Republic Press, forthcoming).

7. See my "Highlife and Nkrumah's Independence Ethos." *Journal of Performing Arts* (University of Ghana, Legon) 4, no. 1 (2009–10): 93–104.

8. See my 1977 interview with him in John Collins, *Music Makers of West Africa* (Washington, DC: Three Continents Press; Pueblo, CO: Passeggiata Press, 1985) and in my forthcoming *Highlife Giants.*

9. About 40,000 Ghanaians saw active combat in the Far East. See Lieutenant Colonel Festus B. Aboagye, *The Ghanaian Army* (Accra, Ghana: Sedco Publications, 1999).

10. E. T. Mensah and his Tempos band were there in 1958, and he mentions that everything useful the French could move was taken back to France, and the rest, including even government uniforms and official stamps, was destroyed. See John Collins, *E. T. Mensah: The King of Highlife* (Accra, Ghana: Anansesem Press, 1996. First published 1986 by Off the Record Press). The Tempos' successful combination of sophisticated Western instruments and African music was also one of the factors that encouraged President Sékou Touré to establish Guinean state popular music bands like Bembeya Jazz, Les Amazons, and so on. See my forthcoming *Highlife Giants.*

11. See A. Thomas, *History of Juju Music,* 82–84.

12. See Ebun Clark, *Hubert Ogunde: The Making of Nigerian Theatre* (Oxford: Oxford University Press 1979), biographical notes 17and 18.

1. The Birth of Afrobeat

1. Moore, *Fela: This Bitch of a Life,* 62.

2. I interviewed Benson on November 14, 2009, at the Wangara Hotel, Accra, after he and I gave presentations together on highlife history at Ghana's National Theatre on November 12 for the "High Vibes" symposium and festival sponsored by the French Embassy and UNESCO.

3. I interviewed him when Professor J. H. K. Nketia and I attended the Afromusique/Africania Colloquium, Grand Bassam, Cote d'Ivoire, in December, at which I read a paper entitled "Goombay: The Impact of Freed Slaves on African Popular and Neo-Traditional Music."

4. From two interviews I did with Helwani in 1997–98, shortly after Fela's death.

5. Johnny Opoku-Akyeampong (now called John Goldy) learnt guitar at

Achimota College Secondary School between 1963 and 1969 and belonged to a pop group called the Psychedelic Experience. Incidentally, he, myself, and Sami Bentil formed a band in 1969 called "Deep Blues Feeling" that played at the university and at a "pop chain" competition at Achimota School and specialized in the music of Jimi Hendrix.

6. Guitarist and singer Alfred "Kari" Bannerman had been previously running a schoolboy band at Adisadel College called the Beavers. He later helped put together the Boombaya (Cosmic Boom) Afro-rock band that went to the UK in 1974.

7. E-mail communication, August 17, 2008, and also November 20, 2013.

8. Note that Faisal Helwani was rather saying that Fela did drink gin at that time.

9. E-mail communication, November 5 and 6, 2013.

10. M. Veal, *Fela,* 63, also mentions the salsa-influenced songs "Abiara" and "Ajo."

11. The *pachanga* (i.e., pacheco-charanga) was created by the New York–based flautist from the Dominican Republic, Johnny Pacheco, and who named it by combining his own name with "charanga," the Cuban orchestras that played mambos, rumbas, and the son.

12. This Freetown band settled in Ghana between 1966 and 1968 and were based at the Ringway Hotel in Accra and made occasional trips to Nigeria—where they became so popular that they moved to Lagos. Francis Fuster was the band's percussionist.

13. A live recording of the Koola Lobitos at the Afro-Spot, recorded in either 1968 or early 1969 (released by Phillips West Africa/Polydor—PLP 001R), was actually named *Afro Beat on Stage*—and included the Latin/soulish song "Ako" that Fela introduced as an Afrobeat.

14. Moore, *Fela: This Bitch of a Life,* 83.

15. It was in 1968, the year that Fela coined the word "Afrobeat," that the Heartbeats settled in Lagos.

16. This was confirmed through discussions I had with Stan Plange who was also present at this meeting that took place at a show in Accra between 1967 and 1968—and well before Fela went to the United States.

17. E-mail correspondence with Tee Mac, November 5, 2013. He is a past president and now executive member of the Nigerian performers' union, PMAN.

18. Tee Mac formed the Afro Collection band with a number of key musicians in Lagos in 1970: Berkley Jones, Laolu Akins, Mike Odumosu, Tunde Kuboye, the Lijadu Sisters, and Joni Haastrup. They played highlife, the music of Jimi Hendrix, Santana, Sly and the Family Stone, and Afro-rock and other Afro-fusion music.

19. The film *Ginger Baker in Africa* was made by Tony Palmer and released in 1971 by Eagle Eye Media.

20. Wings consisted of McCartney and his wife Linda as well as the guitarist and keyboard player Denny Laine, ex-Beatles engineer Geoff Emerick, and two roadies. They stayed in Ikeja, Lagos, between August 8 and September 23 and recorded *Band on the Run* at the EMI Studio and Ginger Baker's ARC Studio.

4. Stan Plange Remembers

1. For more background information about Stan Plange, see chapter 12 of my *Music Makers of West Africa,* and chapter 13 of *Highlife Times* (Accra, Ghana: Anansesem Press, 1996).

6. "J. B." Talks about Fela

1. It was in fact in 1968 that Fela began to call the place the Afro-Spot but continued to do so for a short while after he came back from the United States in March 1970. Then later in 1970 he renamed his club the Africa (or Afrika) Shrine.

2. McCartney, his wife Linda, and other members of Wings recorded mainly at the EMI studio in Apapa—but also did one song at Ginger Baker's ARC Studio.

3. In a later discussion with J. B., I discovered that the Wings members had been coming to the club for several weeks before this confrontation backstage occurred. The Africa 70's Ghanaian bass player George "Fela" McBruce was

one of those being enticed to record with them. Even after this McCartney continued to occasionally visit.

7. The Kalakuta Republic

1. This was part of the Lagos government's current "Operation Ease the Traffic," a draconian policy run by the army man Colonel Tarfa that involved on-the-spot beatings by the police of traffic offenders.

2. FESTAC was the Second World Black and African Festival of Arts and Culture held in Nigeria in January and early February 1977, attracting thousands of black delegates from 62 countries, including Australian Aborigines. Events included traditional Nigerian durbars and regattas, 50 plays, 150 dance and music shows, 80 films, 200 poetry and literature sessions, 40 art exhibitions and a Colloquium on Black Civilization attended by 700 scholars. Fela was initially on the official Nigerian government FESTAC committee but resigned before the event as, with the proposed high entrance fees, he considered it too elitist.

3. Because Abeokuta Rock was the haven for Yoruba refugees fleeing the collapse of the Oyo Empire in the 1820s and 1830s it is known as Olumo, "the place where God has ended our problems." Christians later put a cross on top of it.

4. Fela had a penchant for beautiful Ghanaian women. Emelia Naa Lamiley Lamty was one of the two he kept at hotels in Lagos, paying all their expenses and giving them airline tickets to visit Ghana from time to time. Her biography appears in Carlos Moore's biography of Fela.

5. The force of my blow was confirmed years later by Carlos Moore in 2010 when he came to Ghana to launch a Nigerian reprint of his book *Fela: This Bitch of a Life*. Carlos told me that Fela complained to him in 1982 that I had really winded him and he was aching for days from the fall: but that it was an effective shot.

6. During this spiritual warm-up, conga drums were beaten, and Fela would be surrounded by gyrating female dancers and a shrouded and white-painted figure. This ritualistic side of things became more pronounced in Fela's later

career, when he would slaughter a chicken, and his dancers' makeup became more exaggerated, giving them a traditional masklike countenance.

7. Fela's brother, Beko Ransome-Kuti, was radicalized by the burning of the Kalakuta Republic and Beko's Junction Clinic in February 1977. Later he became the chairman of the Campaign for Democracy in Nigeria and was imprisoned for subversion in 1995 by General Sani Abacha's military government.

8. Ignace de Souza was born in Cotonou in 1937 and became trumpeter for the Republic of Benin's (then Dahomey) first dance band, Alpha Jazz. He moved to Accra, where in 1964 he first joined the Shambros band and then formed the Black Santiagos, the first band to bring live Congo jazz to Ghana. In the 1970s he and his group operated between Cotonou and Nigeria. Sadly, he died in a car crash.

9. Kwese was Faisal Helwani's personal Napoleon Club carpenter, and it was the two of them that designed the stage for Fela's Africa Shrine. They even designed and built Fela's bed, complete with subdued lighting. Shots of Fela having sexual intercourse with one of his girlfriends on this very bed were filmed for "The Black President" production. However, when later in Accra we saw the film rushes at the Ghana Film Industry preview theater we all, except Fela, thought these shots should be edited out.

10. In fact 12 FESTAC buses and 39 cars went missing. Indeed, there was so much confusion at the beginning of the festival that a 13-man military committee was set up just prior to its starting. They immediately dismissed 300 shady drivers and reduced the entrance fee down from the originally proposed 10 to 30 naira (about 5 to 15 US dollars), which was turning the whole celebration into something for VIPs rather than the Nigerian common man.

11. E. T. Mensah (1919–96) was a famous Ga trumpeter and saxophone player who pioneered Ghanaian dance-band highlife in the 1950s and whose Tempos band introduced dance-band highlife to Nigeria in the 1950s. E. T. had the previous year (1976) played at the Africa Shrine when making a Decca/Afrodisia recording for Faisal Helwani entitled *The King of Highlife Is Back Again.*

8. The Black President

1. M. Veal, *Fela*, 161, mentions "Sorrow, Tears and Blood" and "Observation no Crime."

2. Moore, *Fela: This Bitch of a Life*, 160ff.

9. Amsterdam and After

1. Jak Kilby, "Master of Afrobeat," *West Africa*, no. 3518, January 28, 1985, 150–52.

2. Moore, *Fela: This Bitch of a Life*, 302ff.

3. See M. Veal, *Fela*, 226–27.

4. Information on this Liberian trip from the veteran art journalist Basil Okafor during a Felabration 2013 "Post-Fela" discourse panel we were both on in Lagos (October 15); and also Tim Nevin, "Politics and Popular Culture: The Renaissance in Liberian Music, 1970–89," PhD dissertation, University of Florida, 2010, 202–3.

5. From Nana Omane's funeral oration given in Accra, 1997.

15. Nana Danso Orchestrates

1. Besides the already discussed D (dorian) and A (minor) scales/modes' starting points in the circular diagram (that starts in C major), it is also possible to start from the other four "natural" notes E–F–G and B with their corresponding interval patterns—and indeed these were also used in ancient and medieval times (creating the Phrygian, Lydian, and other modes). As there are twelve semitones in all it should also be noted from this circular schema that one can start scales/modes from any of the other remaining six notes, such as F# or the other sharps and flats of the main six "natural" notes. The critical determinant of a scale or mode is therefore not just its starting but also the spacing of its intervals.

2. This trick of improvising melodies a fifth above the original key of the song is also used by blues and jazz musicians.

16. Some Early Afro-Fusion Pioneers

1. Formerly called the Triffis in Ghana (a support band for the El Pollos) and led by keyboard player Lord Lindon.

2. It included drummer Smart Aperh "Pozo" Thompson, keyboard player Malek Crayem, bassist George Allen, and multi-instrumentalist Lash Laryea.

3. In 1973 Oscar Sulley Braima teamed up with the Uhuru highlife big band and singer Eddie Ntreh for an Afrobeat/rock album entitled *Nzele Afrikana* produced by Kwadwo Donkor. The following year I jammed an Afrobeat duet with Oscar on flute and me on the harmonica at the Napoleon Club.

4. I think here that Segun was not only referring to the connection between African and Latin American music stemming from the slave trade, but also that some Latin American freed slaves (particularly Brazilians) settled in Lagos in the late nineteenth century, bringing with them carnival and the samba.

5. The Ghanaian master drummers Okyeremma Asante and Glen Warren (Ghanaba's son) were also members.

6. This is a London-based film company, and the documentary also included interviews with the Lagos Jazzhole club owner Kunle Tejuoso and Femi Kuti representing his father.

7. Quote from his unpublished autobiography *Testament* (page 461) that I helped edit in 1975 for his Accra publisher, Jimmy Moxon.

17. Interview with Fela

1. This tension between Ghanaba and his father is discussed in Ghanaba's unpublished autobiography which I helped edit, receiving it through Ghanaba's English publisher friend, James "Jimmy" Moxon, Ghana's first minister of information and promoter of Louis Armstrong's 1956 trip to Ghana.

2. A well-known Nigerian dance-band musician influenced in the 1950s by the Ghanaian highlife of E. T. Mensah's Tempos band.

3. Faisal Helwani's famous 1970s music spot in Osu, Accra.

4. Here Fela is talking about himself, but could have acknowledged the particular contribution that Tony Allen made to the rhythmic structure of Afrobeat. It is usually accepted by Michael Veal and others that Tony added

to the Koola Lobitos's highlife rhythmic schema techniques borrowed from modern jazz drummers like Gene Krupa and Max Roach (such as cymbal rides, tom-tom and bass drums "bombs" and accents) as well as syncopated soul/funk bass-drum and high-hat patterns.

5. As mentioned in detail in chapter 5, in April 1974 Fela was arrested and taken to Alagbon Close Prison in Lagos.

6. Fela was very supportive of General Murtala Muhammed's government that came to power in a bloodless military coup against the military government of General Yakubu Gowon on July 29, 1975. Fela was even under the impression that Murtala would legalize marijuana.

7. As mentioned in the book, Fela had a serious conflict with the FESTAC organizers. Furthermore, he had a serious problem with General Olusegun Obasanjo who had taken over the running of the country on February 12, 1976, after General Murtala Muhammed had been assassinated in a Lagos "go-slow" traffic jam. It was therefore under Obasanjo's military government that the "Kalakuta" was burnt to the ground on February 18, 1977 and Fela's mother, Funmilayo Ransome-Kuti, fatally injured.

18. Afterthoughts and Updates

1. The *Glendora Africa Arts Quarterly* 2, no. 2 (1997).

2. The Koola Lobitos was formed in London in 1962 from Fela's and J. K. Braimah's earlier Highlife Rakers.

3. A famous Nigerian percussionist who had worked with Ginger Baker, Steve Winwood, Mick Jagger, and Liberia's top singer, Miatta Fahnbulleh.

4. Baaba 2010 obtained his musical training at the Music Academy of Benin City run by the famous veteran highlife musician Victor Uwaifo.

5. Songs like "Kyenkyen Bi Adi M'Awu" and "Hwehwe Mu Na Yo Wo Mpena."

6. Masekela included a version of "Lady" on his 1985 *Waiting for the Rain* album and a "Tribute to Fela" on his 2000 album *Sixty.*

7. These are the percussionist Nii Armah Hammond of the old Hedzoleh band, and Pope Flyn, who was the vocalist for A. B. Crentsil's famous 1970s Ghanaian band the Sweet Talks.

8. As mentioned earlier in the book she also visited Fela in 1976 and recorded "Upside Down" with him.

9. Before this trip Baker had added Joni Haastrup (now living in the San Francisco Bay area) of Nigeria's leading Afro-rock band Mono Mono to his British band Airport. But for Salt Ginger Baker recruited in Lagos the Lijadu sisters, guitarist Berkely Jones, drummer Laolu Akins of the Clusters Afro-rock band, and Tunde Kuboye of Tee Mac's Afro Collection, a band formed in Lagos in 1971 and influenced by Jimi Hendrix, Santana, and Sly and the Family Stone.

10. In the book *Fela: From West Africa to West Broadway,* edited by Trevor Schoomaker (New York: Palgrave/Macmillan, 2003).

11. Afro Moses has relocated to Australia where he has been awarded the 2008–9 Afro-Australian Music Award.

12. This contains their own version of my mid-1970s harmonica Afrobeat "Onukpa Shwarpo," which they retitled "Bokoor of the Mind."

13. The guitarist Jake Solo was originally with the late sixties Hykkers pop band from Enugu and formed the Funkees in 1969.

14. Johnson was based in London and sometimes opened for the Rolling Stones. Olatunji was based in the US and did likewise for the Grateful Dead.

15. Plunky works with the Ghanaian percussionist Okyeremma Asante and had made numerous West African trips.

16. Bob Pinado invented his pop-influenced "sonobete" beat in the early 1970s based on the traditional Efutu rhythms of Winneba. He and I co-ran Szaabu Sounds in the mid-1970s.

17. This famous dance orchestra of the Benin Republic of the 1970s played local Fon music, Congo jazz (i.e., soukous), and Afrobeat.

18. Hippo later released Afro-funk and Afro-rock songs by Ghana's Blay Ambolley and Amartey Hedzoleh.

19. Odumosu had been a bass player in one of Nigeria's sixties pop bands called the Clusters (led by Joni Haastrup) and then moved onto Tee Mac's Afro-Collection, BLO, and Osibisa.

20. He also played with Ghanaian artists Kiki Gyan, Ray Allen, and Eddie "Black Trumpet" Quansah.

21. Jigga Mofy later released in Ghana a remix (done at Mr. Agyemang of

Studio 3, Accra) of this song that appears as "Good or Bad" on his new CD *No Condition Is Permanent.*

19. Felabrations at Home and Abroad

1. King Mensah Ayaovi Papawi played with the prestigious Les Dauphins de la Captitale dance band of Lomé, but left Togo for Paris in the 1990s during President Eyedema's harsh rule.

2. From a list of all Felabration acts at www.felabration.net/inner.php?pg=felabration-artistes. Accessed November 2013.

3. This group included Blackface and Faze and in 2004 released their famous hit "African Queen."

4. "Contemporary R & B" sometimes called "contemporary urban" surfaced in the early 1980s as a high-tech version of older African American R & B combined with funk and disco, pioneered by Michael Jackson, Prince, Jermaine Jackson, Stevie Wonder, Kool & the Gang, Whitney Houston, George Michael, Boyz II Men, etc.

5. The late 1980s fusing of "contemporary R & B/urban" and hip-hop resulted in a variant called "new jack swing" or "swingbeat" by artists like Soul II Soul, Janet Jackson, New Kids on the Block, Madonna, and Bobby Brown. "New jack swing" was followed in the late 1990s by the "neo-soul" of Lauryn Hill, Erykah Badu, and D'Angelo, who added a more 1970s soul sound to hip-hop.

6. Culled from October 19, 2013, Sony Neme of *Saturday* magazine—Weekend Beats. http://www.fela.net/files/felabration/s.

7. For instance, Jazzhole released old palm-wine highlife, juju, and "toy motion" (1950s combination of highlife, juju, and Caribbean music) by Fatai Rolling Dollar, Kunle Tejuoso's older brother Seni Tujuose, and also Sina Ayinde Bakare, son of the juju pioneer Ayinde Bakare.

8. For more on Nkrumah's use of interethnic highlife music to foster national and Pan African identity see my "Highlife and Nkrumah's Independence Ethos," 93–104.

9. She was married to the bass player Tunde Kuboye, who in the early 1970s played with Tee Mac's Afro Collection and Ginger Baker's Salt. In 1981 Tunde

and Fran formed the Extended Family Jazz Band and in the1980 and 1990s ran the important Jazz 38 Club in Ikoyi.

10. Fela's 1975 "Monday Morning in Lagos" is an example of this. It is in 6/8 time, uses a pentatonic scale, and includes *apala*-like chorus chanting.

11. Some of the early names for what was later to be called highlife were *adaha, ashiko,* and *osibisaaba,* and these were played from the late nineteenth century in port towns by soldiers, fisherman, sailors, area boys, and artisans.

12. Fuji was developed in the western Yoruba-speaking part of Nigeria in the 1970s by artists such as Ayinde Barrister and Ayinla Kollington and drew on earlier Islamic-influenced Yoruba music styles like *ajiwere* (or *were*), *waka, sakara,* and *apala.*

13. Shina Peters worked with Segun Adewele in both the Western Brothers Band and in their own Super Stars International. After they split up in 1980 Peters formed his own pop-influenced Afro-Juju Band that released a string of albums, such as his popular 1990 *Shinamania.*

14. Don Jazzy also signed up the UK-based Nigerian naija rap group the 441 Squad.

15. See "Celebrating the Life and Times of Fela in Hipville" by Atane Ofiaja, October 22, 2013, at www.thisisafrica.me/music.

16. These were Kotoja and Ntu Shamala—and he also played with South Africa's Hugh Masekela and the US-based Nigerian master percussionist Babatunde Olutunji.

17. Brian Eno actually came to West Africa in late 1983, invited to Ghana by Faisal Helwani and the Ghana musicians' union (MUSIGA). On that trip he also stayed for a few days with me at my father's farm at Bokoor House and busily recorded the sounds of frogs, crickets, rustling leaves, and seed cases.

18. As mentioned in earlier chapters, Paul McCartney and his Wings band were in Lagos for six weeks to record their *Band on the Run* and often visited the Africa Shrine.

19. An American independent record company set up in 1998 that includes African music in its catalogue, including the music of Fela and his sons Femi and Seun.

SELECTED BIBLIOGRAPHY

Bryce, Jane "'Animal Can't Dash Me Human Rights': Interview with Fela Anikulapo-Kuti." *Index on Censorship* 18, no. 9 (1989): 12–13.

Collins, John. *E. T. Mensah: The King of Highlife.* Accra, Ghana: Anansesem Press, 1996. First published 1986 by Off the Record Press.

———. "Fela and the Black President Film." *Glendora Review: African Quarterly on the Arts* 2, no. 2 (1997): 57–73.

———. "Fela and the Black President Film: A Diary." In *Fela: From West Africa to West Broadway,* edited by Trevor Schoonmaker, 55–77. London and New York: Palgrave/Macmillan Press 2003.

———. *Fela: Kalakuta Notes.* Amsterdam: Dutch Royal Tropical Institute, 2009.

———. "Highlife and Nkrumah's Independence Ethos." *Journal of Performing Arts* (University of Ghana, Legon) 4, no. 1 (2009–10): 93–104.

———. *Highlife Giants: West African Dance-band Pioneers.* Abuja, Nigeria: Cassava Republic Press, forthcoming.

———. *Highlife Time.* Rev. ed. Accra, Ghana: Anansesem Press, 1996.

———. *Music Makers of West Africa.* Washington, DC: Three Continents Press; Pueblo, CO: Passeggiata Press, 1985.

———. "Post-war Popular Bands in West Africa," *African Arts* 10, no.3 (April 1977): 53–60.

———. *West African Pop Roots*. Philadelphia, PA: Temple University Press, 1992.

Collins, John, and Ivor Agyeman-Duah. "The Protestants from Abeokuta: Fela Kuti and His Cousin." In *Crucible of the Ages—Wole Soyinka at 80: Essays in Honour of African Literary and Cultural Studies*, edited by Ivor Agyeman-Duah and Ogochukwu Promise, 177–85. Ibadan, Nigeria: Bookcraft; Oxfordshire, UK: Ayebia Clarke Publishers, 2013.

Emielu, Austin 'Maro. *Nigerian Highlife*. Lagos, Nigeria: The Centre for Black and African Civilisation, 2013.

Erhabor, Uwa. *Kalakuta Diaries*. Bloomington, IN: Authorhouse Publishers, 2012.

Fairfax, Frank Thurmond, III. "Fela the Afrobeat King: Popular Music and Cultural Revitalization in West Africa." PhD dissertation, University of Michigan, 1993.

Goldman, Vivien. "King of Afrobeat Dead at 58: Fela Anikulapo-Kuti 1938–1997." *Rolling Stone*, September 18, 1997.

Graham, Ronnie. "Fela Anikulapo Kuti." *Stern's Guide to Contemporary African Music*, 62–65. London: Zwan/Off the Record Press, 1988.

Grass, Randall F. "Fela Anikulapo-Kuti: The Art of an Afrobeat Rebel." *TDR: The Drama Review* 30, no. 1 (1986): 131–34.

Gray, John. "Anikulapo-Kuti, Fela." *African Music: A Bibliographical Guide to Traditional, Popular, Art and Liturgical Musics of Sub-Saharan Africa*, 295–99. Westport, CT: Greenwood Press, 1991.

Howe, John. "Fela Anikulapo Kuti: An Honest Man." *New Left Review* 225, (September/October 1997): 127–33.

Idowu, Mabinuori Kayode. *Fela: Why Blackman Carry Shit*. Ikeja, Nigeria: Opinion Media Limited, 1986.

———. *Fela Kuti: Lotta Continua*. Viterbo, Italy: Stampa Alternativa, 2007.

Ikuenobe, Polycarp. "African Aesthetics and the Music of Fela A. Kuti: A Semiotic Analysis" *Literary Griot* 6, no. 2 (1994): 1–13.

Jackson-Opoku, Sandra. "Lady in the Slip." *Journal of African Travel Writing* 1, (1996): 64–84.

Kilby, Jak. "Master of Afrobeat." *West Africa* (UK), no. 3518, January 28, 1985, 150–52.

Labinjoh, Justin. "Fela Anikulapo-Kuti: Protest Music and Social Processes in Nigeria." *Journal of Black Studies* 13, no. 1 (1982): 119–35.

Lemi, Ghariokwu. "Producing Fela's Album Jacket." *Glendora Review: African Quarterly on the Arts* 2, no. 2 (1997): 54–56.

Moore, Carlos. *Fela: This Bitch of a Life*. Abuja, Nigeria: Cassava Republic Press, 2010. First published 1982 by Allison & Busby as *Fela, Fela: This Bitch of a Life*.

Olaniyan, Tejumola. *Arrest the Music: The Art and Politics of Fela Anikulapo-Kuti*. Bloomington, IN: Indiana University Press, 2004.

Olorunyomi, Sola. "Fela: Mask on Broadway: A Reading in Aesthetics and Counter-Culture Performance: Halfway Report." *IFRA Ibadan Newsletter* 6, no. 3 (1997): 13–15.

Olatunji, Michael. "Yabis: A Phenomenon in the Contemporary Nigerian Music" *The Journal of Pan African Studies* 1, no. 9 (August 2007): 26–45.

Schoonmaker, Trevor, ed. *Black President: The Art and Legacy of Fela Anikulapo-Kuti*. New York: New Museum of Contemporary Art, 2003.

———, ed. *Fela: From West Africa to West Broadway*. London: Palgrave Macmillan, (2003).

Soyinka, Wole. *Ake: The Years of Childhood*. Ibadan, Nigeria: Spectrum Books, 1981.

Stanovshy, Derek. "Fela and His Wives: The Import of a Postcolonial Masculinity." *Jouvert* 2, no. 1 (1998); online at http://152.1.96.5/jouvert/v2i1/stan.htm.

Stein, Rikki. "Black President." *Straight No Chaser*, no. 43 (Autumn 1997): 20–25.

Stewart, Gary. *Breakout: Profiles in African Rhythm*. Chicago: University of Chicago Press, 1992.

Tannenbaum, Rob. "Fela Anikulapo Kuti: Nigeria's Fabled 'Black President' Makes Music His Weapon." *Musician* 79 (1985): 23–30.

Van Pelt, Carter. "Fela Anikulapo Kuti: Africaman Original." *The Beat* 16, nos. 5–6 (1997): 52–59.

Veal, Michael. *Fela: The Life and Times of an African Musical Icon*. Philadelphia, PA: Temple University Press, 2000.

———. "Jazz Music Influences on the Work of Fela Anikulapo-Kuti." *Glendora Review: African Quarterly on the Arts* 1, no. 1 (1995): 8–13.

Waterman, Christopher. "First Word: Chop and Quench." *African Arts* 31, no. 1 (1998): 1, 4, 6, 8–9.

DISCOGRAPHY BY RONNIE GRAHAM

Ronnie Graham is a historian who specializes in Africa. He was at the University of Ghana from 1975 to 1979 and then Maiduguri University in Northern Nigeria from 1981 to 1984. He then became a freelance writer and journalist who published many articles and wrote two books on African popular music. He was also one of the founders of the London-based RetroAfric record company that released classic works by Ghana's E. T. Mensah, King Bruce, and Kofi Ghanaba, and the Congolese superstar Franco Luambo Makiadi, among others.

Ronnie Graham then joined the British Voluntary Services Overseas (VSO) in Belize where he also helped establish a community recording studio. In 1991 he joined Help-age in Tanzania where he initiated the formation of the Shikamoo Jazz Band that consisted of elderly veteran popular musicians. In 1997 Graham joined the Sight Savers International as regional director for the Caribbean and South Asia and later Eastern Africa. He currently works for the International Agency for the Prevention of Blindness and is based in South Africa. —J. C.

Given that few discographies are ever definitive, this particular effort will focus on the more mundane task of noting the song titles of Fela's full oeuvre, where and when they were first released, and whether they are currently available.

This discography draws on a number of different sources, including the early discographies of Carlos Moore, Ronnie Graham, and the excellently comprehensive and painstaking work of Toshiya Endo, and Michael Veal's published biography of Fela.[1] Additional information is taken from the original releases and unpublished sources.

A discography will never replace firsthand, personal knowledge of the subject, a well-researched biography, or a good music collection. However, a discography can provide a handy guide to the evolution of a musician or musical style; it can highlight the nature of commercial relationships, and it can quantify a contribution often overlooked in more subjective assessments.

This discography of Fela will explore these three dimensions as it objectively tracks Fela's lyrical and musical development, highlights his labyrinthine contractual relationships with national and multinational record companies, and sets the record straight with respect to his phenomenal musical output. In this respect, the discography underpins the key themes of this book.

Lyrics

Lyrically, Fela's career can be divided into a number of defining periods. From the early 1960s to the early 1970s his compositions reflected a broad spectrum of lyrical themes as he tackled a range of issues such as love, nationalism, and Lagosian life. Composition was primarily in Yoruba.

By the early 1970s three new defining themes had started to appear in Fela's compositions; gender, Pan-Africanism, and the struggle of the Nigerian underclass. These concerns were reflected in titles such as "Gentleman" and "Lady"; "Why Black Man Dey Suffer," "Black Man's Cry," and, perhaps most critically as a precursor of things to come, "Go Slow," "Chop and Quench," "Beggar's Song," and "Mattress." The language of expression was now predominantly pidgin English.

1. Carlos Moore, *Fela, Fela: This Bitch of a Life* (London: Allison & Busby, 1982); Ronnie Graham, *Stern's Guide to Contemporary African Music* (London: Zwan Publications/Off the Record Press, 1986), and *The World of African Music* (London: Pluto Press, 1992); Michael Veal, *Fela: The Life and Times of an African Musical Icon* (Philadelphia, PA: Temple University Press, 2000).

Between 1974 and the late 1970s Fela's music entered a true purple patch as he honed his satirical skills with a stream of high-quality invective, taking the themes of unnecessary suffering and Pan-Africanism to a new level of lyrical sophistication. Of course this golden period directly reflected one of the most turbulent periods in his personal life as the Nigerian state exacted revenge on Fela. John Collins witnessed several of the most traumatic episodes of this staggeringly productive period and a flavor of the reality of Fela's life is well reflected in the diary reproduced in chapter 7 of this book. Key compositions of this period include "Alagbon Close," "Expensive Shit," "Who No Know Go Know," "Kalakuta Show," "Monkey Banana," "Sorrow, Tears and Blood," "Colonial Mentality," and the incomparable "Zombie," the most stinging indictment of military rule ever committed to vinyl.

Toward the end of the 1970s, Fela entered a new phase in his lyrical development with the first of many pointed titles, characterized by the use of acronyms. By the age of forty, Fela had witnessed the destruction of his club and home, the murder of his mother, the banning of his music, exile, and a decade of constant police and army harassment. The initialisms and the full titles more or less speak for themselves: "Vagabonds In Power (VIP)," "International Thief Thief (ITT)," "Beasts of No Nation (BONN)," and "Music Against Second Slavery (MASS)."

Alongside his attacks on militarism, perhaps most eloquently expressed in "Army Arrangement" and "Coffin for Head of State," Fela sustained his commitment to Pan-Africanism with such songs as "Africa, Center of the World" and "Movement of the People." Finally, he maintained his almost genetic attachment to the Lagosian underclass with compositions such as "Original Sufferhead," "Perambulator," and "Teacher Don't Teach Me Nonsense." Throughout his career he continued to compose in Yoruba, but as Afrobeat emerged in its full pomp, pidgin became the most favored medium of communication, both inside and beyond Nigeria.

In terms of lyrical development, Fela's career encompassed three distinct periods, as key themes emerged to dominate his compositions. With gathering intensity, these included solidarity with the African, particularly the Lagosian, working class, Pan-Africanism, antimilitarism and anti-imperialism. With a lyrical focus on needless poverty and the brutalization of Africa, Fela's critique remains very much at the heart of contemporary concern.

Music

One can argue that Fela made, and will continue to make, a more lasting contribution to popular African music than many of his contemporaries. He began his career in a unique period of cross-cultural influences, partly reflected in the names of his first bands—Highlife Rakers, Highlife Jazz, Koola Lobitos. He marked the end of his first creative period and the transition into a more militant mode, by creating Africa70 and Egypt 80. Major influences during this formative period included highlife, jazz, calypso, juju, R & B, soul, funk, and Western pop.

By the turn of the decade this sound had been refined down to predominantly funk, highlife, and traditional call-and-response to produce the earliest Afrobeat formulations. Afrobeat grew in potency throughout the 1970s and 1980s until it became the defining style of Fela, bringing a host of African and international stars to pay homage at the shrine. Manu Dibango, E. T. Mensah, and, above all, Hugh Masekela availed themselves of the chance to play with Fela. Paul McCartney, Ginger Baker, and Roy Ayers were the most prominent Westerners prepared to take on the challenge of a visit to Lagos in the 1970s.

By the late 1980s and early 1990s, Fela was adopting a much stricter approach to his music; orchestrating arrangements in a form that could be accurately reproduced. John Collins's book brings this final development to light for the first time, illustrating the very high musical standards Fela increasingly adopted.

Since Fela's death, Afrobeat has grown in recognition, in sharp contrast to the current status of highlife, rumba, and African jazz. His son Femi leads the charge, but numerous Nigerians and others farther afield have not only sustained the legacy but further developed the essence of Afrobeat. From this point of view, Fela's musical legacy is likely to be sustained well into the foreseeable future as younger audiences everywhere come to appreciate the potential political and musical contribution of Fela to twenty-first- century life.

Record Companies

Fela's always difficult relationship with both national and international record companies probably deserves a book in itself. However, though the real lyrical venom was reserved for the international companies, it is important not to overlook his tempestuous times with the Nigerian record business.

Doing business in Africa is never easy, but as a musician of ever-increasing international stature, and an increasingly unorthodox lifestyle, Fela introduced new, and ultimately irreconcilable, contradictions to the process. His reputation, his creativity, the size of his entourage, and his demanding musical standards all made any "normal" promotional effort almost impossible.

During a career spanning four decades Fela, released over two hundred songs on approximately forty different labels, starting in the UK with Melodisc and, for the moment, ending in the UK with the impressive series of reissues from Wrasse Records. In between, Fela worked the music industry spectrum: from the multinational giants and their Nigerian subsidiaries, through the international independents to the homegrown labels. Melodisc (perhaps the first "world music" label) provided Fela with his first contract in the early 1960s, before his return to Lagos and the establishment of a long-lasting relationship with EMI Nigeria. Fela also released material on Philips, Polydor, and Parlophone, and through the Nigerian subsidiaries of these UK-based multinational corporations.

During the 1970s, as the Nigerian economy increasingly came under local control, Fela diversified his commercial base by releasing material on various homegrown labels, including his own Kalakuta and others such as Jofabro, Afrobeat, and Coconut. However, the love-hate relationship with the multinationals (EMI, Decca, Polydor, HMV, and Phonogram) continued throughout the 1970s, intensified by the fact that many of their subsidiaries were by now under local management.

As Fela's international stature grew, two French companies (HMV-Pathé Marconi and Barclay) entered the arena, and Makossa, the rogue African American label, also struck a deal with the rising star. During the decade Fela dealt with a staggering eighteen different companies, illustrating both his growing popularity and commercial appeal and his growing frustration with the new orthodoxy in Africa—corruption.

As the prodigious output of the 1970s slowed to a trickle in the 1980s Fela sustained his personal interest in Kalakuta and sanctioned additional releases on Eurobound and Lagos International, both independent companies. However, he remained tightly contracted to EMI, Decca-Afrodisia, and Polygram, fueling a mounting antagonism between the artist and the companies that had come to represent almost everything Fela had fought against. He sustained his international reach with the link to Barclay and opened up new relationships with the independent American companies Celluloid and Arista.

By the 1990s, only Kalakuta remained a domestic power base for the final few releases before Fela's death in 1997. Almost inevitably, his death sparked off a rush for rights, followed by a flood of compilations, tributes, and "best of" introductions. As the century drew to a close, the family tightened their grip on the increasingly chaotic situation, licensing Sterns for four well-chosen and critical releases before Wrasse Records stepped in with a twenty-two-CD deal in 2000. Over one hundred titles (approximately half of Fela's entire recorded output) are now available on Wrasse, a truly impressive living legacy.

There is no doubt that the influence of Fela and Afrobeat is steadily rising across the world. Numerous bands are currently exploring the musical legacy while the current availability of Fela's most influential recordings testifies to a sustained interest in his life and times. But above all, the deepening crisis in Nigeria bears eloquent witness to accuracy of his lifelong critique of an unjust, brutal, and dehumanizing system.

Fela: The Full Works

Note: Album titles are in italics, a question mark following a title, date, or range of dates means the exact release date is unknown, and songs listed as "Unrecorded" are known to have been performed but were never recorded.

TITLE	FIRST RELEASE	LATEST RELEASE
Abiara	Philips 1965–68	
Africa, Center of the World	Phonodisk 1980	Wrasse 2002
African Message	Decca 1977	
Ajo	Philips 1965–68	
Ako	Philips 1968?	Wrasse 2002
Akunanuna, Senior Brother of Perambulator	Unrecorded	
Alagbara	Philips 1965–68	
Alagbon Close	Jofabro 1974	
Alu Jon Jon Ki Jon	HMV 1972	
Araba's Delight	EMI 1965	
Ariya	HMV 1972	Wrasse 2001
Ariwo	Polydor 1971	
Army Arrangement (vocal)	Celluloid 1985	Wrasse 2002
Army Arrangement (instrumental)	Celluloid 1985	Wrasse 2002
Authority Stealing (vocal)	Kalakuta 1980	Wrasse 2002
Authority Stealing (instrumental)	Kalakuta 1980	Wrasse 2002

TITLE	FIRST RELEASE	LATEST RELEASE
Ayawa Ni	EMI 1965?	
Bamaiyi	Unrecorded	
Beasts of No Nation (vocal)	Kalakuta 1989	Wrasse 2002
Beasts of No Nation (instrumental)	Kalakuta 1989	Wrasse 2002
Beautiful Dancer	HMV 1970	
Beggar's Lament	EMI/HNLX 1975	
Best of the Black President, Volume 1	Bandcamp digital album online store 2010	
Best of the Black President, Volume 2	Bandcamp digital album online store 2013	
Big Blind Country	Unrecorded	
Black Man's Cry	Lumumba 1970	Wrasse 2002
Blacks Got to Be Free	Phonodisk 1989	
Blood Brothers 69	Polydor 1972	
Bonfox	RK 1965?	
Buy Africa	EMI/HNLX 1970	Wrasse 2002
Chop and Clean Mouth Like Nothing Happened	Unrecorded	
Chop and Quench (Jean K'oku)	HMV 1971	
Clear Road for Jaga Jaga	Unrecorded	
Cock Dance	Unrecorded	

TITLE	FIRST RELEASE	LATEST RELEASE
Coffin for Head of State (vocal)	Kalakuta 1981	Wrasse 2002
Coffin for Head of State (instrumental)	Kalakuta 1981	Wrasse 2002
Colonial Mentality	Decca 1976–77	Wrasse 2002
The Complete Works of Fela Anikulapo-Kuti (26-CD box)	Knitting Factory 2012–13	
Condom, Scallywag and Scatter	Unrecorded	
Confusion (vocal)	EMI 1975	Wrasse 2001
Confusion (instrumental)	EMI 1975	Wrasse 2001
Confusion Break Bone (vocal)	Kalakuta 1990	Wrasse 2002
Confusion Break Bone (instrumental)	Kalakuta 1990	Wrasse 2002
Country of Pain	Unrecorded	
Cross Examination	Yaba 1985	
Custom Check Point	EMI 1984	Wrasse 2002
Die Die	Parlophone 1970	
Dog Eat Dog	Decca 1979	Wrasse 2002
Don't Gag Me	EMI/HNLX 1975	
Don't Make Me Ganran Ganran	Kalakuta 1976	Wrasse 2002
Don't Worry about My Mouth-O	Wrasse 2002	

TITLE	FIRST RELEASE	LATEST RELEASE
Egbe Mi O	EMI/HNLX 1970	Wrasse 2002
Egbin	Parlophone 1965–68	
Eke	Parlophone 1965–68	
Eko Ile	Afrodisia 1973	Wrasse 2002
Equalisation of Trouser and Pant	Decca 1977	Wrasse 2002
Everyday I Got My Blues	Philips 1968?	
Everything Scatter	Coconut 1975	Wrasse 2001
Excuse-O	Coconut 1975	Wrasse 2002
Expensive Shit	Soundwork 1975	Wrasse 2002
Fear Not for Man	Decca 1977	Wrasse 2002
Fefe Na Efe	EMI 1973	Wrasse 2002
Fela and the Egypt 80: Big Blind Country—Afrobeat Live (Lekki Beach, 1994)	Yoruba Records, Nigeria 2010	
Fela Anikulapo-Kuti: The Complete Works (5 CD)	Evergreen Company, Nigeria 2007	
Fela Kuti and Egypt 80 Live in Detroit (1986)	Knitting Factory, New York 2012	
Fela Kuti Mixed by Big Chief Xcel	Quantum USA 2004	
Fela's Special	Melodisc 1960s?	

TITLE	FIRST RELEASE	LATEST RELEASE
Fere	RK 1965?	
Fight to Finish	EMI/HNLX 1970	Wrasse 2002
Fire	Parlophone 1965?	
Fogo Fogo	HMV 1972	
Football Government	Unrecorded	
Frustration	Lagos Int. 1981	
Frustration of My Lady	Lagos Int. 1983	
Funky Horn	Wrasse 2002	
Gba Mi Leti Ki N'dolowo	African Music 1976	Wrasse 2002
Gbagada Gbogodo	EMI 1971	Sterns 1996
Gentleman	EMI 1973	Wrasse 2002
Gimme Shit, I Give You Shit	EMI 1984	Wrasse 2002
Ginger Baker in Africa (DVD includes Fela)	Eagle Rock 2006	
Go Slow	Jofabro 1972	Wrasse 2001
Going In and Out	EMI 1972	
Government Chicken Boy	Yaba 1985	Wrasse 2002
Government of Crooks	Unrecorded	
Great Kids	EMI 1969?	
He Miss Road	EMI 1975	Wrasse 2002
He No Possible	EMI 1975	

TITLE	FIRST RELEASE	LATEST RELEASE
Highlife Rakers Calypso No. 1	Melodisc 1960s?	
Highlife Time	1963–69? Wrasse 2001	
Home Cooking	Philips 1965–68	
Igbe (Na Shit)	EMI 1973	Wrasse 2002
I Go Shout Plenty	Afrodisia 1986	
I No Get Eye for Back	Jofabro 1974	
Ikoyi Blindness	African Music 1976	Wrasse 2002
Ikoyi Mentality Versus Mushin Mentality	African Songs 1971	Wrasse 2002
International Thief Thief (ITT) (vocal)	Kalakuta 1979	Wrasse 2002
International Thief Thief (ITT) (instrumental)	Kalakuta 1979	Wrasse 2002
It's Highlife Time	EMI 1965	
Iya Me O Se O	EMI 1969	
J'ehinJ'ehin	EMI/HNLX 1970	Wrasse 2002
J'en Wi T'emi	Afrodisia 1973	
Jean K'oku (Chop and Quench)	HMV 1971	
Johnny Just Drop (JJD) (vocal)	Decca 1977	Wrasse 2002
Johnny Just Drop (JJD) (instrumental)	Decca 1977	Wrasse 2002

TITLE	FIRST RELEASE	LATEST RELEASE
Juju	Polydor 1971	
Just Like That	Eurobound 1989	Wrasse 2002
Kalakuta Show	Kalakuta 1976	Wrasse 2002
Keep Nigeria One	Philips 1969	
Kusimalaya	Parlophone 1965?	
Lady	1972	Wrasse 2002
Lagos Baby	EMI 1965	
Let's Start	Zonophone 1971	Wrasse, 2002
Laise	Parlophone 1965–69	Wrasse 2001
Look and Laugh (vocal)	Barclay 1986	Wrasse 2002
Look and Laugh (instrumental)	Barclay 1986	Wrasse 2002
Lover	Wrasse 2002	
Male	Decca 1975	
Mandele	EMI 1965	
Mattress	Afrobeat 1975	Wrasse 2001
Mi O Mo	EMI 1965	
Mr. Big Mouth and Low Profile	Honest Jons UK 2004	
Mr. Follow Follow	Coconut 1976	
Mr. Grammartology-isationalism Is the Boss	Coconut 1976	Wrasse 2002

TITLE	FIRST RELEASE	LATEST RELEASE
Mister Who Are You?		Philips 1969–70?
Moti Gborokan	Philips 1968?	
Monday Morning in Lagos	HMV 1972	Wrasse 2002
Monkey Banana	Coconut 1976	Wrasse 2002
Movement of the People (Part 1)	EMI 1984	Wrasse 2002
Movement of the People (Part 2)	EMI 1984	Wrasse 2002
Music Against Second Slavery	Unrecorded	
My Baby Don't Love Me	Philips 1965–68	
My Lady's Frustration	1969–70	Wrasse 2002
Na Fight-O	?	
Na Poi	HMV 1972?	Wrasse 2002
Nigerian Natural Grass (NNG)	Unrecorded	
No Accommodation for Lagos	Phonogram 1979	
No Agreement	Decca 1977	Wrasse 2002
No Bread	Soundwork 1976	Wrasse 2002
Noise for Vendor Mouth	Afrobeat 1975	Wrasse 2001
OAU	Unrecorded	
Obe	1969 Los Angeles	Wrasse 2002
Obinrin Le	EMI 1965	

TITLE	FIRST RELEASE	LATEST RELEASE
Observation No Crime	Decca 1977	
Ojo Ton Su	Unrecorded	
Ololufe	EMI 1969	Wrasse 2001
Omo Ejo	EMI 1965	
Omuti Ti Se	EMI 1965	Wrasse 2001
Onijibiti	EMI 1965?	
Oni Machine	Parlophone 1965?	
Onidodo	Philips 1965–68	
Onifere	Philips 1965?	
Open and Close	EMI 1971	Wrasse 2001
Opposite People	Decca 1977	Wrasse 2002
Original Sufferhead	Lagos Int. 1981	Wrasse 2002
Oritshe	Parlophone 1965–68	
Oruruka	Philips 1968?	
Orun	EMI 1965?	
Overtake Don Overtake Overtake (vocal)	Kalakuta 1989	Wrasse 2002
Overtake Don Overtake Overtake (instrumental)	Kalakuta 1989	Wrasse 2002
Palaver (Trouble Sleep Yanga Wake Am)	Jobafro 1972	Wrasse 2001
Palm Wine Sound	Decca 1977	Wrasse 2002

TITLE	FIRST RELEASE	LATEST RELEASE
Pansa Pansa	Kalakuta 1992	Sterns 1992
Perambulator	Barclay 1977	
Power Show	Lagos Int. 1981	Wrasse 2002
Question Jam Answer	Jofabro 1972	Wrasse 2001
Red Hot + Riot (Fela remixes)	MCA 2002	
Roforofo Fight	Jofabro 1972	Wrasse 2001
Se E Tunde	Philips 1965–68	
Sense Wiseness	Coconut 1976	Wrasse 2002
Shakara Oloje	EMI 1972	Wrasse 2001
Shenshema	HMV 1972	Wrasse 2001
Shuffering and Shmiling (vocal)	Coconut 1977	Wrasse 2002
Shuffering and Shmiling (instrumental)	Coconut 1977	Wrasse 2002
Signature Tune	EMI 1965	
Something Nice	Polydor 1971	
Sorrow, Tears and Blood	Decca 1977	Wrasse 2002
Stalemate	Decca 1977	Wrasse 2002
Swegbe and Pako	EMI 1971	Sterns 1996
Teacher Don't Teach Me Nonsense (vocal)	Polygram 1986	Wrasse 2002

TITLE	FIRST RELEASE	LATEST RELEASE
Teacher Don't Teach Me Nonsense (instrumental)	Polygram 1986	Wrasse 2002
This Is Sad	Wrasse 2002	
Tiwa	Polydor 1972	
Trouble Sleep Yanga Wake Am	Jofabro 1972	Wrasse 2001
Underground System	Kalakuta 1992	Wrasse 2002
Unknown Soldier (vocal)	Phonodisk 1979	Wrasse 2002
Unknown Soldier (instrumental)	Phonodisk 1979	Wrasse 2002
Unnecessary Begging	Soundwork 1976	Wrasse 2002
Upside Down	Decca 1976	Wrasse 2002
Vagabonds in Power (vocal)	Kalakuta 1979	Wrasse 2002
Vagabonds in Power (instrumental)	Kalakuta 1979	Wrasse 2002
Viva Nigeria	Lumumba 1970	Wrasse 2002
Wa Ba Mi Jo Bosue	Melodisc 1960s	
Wa Dele	Parlophone 1965–68	Wrasse 2001
Wakawaka	Philips 1965–68	
Water No Get Enemy	Soundwork 1975	Wrasse 2002
Wayo	(1969 Los Angeles)	Wrasse 2002
Who Are You	EMI/HNLX 1970	Wrasse 2002

TITLE	FIRST RELEASE	LATEST RELEASE
Who No Know Go Know	Coconut 1975	Wrasse 2001
Why Blackman Dey Suffer	Africa Songs 1971	
Witchcraft	(1969 Los Angeles)	Wrasse 2002
Yeye De Smell	Zonophone 1971	Wrasse 2002
Yellow Fever	Decca 1976	Wrasse 2002
YeseYese (or Yeshe Yeshe)	Parlophone 1967	
You No Go Die Unless You Wan Die	EMI 1971	
Zombie	Coconut 1976	Wrasse 2002

APPENDIX A:

"Shuffering and Shmiling" Score

SHUFFERING AND SHMILING

Fela Anikulapo-Kuti

(transcribed by Willie Anku)

etc
D
D1
D2
Horn
Solo
Horn
D3
Chorus
etc
Solo
E1
Solo
Every day
etc
E2
Chorus
suffering and
smiling
Solo
E-very day my people de inside bus
etc

chorus
F
etc
F2
Chorus
horns
Solo
keyb
etc
F3
Chorus
horns
call keyb
etc
R
G
Keyboard
Horns

Keyboard
Horns
Keyboard
Horns
Keyboard
Horns
etc

INDEX

Ababio, Desmond, 221
Abacha, Sani, 4, 127, 131, 162, 164, 210, 268, 274
Abami Edo, 1
Abbey Road Studio, 39, 75, 144
Abdulkareem, Eedris, 240
Abeokuta Rock, 88, 91, 273, 386
Abeokuta Secondary Grammar School, 3–4, 44, 86, 99, 259
Abiam, Nana Danso, 136, 183, 186, 191, 221
Abiodum, Dele, 230
Abiola, Moshood, 2, 119, 126–27, 153, 160, 169, 265
Abiza, 221
Abladei, 118
Abosede, Femi, 223
Accra Orchestra, 9
Acheampong, Ignatius Kutu (Colonel), 40, 50–51, 53–54, 61, 76, 120–23, 154–58, 167, 171, 262, 265
Acid Band, 14
Ackah, Jewel, 134
Action Group (AG), 19
adaha, 6, 9, 280n11
Adamu, Danjuma, 219, 223, 254
Addo, Nicholas, 76
Addy, Obo, 223
Ade, Sunny, 6, 16, 131, 219, 224, 230, 239, 254
Ade Bantu Odukoya, 226, 234, 242, 246, 248
Adebimbe, Tunde, 253
Adebiyi, Biodun "Batik," 219, 239
Adedeji, Olamide, 251
Adekunle, Prince, 16
Ademola, Olapado, 4
Adeniji, Olaitan (Heavywind), 251
Aduke, Layoya, 201
Adzo, 118
Africa for Africans, 215
Africa 70, 16, 20, 35, 37, 39–40, 53, 61, 74, 88, 90, 97, 118, 128, 144, 146, 213, 229, 262–63, 265, 272
Africa Shrine, 14, 20, 37–40, 67–69, 71, 75, 77, 104, 111, 117, 128–32, 174, 176, 199, 203, 214, 216, 220, 229, 234, 238–40, 242, 249–52, 255, 262–64, 266, 274, 280

Africa Speaks America Answers, 203
African Brothers, 16, 134, 198
African Connection, 227
African Rhythms, 203
"African Soul Rebels" tour, 214
African Soundz, 203
African Youth Command, 40, 50–51, 134
Afrikaman, Desmond Offong, 242
Afrikan Boy (Olu Shola Ajose), 255
Afrobeat Academy, 226
Afrobeat Chronicles, 219
Afrobeat Crusaders, 225
Afrobeat Down, 223, 241
Afrobeat Eat Osaka (A.E.O.), 255
Afrobeat Experience, 227
Afrobeat Express, 213
Afrobeat Orchestra, 224, 227, 255
Afrobeats (new techno-music), 240, 247–48, 250–52
Afroblend, 250
Afro-Collection, 14, 38, 272n18, 278n19, 279n9
Afro-Cuban, 16
Afrodizz, 223
Afro-funk, 13–15, 223, 229–30, 232, 247, 249, 255, 278n18
Afrofunk Experience, 223
Afro Grooves, 219
Afro Harmony, 252
Afro-hili (music style), 198
Afro-hiphop, 226, 252
Afro-jazz, 23, 98, 195, 197, 202–3, 205, 219, 229–31, 249
Afro-jazz, 203
Afro-juju (music style), 219, 223, 228, 230, 251, 280n13
Afrologic, 242, 248–49
Afro Moses, 225, 228, 247, 255, 278n11
Afromotives, 223
Afro Musia, 223
"Afropolitan Vibes" program, 234, 242, 248
Afropop, 13, 239–40, 251–52
Afro-rock, 13–14, 23, 51 103, 139, 150, 184, 198, 221, 229–32, 253, 261, 272n6, 271n18, 278n9, 278n18, 278n9
Afro-soul, 13–15, 23, 34–38, 197–98, 201, 225, 229, 231, 261
Afro Soul People, 227
Afro Sounders, 26, 201
Afro-Spot, 36–39, 62, 75–76, 111, 222, 261–62, 271n13, 272n1
Afro Waves, 156
Aguda people, 134
Ahenfo, 134
AIDS, 11, 131–32, 162, 214, 253, 268
Ajayi, Bodun, 218
Ajilo, Chris, 11, 80
Akaeze, Eric "Showboy," 201
Akintan, Tunday, 227
Akli D., 214
Akota, 224
Akoye, 224
Akpom, Fidelis, 246
Akuffo-Addo, Nana, 120
Akyeampong, Johnny Opoku (Jon C. G. N. Goldy), 23, 32, 35, 270n5
Alabama Shakes, 253
Alabi, Ekow Savage, 214
Alade, Art, 29
Alagbon Close, 22, 67, 77, 263, 277n5
Alagbon Close, 68, 263, 287
Alariwo of Africa (Rotomi Martins), 219
Albarn, Damon, 213, 228, 234
Albinos, 223
Ali, Prince, 198

Alkebu-Lan, 219
Allen, Tony (Oladipo), 15, 30, 46, 62, 75, 90, 98, 125, 141, 152–56, 203, 212–13, 216, 219, 222, 225–32, 235, 239, 253, 255, 260, 265, 266n4
Alpha Waves, 221
Amala, 218–19
Amanzeba (Nat Brew), 231
Amarfio, Sol, 13, 139, 147
Amartey, Lash Laryea, 220, 278n18
Amayo's Fu-Arkist-Ra, 224
Amboley, Gyedu-Blay, 15
Amechi, Don, 29
Amihere, Annshirley, 32
Amin, Idi, 72
Amnesty International, 1, 128–30, 267
Ampadu, Nana, 16, 134, 198
Amsterdam Woods, 22, 125, 211, 266
Analog Africa label (Germany), 232
Anan, Tommy, 174
Aniboro (Fela's bodyguard), 159
Anikulapo, Jahman Oladejo, 246
Anikulapo-Kuti, Femi, 22, 28, 87, 89, 130, 134–35, 149, 159, 163–66, 211–16, 218–19, 224, 230–41, 245, 250–53, 267–68, 276n6, 280n19
Anikulapo-Kuti, Motun, 241, 256
Anikulapo-Kuti, Seun, 135, 160, 163, 212, 215–16, 218, 237–38, 241–42, 250, 253, 280n19
Anikulapo-Kuti, Sola, 22, 28, 87–89, 92, 127, 132, 210–11, 247, 268
Anikulapo-Kuti, Yeni, 22, 28, 87, 211, 217, 237–39, 241
Animashaun, Lekan, 46, 98, 135, 141, 167, 216
Anku, Willie, 23, 178–79, 181
Anoff, Panji, 218–20, 250
Antibalas, 224, 234, 253–54
apala music, 3, 47, 280n10, 280n12
Apapa, Lagos, 63, 69, 78, 80, 104, 272n2
Aphrodisia, 227
ARC Studio, Lagos, 39, 157, 264, 272n20
Aremu, Isa, 245
Ariya Astrobeat Arkestra, 227
Army Arrangement, 130, 267, 287
Arogundadeot, Lekan, 245
Arpeh, Smart Pozo, 220
Art Ensemble of Chicago, 223
art-music, 136, 194
Asante, Cliff, 220
Asante, Okyerema, 51, 134
Ashanti Wars, 6
Ashiko, 201
ashiko music, 6, 280n11
Ashong, Derrick, 224
Asiko Afrobeat Ensemble, 224
Aso Rock Prison, 161–63
atenteben bamboo flute, 193
Avengers band, 11
Avom, Nicholas, 225
Awadi, 213
Ayers, Roy, 126, 147, 213, 222, 231, 266, 288
Ayetoro, 219, 227, 242, 248, 252
Ayivor, Kofi, 101, 232
Azangeo, Amoah, 110
Azikiwe, Nnamdi (Zik), 4, 18–19, 260
Aziz, Raymond, 36, 261
Azzi, Victor, 81–82, 95

Baba 2010 (Mena Okon Dovie), 219
Ba Cissoko, 214
Baka Beyond, 228
Baker, Ginger, 13, 39, 75, 144, 157, 224, 226, 230, 263, 272n19, 272n20, 272n2, 277n3, 278n9, 279n9, 288

Balewa, Tafawa, 164, 167
Baloji (rap artist), 253
Baltimore Afrobeat Society, 223
Bannerman, Alfred "Kari," 23, 32–33, 198, 227, 271n6
Baranta, 197, 231
Barbecues, 73
Basa-Basa, 14, 20–21, 69–70, 72, 102
"Basket Mouth," 169
Bawasaba, 220, 247
Bayah and the Dry Eye Crew, 254
Beasts of No Nation, 131, 223, 287
The Beatles, 13, 75, 184, 254, 272n20
Bediako, Kris, 198
"Beggar's Song" (or "Beggar's Lament"), 286
Belgian Afrobeat Association, 226
Bello, Abdul "Skilzz," 220, 228
Bello, Olajide, 242
Bellson, Louis, 202
Benders Band, 201
"Beng Beng Beng," 214
Benin City, 20, 70 102, 174, 197, 204, 277n3
Benin Republic, 16, 73, 103, 222, 224, 242, 274n8, 278n17
Benson, Tony, 11, 184, 197, 200
Bia, Baay, 222
Biafra, 58, 78, 261
Big Beats, 16, 75, 197, 233
Big Brovaz, 228
Big Matata, 222
Binete, Smart, 22, 131, 174–75, 177, 267
Biyongi, Frank, 225
Blackalicious, 225
"Black and Proud," 99
Black Angels, 118
Black Beats, 10, 41
Black Egypt, 227
"Black Man's Cry," 223, 286
Black Notes, 253
"The Black President" (film), 20, 53–54, 81, 91, 99–101, 104, 112, 114, 117–19, 122, 134, 179, 211, 214, 229, 235–37, 257, 264–65, 245n9, 275n8
Black Pyramid, 225
Black Santiagos, 56, 70, 73, 80, 141, 274n8
Black Voices, 213
Blay, Ackah, 221
Blekete and the Big Beats, 233
BLO, 14, 70, 230
Blue Diamonds, 165
Blue King Brown, 228
Blue Knights, 198
Blufunk music style, 239
Blum, Bruno, 219, 225
Blur, 234, 213
Bogie, Stuart, 253
Bokoor, 118, 232–33, 278n12, 280n17
Bokoor Beats, 232–33
Boma Boys, 18
Booker T and the MGs, 36
Boombaya band, 14, 198, 271
Booth, John, 119
Botri, Dela, 221, 247
The Boy's Doing It, 201
Braimah, J. K., 4, 22, 27, 53–54, 62, 84, 92–93, 125, 149, 230, 237, 249, 259, 260, 277n2
Brazilian, 16, 98, 159, 213, 229, 276n4
Bread and Bullets (Nigerian play), 19
Broadway Dance-Band, 11, 41, 55, 80, 143, 233–34
Brown, Elvis J., 11, 198
Brown, James, 2, 11, 13, 32, 35–36, 60, 70, 73–74, 99, 201
Brown, Kojo Tawiah, 70

Bruce, Ben Murray, 239
Bucknor, Segun, 11, 15, 23, 36, 80, 197–98, 230, 246, 261
Bucknor, Wole, 29
Buckshot leFonque, 223
Budo, 224
Buena Vibra Sound System, 228
Bugulu Dance Group, 73–74
Bull, John, 29
Bunzus, 14, 20–21, 60–70, 90, 104, 110, 263
Burna Boy (Damini Ogulu), 252
Burning Spear, 131, 267
Bush, Glyn "Bigga," 228
Busia, Kofi, 50, 61, 74, 76, 155, 171, 261–62
Butterfly Six, 134
Byrne, David, 226

Caban Bamboo, 110–12, 194, 197
Café Crème, 225
call-and-response, 16, 99, 180, 182
calypso, 10, 288
Cameroon, 15, 18, 79, 102, 152, 157, 222, 225, 230, 263
Campbell, Ambrose, 27, 98
Cape Coast, 6, 31, 76, 121, 152
Cape Coast Sugar Babies, 5, 7, 9
Captain Thomas Sankara, 131, 171, 267
Captain Yaba (Azongo Nyaaba), 220, 231
Cassava Republic Press, 235, 269n3
Chaka Chaka, Yvonne, 165
"Champion," 136, 221
Charlie Boy, 168, 220
Chase, Biski, 158
Checker, Chubby, 29, 58
Chicago Afrobeat Ensemble, 223
Chicago Afrobeat Project, 240
Chicago, Roy, 10
Chicken George, 241
Chiko, Igo, 29–30
Chimezie, Bright, 219
Chocolate City Music Company, 247
"Chop and Quench (Jeun Koku)," 20, 49, 60, 76, 286
Chopteeth, 224
Clapton, Eric, 13, 39
The Clash, 213
Clegg, Johnny, 14
Cliff, Jimmy, 70, 109, 232, 263
Clinton, George, 223, 230
Club Africa, 230
Clusters, 11, 278n9, 278n19
Coal, Wande, 241
Coffin for Head of State, 1, 124, 219, 287
Coker, Jumoke, 241
"Cold Sweat," 35
Collins, Bootsie, 201, 222
Collins, John, 82, 100–101, 221, 230–33, 244, 263–64, 270n8, 270n10, 287–88
Collins, Obiba Sly, 22, 165
Colonial Mentality, 287
"Colonial Mindstate," 225
Coltrane, John, 15, 98, 205, 249
Comets, 55
Commodores, 159
Common (Lonnie Rashid Lynn), 214–15, 225, 253
The Complete Works of Fela Anikulapo-Kuti, 233
Comprehensive Show, 39, 97, 107, 109
Confusion, 72
Congo, 14, 112, 225, 239, 253, 274n8, 278n17, 285
Cool Cats, 5, 29, 44, 56, 70, 213, 249, 259
Cool Collective, 226
Cooper, Gary, 213
Cream, 13, 39

Crentsil, A. B., 134, 232, 277n7
Crossroads Hotel, Mushin, 83, 85, 95, 109
Crusaders, 201
Cubop, 14
Cumbia Moderna de Soledad, 228
"Custom Check Point," 125
Cyclops, 198

D'Angelo, 214, 279n5
D'Banj (Dapo Daniel Ayebanjo), 240, 251
Dairo, I. K., 6, 47, 239
Dairo, Paul Play, 239
Damisa, Segun, 219, 225
Danjuma, Adama, 219, 223, 253
Danjuma, Theophilus, 116
Danso, Nana, 135, 183, 191, 221
Darko, George, 215
Darling, Tommy (Tamakloe), 15, 98
Davido (David Adedeji Adeleke), 252
Davies, Yinka, 240
Davis, Miles, 15, 28, 98, 202, 205
Dawuni, Rocky, 220, 239
Day by Day, 215, 232
Decca West Africa/Afrodisia, 38, 118–19, 126
De Coque, Oliver, 224
Dede, Amakye, 215
Def, Mos, 214, 224, 241
Deniran, Kunle, 219
De Souza, Ignace, 56, 73, 102, 141, 274n8
Dibango, Manu, 15, 157–59, 216, 220, 225, 230, 288
DiBongue, Claude, 213
Dickson, DK Osei Emmanuel, 221
DJ Ahmir Questlove Thompson, 254
Djan, Kiki, 152
DJ Chief Xcel (Xavier Mosley), 224
DJ Dolores, 229
DJ Eddie Gee (Gboyega Oyedele), 248
DJ Eric Soul, 234
DJ Floro, 225
DJ Frenchman, 234
DJ Jeremiah, 222
DJ Jeremy Sole, 220, 241
DJ Mujava, 222
DJ Tone B Nimble, 240
Don Abi (Adiodun Odukoya), 234
"Don't Gag Me," 194
Dorian mode, 185–90, 192
Dosunmu, Andrew, 235
Dovie Sounds, 219
Downbeats, 10, 42–43, 47, 55–56
Dr. Nico (Kassandra), 14
Drumming Calling, 226
Drum Talk, 228
Dube, Lucky, 239
Duke, Donald, 239
dundun drum, 185, 193
Dusty, Rusty, 105, 110, 111
Dylan, Bob, 2
Dynamite, Pepe, 11

Eager Hands and Restless Feet, 213
Easmon, Charles, 248
Easy Life Top Beats, 201
Edzayawa Pot of Fire, 184
Efya (Jane Awindor), 239
Egypt 80, 22, 125, 128, 130–31, 135, 167, 211, 215–16, 219, 222–25, 227–29, 238, 250, 253, 255, 266–67, 288
Ejiofor, Chiwetel, 235
El Guincho, 226
Ellis, Pee Wee, 223
Ellis, Ray, 55
El Mina Castle, 6, 54, 264
El Pollos, 11, 15, 33, 73–74, 198, 276n1

El Sombreros, 32–33
Emergent Drums, 203
EMI Company, 3; EMI Nigeria, 289; EMI studio, Lagos, 17, 20, 51, 69, 80, 272n20, 272n2
Empire Hotel, Lagos, 10, 40, 67, 69, 79, 97, 104, 143, 147, 153, 204, 262
Eno, Brian, 218, 226, 254, 280n17
Erhabor, Uwa, 235
Esa, Kojo, 220
Eso/Esho, Femi, 239, 241–242
Essiet, Udoh, 225
Evergreen Band, 239, 241, 250
Evergreen Musical Company, Lagos, 233, 241
Everything Scatter, 72
Evi Edna Ogholi-Ogosi, 174
Evora, Cesaria, 231
Excelsior Orchestra, 174
Expensive Shit, 67–68, 97, 150, 263, 287
"Eye Mo De Anaa," 221

Fabija, 152
Fadabasi, 251
Fagbemi, Adedimeji, 216
Fahnbulleh, Miatta, 277n3
Falana, Femi, 239, 241
Fallon, Jimmy, 253
Fanga, Serge Amiano, 225
Fashek, Majek, 157–59, 168, 174
Fashina, Dipo, 239
Fatai Rolling Dollar, 202, 239, 247–48, 279n7
Fear Not for Man, 225
Feelings Lawyer (Wole Kuboye), 70, 72, 79, 86–87, 90, 92–94, 100–101, 105, 110, 118
Fefe Naa/Na Efe (Fefenefe), 168, 221
Felabration, 16, 233, 238–42, 244, 249–55, 258, 268, 275n4, 279n23, 279n6
Fela Debate, 238, 242–43
Fela Live with Ginger Baker, 39, 75
Fela Ransome-Kuti Quintet, 29
Femme Nameless, 224
Ferdinand, Franz, 228
FESTAC, 80, 83, 88, 90, 99–100, 103–4, 107–11, 133, 147, 176, 208, 229, 264, 273n2, 274n10, 277n7
Fight to Win, 214
Firedance Crew, 234
Five Alarm Funk, 223
5Kiem, 222
F. Kenya, 233
Flamingo Dandies, 201
Fokn Bois, 252
Follow Follow, 223
419 Squad, 200, 228
Four Tops, 224
F. Promotions, 30, 32, 57
Francois K., 231
Franco (Luambo Makiadi), 285
Freedom Park, 234, 242, 245, 248, 250
Fresh Jumbe, 228
Friday, Bill, 10, 260
Frimpong, Alhaji K., 221, 231
From Africa with Fury, 216
funk, 13, 15, 34–37, 80, 110, 129, 201, 220–33, 239, 241, 247–49, 252, 255, 277n4, 278n18, 279n4, 288
Funkees, 14, 230, 249, 278n13
Funky Juju, 213
Fuster, Francis, 11, 197, 231, 271n12
Fuzzy Samuels, 145

Gabriel, Peter, 129, 183
Gambia, 11, 185

gandanga music, 222
Gangbe Brass Band, 222, 239, 242
Gardner, George, 22, 120, 123, 265–66
Gaubus, Merrill, 253
gbedu (music style/band), 218, 227
Gene Esposito Band, 202
General Pype, 239
"Gentleman," 49, 221, 286
Ghana Broadcasting Corporation Band, 33, 134, 141
Ghana Film Studio, 22, 81, 83, 86, 106, 114, 118, 236–37, 264–5, 274
Ghanaba, Kofi (Guy Warren), 10, 23, 39, 98, 197, 202–5, 231, 276n5, 276n1, 285
Ghetto Blasters, 225
Gil, Gilberto, 229, 264
Gillespie, Dizzy, 34
"Gimme Shit I Give You Shit," 125
Goldfinger, 165
Goldman, Vivian, 243
Gondola Nightclub, 106
gonje (one-stringed fiddle), 193
The Good, the Bad and the Queen, 213
goombay, 193, 270
Gorrillaz, 213
Go Slow, 254, 286
Graham, Ronnie, 285–86
Granadians, 70
Grass Roots, 152
Gray, Macy, 214
Guinea, 18, 72, 185, 226, 261–62, 270n10

Haastrup, Joni (aka Johnny), 11, 70, 184, 200, 230, 272n18, 278n9, 278n19
Hallelujah Chicken Run Band, 14
Hansen, Jerry, 53
Harare, 14
harmonica, 104, 276n3, 278n12
Harriott, Joe, 28, 111, 116
Harris and McCann's Jazz Group, 110
Hausa, 16, 111, 116, 260
Hayes, Isaac, 201
Heartbeats, 11–13, 33, 35–36, 57, 70, 73, 99, 197, 231, 261, 271n15
Heatwaves, 213
Hedzoleh, 14, 51, 53, 63, 104, 118, 201, 262–63, 277n7, 278n18
Hellborg, Sofi, 226
Helwani, Faisal, 20–22, 30, 32–33, 40, 50, 52–54, 57–59, 63, 69, 116–17, 119, 134, 153, 179, 201, 210, 214, 226, 237, 261–64, 270n4, 271n8, 274n9, 274n11, 276n3, 280n17
Hendrix, Jimi, 13, 270–71n5, 272n18, 278n9
Heron, Gil Scot, 201
Hewale Sounds, 221, 247
higherlife, 219
highlife music, 4–6, 9–23, 27–36, 41, 44–47, 53–56, 59–60, 74, 80, 89, 98, 102, 109, 118, 134, 139–43, 146, 150, 166, 173, 184, 190, 197–98, 201–6, 210, 213–21, 226–27, 230–33, 239, 242–43, 246–52, 255, 259–61, 269n6, 269n7, 270n8, 270n10, 270n2, 272n18, 272n1, 274n11, 276n2, 276n2, 277n4, 277n2, 277n4, 279n6, 279n7, 279n8, 280n10
Highlife Rakers, 27, 89, 102, 260, 277n2, 288
hip-hop, 215, 220–21, 222–29, 231, 240–41, 251–55, 279n5
Hippo Records Holland, 232, 278n18
Hi-Tension, 232
HMV record label, 203
Holck, Gudrun, 225
Homecooking, 213
Honest John label, 214, 226

Honey, Ernest, 152
Hot Four, 11, 198
Hotel X, 223
Howard, Brittany, 253
Hykkers, 11, 200, 278n13
Hypnotic Brass Ensemble, 241

Ian Dury and the Blockheads, 226
Ibadan, 5, 45, 51, 56, 201, 244, 262, 266
Idemudia, Charity ig, 254
Idibia Tuface (Innocent Ujah Idibia), 240, 251
Idonije, Benson, 28–29, 140–42, 216, 235
Idowu, Mabinuori Kayode, 234, 239
Ifudu, Dora, 232
Ihims, 222
"Ijo Soul Ololufe," 201
Ikebe Shakedown, 240
Ikujenyo, Duro, 218, 242
Ikwunga the Afrobeat Poet, 223, 227
Imoudu, Michael, 18
Indian hemp, 60, 67, 69, 77, 79, 120, 126, 132, 169, 171, 263
I No Get Eye For Back, 34
Inspector Reynolds, 81, 90, 94, 100, 218
International Thief Thief (ITT), 2, 22, 126–27, 160, 169, 287
Introducing Hedzoleh, 51, 63
I.Q. Band, 219
Ishola, Haruna, 47, 260
Iszadore, Conrad, 145
Iszadore, Sandra, 37–38, 60, 93, 143–45, 206, 224, 261, 264

Jackson, Lemmy, 165
Jagbanjantis (music style), 251
"James Brown Rides On," 201
Jatt, Jimmy (Jimmy Adewale Amu), 251
Jay-Z, 234
Jazzhole Club, Lagos, 218, 241 248, 276n6, 279n7
Jazz Kings, 9
Jazzy, Don, 239–40, 251, 280n14
JJC (Abdul Bello), 220, 228
JJC (Johnny Just Come), 228
JJD, Johnny Just Drop, 228
Jobe, Badou, 11
Joe Kelly's Band, 10
Jofabro (record label), 289
Johnson, Bola, 201
Johnson, Ginger, 149, 230
Jombo (or Jumbo), Friday, 75–76
Jonathon, Goodluck, 218, 268
Jones, Albert, 70
Jones, Berkely, 70, 200
Jones, Bill T., 233–34
Jones, Grace, 213
Jones, Keziah (Olufemi Sanyaolu), 239, 248
Jones, Thad, 265
Jujuba, 223
Juju Juice, 228
Juju music, 3, 6, 8, 16, 47, 70, 79–80, 131, 150, 213, 219, 223, 227–28, 230–31, 239, 249–51, 269n5, 270n11, 279n7, 280n13, 288
Julius, Orlando Ekemode, 15, 36, 80, 197, 201–2, 219, 230, 261
Juluka, 14
Junction Clinic, 4, 100, 116, 264, 274n7
Jungle by Night, 226, 255
Just A Band, 253
Juwan Ogungbe, 227

Kabaka, Remi, 210
Kabu Kabu, 255

Kadana, Peter (Rescole), 76
Kaikori, Audu, 247
Kakadu Club, 29–31, 36, 39, 62, 75, 260–62
Kala-Kosa jail, 84
Kalakuta Museum, Gbemisola Street, Ikeja, 255
Kalakuta Republic, 4–5, 20, 67–68, 81, 83, 85, 87, 89, 104, 117–18, 124, 131–32, 176, 179, 204, 207, 235, 255, 263–66, 274n7
Kalakuta Show, 72, 82, 105, 204, 263, 287
Kaleta (Leon Ligan-Majek), 224, 253
Kamanzi, Robert, 222
Kante, Mory, 226
Kapingbdi, 14
Kara Kata, 254
Karikari, Kofi, 219
Kasule, Bobbin, 222
Kayode, Samuel, 213, 227
Kaysha (Edward Mokolo), 225
Kazz, 165
Keane, Shake, 28
Keazor, Emeka, 242, 249
"Keep Nigeria One," 37
Keita, Salif, 213
Ken, Baba Okulolo, 219, 223
Kennies Music, 252
Kenny Ogungbe (Kenny Saint Brown), 252
Khoung, Yves "Korbo," 225
Kidjo, Angelique, 220, 253
King, Nana, 136, 221, 247
King, Peter, 75, 230
King Ayisoba, 220
King Chango, 224
King Scratch, 240
Kinomo, Ras, 165
Knight, Gladys, 201, 224
Knitting Factory (record label), 215, 233, 241, 253, 255
Kofi, Henry, 76
Kofi Omane, Nana, 51, 134
Kokolo Afrobeat Orchestra, 224
Kolade, Foly, 224
koliko (or kologo) lute, 220, 231
Kologbo, Oghene, 88, 90, 102–3, 157, 226, 234
Konadu, 165–66
konkoma (konkomba) music, 5, 255
kon-kon rhythm, 200
Koola Lobitos, 16, 19, 27, 29–34, 46, 49, 54–56, 73, 98, 125, 141–46, 154, 184, 205–6, 210, 213, 229, 260–61, 271n13, 277n4, 277n2, 288
Koomson, Abena, 254
Koranteng, Daniel "J. B.," 22, 39, 73–74, 262
Kotoja Afrobeat Band, 219, 223, 280n16
Krane, Dammy (Oyindamola Johnson Emmanuel), 252
Krio, 6
Kru (or Croo), 6
Kruper, Gene, 202, 277n4
Kuboye, Fran, 94, 247
Kuboye, Tunde, 94, 247, 272n18, 278n9, 279n9
Kuboye, Wole. *See* Feelings Lawyer
Kukrudu, 223
Kumapim Royals, 134
Kunniran, 220
Kusun Ensemble, 221
Kuti, Kayode, 253
Kutiman, 225
Kwessie, Richmond Kwame, 227
"Kyen Kyema Osi Akwan" or "Kyenkyemma," 75, 197

Lady, 49, 60, 76, 136, 194, 221, 277n6
Lady Jaywah, 252

Lady Seyi Shay, 251
Lagbaja (Bisade Ologunde), 135, 219, 239
Lagos Jump, 230
Lagos No Shaking, 213
Lagos Roots Afrobeat Ensemble, 254
Lampty, Naa Limley (Emelia), 90
Lante, Knii (or Khini), 252
Lasisi, Najim, 219, 223
Laswell, Bill, 130, 222, 267
Latin music, 10–13, 16, 32–34, 200, 227, 252, 271n13, 276n4
Lawal, Gaspar, 230
Lawson, Rex, 10
Lawson, Theo, 241–42, 245, 256
Lemi, Ghariokwu, 82, 204, 234, 242, 263
Leo, Bukky, 227
Les Frères Smith, 225
Les Nubians, 225, 239
Lijadu Sisters, 16, 224, 230, 272n18, 278n9
Like Water for Chocolate, 214
Lindon, Lord "Akakpo," 74, 233, 276n1
Lion Head label UK, 228
Live at the Shrine, 214
Live in Amsterdam, 242
Local Dimension, 221
Long John, 219
Longomba Awilo, Congolese singer, 239
Lord of Ajasa, 239
Lougah, François, 103, 264
Louna, Jeff, 179
Luhn, Chris, 220
Lumumba Duke (Kwerku Baidoo), 80, 143, 261

Maal, Baaba, 234
Mabiaku, Dede, 135, 218
Macaulay, Herbert, 18, 30
Magic Aliens, 15, 198
Maiga, Sidy, 241
Makossa label, 289
Malone, Kyp, 253
Maluka, 225
Mamelo Sound System, 229
Mandators, 174
Mangwana Stars, 233
Many Things, 216
Mapfumo, Thomas, 14
maringa music, 6
Marley, Bob, 2, 51, 242–43, 245, 249, 251
Marley, Kymani, 242, 250
Marley, Rita, 242–43
Marsalis, Branford, 223
Martins, Bayo, 22, 27, 29, 49, 148, 210, 260
Masekela, Hugh, 16, 51–53, 63, 143, 159, 171, 201, 220, 222, 230, 239, 262, 277n6, 280n16, 288
Masima, Okes, 225
Massak, 225
MASS: Movement Against Second Slavery, 214, 287
Mathambo, Spoek, 253
"Mattress," 286
Matwawana, Edo King, 223
mbaqanga music, 15
Mbulu, Letta, 230
MC Breis, 220
McBruce, George 198, 272
McCartney, Paul, 133, 29, 75–76, 216, 254, 262, 272n2, 273n20, 280n18, 288
Mchunu, Sipho, 14
McQueen, Steve, 235
Mdungu, 226
Meissonier, Martin, 216
Melodisc label, 289
Mena, Carlos, 241
Mensah, E. T., 5, 9–11, 53, 56, 98, 109, 111,

118, 146, 202, 232, 264, 269n6, 270n10, 274n11, 276n2
Mensah, Joe, 222, 41, 56, 134, 210, 232, 260
Mensah, King, 239, 279n1
Mensah, Kwaa, 118
Mensa (Mensah Ansah), 252
Menson, Techi, 165
Mercury Dance Band, 231
Metropole Club, Accra, 141
Mighty Canary, 107
Miller, Bala, 16
Mipakuko, Charles, 222
"Mister Who Are You," 20, 49, 262
modal jazz, 15, 37
Modern Aces, 201
Modern Ghanaians, 220
Modinaires, 143
Mofy, Jigga, 233, 278n21
Mohammed, Murtala, 54, 208, 263–64, 277n6, 277n7
molo (Yoruba lute), 186
Monjolo, 229
Monk, Thelonious, 202
Monkey Banana, 287
Mono Mono, 14, 184, 200, 230, 278n8
Moore, Carlos, 27, 36, 121, 128–29, 233, 235, 239, 269n1, 273n4, 273n5, 286
MOP. *See* Movement of the People
Moreson, A. J., 85–86, 116
Mos Def, 214, 224, 241
Moss, Sid, 29
Movement of the People, 124, 249, 287
Movement of the People (political party), 123, 219, 243, 249, 257, 265
Mr. Follow Follow, 89, 223
Mr. Incredible or M.I. (Jude Lemfani Abaga), 251
Mr. Something Something, 223
Musa, Bamaiyi, 131
"Music Against Second Slavery (MASS)," 287
Musicians' Union of Ghana (MUSIGA), 41, 134, 139, 210, 280n17
Music Is the Weapon (film), 128, 266
Musiki w'Afrika, 220
mutaba music style, 15, 197
Mwanbu, 222
My Life in the Bush of Ghosts, 226

Nação Zumbi, 229
naija (rap), 25, 280n14
Namukasa, Milly, 222
Na Poi, 24, 61
Napoleon Club, Accra, 51, 53, 87, 90, 118, 121, 205, 210, 220–21, 264, 274n9, 276n3
Nas (Nassir Jones), 225
native blues music, 6
Native Spirit, 220
Nat's Club de Paris, 42
Ndagire, Sarah, 222
Ndaro, Konikima "Kilimanjaro," 219
N'Dour, Vivianne, 231
Negrissim, 222
Nelson Cole brothers, 196
neo-soul music, 240, 254
Nepa (Fela's electrician), 91, 109
N.E.P.A. (Tony Allen recording), 213
Neville Brothers, 129
New Africa Shrine, Ikeja, 128, 214, 234, 238, 240, 242, 249–50, 252, 266
New Hedzoleh, 118, 263
Ngenya, Moses, 15
Ngomalio, Emmanuel, 29
Nielson, Fransesca, 165
Nigerian (Biafran) Civil War, 19, 37, 58, 155

Nigerian Broadcasting Corporation (NBC), 29–30, 140, 253
Nigerian Campaign for Democracy, 4, 268
Nigerian Electrical Supply Authority (NEPA), 38, 90–91
Nigerian natural grass (NNG), 67, 95
Nigerian Union of Musicians, 55
Nigeria 70, 16, 37, 75, 144, 230, 262
Nigga Raw (Okechukwu Ukeje), 240
Nightingale, Tunde, 6
9ice (Abolore Akande), 240
Ninkribi, 231
Nkengas (or Ikengas), 230
Nketia, J. H. K., 178, 270n3
Nkrumah, Kwame, 4, 10, 17–20, 40, 51, 58, 72, 89, 97, 123, 131, 140, 142, 154, 170–71, 202–3, 243, 259–62, 265, 269n7, 279n8
Nneka (Lucia Egbuna), 220, 240
"No Agreement," 134–35, 189–90, 193, 221
No Discrimination, 213
No Place for My Dream, 215
Norris, Agu, 213
Nortey, Nii Noi, 220
Northern Pyramids, 16, 111
Nswewi, Meki, 22, 29
Ntu Shamala, 223, 280n16
Nubuke Foundation, Accra, 235
Nurban music style, 247
Nuweku, Yusu, 226
Nyame, E. K., 22

Obasanjo, Olusegun, 22, 123–24, 153, 173, 263, 266, 277
Obey, Ebenezer, 6, 239
Obot, Sammy, 32
Octopus Hotel, Surulere, 176
Odebunmi, Olufemi, 241
Odukogbe, Soji, 219, 223
Odumosu, Mike, 200, 232, 272n18, 278n19
Odunesu, Emmanuel, 17
Oduro, Alex Ekow, 20, 53–54, 85–86, 92, 95, 106, 149, 237
Ofege, 14, 200
Ofo and the Black Company, 14, 200
Ogunde, Hubert, 18, 270n12
Ogundipe, Funsho, 219, 227, 242, 246, 248, 252
Ogunkoya, Kola, 135, 218
Ojah (band of Afro Moses), 225, 255
Ojah (band of Hugh Masekela), 201
Ojukwu, Emeka, 58, 261
Okafor, Basil, 249, 275n4
Okoli, Chris, 31, 201
Okonta, Eddie, 10
Okoro-Idogu, Gregory, 130
Okosun, Sonny, 11, 14, 80, 200, 230
Okukuseku, 31, 134, 166
Okulolo, Baba Ken, 219, 223
Oladende, Folake, 69
Olaiya, Victor, 5, 10–11, 20, 29, 44, 55, 69, 98, 141, 146, 202, 205, 213, 227, 239, 247, 249, 259
Olajide, Kayode, 135, 218–19, 242
Olatunji, Babatunde, 230, 278n14
Olorunyomi, Shola, 244
Olota, Seun, 242, 247
Olu Maintain (Olumide Edwards Adegbolu), 240
Olumo Rock, Abeokuta, 88, 256
Oluwafunso, Taiwo, 242
Omadhebo, Geoffrey, 253
Omatshola, Tee Mac, 14, 22, 37, 272n17, 272n18, 278n9, 278n19, 279n9
Onola band, 223, 254
"Onukpa Shwarpo," 232, 278n12
Onyia, Zeal, 29–30, 56, 98, 133, 141, 150

Open and Close, 49–50, 76
Opposite People, 119, 253
Opus One, 183
Oputa, Charlie Boy, 220
Orange Juice, 228
Orchestra Jazira, 226
Orchestra Polyrhythmic de Cotonu, 232
Orezi (Esegine Allen), 252
Original Sufferhead, 287
"Oritshe/Orise," 34
Osei, Teddy, 13, 129, 143, 147, 232
Osibisa, 13, 23, 80, 103, 107, 111, 139, 144–455, 147, 149–51, 198, 220, 232, 261, 264, 278n19
osibisaaba music style, 6, 9, 280n11
Osibisa Kete, 140
Osinbajo, Yemi, 239
Ostinato, 180, 182, 186, 193
Otrabanda label Holland, 232
Ott, Pascal, 246
Oxford Quintet Foals, 228
Oyedele, Gboyega, 242, 248
Oyelana, Tunji, 201
Oyemi, 242
Oyijide, Wale, 220
Oyikwan Internationals, 233
ozzidi music style, 228, 14

pachanga, 34, 271n11
Palava (or *Palaver*) (*Trouble Sleep Yanka Wake Am*), 134, 253
palmwine drink, 95
palm-wine music style, 6, 239, 279n7
Pan African Orchestra, 23, 135–36, 183, 185, 192, 194, 247
Papingo Nightclub, 14, 20, 69–70
Papoti, Nii, 97, 99–100, 102, 104, 109–10, 112
Parker, Charlie, 28, 98, 202
Parliament/Funkadelic, 213
Parlophone label, 289
Pastor Thomas (Fela's maternal grandfather), 3
Pasuma (Wasiu Alabi Ajibola Odetola), 251
Payne, Kole Israel, 214
Peacocks, 230
Penta Hotel, Accra, 153, 175, 177
Pentatonic, 16, 99, 108, 179, 190–92, 196, 280n10
"Perambulator," 287
Peters, Pick, 16
Peters, Shina, 224, 228, 230, 251
Phonodisc record factory, 271n13
Phonogram, 289
Pickett, Wilson, 11
Pidgin Music, 252
Pinkett-Smith, Jada, 234
Pino, Geraldo, 11–12, 33, 36, 57, 73–74, 99, 197, 231, 261
Pinodo, Bob, 15
Plange, Stan, 10, 22, 40, 53, 55, 59, 80, 130, 133–34, 140–41, 149, 214, 261–62, 271n16, 272n1
Plantashun Boiz, 240
Plunky's Oneness of Juju, 231, 278n15
"Pocket Your Bigmanism," 198
Poets of Rhythm, 226
Polydor label, 27n13, 289
Polygram label, 229, 290
Polyphonic, 6, 180
Poly-Rhythmic Orchestra, 16
Pono, Yaa, 252
"Poor Man No Get Brother," 198
Port Harcourt, 167, 252
Positive Force, 130, 135, 214–16, 219, 224, 238, 250, 253, 267

Positive Live Soul, 213
Postmen, 11
Pozo, Chano, 34
Preachers, 165
premprensua hand-piano, 193
Presidential Hotel, Accra, 76
Professor Fats (Fru "Fats" Tanga), 152
Professor Hindu (Kwaku Addaie), 127–29, 158, 171, 266
Professor Peller, 128
Psychedelic (Magic) Aliens, 213
"Psychedelic Afro Shop," 201
Psycho On Da Bus, 213

Quansah, Eddie, 55
Quaye, Asebre, 221

Rafiatou, Fifi, 225
Ramblers, 57
Ransome-Kuti, Bekolari (Beko), 3–4, 22, 78, 100–101, 116, 130, 209–10, 241, 249, 257, 259, 264, 268, 274
Ransome-Kuti, Funmilayo, 3–4, 18, 22, 38, 87, 94, 116, 118, 124, 129, 249, 259, 264, 266, 277
Ransome-Kuti, Nike, 241
Ransome-Kuti, Olikoye, 3, 132, 259
Ransome-Kuti, Oludulopa (Dolu), 3, 22, 94, 132, 209
Ransome-Kuti, Remi, 22, 27, 62
Ransome-Kuti, Reverend J. J., 3, 88, 204, 210
Ransome-Kuti, Reverend Oludotun, 3
Ransome-Kuti, Yemisi, 241, 243–44
RAS, 226
Rastafarian, 157, 244
Rawlings, Jerry John (Flight Lieutenant), 123, 171, 265, 268
Ray, Rita, 228, 231
Real World Studio, 183
Red Hot Collective/Foundation, 224, 253
Red Hot + Fela, 253–54
Red Hot + Riot, 253
Red Spots, 10
Reggae Sunsplash '88, Liberia, 131, 249, 267
Reinhardt, Max, 228, 231
Reixa, Pablo Diaz, 226
Remember Fela, 222
RetroAfric label, 231, 285
Revolution, 36, 198, 200
Reynolds, John, 218
Rhodes, Steve, 29, 31, 230
Rhythm Aces, 10
Rhythm Funk Masters, 225
Rhythmology, 232
Rhythm Taxi, 226
Rich, Buddy, 202
Richardson, Wendel, 145
Rimitti, Cheikha, 231
Ringway Hotel Accra, 56–57, 141, 271n12
River Niger, 225
Roach, Max, 202–3, 277
Rocket Juice and the Moon, 214
rock music, 13, 32, 215, 251
rock 'n' roll, 11, 13, 150, 188
Rockstone, Reggie, 221, 247
Rofo Rofo Fight, 49
Rogers All Stars (record company), 266
The Rolling Stones, 33, 184, 278n14
Ronnie Scott's Club, London, 227
The Roots (hip-hop/neo-soul band), 254
Ross, Edmundo, 10
Ruggedman (Michael Ugochukwu Stephens), 240

Sahr, Ngaujah, 254
Saint Brown, Kenny, 251–52
sakara music, 3, 280n12
Sakara (or *Shakara*) *Oloje*, 49
salsa music, 16, 34, 36, 250, 271n10
Samiana, Inemo, 227
Sammy, Kofi, 134, 165
Samuels, Ebenezer Kojo, 14
Samuels, Fuzzy, 145
Sanekoye, 221
Santamaria, Mongo, 200
Santana, 13, 200, 272n18, 278n9
Sappers, 153
Saro-Wiwa, Ken, 268
Saunders, Red, 203
Savage, Tiwatope "Tiwa," 240
Savannah Breeze, 232
Sawaaba Sounds, 16, 198
Schälsick Brass Band, 226
Schoonmaker, Trevor, 224
SECAPS Hotel Accra, 174
Secret Agent, 213
seprewa (Akan harp-lute), 195
Shagari, Shehu, 124, 171, 266–67
Shambros, 31, 274
Shankar the Amuludun (Ogunbadewa Ayodele Peters), 219
Shawa, 225
Shayo High-Life Music, 218
Shibabaw, Ejigayehu "Gigi," 222
Shikamoo Jazz Band, 285
Shuffering and Shmiling, 119, 135, 178, 181, 189, 193, 221
Sierra Leone, 3, 6, 11, 13–14, 36, 73, 99, 222, 231
Siisi-Yoyo, Frank, 22, 152, 219, 265
Sila, Victor, 222–23
Simonon, Paul, 213
Simpson, Kojo, 32
Sinclair, Bob, 225
Sir Afro-Fifi, 199
Skales (Raoul John Njeng-Njeng), 251
Sly and the Family Stone, 13, 272n18, 278n9
Small, Millie, 29
Smith, Will, 234
Solanke, Jimi, 239, 242, 247
Sole, Jeremy, 220, 241
Solo, Jake, 230, 232, 278n13
Sorrow, Tears and Blood, 110, 244, 275n1, 287
Sosimi, Dele, 33, 216, 219, 227, 255
Soul Assembly, 36, 198, 200
Soulfege, 224
Souljazz Orchestra, 223
"Soul Makossa," 15, 225
soul music, 4, 11–16, 32, 33–37, 60, 73–75, 99, 110, 135, 153, 197–98, 200–201, 222, 230, 240, 248, 261, 271, 277n4, 279n5, 288
Soul Providers, 224
Sound of Aquarius, 218
Sound Sultan (Olanrewaju Fasasi), 251
Soundway label UK, 231
South African Jam Band, 222
Soyinka, Wole, 230, 238, 246
Stan Kenton's Afro-Cubists, 34
Stargazers, 55
Star Hotel, Accra, 32, 54, 62, 175, 177, 264
Stein, Rikki, 130, 233, 255, 267
Sting, 129
Strangers, 11
Strayhorn, Billy, 202
Stride Band, 228
Strut record label UK, 213, 230
sufferheads, 1, 68, 234
"Suki Shy Man," 14

Sukura, Aaron Bebe, 221
Sulley, Oscar, 198, 232, 276n3
Sun Ra, 264
Super Afro-Soul, 201
Super Combo, 14
Super Eagles, 11
Superkali, 223
Superpowers, 223
Surulere Club, 109, 263
Surulere Football Stadium, 109, 263
Sweat Band, 223
"Swegbe and Pako," 60–61
swing music, 9–11, 32, 252
Switch, Kay (Kehinde Oladotun Oyebanjo), 251
synchro system, 16

Tafa Belewa Square, 164
Takashi, 220, 247
Taylor, Ebo, 15, 134, 221–22, 247, 255
Taylor, Kobina, 141
T Boys, 225
Teacher Don't Teach Me Nonsense, 225, 287
Tejuoso, Kunle, 241, 276n6, 279n7
Telfer, Ricky, 198
Tempos, 5–6, 9–10, 19, 56, 118, 202, 232, 264, 270n10, 274n11, 276n2
Temptations, 224
Tenor, Jimi, 213
Terracota, 165
Tetteh, Nii Tettey, 221
Tetty Addy, Mustapha, 134
Tetuila, Tony (Anthony Olanrewaju Awotoye), 220–21
Themes for African Drums, 203
Think Africa, 216
Third Phase, 203
Third World reggae group, 159, 171
Tic Tac, 221, 247
Timbaland (Timothy Mosley), 225
Timbuctu (rapper), 226
Tiptoe Club, Accra, 73, 76, 118, 141–42
Tizzle, Seun (Seun Morihanfen), 251
Todd, Stanley, 11, 51-52, 198
Tong, Simon, 213
Tontoh, Mac, 220, 232, 261
Tony Allen Live, 213
Tosh, Peter, 131, 159, 267
Touray, Paps, 11
Toure, Sekou, 18, 72, 262, 270n10
Towobola, Depo, 245
Tribez band, 228
Triffis, 74, 276n1
Tropicalia movement, Brazilian, 229
Trouble Sleep Yanka Wake Am (Palaver or *Palava)*. See *Palava* (or *Palaver*) (*Trouble Sleep Yanka Wake Am*)
Tsiboe, Nana, 227
Tune Yard, 253
Turrierand, Gecko, 226
Tutu, Osei, 179, 231
twist dance, 11, 13, 29, 58

Uhuru, 19, 23, 32, 41, 45, 55–59, 63, 73–74, 80, 118, 139–43, 232, 241, 260–62, 276n3
Umoja, 201
Underground Sound, 218
Underground System, 131
University of Ghana, 20, 23, 49–50, 73, 93, 52, 178, 183, 269n7
Unknown Soldier, 116–17, 219, 265
Upside Down, 38, 108, 125, 189, 264, 278n8
U2, 129
Uwaifo, Victor, 15, 20, 102, 197, 204, 230, 277n4

Vampire Weekend, 228
Vector (Olanrewaju David Ogunmefun), 251
VIP (Vagabonds in Power), 119, 274n10, 287
VIP hiplife group, 239
Voices of South Labone, 118

Wanluv the Kubolor (Emmanuel Owusu Bonsu), 252
Wantu Wazuri, 15, 198
Warren, Guy. *See* Ghanaba, Kofi
Washington, Grover, 36
Water No Get Enemy, 34, 98, 190–91, 198, 225
Weavers, 219
"We (or Wa) Dele," 34
Weird MC (Adesola Adesimbo Idowu), 36, 220, 251
Wells, Mike, 63
West African Swing Stars/Rhythm Brothers, 27
Western Toppers, 213
Weston, Randy, 213
Whitfield Brothers, 226
Who No Know Go Know, 20, 34, 53, 257, 287
Why Black Man Dey Suffer, 286
Williams, Shina, 230
Williams, Tunde, 108, 216, 224, 254
Wint, Eleanor, 243, 257
Wizkid (Ayo Balogun), 251
World Music and Dance (WOMAD), 183
Wrasse Records, 214, 289–90
Wright, Jaguar, 214
Wunmi, 227, 247

Yaaba Funk, 227
Yaanom, 231
yab (or "yabbis"), 40, 50, 53, 68, 99, 108–9, 147, 160–62, 170, 173
Yaba College, 58–59, 218, 246
Yankson, Papa, 134
Yawo's Afrobeat Band, 222
"Yeah Yeah Ku Yea," 233
"The Year 2000 Got to Be Black," 126
Yellow Fever, 60, 108
Yerba Buena, 224
"Yeshe Yeshe" (or "Yese Yese "), 30, 59, 141
Yorubeat (music style), 227
Young African Pioneers (YAP), 83, 218

Zantoba Mark Three band, 153
Zanzibar Club, Los Angeles, 220, 241
Zimba, Atongo, 220, 232, 247
Zimbabwe, 14
Zimbabwe Spirit, 222
Zitte, Alex, 165
Zombie, 2, 114, 117, 120, 150, 175, 194, 223, 228, 264–65, 287
Zonglo Biiz, 14, 198
Zozo Afrobeat Band, 224, 241, 253
Z Plus, 222
Zulwannsago, 226

Music:Interview

A SERIES FROM WESLEYAN UNIVERSITY PRESS

Edited by Daniel Cavicchi

Yip Harburg: Legendary Lyricist and Human Rights Activist
by Harriet Hyman Alonso

Fela: Kalakuta Notes
by John Collins

Reel History: The Lost Archive of Juma Sultan and the Aboriginal Music Society
by Stephen Farina

Producing Country: The Inside Story of the Great Recordings
by Michael Jarrett

Always in Trouble: An Oral History of ESP-Disk,' the Most Outrageous Record Label in America
by Jason Weiss

The Music/Interview series features conversations with musicians, producers, and other significant figures in the world of music, past and present. The focus is on people who have not only made good music but also have insightful and profound things to say about creativity, politics, and culture. Each Music/Interview book presents an original approach to music-making, showing music as a vehicle for inspiration, identity, comment, and engagement. The interview format provides conversations between knowledgeable insiders. By foregrounding individual voices, the series gives readers the opportunity to better appreciate the sounds and music around us, through the voices of those who have experienced music most directly.

ABOUT THE AUTHOR

JOHN COLLINS first went from Britain to Ghana in 1952 as a small child when his father helped establish the University of Ghana. Collins has been actively involved in the Ghanaian and wider West African music scene since 1969 and is now a naturalized Ghanaian. Over the years he has been a musician, bandleader, recording producer and engineer, music-union executive, archivist, writer, and music journalist. He served on the executive board of the Musicians' Union of Ghana (MUSIGA) in the late 1970s and from 1991 to 1998 was a trustee on the Ghana National Folklore Board/Copyright Administration.

He is currently a professor in the music department of the University of Ghana, chairman of the Bokoor African Popular Music Archives Foundation (BAPMAF), manager of the Bokoor Recording Studio, co-leader of the Local Dimension highlife band, and a patron of the Musicians Union of Ghana (MUSIGA)

He has published numerous articles on West African music and over the past forty years has influenced and inspired countless other activists, journalists, writers, historians, musicologists, and musicians. Some of his earlier books include *African Pop Roots: The Inside Rhythms of Africa* (1985); *Music Makers of West Africa* (1985); *E. T. Mensah: King of Highlife* (1986 and 1996); *West African Pop Roots* (1992); and *Highlife Time* (1996).

BANNING EYRE has performed and written about international music since 1988. He has traveled extensively in Africa and has produced many programs for the award-winning public radio series *Afropop Worldwide,* where he is senior editor of afropop.org. He is the author of *Afropop: An Illustrated Guide to Contemporary African Music* (Saraband, 1997) and *In Griot Time: An American Guitarist in Mali* (Temple University Press, 2000).